The DETECTIVE BRANCH

ANDREW PEPPER

Weidenfeld & Nicolson
LONDON

First published in Great Britain in 2010
by Weidenfeld & Nicolson
An imprint of the Orion Publishing Group Ltd
Orion House, 5 Upper St Martin's Lane
London WC2H 9EA

An Hachette UK Company

A CIP catalogue record for this book is
available from the British Library

ISBN 978 0 297 85527 9 (cased)
ISBN 978 0 297 85528 6 (trade paperback)

Typeset by Input Data Services Ltd,
Bridgwater, Somerset

Printed and bound in Great Britain
by Clays Ltd, St Ives plc

The Orion Publishing Group's policy is to use papers
that are natural, renewable and recyclable products and
made from wood grown in sustainable forests. The logging
and manufacturing processes are expected to conform to
the environmental regulations of the country of origin.

www.orionbooks.co.uk

The DETECTIVE BRANCH

Andrew Pepper lives in Belfast where he is a lecturer in English at Queen's University. His first novel, *The Last Days of Newgate*, was shortlisted for the CWA New Blood Dagger.

Also by Andrew Pepper

The Last Days of Newgate
The Revenge of Captain Paine
Kill-Devil and Water

For Michael and Lucy

It is criminal to steal a purse, daring to steal a fortune, a mark of greatness to steal a crown. The blame diminishes as the guilt increases

Friedrich Schiller

Paternoster Row

NOVEMBER 1808

He had been looking for his mother among the prostitutes and brothels of the Ratcliff Highway when they had seized him; two pairs of hands that had clasped his coat at the shoulder and lifted him clean off his feet.

A week later, he had been taken to a gloomy building in the shadows of the giant dome of St Paul's which he later discovered was an orphanage. He hadn't known at the time that he was an orphan. He hadn't known what an orphan was.

The dormitory where he and fifty other boys slept, two or three to a bed, was cold and damp. The wind blew right through it and even though they huddled together under a thin blanket for warmth, it was never enough. That first night had been the worst; he hadn't snivelled or cried like some of the boys but he had been so cold that he hadn't been able to stop shaking. Every hour bells would chime and it was difficult to sleep. Occasionally they whispered to one another under the blanket, even though talking at night was strictly prohibited. They lied about their circumstances and what had brought them there; the truth, for most of them, was too painful to bear. Nobody said what they all knew to be true: that they had no one; they had been abandoned and were alone in the world.

The Owl didn't make his rounds the first night he was there. It was said by some of the boys, maybe out of wishful thinking, that the man was suffering from a fever, since he never missed his rounds. But the next night the Owl was back. Alongside the other boys, he shivered and hid under the blanket. They heard the door first of all, creaking on its hinges, and then a thin shaft of light cut through the darkness filtering through the thin fibres of the blanket. After the door had groaned to a close, returning the room to darkness, they could see nothing but they could hear him; the same steady, deliberate footsteps that, over the following year, would become terrifyingly familiar to him. The Owl, he was told, always took his time. He would undertake a couple of lengths of the room, up and down past the beds that were arranged in rows, heads facing the walls, before the footsteps came to a halt; before he had made his choice. As he walked past their bed, they held their breath; no one flinched; no one even blinked. They could smell the pipe tobacco over the odour of floor polish. When the footsteps continued, when they didn't stop, when he was far enough away so he wouldn't hear, they let out a collective sigh of relief. You could see his eyes in the dark, it was said. That was why they called him the Owl. On that second night, he stopped somewhere up at the other end of the narrow room. They didn't hear whose name he called out. The next morning someone told them that it had been Tamworth. As was the unwritten rule, no one sat next to Tamworth the following day while they scoffed their breakfast gruel. It was as though his unhappiness was contagious.

It was not until his third week there that the Owl stopped at the end of his bed. The smell of pipe tobacco was thick in the air, and no one in the bed moved. They heard the Owl take a step in their direction and next to him, Simms flinched. He had been there the longest and knew the most; he knew the worst. They waited. It was clear that the Owl was perched over them, for they could hear him breathing; it was just a question of which one of them he would choose.

Even before the Owl had spoken, somehow he knew that his name would be called out; and he was right.

'Pyke.'

Pyke felt the other two relax but curiously he wasn't afraid; he would face this man in person and he would not be afraid.

4

Drury Lane

JULY 1844

ONE

According to a passer-by, three pistol blasts shattered the calm of a trading morning on Drury Lane. They came from inside Cullen's pawnbroker shop. According to the witness, Robert Morgan, a printer who had once served in the merchant navy and who'd been walking past the shop, the shots were fired in rapid succession. As he later told the police, he stepped into the dingy shop and through the waft of dust and powder he saw two bodies sprawled out on the tiled floor. The owner of the shop, Samuel Cullen, lay on his back in front of the counter, blood seeping from his stomach, his expression oddly resigned. The other man had been shot in the back and had tried to crawl towards the door, perhaps to get help, and a trail of his blood was smeared across the tiles. When Pyke inspected him a few hours later, his hair was matted with blood and his lips were caked with dust. Pyke found the third man under the stairs at the back of the shop, curled up like a baby, and when he laid him out, he saw that the blast must have caught the man in the face because there was almost nothing left of it. His chin, mouth, cheeks and nose had all been pulped by the ball-shot.

The shop was located on Shorts Gardens between a ginnery and an eating house where, on a normal day, a woman with black hair and thick ankles would have been ladling tripe stew into thruppenny bowls. The street name may have conjured images of bucolic tranquillity but in reality it was a narrow, dirty lane in one of the most run-down parts of the city, a tangled knot of decrepit tenements and open cesspools. Children with wan, malnourished faces squatted barefoot in the filth while wolfish dogs scoured the gutters for scraps. Usually the street itself would be choked with fish and vegetable barrows, and donkey carts laden with coal, but because of what had happened, barricades had been erected at either end, and although curious bystanders had begun to mass behind them, it was still eerily quiet.

The pawnbroker's shop was where the neighbourhood's poor came to trade their last possessions – silver lockets left to them by their grandmothers and, if they were desperate enough, the boots straight off their feet. The pawnbroker would give them a fraction of the true value of the item they brought in, and a slip of paper allotting sixty days in which to reclaim their property. People rarely did; in which case the items were sold for five or six times more than the pawnbroker had paid.

Cullen's shop was typical of its kind and nothing about it suggested that its owner possessed – or had ever possessed – something that might be worth killing for. The makeshift shelves were stacked with pairs of old boots, petticoats, dirty cotton-print dresses, soldiers' uniforms dating back to the time of Napoleon, braces, broken umbrellas, cheap metal combs, mildewed bonnets, torn books and magazines.

Having arrived with two of his sergeants, Whicher and Shaw, Pyke had cleared the shop and inspected the dead bodies. He didn't know, and had never come across, Samuel Cullen – another indication of the man's lowly status. Cullen had been identified by the owner of the neighbouring ginnery, who had peered down at the other victims and declared he'd never seen them before. But Pyke had. When he'd rolled over the corpse of the man who'd been shot in the back and had tried to crawl out of the shop, he found himself staring at a face he knew. He stood up suddenly, held his breath and wiped his upper arm across his forehead. Harry Dove was the friend of a friend. A friend, if that was the right word, who wouldn't want his name dragged into a murder investigation.

'Know him, then?' Whicher said, perhaps because he'd seen Pyke's reaction.

'I thought I did, for a moment,' Pyke said, turning away from Whicher to shield his expression.

'Oh.' If Whicher didn't believe him, he hid the fact well.

'You?'

Whicher shrugged. 'What about the other fellow, the one you found under the stairs.'

'What about him?'

'Any idea who he is?'

Pyke opted to ignore the question. 'Is Shaw upstairs with the passer-by?'

Whicher nodded. He was short, for a policeman. Just five foot eight, the minimum height to gain entry to the force. His dark hair was closely cropped and his clean-shaven face was pitted with smallpox scars. But it was his eyes which stood out: they were emerald green and shone with understated intelligence. He didn't say much but he had a keen eye for detail and a sharp memory. Although the man was young, Pyke already regarded him as his natural successor, or at least the one most capable of taking charge of an investigation. Whicher was cool, methodical and, equally important, he kept himself to himself outside work hours. The others, Pyke had heard, regarded him as aloof.

'Shaw is taking care of the wife, too,' Whicher said. 'She was out running errands when the robbery took place. Came back to find her shop crawling with policemen. She collapsed on the floor and had to be restrained.'

'You're calling it a robbery, then?'

'Why? You don't think it was?' He gave Pyke a sceptical look.

Earlier, they had come across the pawnbroker's safe, behind the counter at the back of the shop. It had been opened and emptied. The key was still in the lock.

'The passer-by said he heard three shots in quick succession. Said he entered the shop almost immediately.'

'So?'

'Let's assume that the safe was cleared before the men were shot.'

Whicher put his hands on his hips while he considered Pyke's hypothesis. 'That sounds about right.'

'So why did the gunmen open fire on Cullen and the other two *after* they'd got what they'd come for?'

Whicher shrugged. 'You think there was more than one of them?'

'Three shots were fired. In rapid succession. That's what the witness said, wasn't it?'

'Yes.'

'In which case, a single gunman wouldn't have had time to reload his pistol.'

9

Pyke turned his thoughts back to Dove and whether he should own up to recognising him, what the consequences might be. He looked down at the bodies, and tried to reconcile the conflicting sentiments assailing him. It was his job to remain detached, to see things as they were, but it was hard to look at the crime scene and not feel a twinge of excitement. An abomination had been perpetrated and it was his job to find the man or men responsible. At bottom, it was why he'd agreed to join the police force; because he loved the thrill of the chase.

A little later Cullen's wife confirmed the identification of her husband with a nod and sniffle but said she hadn't ever seen the other two men before.

'And before you ask,' she said, wiping her nose on the sleeve of her dress, 'I don't know nobody what'd want to kill my Sammy, neither.'

'But he can't have been a popular man, given how he earned his living.'

That made her snort. She was fifty, Pyke estimated, a few years older than her husband, and had probably done well to marry at all. Her skin was dark and tough, her eyes small and quick, like a magpie's.

'Sammy didn't force folk to do business with 'im. And he gave 'em a fair price, compared to some of them others. Else they wouldn't come back.'

Pyke nodded. Anyone with a petty grievance against Cullen wasn't likely to go to the shop armed with a pistol or blunderbuss. 'Had your husband ever been in trouble with the law?'

The wife glowered at him and folded her arms.

'Was your husband ever convicted of a crime, Mrs Cullen?'

She refused to meet his stare or answer his question and Pyke decided not to force the issue. If Cullen had been arrested or convicted of fencing stolen goods, they would find out soon enough.

'Has anyone made threats against your husband recently?'

This time Pyke saw that he'd struck a nerve and, before Cullen's wife could deny it, he added, 'If they didn't find what they were looking for, they'll be back, you know that.'

'Like you said, some folk round 'ere don't care for how we earn our bread. But we ain't got no problems with our neighbours. Ask 'em if you don't believe me.'

Pyke stole a glance at Whicher. 'Was your husband expecting someone this morning? Did he say anything to you about a visit?'

She assessed him coolly. 'He did say something over breakfast this morning. Said someone was comin' to see him, an' it might be good for business. Truth be told, he seemed quite excited.'

'Did your husband mention any names?'

Biting her lip, Cullen's widow looked into Pyke's face, the extent of her grief apparent for the first time, and shook her head.

The full complement of the Detective Branch assembled in the back room of the shop just after five.

Two members had left or been promoted in recent months, which meant there were now just four of them, five including Pyke. Frederick Shaw was the youngest and the one who deferred to Pyke's authority the most. Pyke didn't encourage this and found it more irritating than endearing, but while he felt Shaw was too timid and too beholden to the rules, the man had a quick mind and was willing to learn. He also had the kind of uniform, nondescript features that were useful in their line of work, meaning he could disappear easily into a crowd. He was average height, average build, average weight, with short brown hair and no sideburns or whiskers, as was the fashion. William Gerrett, on the other hand, always drew attention to himself. In some ways, this wasn't his fault. At six foot three inches, he was a head taller than anyone else in the room and had the kind of weak chin that disappeared into the flesh of his neck. He was flabby and heavy boned, too: a farmer's lad who had never quite outgrown his natural talent for tilling the soil and who was quite unsuited to the careful, painstaking logic of police work. He had made a name for himself by being an intimidating figure on the beat, but those skills had little value in the Detective Branch and Pyke had often wondered why he'd been chosen as a detective in the first place. Pyke didn't care for the man's looks or his poor personal hygiene, but it was the man's sloppiness that he couldn't forgive. Often Gerrett would forget to file even the most rudimentary pieces of information and needed to be reminded, two or three times a day, what he was supposed to be doing.

Shaw, Gerrett and the fourth member of the Branch, Eddie Lockhart, all lived together in a boarding house with the other single officers in Great Scotland Yard. As far as Pyke could tell, Gerrett and Shaw were friends, but Lockhart was the linchpin of the group and, by some margin, the most charismatic and handsome of them. At six feet tall, he was about the same height as Pyke but he was thinner and wirier, and wore the thinnest of moustaches, which he doubtless had to trim each morning. He had a natural confidence and an easygoing manner which worked well for him in the job, as witnesses and even suspects felt comfortable talking to him. But he was also the member of the Branch that Pyke knew the least about and the one who kept his assessment of Pyke closest to his chest. In fact he had seemingly made a conscious decision to keep his distance from Pyke and perhaps resented the fact that Pyke tended to consult first with Whicher rather than him, even though he was older. Lockhart was also intelligent, which made him either a useful ally or a potentially awkward presence in the team. Thus far, Pyke had found him to be the latter.

Pyke told them to gather round and ran through what had happened. Their eyes glistened with alarm and excitement. They might all have worked on murder investigations before but Pyke suspected that none of them had been in such close proximity to three dead bodies. Even Lockhart had baulked when he'd first stepped into the shop. Pyke examined their faces. They were all men he had inherited when he'd assumed the position of head of the Detective Branch at the end of the previous year. At the time he had been told he would be able to recruit two additional men of his own choosing, but now he had been informed that he would have to wait for replacements for the two who had left.

'Whatever else you were working on, gentlemen, this now takes priority. There will, of course, be immense pressure on us to find and arrest the person, or persons, who committed this act. I'll expect your full co-operation. Is that understood?'

They all nodded. The air around them was still thick with the scent of fresh blood.

'Let's start with Cullen, then. From the look of his shop, I'd say he wasn't too successful as a pawnbroker. Was he a fence, too? Perhaps. The wife as good as admitted he sometimes dabbled in stolen goods. I'll need a volunteer to visit Bow Street first thing in the morning, go through the records there, and find out if he was ever convicted of a crime.'

Shaw put up his hand. 'I'll do it, sir.' He was always the first to volunteer and insisted on calling Pyke 'sir', even though Pyke had repeatedly told them to call him by his name.

'Good.' Pyke paused, looking at his men. 'We don't know who the other two victims are. We need to identify them as quickly as possible, and find out what they were doing in the shop.' Pyke said this even though it was clear to him that a man like Harry Dove wouldn't have been there to buy a gnarled pair of boots or a broken umbrella.

'After the inquest, I've arranged for the bodies to be laid out in an upstairs room at the Queen's Head, just across the road. When news of this spreads, people will want to come and look. Someone, somewhere will know the identity of these two men, so I need one of you to remain with the bodies.'

When no one else put their hand up, Gerrett made a half-hearted gesture. Secretly Pyke was relieved; it was the least taxing of the tasks and hence the one most suited to Gerrett's capabilities. Pyke thanked him and moved on.

'The fact that the safe was open and its contents had been removed suggests robbery as the likely motive. But the three men were shot dead *after* the gunman or gunmen had got what they wanted. Why would they do that? Did Cullen or one of the others try to disarm the gunman and fail?'

Pyke stared at their faces. He didn't get an answer, nor did he expect one. 'If it was, in fact, a robbery, we need to work out what was taken.' He looked at Whicher. 'I want you to have a look at Cullen's books. Talk to the wife, if you have to. Make a list of what was stolen. There'll also be a record of what people brought in to be pawned. Look for anything unusual or valuable and make a note of it.'

Next, Pyke turned to Lockhart. 'I want you to knock on doors and speak to the neighbours. The man or men we're looking for might've entered the shop from the street or from Drury Lane. Someone might have seen them. Similarly I'm guessing they left through the backyard. Again, someone living in one of the tenements might have seen something. Talk to people, try to jog their memories.'

Lockhart nodded curtly but said nothing. He seemed almost jittery and couldn't bring himself to look at the corpses.

'Whoever did this,' Pyke said, 'came prepared. They came with loaded pistols. The witness heard three shots in rapid succession. That tells us they didn't have any qualms about pulling the trigger.'

Pyke thought about the bodies laid out in the adjacent room. Briefly, he tried to imagine someone walking into Cullen's shop, pistol already drawn; imagined this man ordering Cullen to open the safe and empty the contents into a bag; imagined him turning on Cullen and firing. Perhaps it had been a double-barrelled pistol, in which case he could have turned it on Dove or the other man and fired again. But a man like Harry Dove wouldn't have given him the time to reload. So maybe the gunman had used two pistols, or maybe there had been two gunmen after all?

Killing someone was never easy, but whoever had done this had moved from man to man, seemingly firing at will. Pyke closed his eyes and tried to picture the scene: the jolt of the pistol as the shot was discharged, the tearing of flesh, the screaming, the acrid whiff of burnt powder. None of this had put off the gunman. Rather he had gone about his task with methodical precision. One shot, followed by another, followed by another.

It struck Pyke later that he wasn't looking for a robber. He was looking for an assassin; someone who liked to kill.

'How's your uncle?' Edmund Saggers asked. He had managed to push his considerable bulk to the front of the barricade and persuade one of the uniformed constables to let him talk to Pyke.

'He's been better,' Pyke said, glancing at the shining faces of the mob gathered behind him. 'He's been worse, too.'

As a reporter for the *London Illustrated News* and, before that, a freelance penny-a-liner, Saggers had met up with Godfrey Bond every month for the past ten years to talk about literary tittle-tattle over a table full of food and as much wine as both men could pour down their throats. He had also become Pyke's friend – or a friend of sorts. From time to time, Pyke found it useful to get Saggers to highlight stories arising out of particular investigations and most of the time Saggers was willing to oblige, in return for an exclusive at some later date.

'I heard he's given up his apartment in Camden and moved in with you,' Saggers said.

'That's right.' Pyke hesitated, wondering whether to voice his concerns about his uncle. 'How did Godfrey seem to you, the last time you met for lunch?' In Pyke's opinion, his uncle's health had deteriorated since the start of the year but he didn't want to articulate this to Saggers. He didn't even want to acknowledge it to himself. Although Godfrey was in his seventies, the notion that the old man's health might be failing was too much for Pyke to bear.

Saggers considered the question. He was wearing a tweed coat and matching trousers that had been made for him and which he rarely, if ever, changed out of. 'Between the two of us, he didn't finish his wine.'

Pyke nodded. It confirmed what he'd suspected for a while. The idea panicked him, as much for Felix's sake as his own. His fourteen-year-old son was devoted to the old man. It was also true that Godfrey was the only father he, Pyke, had ever known.

Saggers gestured at Cullen's shop. 'I heard there are three dead including the owner. Shot by a person or persons unknown.'

'What else did you hear?'

Saggers let his gaze drift over Pyke's shoulder. 'Hard to understand 'em, to be honest.' He stared up at a soot-blackened building. 'This place shouldn't be called Little *Dublin*. From the accents I'd say Little Cork would be more accurate.'

'People gossip,' Pyke said. 'You must have overheard something.'

'Have you heard of the Raffertys?'

That got his attention. 'No. Should I have?'

'Three brothers from County Cork, or so I gather. Talk is, they've started their own gang.'

Pyke looked into Saggers's eyes; they were almost translucent in colour, half buried in two deep pits of flesh. 'Do people think they might be responsible for the murders?'

'I've been standing here for about an hour and I've heard the same name whispered three or four times. Draw your own conclusions.'

*

Ned Villums was sitting at his functional desk in his plain office in a residential street in the middle of Clerkenwell. He barely looked up when Pyke was ushered into the room by one of his assistants.

'I'm here about the Shorts Gardens robbery.'

Villums finished what he'd been reading and raised his eyes. 'I've already heard about it. Three dead, if my information's correct. Nasty business.' He waited for a moment, then added, 'For what it's worth, Cullen was a stupid, shambling wreck of a man.'

Pyke wiped the sweat from his forehead with a handkerchief. 'I'm sorry to have to tell you this, Ned, but Harry Dove was one of the victims.'

'Harry? You mean . . .' Villums struggled to come to terms with what Pyke had just said.

'Shot in the back.' Villums's eyes shifted focus and instinctively he gripped the desk. 'Like I said, Ned, I'm sorry. I know how much the lad meant to you.'

To look at, Villums was as insignificant as the next man. His greasy hair had no particular style and his ill-fitting jacket and matching corduroy breeches made him look more like a coster-monger than one of the shrewdest, most revered men in the city's sprawling underworld. That was exactly why he'd risen to the position he had when others had died or gone to prison. He didn't draw attention to himself; he was a good judge of character; he dealt only with people he knew and trusted; and if crossed, he could be as ruthless and cruel as the worst of them. Pyke had known and traded information with him for more than twenty years, and while he didn't exactly consider Villums to be a friend, there was, Pyke felt, a mutual respect. Knowing what they were both capable of, they had been careful not to antagonise one another. Villums was certainly not the kind of man you wanted to turn your back on.

'Jesus Christ. Sit down and tell me what happened.' Villums fetched a bottle of whisky from the shelf behind his desk and poured them both a glass.

Pyke did as Villums asked, leaving nothing out. Villums didn't interrupt. Even after Pyke had finished, he just sat there quietly, assessing what he'd been told. Pyke didn't know how Dove had first come to Villums's attention but he had become one of the man's most trusted associates.

Eventually, after rearranging some items on his desk, Ned sat forward. 'I've heard about the men you're interested in. The Rafferty boys. Nasty types. I'm told they sometimes play cards in the King of Denmark but more often you'll find them at the Blue Dog on Castle Street.'

'But are they capable of walking into a pawnbroker's shop in broad daylight and killing three men?'

Villums shrugged. 'Rumour has it they hung a police informer on a meat hook, slit open his stomach and pulled out his intestines inch by inch.'

'Why haven't I heard of them?'

'They do robberies, mainly. Houses, shops, warehouses, even banks. They're careful, though. Makes me wonder whether they would walk into a pawnbroker's shop in the middle of the day like that.'

Pyke picked up the whisky glass Villums had filled for him. 'The bodies of two as-yet-unidentified men will be laid out for public viewing. Sooner or later someone will recognise Harry.'

Villums nodded. 'And you think I'll be dragged into the investigation?'

'Your connection to Harry isn't exactly a secret.'

'But you're in charge of the investigation.'

Now they were getting down to it. Pyke sat back in his chair and drank some whisky. 'You're asking me to keep your name out of it?'

'If people know about my connection to Harry, they might find out about my association with you. If that becomes public knowledge, it wouldn't be good for either of us.'

Pyke tried to assess whether this constituted a threat or not. He had traded information for money with Villums and subsequently a pickpocket ring and a gang of housebreakers had been tried and convicted. He had also been paid for arresting Villums's enemies. Pyke was happy to leave the ethics of his actions for others to worry about: the convictions had put men who stole for a living behind bars and had been instrumental in consolidating Pyke's status in the Detective Branch and the New Police. It was also true that Pyke had plenty of enemies, men who had opposed his appointment and who would dearly love to expose him as a liar and a criminal.

When he'd first found out that Pyke was going to join the Detective Branch, Villums's reaction had surprised him. Pyke had expected suspicion, even hostility, but Villums had welcomed the news. 'Don't you see?' he had said. 'You'll be on the inside. I'll finally have someone on the inside.' At the time, Pyke didn't try to dampen Villums's enthusiasm. He'd certainly profited from the information Villums had passed on to him but he had also tried to distance himself a little from his former associate.

'Do you know what business took Harry to Cullen's shop in the first place?' Pyke asked, deciding to change the subject.

Villums didn't seem to have heard the question. Instead he picked up the whisky bottle and poured himself another glass. 'Harry was no fool,' he said eventually, his calloused fingers wrapped around the tumbler.

'I didn't say he was.'

'You want me to be blunt, Pyke, I'll be blunt,' Villums said, suddenly. 'You're a policeman now. Keep Harry out of the investigation.'

Pyke looked into Villums's slate-grey eyes and held his stare. 'As I said, someone will recognise him sooner or later. It's inevitable.'

'Then just make sure my name isn't brought into the conversation,' Villums said.

'I'll do what I can, but I can't make any promises.'

Villums sat forward, drumming his fingers on the edge of his desk, his eyes glowing. 'We've had a good understanding for a number of years. I might even count you as a friend. But rest assured, Pyke, if I was ever faced with the choice of protecting you or saving myself, I'd do whatever was needed.'

'Then we both know where we stand.'

Villums stared at him, contemplating his next move. 'I'll ask around about Harry.'

Standing up, Pyke felt a rush of blood to his head. Or perhaps it was just the whisky. He walked to the door, then turned around. 'Ned.' He waited for Villums to look up at him. 'We've always got along by respecting each other's privacy and not interfering in each other's business.'

'So?'

'This is *my* investigation, Ned. I'm a policeman now.'

Villums seemed disappointed by this response. 'You're your own man, Pyke. Always have been, always will be.'

When he got home that evening, Pyke ate the supper left for him by his housekeeper, a middle-aged spinster called Mary Booth, and looked in on his son, Felix, who was asleep in his room. For a while, he lay on his bed reading, but sleep was beyond him so he put on his boots and let himself out into the garden of his Islington town house. It was a cooler night than the previous few and the wind was now coming from the west, carrying the hint of rain. He wandered down to the bottom of the garden where the sty was located and saw that one of his pigs, Alice, had escaped and was rooting around in his neighbour's vegetable patch. Pyke was joined by Copper, a three-legged mastiff and former fighting dog he'd acquired and now kept as a pet, and between the two of them, they managed to herd the long-bodied pig back into the sty.

A year earlier, Pyke had employed Villums to dispose of thirteen gold bars he'd illegally acquired from the bullion vault of the Bank of England and he'd used the proceeds to buy the house where his family was now living. It was a stout, respectable terrace in Islington; strangely only a few streets away from the house on Cloudsley Terrace that his deceased wife, Emily, had inherited from her father and where they had lived in the first years of their marriage. Pyke had wondered about the wisdom of buying a house in an area that held so many memories for him but Felix had been insistent, for although he had been too young to remember the old house, he had liked the idea of living in a part of the city his mother had known.

It had almost been ten years since her death and they hardly ever talked about her. Perhaps this was as it should be, Pyke thought, as he climbed the stairs. Perhaps you ran out of things to say about someone who had been dead for so long. But late at night, when he couldn't sleep, Pyke would lie in his bed, staring up at the ceiling, and he would think about their time together, trying to remember the small details; the shape of her mouth, the touch of her fingers, the crease just above her nose that deepened whenever she became irritated or angry. Sometimes his thoughts would also turn to Jo, Felix's nursemaid and then his nanny. Pyke had had a brief and unsuccessful dalliance with her a few years earlier, and he would wonder where she was now and what she was doing. In the end, his mind always wandered back to Emily, and as Pyke lay there listening to the shutters rattle against their jambs, he thought about what had been lost and what he would never get back.

TWO

Grief affects people in different ways but Pyke had always thought that it was a luxury of the indolent. The next morning, he found Cullen's wife at the front of the shop. On her hands and knees, and wearing a tatty apron, her hair tied up in a bun, she was scrubbing the floor with a wire brush. Her face was rigid with concentration as she drew the bristles back and forth across the dark stains, as though the act itself could somehow erase the memory of what had happened. Pyke let the door close behind him and coughed. She looked up, startled, and then allowed her gaze to return to the stain in front of her. 'What do you want?'

'Tell me about the Rafferty brothers.'

Pyke saw at once that his words had rattled her. She stared down at the damp, soapy residue on the floor. 'What about them?'

'You know who I'm talking about, then?'

'There's not many folk around 'ere what don't know the name.'

'Yesterday I asked you whether anyone had threatened your husband. You gave me an equivocal answer.'

This time she stopped scrubbing, put down her brush and looked up at him. '*Equivocal?*'

Pyke nodded, acknowledging her subtle rebuke. She wouldn't have known it from the way he spoke, he thought, but he came from the same background she did. 'The Raffertys or someone from their mob came to the shop, didn't they?'

Cullen's wife hauled herself up off her knees and stretched. 'You seem to have all the answers.'

She started to walk away but Pyke grabbed her wrist. 'I'm trying to find the man or men who killed your husband.' The woman tried to shake him off but he wouldn't let go.

Her small, quick eyes hardened. 'Folk like us don't say no to the likes of the Raffertys.'

Pyke let go of her wrist. 'What did they want with your husband?'

She put her hands on her hips and sniffed. 'Fence some of their loot.'

'And he agreed?'

''Course he agreed. What choice did he 'ave?'

Pyke paused for a moment, listening to the jangling of knives and spoons from the eating house next door. 'Maybe your husband tried to pull the wool over the Raffertys' eyes and they came here to teach him a lesson?'

That elicited a hollow chuckle. 'My Sammy weren't a brave man but he weren't stupid, neither. If the Raffertys told him to dance a barefoot jig on a bed of hot coals, he woulda done it with a smile on his face.'

'You don't think it was the Raffertys who killed your husband, then?'

Cullen's wife dug her hands into the pouch of her apron. 'Like I said yesterday, Sammy was excited 'bout something, a cull comin' to see him. If he was expecting the Rafferty boys, he would've been quakin' in his boots.'

It was still early but the street outside was thronging with people and no one was paying much attention to the shop, as though what had happened the day before had already been forgotten. Pyke walked under a line of dripping clothes and stepped out on to Drury Lane, where an endless procession of cabs, drays and costermongers' barrows were crawling in both directions. The pavements were full, too; navvies in their white moleskins and laced boots idling on the corner, an old man blowing on Irish pipes, a younger man carrying a sign advertising a camphor emetic. From the upper-floor windows, Pyke could hear crying and screaming, men still drunk from the night before berating their wives and children. All around, men and women dressed in work clothes were readying themselves for the day ahead; some would find work pulling up potatoes or picking hops in Bromley and Bow, others would lump coal or lay bricks. Some would set up makeshift stalls on the city's streets selling oranges and potatoes. In the window of a baker's there was a placard declaring 'No Popery'. Next door, outside a ginnery, was a board advertising Dublin stout. A newspaper seller stood on the next corner holding up a copy of the *London Illustrated News*. Doubtless its revelations, and its lurid description of the murders, would further fan the flames of discord: Catholic Ireland bringing its barbarian ways to the streets of Protestant England. Pyke knew there were around fifty or sixty thousand Irish in St Giles alone. What would happen, he wondered, if the Catholics and Protestants living alongside each other in the rookery really did turn on one another?

On the other side of the street, Pyke saw Lockhart emerge from a butcher's shop. Cutting in between a brewer's dray and a hackney carriage, he caught up with the man outside the Queen's Head.

'I've just talked to an old man who lives in one of the tenements at the back of Cullen's shop,' Lockhart said, breathlessly.

They looked at one another warily as Pyke waited for Lockhart to catch his breath. Personally Pyke felt his colleague's face was too gaunt and his eyes were too close together but he'd heard it said, by Gerrett when he was drunk, that he, Pyke, was jealous of Lockhart's youth and good looks.

On this occasion, Lockhart seemed excited rather than diffident. He told Pyke that a witness, a retired coal-whipper, had seen a well-dressed man, tall, with dark hair and swarthy skin, in the alley behind the pawnbroker's just after the shooting. The man had been carrying a large pistol. The coal-whipper reckoned he'd be able to recognise the gunman if he ever saw him again.

A cart piled high with wooden crates rattled towards them, the harness clanking loudly as the iron-shod wheels rolled over the cobblestones. Pyke waited for it to pass. 'That's fine work, Detective.' He thought he saw Lockhart smile. 'Keep it up and I'll see you back in the office at five.'

About lunchtime it started to rain and by early afternoon a brown slush had collected at the sides of the street and was sprayed up on to the pavements by the passing traffic. It meant there was standing room only in the taproom of the Blue Dog, traders from the nearby market taking refuge from the downpour alongside knife-grinders, basket sellers, hawkers, balladeers, oakum pickers and cos-termongers. Steam rose from wet clothes, creating a fug that smelled almost as bad as the rotten vegetables on the pavement outside. Pyke approached the zinc-topped counter and asked to speak to the landlord. No one took much notice of him until he said he was there to 'rattle the cage' of the Rafferty boys. The pot-bellied landlord folded his arms and smiled. Almost immediately, conversation in the vicinity of the counter stopped.

'And who, sir, are you?' The landlord's moustache twitched.

'Pyke.' He waited. 'Detective Inspector Pyke.' As he said it, he could almost feel the walls closing in on him.

'A Jack, eh?'

'You want to point me in the direction of the Raffertys or do I have to arrest you for being fat and ugly?'

'Tough-talking, too.' The landlord's eyes were as dead as a filleted mackerel's. 'You here on your own?'

'I see you can count to one. I'm impressed.'

That drew a smirk. 'A brave man. Or a stupid one.' A few men within earshot laughed.

'You can talk, surely you can, friend, but I wonder if that's all you've got,' a voice said behind Pyke. An Irish brogue.

Pyke turned and found himself staring at a man in his forties, with unkempt, reddy-brown hair, a sunburnt face with a six-inch scar running down one side of it, a neck as thick as the stump of a small tree, and arms that had doubtless crushed men to death. He was the kind of man who could plunge a knife into your belly as easily as he could drink a mug of ale. Pyke noticed, too, that a path had cleared around him.

'Your name Rafferty?'

'Might be. Then again it might be O'Shaunessy or Cleary depend-ing on who's askin' the question.' A few nervous laughs rippled around the taproom.

'Yesterday morning, three men were shot and killed in a pawn-broker's just off Drury Lane. The rumour is that you or one of your brothers might have pulled the trigger.'

His expression didn't change. 'Is that so? And why would we want to go and do a thing like that?'

'That's what I'm here to find out.'

The man studied him with a disconcerting mixture of curiosity and indifference. 'Where I come from, a Peeler dares enter a place like this, he leaves in a box.'

'Lucky for me we live in a more civilised part of the world.'

'You saying me or my brothers had anything to do with that shootin'?' the man asked.

'That's what I'm here to find out.'

'Has the widow been talkin'?'

Pyke took a moment to assess the threat he'd implicitly made against Cullen's wife. 'If you or your brothers touch a hair on her head, or even go within fifty yards of her shop, I'll dunk you in a cesspool until you choke.'

Rafferty seemed amused, rather than unsettled, by Pyke's words, as if he knew that the threat was a hollow one. 'Cullen was nothing. Not worth the steam risin' off my piss. The fact he was shot has nothin' to do with us.'

Pyke studied Rafferty's face for signs that he might be lying but his ignorance appeared to be genuine. 'So where were you and your brothers yesterday morning between the hours of ten o'clock and midday?'

'Right here,' Rafferty said, without hesitation. 'In full view of a hundred men.'

'And people here would be happy to swear an oath to that effect?' Pyke looked at the faces flanking Rafferty. Of course they would be happy to swear an oath, he thought. They were all completely terrified of him.

Rafferty just shrugged. 'Ask 'em yourself.'

Pyke turned to the landlord. 'Well?'

The pot-bellied man grinned. 'None of 'em Raffertys even slipped out back to relieve 'emselves.'

A chorus of validations echoed around the taproom. Rafferty stood there, arms folded. Pyke turned back to face him. 'So which Rafferty are you?'

'Conor.'

'I'll come back soon and we'll continue this conversation.'

Rafferty smiled. 'Any time, Peeler.'

Later Pyke learned that Conor Rafferty had once taken a hammer to a man who'd slept with his sister and systematically broken every bone in his body. The person who told the story added that Conor was the least cruel of the brothers.

The address of the New Police's headquarters was 4 Whitehall Place but the entrance was in Great Scotland Yard. The building housed the police's administration, the offices of the two commissioners, the men of the Executive Division, the newly instituted Criminal Returns office, which compiled information and statistics to show the prevalence of crime in particular districts, and the accounts department. While the commissioners enjoyed views that took in the river on one side and St James's Park and Horse Guards' Parade on the other, the Detective Branch occupied three poky rooms on the ground floor that looked directly on to a brick wall. Pyke found the view oddly reassuring. As he sometimes told his men, it gave them a proper sense of their place in the New Police's hierarchy.

As a detective, Pyke didn't have to wear a uniform, something he was very grateful for. Even though he had been doing the job for over six months, he still didn't feel wholly comfortable with his new-found authority and he was glad not to be reminded of it each time he walked past a mirror. It was a long time since he had served as a Bow Street Runner and it had taken him a while to find his feet and adjust to being part of a large organisation again. Still, his time as a Runner had taught him the rudiments of detective work and, more than this, how a detective branch should function. For many years, his mentor at Bow Street had failed to convince successive home secretaries about the merits of creating a centralised, dedicated detective department. Tory and Whig politicians had felt that the true role of the police should be to deter crime from happening in the first place and that detectives were akin to spies whose unseen presence on the streets threatened the very notion of liberty. Now, though, the political wind had changed and Pyke had been given the chance to turn his mentor's vision into a reality.

Pyke kept one of the rooms for himself. The second room, also small, was used for questioning witnesses and interviewing suspects. The largest room housed desks for all the other detectives, together with a row of filing cabinets that contained a growing library of cards. These cards detailed the criminals or suspected criminals known to them and were arranged according to their particular skills. There were sections for pickpockets, lumpers, footpads, magsmen, swell mobs, sharpers, prostitutes, pimps, house burglars, horse thieves, rushers, receivers, murderers, rapists, sodomists, shoplifters, screevers and cracksmen. Each card listed the person's name, their aliases, all known acquaintances, their current residence, all former residences, a list of any convictions and details of time served in prison. This information was then cross-referenced with the names of other known or suspected criminal associates. Each section was arranged alphabetically, according to surname, and the idea was that any piece of information they came across, no matter how trivial it seemed at the time, would be added to a person's card. Additionally the cabinets contained copies of the daily crime reports circulated by the assistant commissioner's office to all divisional superintendents, providing descriptions of suspects, missing persons and stolen property.

Sometimes Pyke wondered what his wife, Emily, would have made of his decision to join the police force, whether or not she would have been surprised. Part of her, he suspected, wouldn't have batted an eyelid, even though he had once told her, after leaving the Runners, that he would never go back. Throughout their marriage, Emily had known that he missed his former profession: the excitement and even the grubbiness of the work. But he had changed in the years since her death. As a young man, he had been as much concerned with lining his own pocket as locking up malefactors. Those ambitions hadn't deserted him entirely but these days he'd come to believe that the law, even if imperfect, was both a necessary and an inevitable part of civilised existence. Part of him also knew she would have been disappointed in his decision. He could hear her voice: telling him that by becoming a policeman he was colluding with a system that was founded on unfairness. She had been a firebrand radical, a socialist, someone who'd believed passionately, naively perhaps, that the world could be altered by the words and deeds of those with political commitment.

Pyke checked to make sure there wasn't a card made up for Harry Dove and that his name wasn't listed in connection with other known receivers. When he was satisfied of this, he walked up the staircase to the office of the two commissioners and knocked on the door of Sir Richard Mayne, entering before being invited to do so.

Mayne was sitting behind his gargantuan desk. He was youthful in looks, despite his fifty years, with a smooth, oval face, brown hair that was greying at the edges, and a hard, compressed mouth. He was cold and taciturn but, as a former solicitor, he had a good brain for police work and it was he, rather than the other commissioner, who had argued for the creation of a specialist detective department. Some liked to compare Mayne to Peel, and Pyke could see the similarities. Like Peel, Mayne could be stern and humourless; Pyke rarely saw him relax and he never spoke an unnecessary word. But Mayne could be loyal, too, and while he hadn't exactly warmed to Pyke as head of the Detective Branch, Pyke knew he had vigorously defended him to outsiders and at his twice yearly appearance before the parliamentary select committee.

With him in the room was Walter Wells. Wells had just been promoted to the rank of acting superintendent of the Executive Division, the largest and most prestigious of all of the New Police's divisions and the only one based at the headquarters in Whitehall Place. It was the most senior position in the New Police after the two commissioners and the post of assistant commissioner. Wells was about the same age as Mayne but his hair was still thick and black and looked as if it had been cut with the aid of a pudding bowl. His head was the size of a pumpkin and his skin seemed to have the consistency of hard wax. Even when he smiled, it didn't move. He had joined the police force ten years earlier and had risen steadily through the ranks. As a soldier, he had been decorated for his service to the Afghan campaign, during which it was said he'd single-handedly fought off a mob of tribal warriors for two days until reinforcements had arrived. There were a lot of former army men in the New Police, and many of these spoke highly of Wells. Pyke had yet to make up his mind, and he was irritated by Wells's mostly crass attempts to ingratiate himself with whoever he was talking to.

Briefly Pyke told them what had happened at the pawn shop, that three men including the owner had been shot and killed, then he outlined how the investigation was proceeding. Both men seemed happy enough with his account, but the fact that Wells had been invited to this meeting in the first place worried Pyke. The Detective Branch, with just five men, was a minor department, and although it answered directly to the office of the two commissioners, this autonomy was constantly under threat. Each of the divisions had its own area of jurisdiction and some superintendents resented the fact that crimes committed in their patch could be handed over to the Detective Branch. Some argued that the Detective Branch wasn't strictly necessary and that crimes committed in their areas could be investigated just as well by their own men.

When Pyke had finished talking, Mayne invited Wells to respond and the acting superintendent told them about some Irish ruffians who had been seen firing their pistols on waste ground near King's Cross. Pyke's thoughts immediately turned to the Raffertys, and when Wells added that these Irishmen had been spotted drinking in the King of Denmark on Long Acre, the place Villums had mentioned, he knew they were talking about the same men.

Mayne turned his gaze towards Pyke. 'In the last hour, and with my approval, Walter has dispatched a group of officers from the Executive Division to pay this establishment a visit and, I hope, apprehend the men in question.' He looked across at Wells. 'Do you have their names, Walter?'

'No names, I'm afraid. Just descriptions.'

'I see.' Pyke took in this information, wondering whether any of the descriptions would match Conor Rafferty. 'Does this mean I'm no longer in charge of the investigation?'

'Not at all. But we both felt that, in the circumstances, time was of the essence. In view of the seriousness of the incident, I feel that the investigation would benefit from Walter's expertise and experience.'

Pyke glanced across at Wells. 'And who would be in overall charge of the investigation?'

'You would still run the day-to-day affairs.' Mayne tapped his fingers on the desk. 'This is about co-operation between departments. Anyway, you'll be snowed under as it is. Another pair of hands can't do any harm.'

'You don't seem especially convinced by the course of action we've taken,' Wells commented, trying to smooth over the situation.

'You're a plain-speaking man by reputation. I'd like to hear what you've got to say.'

Pyke shrugged. He considered telling them about the Rafferty brothers but decided this would only stoke Wells's rash decision-making. 'What evidence is there to indicate that these men were involved in the robbery?' He waited. 'Aside from the fact they're Irish and were seen in a pub on Long Acre?'

When neither of the men answered immediately, Pyke added, 'And to date, our enquiries have led us to believe we're looking for a single gunman, not a mob.'

Mayne's jaw hardened and he shook his head. 'A single gunman couldn't have fired all three shots.'

Wells leaned back against his cushioned chair and extended his arms upwards. 'Perhaps I might ask, Detective Inspector, what is your opinion of the Irish?'

'The Irish?' Pyke turned to look at him. 'I know a few, rich and poor, and I couldn't generalise.'

'Perhaps you should spend more time in places like Saffron Hill or Little Dublin. Ten or fifteen to a room, fifty in every building. More arriving by the day and reproducing quicker than vermin.'

'If we peddle that notion to the newspapers, I guarantee we'll see Catholics hanging from gas-lamps by the end of the week. Is that what you want? Mobs of irate, self-righteous Englishmen burning people out of their homes?'

Wells clenched his jaw but said nothing.

'Enough of this,' Mayne interrupted. 'Personal views aside, we are following up on this line of enquiry because it is, or might be, pertinent to your investigation.'

Pyke was surprised that the commissioner had again referred to it as his investigation and wondered to what extent this was true.

'More to the point,' Mayne added, 'I want the two of you to co-operate with the new superintendent of Holborn Division.'

'I thought that position hadn't been filled,' Pyke said. He'd heard that the old superintendent had retired but that a replacement still hadn't been found.

'It hadn't,' Mayne said carefully. 'Until this afternoon.'

'Oh?'

'In light of the events that have brought us all here I felt it was imperative to make an appointment. And as fortune would have it, there was a suitable man willing to put himself forward.'

There was a knock on the door. 'Come,' Mayne barked, adding, 'That should be him. I asked him to attend this meeting.'

Benedict Pierce strode into the room and nodded politely at Wells. Ignoring Pyke, he said, 'Sir Richard,' and waited for Mayne to invite him to sit. He had the stiff demeanour of a military man but, unlike Wells, Pyke knew for a fact he had never seen, or been anywhere near, active service. All of the buttons on his frock-coat had been polished and there was a perfect crease running down the length of his trousers. Not a single hair on his head was out of place and his chin was smooth and clean shaven. He removed his stovepipe hat, sat down on the empty chair next to Wells and crossed his legs.

Pyke considered his options. He could refuse to work with Pierce and see what transpired, or he could say nothing and find out what kind of game Pierce was playing.

'You know Walter, of course. Pyke, too.' For Pyke's benefit, Mayne added, 'I'm pleased to say that Superintendent Pierce has agreed to assume control of E Division with immediate effect. Any questions?'

Pyke smiled, deciding to keep his thoughts to himself. 'I'm pleased, for your sake, that you were able to fill the vacancy at such short notice.'

There were many reasons why Pyke disliked Pierce. The fact that the man was punctilious, vain and self-regarding was almost beside the point. Pyke didn't hold Pierce's rampant ambition against him either, even if this meant he had risen with an almost obscene swiftness through the ranks of the New Police. What rankled most was that this success was not due to Pierce's skills as an investigator or even an administrator but rather because he had always sought out the right connections. He belonged to the clubs that mattered and had even joined a Masonic lodge. Pyke had traded with men like Villums and the information he had bought and sold had secured his position in the New Police. But while he had turned a blind eye to some of Villums's activities, he had never accepted a bribe to cover up someone's involvement in a murder and had never allowed the rich and powerful to tell him how to do his job.

Pyke suspected this wasn't true of Pierce, but it was the man's hypocrisy which galled him most of all; the fact that the new head of E Division could let a rich man who'd strangled his servant live out his days in peace and yet would make sure a poor man who had stolen in order to feed his starving family was sent to the scaffold.

'Good.' Mayne glanced at Wells and turned to Pierce: 'I take it you've now had a chance to visit St Giles for yourself.'

Pierce nodded. 'I'm pleased to report that the crowds have diminished and that my men have secured the premises.' Uncrossing his legs, he glanced across at Pyke and added, 'In fact, I believe I've come across some information which may be of use to the investigation.'

'Go on, Benedict.'

'One of the victims, the pawnbroker, Cullen, was threatened only the other week by a couple of brutes with Munster brogues.'

Pyke felt the muscles in his stomach tighten. 'You must have talked to the wife.' He paused, trying to gather his wits. 'But it's not your investigation.'

'I was just trying to apprise myself of the situation.' Pierce looked around the room and realised that this was new information. 'And it's lucky I did because it looks like Inspector Pyke has omitted to share this piece of news.'

'A troublesome oversight, indeed, especially in the light of Walter's suspicions about the Irishmen who were seen firing their pistols.' Mayne stared at Pyke and shook his head.

Pierce asked Wells to elaborate, and when Wells had finished Pierce nodded then turned to Pyke. 'Then it seems we have our men already.'

'Except Pyke doesn't seem to concur with this view,' Mayne said.

Pyke did his best to hide his anger but the sudden rush of blood to his neck must have given him away.

'No? Already trying to do things your own way, Pyke?' Pierce taunted him.

Not for the first time it struck Pyke what an outsider he was in their company. Ostensibly, he dressed as they dressed and spoke as they spoke, but whereas Mayne and Wells had come from upstanding, landed families and Pierce had bought his way into the right clubs and associations, Pyke had grown up in the rookery and would never be accepted as their equal. Most of the time, Pyke was unconcerned by their efforts to disparage and exclude him, and the idea of ever wanting to join their clubs appalled him, but every now and again their high-handed manner rankled him. If he was honest, Pyke was most angered by the idea that someone in the Branch might be passing information back to Pierce. For how else would Pierce have known so quickly about the Irishmen who had been to Cullen's shop? Pierce had been the head of the Detective Branch before him and still had contacts, perhaps even friends, among the detectives and the clerks. Pyke had been told that Eddie Lockhart had been Pierce's favourite.

'I'll ask you again, Sir Richard,' Pyke said. 'Is this my investigation?'

Mayne gave Pyke a cool stare and reiterated the importance of co-operation between divisions.

'I asked a question, sir, and I'd appreciate an answer. Is this my investigation?'

'Yes, for land's sake, I told you it was ...'

Pyke stood up and straightened his frock-coat. 'Then until I'm told differently, I'll run it as *I* see fit.' He didn't take another breath until he was out of the room, and he waited until he was halfway along the corridor before he punched the wall.

THREE

While his men were gathering in the main office, Pyke was able to open a note from Ned Villums. It had been left for him by one of the clerks. The note simply said: *Harry Dove went to shop to inspect a jewelled crucifix, very valuable.* Pyke put the note in his pocket and turned this new information over in his mind. So Dove had gone to Cullen's shop on business. For some reason, the mention of a jewelled crucifix seemed familiar and he made a note to check the daily route-papers detailing items that had been reported as stolen.

As soon as Pyke stepped into the main office, the four sergeants looked up at him and their conversations ceased. It was always the way, and Pyke had increasingly been trying to interpret their reticence in his presence. Shaw, he felt, was afraid or in awe of him whereas Gerrett resented him in the way a stupid, lumbering dog resented its master. Whicher didn't say much to the other men and had either excluded himself from their social circle or been excluded; Pyke didn't know which. But it was Lockhart's silence which Pyke found the hardest to read. Aside from Whicher, he was the most intelligent of the detectives and his work was thorough and imaginative, but Pyke couldn't help feeling that Lockhart resented him in some way. Pyke recognised Lockhart's indifference because he had once behaved in a similar manner with his superiors. As a Runner, Pyke had operated according to his own agenda and had had little time for the chief magistrates he'd served under. Now he was head of a department, he had to inspire men to do their best for him, and this meant making sure they either respected or feared him.

Pyke's detectives had come from working-class backgrounds and, like most working lads made good, they were used to taking their orders from men like Mayne or even Benedict Pierce, who had been able to reinvent himself as a blue-blooded defender of Church, Crown and Empire. But Pyke had no idea what they made of *him*, whether they saw him as an establishment figure or an outsider. They would have heard a little about his past, of course, because it had been openly aired at the time of his appointment; they would know, for example, that he had once been convicted of murder and that he had been sentenced to hang before escaping from Newgate and earning a pardon. Or that more recently he'd served nine months in Marshalsea prison for not paying his debts.

Two days earlier, following an arrest that Gerrett had made, a shoemaker and a father of four from Shoreditch had been convicted at Bow Street for stealing a gentleman's greatcoat. The man's pleas for clemency had fallen on deaf ears and the magistrate had sentenced him to serve eight years in the House of Correction for the County of Middlesex, otherwise known as Coldbath Fields. Gerrett had gone around the room seeking the acclaim of the other men. When he'd come to Pyke, he had stood there like a schoolboy waiting to be praised. Pyke had congratulated him on a job well done and then reminded him that a poor man with four children had been sent to prison for eight years for stealing a coat. He had also mentioned the case of a stockbroker who'd defrauded investors of thousands of pounds and who had walked out of the courtroom without incurring a fine. Only Jack Whicher had seemed to have understood what he'd meant.

Pyke invited the men into his office and waited for them to file into the small room and take their place in a semicircle around his desk. He started by telling them about the suspicions regarding the Raffertys; the fact that they had visited Cullen's shop a few weeks earlier and pressed the pawnbroker to receive stolen goods and that some men, possibly the Raffertys, had been seen firing their pistols on wasteland behind King's Cross. He also described his encounter with Conor Rafferty and said that a roomful of people were willing to swear the Raffertys had been drinking in the Blue Dog on Castle Street at the time of the shooting. For the time being, he decided not to say anything about the crucifix.

He turned to Shaw. 'Tell us how you fared at Bow Street. Was Cullen's wife telling the truth when she intimated Cullen had never been convicted of a crime?'

Shaw took out his notepad and wiped his nose. 'Cullen's served two prison sentences. One as a debtor, six months in the Fleet. The other for receiving stolen goods. Two and a half years in Coldbath Fields.'

There was a murmur of approval from the others.

'When was that?' Pyke asked.

'About four years ago.'

Pyke digested this information. It didn't change much – in fact, it only confirmed what he'd already suspected: that Cullen was a disreputable but insignificant figure, a man on the fringes of the city's underworld.

'Good work, Frederick.' The others congratulated him, too. Shaw stammered that he'd been lucky.

Turning to Gerrett, Pyke tried not to pay too much attention to the disgusting mound of wobbling flesh around the man's neck. 'What news from the inquest?'

'The jury ruled the deaths to be wilful murder committed by a person or persons unknown.'

'And are the bodies still at the Queen's Head?'

'In the upstairs room.' Gerrett shot a sideways glance at Lockhart. Most of the time, he didn't breathe without Lockhart's approval. 'The landlord said the bodies can stay where they are; he's happy to let people traipse upstairs to see them, thinks they'll stop for a drink after. He didn't need any convincing it would be good for business.'

'Anything else from the inquest?'

'No, I don't think so,' Gerrett said, his hands in his pockets.

'I'm presuming it didn't shed light on the identity of the other two victims?'

'You presume right.' Gerrett folded his arms and sniffed.

Pyke chose to ignore the big man's attempt to needle him. 'Well, someone will recognise them soon enough, at least the one who was shot in the back rather than the face.' Pyke made sure he didn't meet Jack Whicher's stare.

'There's already a queue outside the Queen's Head stretching back as far as the Theatre Royal,' Gerrett added.

'I want you there as soon as the landlord opens his doors.' Pyke paused, wondering whether he should assign Shaw to help. 'Some of those waiting in the queue will be desperate to convince you the dead are their friends or loved ones. Don't ask me why, because there's no financial advantage in it, but people like to be associated with something like this. Your job is to sort out the wheat from the chaff. So don't be afraid to ask difficult questions and, remember, to make a positive identification, you'll need corroboration from two independent witnesses.'

Pyke turned to Whicher, who didn't seem particularly enthused by his discoveries. 'Your turn, Detective.' He didn't like to call him 'Jack' in the company of the others, because this singled Whicher out as his favourite.

'The wife's disorganised so the books are in a real mess,' Whicher said, looking at Pyke. 'I'd say it's a small operation; it doesn't seem to make more than a few pounds a month, barely enough to pay the rent.'

'That's a good start,' Pyke said. 'But now, I'd like you to focus on something else.' Pyke glanced across at Lockhart and quickly explained that the detective sergeant had found an eyewitness and gave a description of what the elderly man had seen: a single figure fleeing the scene, brandishing a large pistol.

'The man walking past the front of the shop, Morgan, told me he heard three shots fired in rapid succession. If they all came from a single gun, we can rule out a conventional flintlock pistol. But I've read about a new gun called a revolver that some gunsmiths have begun to import from America.' Looking at Whicher now, he added, 'I'd like you to visit every gunsmith you can think of and get names and descriptions of anyone who's purchased one of these weapons in, say, the last month.'

Whicher nodded briskly. He seemed happy about the prospect of not having to return to the pawnbroker's shop.

Pyke turned to Lockhart. 'I hope you don't mind me telling the men about your findings, Detective.'

To his credit, Lockhart shrugged and said he wasn't concerned. 'I sat with the witness for quite a while,' he added, looking at Whicher and Shaw. 'In the end, he gave me quite a reasonable description of the gunman. Our suspect is at least six foot tall, well built, with short, black hair. He's swarthy, clean shaven, and wears expensive clothes.'

'A gentleman rather than a poor Irishman, then?' Pyke asked.

Lockhart made a point of avoiding his eyes. 'It could have been a disguise.'

Pyke nodded. He didn't like the men arguing with him but Lockhart was right; it was wise to keep all avenues of enquiry open.

'Actually there was something else,' Lockhart said, sensing that Pyke was about to move on.

'Yes?'

'A crossing sweeper by the name of ...' Lockhart had to look down to consult his pad. 'Jervis. He reckons he saw a policeman in the vicinity of the pawnbroker's around the time of the shooting.'

This was new and potentially important information. 'Before or after?'

'The sweeper said just before. Then he heard the shots. He told me he looked round and the policeman was gone.'

Pyke turned to Whicher, not bothering to hide his concern. 'Who was the first to arrive at the scene?'

'Constable Kent, E Division. Badge number E78.' He paused while he read through his notes. 'The witness, Morgan, ran up to him outside the Theatre Royal on Drury Lane.'

'So this policeman the crossing-sweeper saw, or thought he saw, outside the shop on Shorts Gardens couldn't have been Kent.'

Whicher shook his head.

Pyke turned back to Lockhart. 'Are you absolutely sure your witness wasn't having you on?'

'He was adamant.' Lockhart folded his arms. 'He gave quite a detailed description, too. Said the man had black bushy hair under his stovepipe hat and a bad limp.'

Pyke took a moment to ponder what he'd just been told. It made no sense. If a policeman had been near the shop at the time of the robbery, he would at least have raised the alarm. Still, if the crossing-sweeper was telling the truth, it was good detective work on Lockhart's part.

'I'll look into this. But tomorrow I'd like you to find this new witness and bring him here so I can talk to him.'

Lockhart pursed his lips. 'He'll just tell you exactly what he told me.'

Pyke was about to respond but he managed to restrain himself.

As he looked around the room, he could feel the heat rising in his neck.

Lockhart leaned over and whispered something in Gerrett's ear. The taller man grinned and, as he did so, he looked at Pyke.

'Something amusing, Billy?'

Gerrett reddened but said nothing. Next to him, Lockhart's smile turned into a smirk.

Rankled, Pyke stared Lockhart down. 'I want to make one thing perfectly clear: what we discuss in this room goes no farther.'

No one spoke or even moved. 'And let me say this: if I find out that *any* of you have been passing information about this investigation to parties not present in this room I'll drum you out of this office and back into uniform quicker than you can say Benedict Pierce.'

Later, when Pyke returned home, he found Godfrey in ebullient mood, railing against the latest income tax demand he'd received, and Felix lying next to Copper, seemingly picking fleas from the mastiff's tawny fur. Felix's face was rigid with concentration. It was the same expression he had while reading or doing school work. In these circumstances, it was almost impossible to rouse him, even to come to the table to eat. Pyke found Felix's dedication to his studies commendable but he also worried about his son becoming too closeted from the world around him.

'I told the buggers I no longer earn an income. I'm a destitute old man in the twilight of his life.' Godfrey's face was the colour of a ripe beetroot and his hand was nursing a glass of claret.

'You'll outlive us all,' Pyke said, waiting for Felix to look up and acknowledge him. Hearing Pyke's voice, Copper lifted his head and started to wag his tail.

'God forbid it.' Godfrey chuckled.

'Good day at school?' Pyke asked Felix.

Felix's face was blank, almost bored. 'Same as always.'

Pyke nodded. This was about as much as he ever got out of his son. It was the way of the world, he supposed. Fathers and sons. It wouldn't have bothered him except that he knew that the lad confided in Godfrey, poured out his heart to the old man. In one sense, Pyke was grateful that Felix had someone he felt he could talk to, but in another, he wondered why such a chasm had opened up between himself and the boy. Perhaps it was just his age. He had heard someone say that fourteen-year-olds rarely opened their mouths in the company of adults. Briefly he wondered what Felix was like at school, how he related to his peers and his teachers.

Godfrey sat down in one of the armchairs and groaned. He had lost a lot of weight in recent months and his once lustrous mane of white hair had thinned considerably. Earlier in the summer, he had taken Pyke to a place called Bunhill Fields and explained that he had bought one of the plots there. It was, he'd said, the only non-denominational burial ground in the city; a place that housed the graves of men such as Blake and Defoe. Godfrey had made Pyke promise not to give him a Christian funeral when he died. Pyke had assured him that he needn't worry about being accepted into heaven.

'Felix, dear boy. Will you be so kind as to fetch your favourite uncle another glass of claret?' He poured the rest of the wine into his mouth and held up his empty glass.

Almost at once Felix rose to his feet and took the glass from Godfrey's hand. He didn't think to offer a glass to Pyke.

If Godfrey saw the hurt in Pyke's expression, he didn't mention it. Instead he sat forward and whispered, 'Actually, I wanted to talk to you about the boy ... something he said to me.'

Pyke's expression remained opaque because he didn't want the old man to see that he was envious of the easy manner that Godfrey had with his son.

'He's tried to initiate a few conversations with me over the past month or two about Christianity; whether I have any faith, what I think about the crucifixion, the resurrection.'

Pyke assimilated this piece of information. Eventually he said, 'You think it's been on his mind.'

'I'd say so.'

'Did he say anything else?'

'In what sense?'

'Where this interest has come from, for example?'

That drew a sharp frown. 'He's fourteen. He's old enough to have his own questions.'

Pyke wondered whether someone at the school had been

40

encouraging his son, but then dismissed the thought. One of the reasons Pyke had chosen the school in the first place was its non-denominational status and the fact it offered no religious instruction.

They heard Felix's footsteps returning and Godfrey whispered, 'I don't want you to say anything to the lad just yet ...'

They both looked up at the same time. Felix, who was almost as tall as Pyke and the spitting image of his mother, cocked his head and said, 'Were you talking about me?'

Godfrey held out his hand to receive the glass of claret. 'I was just asking your father about the Drury Lane murders. The three men shot dead in the pawnbroker's.'

'Oh.' Felix thought about this for a moment. 'It looked like you were talking about me, that's all.'

'Well, I was just asking your father whether you'd expressed an interest in the case,' Godfrey added.

Pyke would have liked Felix to have been more interested in what he did for a living but the lad seemed to regard his work as vulgar. Long gone were the days when Felix had devoured the tales of the *Newgate Calendar*. Now, he was far more likely to have Plato's *Republic* or a book about Florentine art on his bedside table.

'Why on earth would I be interested in the exploits of criminals?'

'You'd prefer it if such actions went unpunished? That men be permitted to kill each other with impunity?' Pyke tried – and failed – to keep the irritation from his voice.

'Maybe you're right, Pyke, but the world can be such a beautiful place.' Felix had taken to calling him Pyke in recent months, just like everyone else. He had also adopted an affected way of speaking and, on occasions, Pyke had come close to slapping him.

'Beautiful for those who can afford beautiful things. For those who can't grub together enough to live, it's a different story.'

Felix shrugged. 'Does the sunset cost anything? Or the view from the top of Primrose Hill?'

'I don't suppose someone living in the middle of Spitalfields has ever heard of Primrose Hill.'

Felix looked at him and glared. He was now caught in an argument he couldn't win.

Later Pyke wondered whether he might have pressed his point too hard because Felix stood up suddenly and left the room without saying another word.

'It's just a phase, dear boy,' Godfrey said gently.

'I hope so.' Pyke looked at his uncle and shook his head. 'For the lad's sake as much as mine.'

That night, Pyke lay in bed thinking about Felix and how different his life was to the one Pyke had known as a boy. He often wondered what his own childhood had really been like, whether it had been as good or as bad as he remembered. It was true that prior to his father's death they had been poor, but he wouldn't have known it at the time. Felix took so much for granted because for the most part he'd always been comfortable, well provided for. Pyke remembered sleeping under hessian sacks that scratched his skin; he remembered roaming the streets with other children, stealing his first apple; he remembered the hunger pains in his stomach when he had to go to bed without a meal and the smell of the Macassar oil that his father used to put in his hair before going to the tavern. It was funny what you remembered as you got older, things that you thought were lost for ever. When Felix was born, Pyke had never known a joy like it, and when his son was a young boy, Felix's adoration had carried him through many a dark hour. Now all of that was gone, and though he wanted to be a better father he didn't know how.

Lying there in the dark, his thoughts turned to Godfrey and how different life would be without him; mostly how different it would be between him and Felix. With Godfrey gone, it would just be the two of them, no one to mediate between them as the old man had done for as long as Felix had been able to talk. Why was it, Pyke wondered, that he didn't know what to say to his son, how to talk to him? And why did he always feel he wasn't doing enough for the lad? That he'd always somehow let Felix down? Or that he was a disappointment or an embarrassment to him? Still unable to sleep, Pyke turned his thoughts finally to the robbery. He imagined the first shot being fired, the gunman waiting for the smoke to clear, then firing again and again, until the room was silent. He thought about Walter Wells and his desire to cast the Irish as villains; about

Pierce and his apparently 'magnanimous' decision to take up the vacant position as the head of Holborn Division; and finally about the detectives under his own command. But the last face he saw before he drifted off to sleep was Harry Dove's: it was pressed against a dirty pane of glass, twisted and contorted, mouthing something that Pyke couldn't quite fathom.

FOUR

The sky was the colour of dishwater, the air still damp from the rain that had swept in from the west, accompanied by a vicious wind that had torn lead slates from the roofs. It was no longer raining; a faint drizzle, almost a mist, had succumbed to the mild glow of the sun rising in the east, and the pavements and cobblestones were just beginning to dry.

The first wagon stopped at one end of Buckeridge Street and six police constables in uniform – long-tailed coats and top hats – alighted; a few minutes later, a second wagon pulled up behind it and then a third, just short of twenty hand-picked men assembling on the corner of Buckeridge and Church Streets, trying not to make a noise or draw attention to themselves. From within the rookery – a dense jumble of decrepit tenements, alleyways and courts that extended as far north as the British Museum – a cockerel crowed and a dog barked. The men conversed in whispers, glancing nervously up and down the narrow street as a shaft of watery sunlight cut through the surrounding rooftops. Finally a fourth wagon arrived and Walter Wells alighted. The acting superintendent stepped over the water pooled in the gutter and strode out in front of the other officers, the military man in his element, inspecting his troops before battle. Wells inhaled a pinch of snuff and wiped his forehead with the sleeve of his coat. The men had breakfasted well, Wells had seen to that; as a soldier, he knew that any army marched and fought on its stomach. Everything seemed to be in order.

Some of the dwellings were derelict – Buckeridge and Bainbridge Streets had both been earmarked for demolition; a new road linking High Holborn in the east and Oxford Street in the west was planned, cutting a swathe through the worst part of the rookery. Most of the buildings, however, were still occupied, if only by squatters, the poorest of the poor, who slept eight or ten to a room, defecated in the street, and cooked food on open fires in the yards or courts.

Wells took out his truncheon and indicated for his men to do likewise. Raising it up in the air, he waited for a moment, like a conductor, and then brought it down with a sudden jerk of his wrist. The constables filed out along the street, two congregating at each door. When they were all in place, Wells gave the signal and they issued a collective belly roar and crashed through the doors in unison, the noise shattering the silence and echoing up and down the narrow street. Wells stood there, sniffing the air, as the first bedraggled men were slung out on to the street, arms protecting their heads, while other policemen moved forward to throw them into the waiting wagons. Ignoring the screams of women and children, who had also been herded into the street, the policemen moved systematically from house to house, not stopping until the entire street had been cleared, and their truncheons were coated with a patina of blood. Only then did they consider the desolation they had caused, the screaming and the wailing as the first of the wagons, jammed full of bodies, lurched forward, the horses buckling under the strain despite the crack of the driver's whip.

Wells gave Pyke a full description of what had happened later that morning when Pyke found him in the corridor outside the holding cells underneath the old watch-house. Wells's division and number – A1 – was manifest on the collar of his coat; his truncheon was clipped to his belt.

The cells were full to the point of overflowing and the confined space smelled of body odour and gin. Wells greeted Pyke enthusiastically and told him that the raid had been a qualified success. They hadn't found the gunmen but he assured Pyke that it would only be a matter of time.

Pyke listened, trying to reconcile his anger with the notion that Wells outranked him and hence wouldn't welcome the criticism. It was stupid, what they had done, stirring up unnecessary trouble, but Pyke didn't want to make an enemy out of Wells just yet.

'I spoke to one of the Rafferty brothers yesterday at the Blue Dog on Castle Street. He told me that a hundred men would vouch that he and his brothers were there at the time of the robbery.'

'And you didn't think to share this information with me?'

'Your mind seemed to be made up.' Pyke waited. 'Just because a handful of Irishmen were seen firing their guns on wasteland doesn't mean they walked into Cullen's shop and shot three men in cold blood.'

Wells eyed him suspiciously. 'I don't like to say it, sir, but you're beginning to sound like a papist appeaser.'

Pyke let the insult linger in the air between them. It didn't especially bother him – he'd been called a lot worse.

Perhaps sensing he'd pushed the matter too far, Wells softened his expression. 'Notwithstanding the smoke and mirrors of their idolatrous religion, if you'd seen what I saw this morning, *fifty* men, women and children crammed into dwellings that weren't built to house more than ten, you might agree that we are being overrun by papists.'

'And beating a few of them over the head with truncheons is going to take care of the problem?'

Wells looked up and down the narrow corridor and shook his head, disappointed by Pyke's response. 'I see we're never going to agree on this issue but perhaps, Detective Inspector, I could have some assurance that in the future you will keep me informed on matters pertaining to this investigation?'

'If you'll let me know when you intend to drag half of the Irish poor in here to answer questions.'

They regarded one another for a moment or two but it was Wells who broke the silence. Brightening, he slapped Pyke on the arm and said, 'I'll do what I can, Detective Inspector. I hope you'll do likewise.' When Pyke nodded, he smiled and added, 'I'm quite certain we will get along together just fine.'

Pyke said he hoped this would be the case and waited. He could tell that Wells had something else on his mind.

'Actually, Detective Inspector, I wanted to talk to you about Superintendent Benedict Pierce.'

'Pierce?' As ever, when the man's name was mentioned, Pyke felt his skin prickle.

'Your antipathy towards him is hardly a secret. And by all accounts he is less than fond of you. I heard that he sought to thwart your appointment as head of the Detective Branch?'

Pyke just shrugged. He'd heard the same rumour and suspected it to be true. 'I've made no secret of my low opinion of Pierce.'

'Quite, quite,' Wells said, suddenly adopting a more amicable tone, 'and between you and me, I commend your judgement. While I would never articulate such thoughts in public, I am happy to concede that I find the man to be untrustworthy and unctuous. I am telling you this in confidence, of course.'

'Fine,' Pyke said, trying to assess whether Wells's disparagement of Pierce was genuine or not – and why he had chosen to talk to Pyke about it.

'You will perhaps have wondered why Superintendent Pierce volunteered to assume command of the Holborn Division.'

'I have my ideas.'

'Such as?'

'He intends to meddle in this investigation. Perhaps he wants to take the credit for any success, or he simply wants to show me up. He still has his admirers in the Detective Branch.'

Wells considered this. 'Perhaps you know information that could scupper his ascent up the greasy pole.'

A moment's silence passed between them. Pyke held Wells's gaze and tried to work out whether he was just fishing for information. 'Perhaps, but I'm sure he knows things about me that could be just as damaging,' Pyke said, eventually.

'Then it might be as well to collect as many friends in high places as possible.' Wells paused. 'Perhaps you know that the assistant commissioner's position is soon to be filled. What you may not know, however, is that Pierce intends to offer himself as a candidate.'

'But he's only just been appointed as superintendent of the Holborn Division.'

Wells shrugged. 'You'll understand, Pyke, I am not without self-interest in this matter. I've made no secret of the fact that I consider myself to be a worthy candidate for the position – or at least more worthy than Pierce.'

'If it came down to a straight choice between you and Pierce, you can rest assured that I wouldn't recommend Pierce.'

That seemed to gratify the former soldier and he grinned and clapped Pyke on the back. 'Capital, old chap. Capital. And I'll do my utmost not to interfere in your investigation. How does that sound?'

When Lockhart brought the crossing-sweeper to Pyke's office later that day, the dishevelled and slightly pungent man kept to his story and confirmed everything that Lockhart had said. As soon as the shots were fired, the crossing-sweeper said, the policeman had hurried off in another direction. That was how he knew the man had a limp, he added. Lockhart remained in the room while Pyke questioned the sweeper, his expression slightly smug. Once the man had said his piece, Pyke thanked both him and Lockhart and gave the former a few shillings for his time.

Pyke barely had a moment to gather his thoughts when Billy Gerrett knocked on his door and fell into the room. His large, round face was still glistening with sweat from the run up the stairs. 'We know who one of the victims was.'

If it had been Whicher or Lockhart, they might have seen Pyke's involuntary flinch. As it was, Gerrett was too wrapped up in his news.

'Who?'

A drop of sweat fell from Gerrett's chin and landed a few inches from the tip of Pyke's boots.

'Harry Dove,' Gerrett said. 'The one who was shot in the back.'

'And this identification has been corroborated?'

Gerrett nodded briskly. 'Two independent witnesses. Both credible.'

Pyke stared up at Gerrett's jowly face and his mop of greasy blond hair. 'And what could they tell us about this man?'

'One said he used to work at the Old Cock in Holborn; the other that he lives somewhere on Finsbury Square.'

'Who else knows about this?'

'Well, I told Lockhart and Shaw ...'

'That's fine,' Pyke said, trying to appear more genial. 'Just don't divulge his name to anyone outside the department. That understood?' When Gerrett nodded, Pyke added, 'Have you checked the files?'

Again Gerrett nodded.

'And?'

'There's nothing on Dove.'

Pyke knew this already, but he tried to appear sanguine. 'Of course, it could be that he was just a customer. Unlucky man finds himself in the wrong place at the wrong time.'

But the implications were lost on Billy Gerrett. He nodded blankly and waited for Pyke to congratulate him on a job well done.

After Gerrett left, Pyke opened the filing cabinet, removed a wad of route-papers from the previous six months and put them on his desk. It took him half an hour to find what he'd been looking for. On the fifth of March, a burglary had been reported at the private residence of Archdeacon Wynter; the items stolen included a communion plate and a jewelled cross. Pyke made a note of the archdeacon's address, put the reports back in the cabinet, and sat in his chair, trying to recall why no one in the Detective Branch had been asked to investigate this particular burglary.

The following day, a Sunday, Pyke spent the morning with Felix, a ritual they had fallen into following Emily's death. At first it had been a genuine pleasure to go for a walk or a ride in a carriage with his son, a weekly event he would look forward to and which the boy seemed to enjoy as well. In the last few years, however, this ritual had dwindled from a weekly event to a monthly one, a slow, unspoken retreat from the intimacy they'd once known, and now, when Pyke suggested they go to the zoo or take a ride out to the country, his son responded with a dead-eyed shrug, not rejecting the idea but not showing any enthusiasm either. Pyke wasn't necessarily upset by this but he couldn't stand Felix's distance, the fact that the lad spent so much time with his head in a book. He'd tried to ask, on a few occasions, what interested the boy or what exactly he saw himself doing in the future, but Felix would only look at him with a pained expression and say he didn't know. Pyke loved him, of course, but he worried about what the school that cost him so much money was turning Felix into. Privately he was glad Felix had not yet become some kind of adolescent gentleman, but the lad's apparent thirst for knowledge had turned him against more earthly pursuits.

That morning, they had aimlessly toured the deserted streets of the West End in the back of a hackney carriage, then Pyke had given up the carriage and made them walk from the edge of Regent's Park all the way to Holborn. It had started to rain after the first ten minutes and they completed the hour-long stroll in grudging silence, Felix a few steps behind him, hands buried in his pockets.

'There's a man I need to talk to,' Pyke said, as they neared his intended destination. He reached into his coat and retrieved a few coins. 'Here, that's for the fare home.'

Felix took the coins, his eyes barely acknowledging Pyke. Pyke supposed no more would be said, but then the lad surprised him.

'Why don't we go to church on Sundays like everyone else?' There was a note of confrontation in his voice.

Pyke knew that Felix had started to exhibit an interest in such matters but he'd made a point of not encouraging him. 'You don't like our Sunday mornings?'

Felix knew better than to confront Pyke directly but he elected not to answer the question.

'If you like, you can come with me while I visit this man. Perhaps you'll understand my reasoning better once you've met him.'

Pyke didn't know for certain that Archdeacon Wynter was the objectionable creature he suspected but he felt on reflection that it was highly likely.

'Who is he?' Felix wanted to know, a little intrigued now.

'The archdeacon? One of the most powerful church figures in the whole city.'

'And why do you need to see him?'

'A crucifix was stolen from his private safe a few months ago. I think it was the reason those three people were killed in the shop near Drury Lane.'

But already Felix's interest had waned. Just as a hackney carriage drew alongside them, and without discussing the matter, the lad thrust out his arm. Felix looked at Pyke and shrugged. 'I wouldn't want to get in the way of your work.'

In matters of religion, Pyke was unusual, he supposed, insofar as he didn't just doubt God's existence; rather, he was certain, in his own mind at least, that to presume the existence of God was the height of folly. Pyke didn't shout his views from the rooftops. He was astute enough to realise that such ideas weren't merely unfashionable in the current climate; they were downright inflammatory. In private, Pyke would describe the Roman religion as mysticism and obfuscation, and the Protestant faith as dour and joyless, a practice whose main function seemed to be social rather than spiritual: to make the unruly docile and compliant. In public, though, he would bow his head if a prayer was said or if God's wisdom was called upon. He might give a sardonic smile if he was in polite company and grace was being said, particularly if the recipient of his smile was passably attractive and suitably unimpressed with her husband. To such women he would try to appear as irreverent and worldly because, as everyone knew, Christians were earnest hence unattractive, and they made terrible lovers. He would let these women see that he was dangerous and had a bit of the Devil in him, and later, when he was fucking them in the cloakroom or outside in an alleyway, they would know this for themselves.

Wisdom and experience had taught Pyke not to antagonise the pious unnecessarily, but when he met men like Adolphus Wynter, it was hard not to fall back into old habits.

The archdeacon was the kind of man whose smile put you in mind of fingernails being scraped down a schoolroom blackboard. He was about fifty or thereabouts and still looked in rude health, with a ruddy jowl and the kind of sagging chin that came from overindulgence, and when he shook hands, he squeezed hard, as if the ritual weren't simply a greeting but a test of strength. The ring on his finger told Pyke he was married and later, when Pyke was introduced to his wife, he knew instinctively that the marriage wasn't a happy one. Sometimes you could just tell. The archdeacon wore a black gown and cassock and Pyke could see that he was the kind of man who felt comfortable in this attire, as though it confirmed to others that he had been chosen by God. But it was Wynter's eyes which really caught Pyke's attention. In all the time Pyke was in the man's presence, he almost never blinked.

'You'll understand, I can't possibly entertain your enquiry today. In fact, I'm surprised you should even think to bother me on the Sabbath.'

They were standing in the entrance hall of Wynter's impressively proportioned town house on Red Lion Square.

'Well, I am a little surprised to find you at home but since you are here, I think it would be best if you could grant me a few minutes of your valuable time.' In actuality, Pyke had been told that Wynter always took his Sunday lunch at home before returning to St Paul's for the evening service.

'You are working, sir, and therefore breaking the Sabbath, and if I should indulge your blasphemy, I should be breaking the Sabbath too.'

Pyke ignored the butler who was standing next to the open door. He took another step into the hall and noticed the paintings hanging on the wall. A Gainsborough and, if he wasn't mistaken, a Titian, too. 'My visit concerns the theft of a number of valuable items, including some kind of cross, from this property a few months ago.'

Wynter moved to block Pyke's path into the rest of the house. 'As I just explained to you, sir, I cannot answer your questions today.'

'You're quite sure about that?'

'As sure as the man who built his house on a rock foundation.' The archdeacon smiled for the first time, revealing teeth that were straight and white. 'Matthew seven, verses twenty-four to twenty-seven.'

'So what if I were to tell you that tomorrow the newspapers will carry a story describing how the men shot dead in a pawnbroker's shop on Friday morning were killed because of the cross stolen from this address?'

That wiped the smile from his face and, for a few seconds, the archdeacon was lost for words.

'You did read about the incident? Three men shot in broad daylight in a busy shop just off Drury Lane.'

'Yes, yes,' Wynter snapped. 'I suppose I can spare you five minutes.' He motioned for the butler to close the front door. 'Quickly, man. In the drawing room.'

Wynter led Pyke down the hall to a plush room with elaborately corniced ceilings and a silk damask hanging on the wall. In fact, Pyke was quite taken aback at how large and well appointed Wynter's house was, and he wondered how a man on a church salary could possibly afford such a home, let alone find sufficient funds for its upkeep.

'Perhaps you could tell me what happened and what was taken?' Pyke said, inspecting the towering Georgian window that looked out on to the street.

'Is this really necessary? I went over it with one of your colleagues.'

'But not someone from the Detective Branch.'

Wynter sighed. 'Look, as I told the superintendent at the time, a burglar entered the house through an upstairs window while my family and I, and indeed most of the servants, were attending the evening service at St Paul's.'

Pyke noted that Wynter had referred to a superintendent. This was unusual. In Pyke's experience, such high-ranking figures rarely, if ever, took personal charge of anything as run of the mill as a burglary.

'Perhaps you might tell me whether the items were stolen from a safe?'

'Yes, the one in my study.'

So it had been a professional job. While it was easy enough to break into a safe, you needed to be a trained cracksman to do so.

'Then I'll need to see your study.'

'Why? The safe has been replaced. There's nothing to see.' Wynter glanced at his fob-watch. 'I really do have to insist that we conduct this meeting at some other time.'

'Well, could you just tell me what was taken? As I said, I'm especially interested in this cross.'

'A Saviour's Cross. It's made of solid gold and adorned with precious stones. It's more than three hundred years old, one of the few examples of its type that survived the clutches of Henry VIII's men.'

'And it's valuable?'

The archdeacon glanced again at his fob-watch. 'I couldn't put a price on it but the precious metal and jewels alone would be worth a fortune.'

Pyke allowed his gaze to wander around the room while he pondered the likelihood of a jewelled crucifix turning up in a pawn shop in St Giles. He had taken an instant dislike to the archdeacon but this did not necessarily mean that the man wasn't telling him the truth.

'What else was taken?'

'A solid gold communion plate, a gold cup, a silver pocket watch that belonged to my grandfather and a small amount of money.' He let out a heavy sigh. 'Nothing when compared to the value and importance of the Saviour's Cross.'

Pyke took out his notepad and flicked over the pages until he saw what he was looking for. 'And I'm right in thinking this burglary took place on the first Sunday in March?'

'Yes, man, March, that's correct. Now please, I'm going to have to ask you to leave. I have some very pressing matters to attend to.'

'I take it the cross hasn't been recovered,' Pyke said, ignoring the archdeacon's efforts to usher him out of the room.

'No, it hasn't.' The archdeacon was standing by the door but his curiosity got the better of him. 'You say that the cross has turned up at the shop where those three men were killed?'

'Not turned up. But I'm led to believe that a desire to buy or sell the cross was the reason why at least one of the men was there. Could you tell me the name of the superintendent who investigated the burglary?'

'Look, sir, I have been more than accommodating ...'

'His name, or else I'll go straight to see a journalist I know. He works for the *London Illustrated News*.'

'I made the request, sir, that he attend to the matter in person, given the sensitive and extremely valuable nature of what was taken.'

'I asked for the man's name.'

The archdeacon puffed out his chest. 'You'll get nothing more from me, sir. In spite of your impertinence and threats. Now I'll bid you good day.'

'Then you force me to make an educated guess,' Pyke said, stopping almost directly in front of Wynter. 'Benedict Pierce.'

The archdeacon looked dumbstruck.

The following morning, a Monday, Pyke found Benedict Pierce at his desk on the first floor of the E Division station house on Bow Street. It was the same building that the Bow Street Runners had once occupied and where he and Pierce had started their careers.

Unsurprisingly, Pierce had selected the large walnut-panelled office at the front of the building for himself.

'The Saviour's Cross; it was stolen from the safe of Archdeacon Wynter's private home on the fifth of March this year.'

Pierce didn't look up from the papers he was inspecting. 'Nice to see you, Detective Inspector. But next time, do you think you could knock?'

'The archdeacon specifically asked for you to lead the investigation. Why?'

Pierce held his breath for a moment, as if weighing up the question. 'Is there a reason for this most unwanted intrusion?'

'I've reason to believe that this same item was the target of the robber or robbers who killed the men at the pawnbroker's in St Giles.'

Pierce assimilated this news. 'And what, exactly, has led you to such a conclusion?' There was a note of caution in his tone.

Ignoring his question, Pyke said, 'I want to know how you investigated the robbery at the archdeacon's home and whether you recovered any of the stolen items.'

'If I had recovered the Saviour's Cross, it would be back in the archdeacon's possession, not being hawked to a pawnbroker.'

'Tell me about the investigation.'

'What's to tell? I pursued a number of avenues of enquiry. I'm afraid to say that none of them came to anything.'

'Any suspects?'

Pierce looked around the spacious room and yawned.

'I'm sorry. Am I boring you?'

'Boring me? Of course not.' Pierce smirked. 'I've just got very little of consequence to tell you.'

Pyke looked around the man's office, trying to remember what it had looked like when he'd been a Runner. 'Why did Wynter ask for you personally? Wasn't that unusual, given you were based in Kensington at the time?'

'The archdeacon is a good friend of mine. Is it any wonder he should prefer me to the barbarian currently commanding the Detective Branch?'

The idea of Pierce kneeling before the robed Wynter awaiting his communion made Pyke feel physically ill.

'I'm curious as to why you decided to take up this position, Pierce. I would have thought you had your eyes set on greater things.'

This time Pierce did look up at him, something bordering on concern or interest etched on his face. 'Such as?'

'I heard a rumour that the assistant commissioner's position is soon to be filled.'

Pierce controlled his reaction. 'But can you trust what people tell you? That's the question. For example, I was told recently that your search for the pawnbroker's killer has narrowed considerably. A man of about six feet with dark hair and wearing a gentleman's cloak.'

Pyke did his best to hide it, but Pierce seemed to know at once that he'd won this little exchange. As he left Pierce's office, Pyke was determined to find out the source of Pierce's information.

Pyke waited at the mouth of the street, the buildings on either side towering above him. Sometimes it felt as if the city might open its jaws and consume him whole. Especially in this part of the city, around Saffron Hill and Field Lane, where the buildings seemed to have been constructed almost on top of one another, endless tracts of soot-blackened brick and plaster. It was where the poor came to live and die; where swell mobs planned their next robberies, coiners oxidised their metal, pickpockets and mashers waited in the shadows. The police rarely entered such places, for obvious reasons. It was almost impossible to apprehend a fleeing suspect, and it was dangerous, too: the police weren't popular with the poor.

The city elders often talked about demolishing the rookeries and replacing them with wide avenues and stout, respectable terraces where the middling classes could venture without fearing for their lives. New roads that would cut directly through the worst slums had been planned for St Giles, Spitalfields and Devil's Acre, behind Westminster Abbey. Still, in spite of these grandiose visions not much had changed in this part of the city for decades; if anything, the houses were a little more slipshod, the area a little more dangerous, the rats a little larger. And Wells was right: all of this had been made worse by the never-ending flood of men and women from the countryside and abroad, trains arriving at Euston,

Paddington, London Bridge and Shoreditch spewing thousands of people into the maw of the city, a bloated sponge absorbing everything into its midst.

Villums appeared from the shadows; he was swaying slightly and his breath smelled of whisky. 'Let's walk,' he muttered.

'Someone identified Harry's body,' Pyke said. 'He's now part of the investigation, Ned. There's nothing I can do about it.'

They walked for a few yards in silence. 'But you can stop it getting any closer to me, can't you?'

Pyke shrugged, unsure what kind of assurance he could give. 'Harry was careful, wasn't he? Didn't draw attention to himself, kept his circle of acquaintances small.'

'Clearly he wasn't careful enough,' Villums replied.

'I'll do what I can, Ned. That's the best I can promise.'

Villums stopped and turned to face Pyke. 'And what about the animals who did this to my boy?'

'If I find them, I'll make sure they're punished to the full extent of the law.'

'Is that it?'

Pyke looked into his face. 'Isn't that enough?'

'You forget, Pyke, I know what you're capable of.'

It was true that Pyke had killed men, but not gratuitously and never because he'd been paid to do so. 'I'm a police detective now, Ned.'

The disappointment was tangible in Villums's eyes. 'I said I'd do what I could to help you and I'm a man of my word.'

'You have more information for me?'

'I'm reliably informed that a fence by the name of Alfred Egan is due to meet a man, I don't know who, regarding this cross.'

'When? Tonight?'

Villums nodded. 'Early evening. The Red Lion Inn, Field Lane.'

Pyke knew better than to ask for more information. Instead he patted Villums on the arm and left him to contemplate the scene on the other side of the street, a blind man trying to hit a stray dog with his walking stick.

FIVE

The odour of putrefied flesh wafted on the stiff breeze. Smithfield, with its twice-weekly sheep and cattle market, was near by, as were numerous fat-boilers, tripe-scrapers, dog-skinners and underground slaughterhouses, all contributing to the rank unpleasantness of the air. Rain lashed the cobblestones outside the Red Lion Inn, and women in flounced crinoline skirts tried in vain to lift their hems up out of the mud. Inside, drove-boys rubbed shoulders with butchers, market inspectors and animal traders, and everywhere you looked there were people, heads glistening under the flare of gas-lamps. The Red Lion was a veritable rabbit warren, which was perhaps why Egan had chosen it as a meeting place. In one nook, a fiddle-player was cutting loose while drunken revellers cavorted with one another, their arms linked as they moved in dizzying circles. In another, dead-eyed men were playing cards, winning – and more often losing – a week's wages on the turn of a single card. The walls and ceilings were as black as tar, stained by pipe tobacco and cheap tallow, while the wooden floors were covered with clumps of wet butcher's sawdust and discarded oyster shells. There was a smell, too, that Pyke couldn't quite put his finger on until he saw the prostitutes leading swaying men outside into the alley.

At the counter, Pyke ordered and paid for two gins, pushing one of the glasses towards Whicher. The others – Shaw, Gerrett and Lockhart – were outside, watching the various doors into the tavern. An awkward silence followed as Whicher took the glass and placed it in front of him without taking a sip.

'To working boys made good,' Pyke said, holding up his glass, before tipping the spirit down his throat.

Whicher looked at him with evident surprise. Clearly he hadn't imagined Pyke as a working boy.

'What?' Pyke laughed. 'You think I was born with a silver spoon in my mouth?'

Whicher was bemused. 'I heard a rumour that you married into the aristocracy, that's all.'

This much was true. Emily's father had been related, by marriage rather than blood, to the first duke of Norfolk. But Pyke had never been comfortable in that environment and in the legal wrangling that followed Emily's death, a Chancery judge had eventually ruled in favour of Emily's male cousin. Pyke had never been back to her family's seat – Hambledon Hall – fifteen miles north-east of the capital.

'For the first few years of my life, I lived in St Giles,' Pyke said, by way of explanation. Whicher would know well enough what this meant.

'I was born and grew up in Camberwell.'

Pyke nodded. 'So what made you want to be a policeman?'

'Sometimes I wonder.' Whicher's laugh was defensive rather than humorous.

'How so?'

'A man is killed and every effort is made to apprehend the murderer. But hundreds, thousands, die each year, from starvation, disease and poverty, and we act as if it doesn't matter.'

It was unusual to hear a policeman articulate such a notion, and it reminded Pyke about the other detectives' reaction to the fate of the shoemaker who had stolen the gentleman's coat.

Pyke looked around the crowded room. 'This man we're expecting. He's a crafty operator. One sniff of danger and he'll be off. He knows me by sight. That's why I want you to approach him, make an arrest if you have to. I'll go after the person he's here to meet.'

They turned to watch the men entering and leaving the taproom, Pyke scrutinising their faces. A pot-boy in a black and white apron swept past them with a tray of drinks.

'Are the men happy with how things are progressing?' Pyke asked, suddenly.

'You mean the investigation?'

'Or generally.'

Whicher shrugged. 'They seem to be.'

'You don't talk to them?'

Whicher seemed to consider this for a moment. 'I wouldn't call any of them my friend.'

Pyke was emboldened by this response. 'But they talk to you. Particularly Lockhart.'

Whicher took a sip of gin. 'We talk but given our work together, what we do, that isn't a surprise.'

Pyke nodded, wondering whether in his eagerness to extract information from Whicher he had overplayed his hand. He was about to make light of it when he looked up and saw Alfred Egan wander into the room. Grabbing Whicher's arm, Pyke whispered, 'You see the one in the shooting jacket? That's him.'

Whicher's body stiffened. Pyke said, 'Stand by the door. But don't make a move until I give you the sign. Pretend you're waiting for someone.'

He watched as Whicher pushed through the crowd of bodies. Nervous all of a sudden, he tried not to think about all of the things that could go wrong. Egan was just as Pyke remembered: a slight, nervy, hatchet-faced man. If the fence caught the slightest glimpse of him, he would head straight out of the door. As it was, Egan sat down at one of the tables, his billycock cap resting on his lap. His gaze swept around the room before settling on the door he'd just come through. Whicher took up his position with his back turned to Egan. The fence didn't seem to notice him.

About five minutes later, the door swung open and a tall man wearing a dark cloak stepped into the taproom. Pyke felt the skin around his temples tighten. There were many tall men in the city and it would be too much to hope that this might be the same man the witness had seen running away after the shooting. Pyke took a moment to memorise his features: his muscular frame, slightly receding hairline, beaked nose and thin, almost non-existent, lips. Egan stood up and sidled towards the new arrival. Whicher noted this and moved to block their access to the door. Pyke was moving, too, trying to remain hidden among the mass of bodies milling around the counter. Heart thumping, he made it to within ten feet of Egan before the fence saw him, and immediately tugged at the taller man's sleeve, turning for the door. Whicher was there to block him but the other man had already sensed the danger. Dropping his shoulder, he sent Whicher tumbling to the floor. Pyke arrived in time to hit Egan with a cudgel, but too late to stop the other man from bolting.

Outside, Pyke found little Frederick Shaw lying on the ground. He had been no match for the man, who was now halfway across Field Lane.

Pyke tore off in pursuit of the man, who was now about twenty or twenty-five yards ahead of him. The man noticed he was being followed and darted into one of the alleys zigzagging off the main street, hoping to lose Pyke in the labyrinth of lanes, yards and courts. Underfoot, the ground was slippery and Pyke nearly lost his footing. Each time he turned a corner, he feared that he had lost his prey, but the man ahead of him wasn't thinking as he should have; he was concerned only about putting as much distance as possible between himself and Pyke rather than trying to hide from him. The man was taller than Pyke and should have been quicker, but he was less agile over the spongy ground. Pyke sensed he was catching up even before the man tripped on a piece of discarded furniture. But just as the man fell, a young girl, oblivious to what was happening, stepped out in front of Pyke. Later he would remember the feeling as he clattered into her, but he managed to maintain his footing, careened on towards the man and launched himself through the air, tackling the man and sending them both sprawling into the mud.

On the ground, the advantage ceded to the taller, stronger man. The chase had taken more out of Pyke than he'd realised, too. He tried to stand up, reasoning that if he could make it on to his feet, he stood a better chance of being able to finish off his opponent: a kick to the groin, a stamp to the head. This was how street fights were won. The man sensed this, and pulled him back down into the mud, wrapping his giant arms around Pyke's chest and squeezing. There was little Pyke could do. The man's grip was like a vice and Pyke thought at one point that his shoulder had been wrenched out of its socket. Red faced and perspiring, Pyke looked up and saw a smudged face and a pair of white eyes looking out from one of the broken windows of the tenements. Others had gathered around them; the fight a diversion from their routine. They could tell it was serious, too – an awed silence had fallen over the alley. Just as he feared he might pass out, every last breath crushed from his chest, Pyke managed to free one of his arms and with as much force as he could muster, he drove his elbow back into the man's stomach. Doing so created sufficient room for Pyke to drive the other elbow up into the bridge of the man's nose. Free at last, he rolled over and brought his forehead down hard against the man's already shattered nose. That drew a shriek of pain.

Up on his feet, Pyke drove the heel of his boot on to his opponent's hand but the man was quick and scrambled to his feet as well, then charged at Pyke, catching him off balance. They crashed through the half-open door of one of the tenements. Too late, Pyke realised that the man had managed to retrieve a knife from his boot. In the next instant, he slammed the knife down, Pyke moving quickly to one side, the blade slicing through his coat and shirt. At first, Pyke felt nothing, then a wetness. The pain hit him only later. The man vacillated as Pyke sank to the ground, perhaps trying to decide whether to finish him off or run. Pyke took advantage of his hesitation, grabbed hold of the man's ankle and twisted it in a sudden, circular movement. There was the sound of bone snapping and what tumbled from the man's mouth seemed inhuman. The knife fell from his hand and he collapsed to the floor. Pyke tried to crawl away but the man wouldn't let him. Pulling Pyke back towards him, he seemed to have made up his mind. His hands slid around Pyke's neck and he started to squeeze. Pyke could see the man's eyes, smell his rage. Choking, he tried to pull the man's hands away from his neck, to no avail. Suddenly light headed, he tried to resist the urge to panic, to give in. That would lead to certain death. With his last reserves of strength, Pyke ran his fingers over the man's face and then gouged his thumbs into his eyes, breaking his opponent's grip. Pyke staggered to his feet and aimed a wild kick at the man's head. Then he heard rattles and saw Shaw and Whicher at the door, a constable in uniform, too, and he felt one of them – Whicher perhaps – pulling him away as someone else uttered, 'He's lost a lot of blood.'

The wound wasn't a deep one. It was what doctors called a flesh wound. Still, Pyke couldn't remember much about being carried to

St Bartholomew's or being stitched up by a surgeon. He put this down to exhaustion – and the effects of the laudanum they'd fed him. Later in the night, he woke up, disoriented, asking for Emily. She came to him, her face clear in a way it hadn't been for years. The room smelled of camphor. He tried to reach out and touch her but there was nothing there. Outside, the rain was pelting down against the windowpanes but the room – and the hospital – was absolutely quiet. Pyke lay there, not daring to move, thinking about the man he'd fought and whether the Saviour's Cross had been recovered from one of his pockets.

Finally Pyke fell asleep until the light raised him; he lay there for a moment, blinking, trying to remember what had happened. As he sat up, a sharp pain bolted down one side of his body. He peeled off the bandage and inspected the wound; it was six inches long and criss-crossed with stitches. It wasn't bleeding, though. That had to be a good sign. He tried to swallow but couldn't; his mouth was dry, all the moisture leached from his body like water evaporating on a hot grate.

Jack Whicher came to see him in the middle of the morning. He offered Pyke the best wishes of the other detectives and told him that he'd passed a message on to his housekeeper, telling her that Pyke had been injured but that she wasn't to worry. Pyke thanked him for remembering this detail and tried to sit up.

'Are you badly injured?' Whicher asked. To Pyke, the concern in his voice seemed genuine.

'If it wasn't for the laudanum, I'd feel it right enough. But I'll live. And I'll be back at work in a few days.' Pyke pushed his back into the pillows. 'Tell me about the man. I assume he's under lock and key.'

'He's not going anywhere.'

'Egan, too?'

Whicher nodded. 'Cells at different ends of the passageway.'

'That's good.' It wouldn't give them the chance to concoct a story. Pyke took a breath. 'For God's sake, man, put me out of my misery. Did you find the cross?'

'I'm afraid not. And so far he's refused to say a word, he won't even tell us his name. There wasn't anything in his pockets to help us identify him.'

Outside the room, a porter rattled by with a trolley. Pyke waited until he had passed. 'I don't know if you've thought about finding the second witness, the coal-whipper who saw the man in the cloak ...'

'Gerrett and Shaw have gone to find him, to see if he can identify the man we've arrested.' Whicher paused. 'I might've found a gunsmith on the Strand who sold a revolving pistol to a man matching his description.'

A sudden pain across Pyke's midriff caused him to wince. Looking up, he saw the excitement on Whicher's face. This was the best part of the job and he was sorry to be missing it: the noose was already halfway around their suspect's neck. He asked about the man's condition.

'Broken nose, broken ankle. Might lose an eye, too. A doctor visited him last night, put a splint on his ankle and gave him some laudanum for the pain.'

'I'd like you to take charge of the interrogation. Press him for a name, at the very least. And let me know as soon as possible if he's identified as our gunman.'

'And Egan?'

'He'll deny knowing the other man. He'll tell you he hasn't done anything wrong and in a way he's right. He hasn't. He'll demand to be released. Just keep him locked up until I'm well enough to make it to Scotland Yard. And whatever you do,' Pyke added, 'don't let anyone else go near the prisoners. And certainly no one outside of the Branch.'

Nodding, Whicher went to check his pocket watch. 'I meant to say; your son's waiting outside. I asked him if he wanted to see you first but he said you'd probably prefer to talk to me.'

A sharp, searing pain streaked up and down his entire left side but Pyke tried to smile. 'Tell him to come in.' At the door, Whicher paused and Pyke said, 'It's good of you to come and see me, keep me informed.'

Pyke had expected Felix to be his usual nonchalant self but as soon as the lad stepped into the room, he rushed over to the bed and embraced him, suppressing a sob. He assured Pyke that he'd come as soon as he'd heard, even though Mrs Booth, the house-keeper, had told him not to. It took Pyke a few minutes to calm his son and convince him that the injury wasn't a serious one. When he showed Felix the wound, the lad pressed his nose against it, and informed Pyke that it didn't smell. This was a good sign, Felix assured him. Pyke sat there, staring at his son, surprised at how much the lad's concern had touched him. He wanted to say something but couldn't find the right words.

'What?' Felix withdrew from him, aware that he was being watched.

'Nothing. It's just good to see you, that's all.' Pyke smiled.

Felix looked away awkwardly. He stood up and wandered over to the window. 'So what happened?'

'I was chasing a suspected robber and I caught up with him. We fought. He did this to me with his knife.'

'Did he get away?'

Pyke didn't feel like boasting about the arrest so just shook his head.

'What had this man stolen?'

'A crucifix.'

'That's what you went to see the archdeacon about, wasn't it?'

Pyke smiled. 'Well remembered.' The lad might not be the strongest fourteen-year-old but he had a quick mind.

Something outside had caught Felix's attention, and when he eventually turned around his expression was serious. 'When I first heard, when that policeman knocked at the door, and said you'd been injured, I thought ...' But tears had filled his eyes and he couldn't carry on.

Ignoring the pain, Pyke reached forward and held out his hand. He could still remember what it felt like to be an orphan. For a moment, Felix remained where he was, unsure what to do, but finally he relented and sat down on the edge of the bed.

The surgeon was a short man with a limp handshake and prominent teeth. He inspected the wound and told Pyke that it was healing well but that he should remain in the hospital for another couple of days. When he had left, and with the help of some laudanum, Pyke tried to get up, but an acute pain scudded down one side of his body. Still, he made it as far as the commode and emptied his bladder. He had just staggered back to bed when Whicher put his head around the door.

'We put the suspect in a room with ten other men. The coal-whipper picked him out.'

This was good news. 'What about the gunsmith?'

Whicher was grinning now. 'He picked out our man, too. According to his records, our suspect's name is Sharp.'

'Sharp.' Pyke weighed the name in his mind. 'I take it there's been no confirmation of his name from Sharp himself?'

Whicher shook his head. 'Still hasn't said a word.'

Pyke thought briefly about their next move. There was no physical evidence against the man but the circumstantial evidence was strong, certainly enough to take the case to a magistrate. 'What about Mayne and Wells?' he asked.

'Mayne's cock-a-hoop. He told me to pass on his best, offer you his congratulations. I haven't seen Wells.'

Pyke's thoughts turned back to the evidence. 'We still need more. All we've got is an old man who says he saw Sharp in the vicinity of the pawnbroker's at the time of the robbery. The gunsmith's evidence is good but it's not enough. If we're to send this man to the gallows, we need to find the pistol. And a motive . . .'

'I'm afraid there was nothing on Sharp's person to indicate where he lives. Unless he speaks, or someone else comes forward, we're stuck.'

'You need to put pressure on Egan. He knows something about this man. He must do. We need to find out how and why Sharp contacted him in the first place.'

'Egan isn't saying anything. He knows we don't have anything on him.'

Pyke nodded. He couldn't ask Whicher to do what he would do: take a cudgel and beat the truth out of Egan. He tried to get comfortable in the bed. 'Jack?'

Whicher stared at him, surprised to be called by his first name.

'Thank you.'

Even with the laudanum he'd consumed, Pyke was finding it difficult to sleep, and as he lay still, listening to the bleating of sheep being herded into nearby Smithfield for the market the following morning, he found himself thinking once more about Emily. In order to sleep, she had often resorted to doing what she'd done as a child: listing the names of the tenant farmers on her father's estate. *Anderson, Blake, Cant, Curtis, Dawson, Edwards.* It was funny that he could still remember the names so clearly; and that he could hear them in his dead wife's voice, her low, polished tone. Later, he slipped in and out of dreams that unsettled him but which he couldn't quite recall when he woke up. The air in the room was fetid and the bed sheets were soaked with his perspiration. Outside, he could still hear the animals, but he had grown used to the noise and he even found the bleating reassuring in its monotony. For some reason, he now found himself thinking about Jo, her red hair and her soft white skin. They had been happy for a time, the three of them, four if he counted Godfrey, until he had cajoled Jo into his bed. He hadn't heard from her in more than two years and briefly he wondered what had become of her. Sleep finally came to him just as the sun was rising, pale and orange, in the east.

'Pyke.'

He felt someone roughly shaking his arm.

'*Pyke.*'

Opening his sleep-encrusted eyes, Pyke saw Jack Whicher standing over him. Instantly he could tell from Whicher's expression that all was not well.

'What is it?' His head was still groggy from the laudanum and there was a dull ache in his side.

'Very bad news, I'm afraid.'

Ignoring the pain, Pyke sat up and rubbed his eyes. 'What's happened?'

'The man you fought, Sharp ...' Whicher hesitated, not sure how to continue.

'What about him?'

'The gaoler found him in his cell first thing this morning. He hanged himself some time in the night.'

Whitechapel High Street

DECEMBER 1844

SIX

One of the clerks ran into Pyke's office, red faced and out of breath. He stood there for a few moments panting. 'A man's been attacked, possibly killed. A policeman saw it happen, in the churchyard next to the police station house on Aldgate High Street. Everyone from K Division is out looking for the murderer and Wells is rounding up as many men as he can find. He told me to come and get you, and anyone else from the Detective Branch.'

It was late, after nine, and Pyke had just been about to go home. The other detectives had already left. Taking his greatcoat from the stand, he followed the clerk along the corridor and outside into Scotland Yard, where constables in uniform were streaming out of the single men's quarters and getting into the carriages that were lined up, one behind the other, to take them to the East End.

'What do you know?' Pyke asked, as soon as he found Wells, who was instructing the driver of one of the carriages.

It was a grim, wet night and the strong easterly breeze was driving the icy rain directly into their faces.

'An officer from K Division saw it happen; called for reinforcements and gave chase. They followed the culprit all the way along Whitechapel High Street and now they think they've got him cornered in the area just south of the railway tracks, a little farther along from the new station at Shoreditch.'

Wells climbed on to the roof of one of the carriages and pulled Pyke up next to him. Moments later, they were moving, eight or ten men inside each carriage, another four on the roof.

For a while they sat in silence, as the empty pavements and shuttered shops of the Strand passed by in a rain-soaked blur. Pyke had not seen much of Wells since he had returned to work a few months before, and had not missed the man's irascible temper and his unctuous ways. Nor had Pyke heard anything more about Wells's tussle with Benedict Pierce to succeed Tilling as assistant commissioner. Some time in the autumn, Pyke had concluded that Wells had exaggerated his antagonism towards Pierce in order to try to befriend him. This meant that on the few occasions when Pyke had bumped into Wells at the station house, the acting superintendent had wanted to stop and talk as though they were more than just colleagues.

Pyke knew that Wells and Mayne were happy enough with the outcome of the robbery investigation, even if the likely culprit, Sharp, had hanged himself in one of their cells. The fact that they didn't know why Sharp had shot and killed three people, including the owner of the shop, or that the likely cause of the shooting, a jewel-encrusted crucifix, had not been found, didn't appear to concern them.

For his part, Pyke was not prepared to accept, without cor- roboration, that Sharp had killed those men in Cullen's shop. It was true that the evidence pointed in that direction but the apparent lack of motive concerned him. When he'd finally returned to work after his injury had healed, Pyke had been less than impressed by the investigation into Sharp's suicide. The gaoler, who had been sleeping at the time under the influence of his nightly dose of porter, had shouldered much of the blame and had subsequently been dismissed. But he'd denied providing Sharp with the means of killing himself and the official report had been unable to determine how Sharp had managed to requisition sufficient rope to hang himself with.

It was true that Pyke had emerged from the events of the summer with his reputation and position intact. With Sharp dead, no one had bothered to look too carefully into the background of Harry Dove and the third victim, who had been identified as John Gibb. The fence, Egan, had been released without charge. He'd protested his innocence throughout and with no evidence to support a prosecution, they had had no choice but to let him go. The only fall-out from what had happened had been Pyke's association with Ned Villums. Pyke hadn't seen or heard from Villums since July, nor had he made any effort to get in touch with the man himself.

As the carriage turned on to Fleet Street, the taller buildings and narrower street afforded them more protection from the rain, enough to allow a conversation.

'Do you know who the victim is?' Pyke asked, wiping water from his eyes.

'I was told he might be affiliated with St Botolph's,' Wells said.

Pyke nodded. It was just as the clerk had explained: the church next door to the station house on Aldgate High Street. 'You know we'll never find the culprit. Those alleyways and courts could hide a whole army of murderers.'

Wells pulled up the collar of his coat and dug his hands into his pockets. Pyke could tell he was in his element. For once his eyes were bright whereas usually they were hard. Perhaps this kind of excursion reminded him of his time in the army.

The journey took just half an hour. They turned up Brick Lane and passed under the Eastern Counties railway line. In fact, the carriage stopped in the tunnel, to give the horses protection from the rain. They were met by Superintendent Edward Young of Stepney Division, who told them that his men were now searching the area to the north of the railway line. Wells climbed down to instruct the men who'd travelled with them and another lot who'd just arrived.

'Any further information about the victim?' Pyke asked the superintendent.

'Dead as they come.'

'Has anyone identified him?'

Young shook his head. 'I'm told the victim was hit in the face, repeatedly, with some kind of heavy instrument.'

Ahead of them, drinkers from the Windmill and the pub across the street, the George, were spilling out of the respective taprooms, some still holding tankards in their hands.

'When and where was the most recent sighting of the perpetrator?'

'A witness saw a man running along Hare Street about ten minutes before you arrived. My men are searching every house, on both sides of the street.'

'Not going to be popular with the locals.' Pyke gestured towards the growing crowd in front of the two pubs. A few men were shouting obscenities at the uniformed officers.

Wells rejoined them. 'Last sighting on Hare Street. I've sent one group of men up as far as Church Street and they'll work their way back towards us, and another group as far west as St Matthew's. If this man's still in the area, we'll get him. I can feel it in my bones.'

Pyke had no such confidence, but that was because, unlike Wells, he had first-hand experience of what it was like to chase someone through the lanes and alleys of one of the poorer districts.

He told Wells and Young that he wanted to reconnoitre the area and that he would meet them back at the carriages in about an hour. At first Wells insisted on accompanying him but Pyke put him off, saying he preferred to work alone. Thrusting a rattle into his hand, Wells told him to use it, either if he saw the suspect or if he ran into trouble with any of the 'natives'.

If anything the rain had become heavier and more persistent and every item of Pyke's clothing was sodden. In the deep pocket of his greatcoat, he touched the smooth wooden handle of the pistol which, as an inspector, he was permitted to carry, as he made his way along John Street to the north side of the railway line.

In the distance Pyke heard the sound of glass breaking. Something moved ahead of him and instinctively he stiffened; a stray dog darted out of the shadows and slipped into an alley on the other side of the street.

John Street petered out a few blocks later and Pyke cut through one of the open courts to Hare Street, where the main search was taking place. He showed his warrant card to one of the uniformed officers and was ushered through the checkpoint. Ahead was the church Wells had mentioned. St Matthew's. It looked horribly out of place among the slums; its gleaming façade towering over every edifice in the area.

At the far end of Hare Street, near the Windmill and George pubs, Pyke could see that a sizeable crowd had now formed. He heard chants and glasses being smashed. A little later, a small group of men overwhelmed the police barricade, and they were followed by others, bellowing and waving whatever they'd been able to find: chair legs, tankards, knives and sticks. The policemen who'd been conducting searches of the houses spilled out on to the street, truncheons drawn, and then it was hard to tell who was hitting who, a mass of arms and bodies flailing in the dark. Pyke, who was at the far end of the street, opted to avoid the fighting. Instead, he crossed another yard and found himself on derelict land at the back of St Matthew's. He paused and looked around him. The rain and the wind had eased and the air around him smelled of wet leaves. In the distance, he thought he saw someone or something move, and he shouted. Whoever it was looked up, dropped something, and bolted. Pyke followed the man around the church and over boggy ground as far as the Bethnal Green Road. The fleeing man had a limp and Pyke caught up with him easily.

Drawing his pistol, Pyke held it steady and said, 'Get down on to your knees and hold your hands above your head.'

The man's appearance was dishevelled and his clothes were filthy; if Pyke had to guess, he would have said he was a tosher or mudlark, even though they were a good half a mile from the river.

'Don't shoot, mister. I ain't done nothing.'

Everything in Pyke screamed that this wasn't their man.

It was midnight by the time Pyke made it back to St Botolph's on Aldgate High Street. He showed his warrant card to the constable manning the entrance to the yard and was told that the body had been moved into the church itself. Earlier, he had learned that their suspect hadn't yet been apprehended but they weren't abandoning their search. Three constables had suffered cuts and bruises in the melee on Hare Street and a number of arrests had been made. Pyke found Walter Wells in the church's nave, talking to one of the wardens. When he saw Pyke, Wells excused himself and came over to join him.

'So it would seem the man who did this has managed to slip through our fingers.' The blood was vivid in Wells's neck and cheeks.

'What exactly did he do?'

'I'll show you the corpse in a moment. I'm afraid it's not a pleasant sight.'

'They never are.' Pyke looked around the church and yawned. He had hoped to be home by now. Felix would be expecting him and the lad had already spent too much time at Godfrey's bedside since the old man's heart attack. Being at work distracted Pyke from what was going on at home and at times he welcomed this respite; the chance to forget, if only temporarily, that his uncle was dying. But he also knew that his absence placed too much of a burden on Felix, and that his son had started to resent the lack of time he spent with them.

'You have a name?' Pyke asked.

'The rector,' Wells said. 'Isaac Guppy.' Even though they were out of the cold, Pyke could still see Wells's breath in front of his mouth.

'The superintendent from Stepney said he'd been attacked with a heavy implement of some kind.'

'A hammer, we think. One was found next to the body.'

The body had been laid out in one of aisles and covered with a white dustsheet. Wells bent over and drew it back.

There was hardly anything left of the man's face, and what remained was a grotesque amalgam of broken bones, dried blood and torn, bruised flesh. Nothing else, apart from the man's face, had been affected: the rector's body was pale, fleshy and unremarkable. They didn't need a doctor to tell them how he had died: his skull had been shattered by repeated blows of a hammer.

The implement in question was retrieved by one of the constables.

'Did this constable actually *see* the attack taking place?' Pyke asked.

'No, but he did see a man standing over the body. You can interview him yourself. I'm told he can provide a fairly detailed description. He shouted at the man not to move but the man ran. He followed him as far as Bethnal Green but then lost him.'

'What did the churchwarden have to say?' Pyke could see from the gleam in Wells's eyes that he had additional information, either about the victim or the suspect.

'The description of our suspect matches someone who works here and at the rectory. Francis Hiley. The warden let it slip that he already has a criminal conviction.'

'For what?'

'The warden didn't know. Apparently Hiley slept rough in the church. There's no sign of him, of course.'

Pyke understood that Wells had already made up his mind: Hiley was their man. It didn't matter that there was no physical evidence to underscore this belief. The man was an ex-felon and he had run away from the scene of a crime. But what did this actually prove?

Wells, however, was in no mood to be put off. In his mind, the murderer was as good as caught and his entire demeanour reeked of self-congratulation.

'We can visit the rectory any time we want. Guppy's wife and his household are expecting us.'

Pyke looked at him and licked his lips. 'I've sent word to Jack Whicher to meet me at the rectory.'

For a few moments, neither of them spoke. Wells's face reddened slightly and his jaw tightened. His responsibilities, as they both knew, were primarily administrative. 'Very well, sir. If you have no further call for my services ...'

'Walter.' Pyke reached out and touched his arm. 'Your good work tonight hasn't gone unnoticed. Perhaps you could be persuaded to remain here for a while longer and talk to the coroner when he arrives?'

Wells seemed satisfied with this and even managed a wry smile.

The rectory was a good five-minute walk from the church and it wouldn't have looked out of place in the manicured grounds of a country house. It was a gabled brick-and-flint building with stone dressing and mullion windows. As well as having a drawing room, library, study, ballroom and numerous living areas on the ground floor, there was enough room upstairs for Guppy and his wife, his three children, and an annexe for five servants, a gardener and two stable boys.

It wasn't long before Whicher joined Pyke in the drawing room. Upstairs he could hear the children sobbing. He had been met by the same warden he'd seen in the church and shown into the drawing room. Whicher was now conferring with the parish beadle, a rotund, punctilious man called Tobias Nutt. In spite of the lateness of the hour, they were, Nutt informed them, awaiting a visit by the archdeacon himself, who had been told the terrible news.

Perhaps there was nothing out of the ordinary about the archdeacon's visit. After all, one of his flock had just been murdered. And perhaps it was the archdeacon's particular duty to deal with this kind of occurrence, though Pyke was reasonably sure that a man of the cloth had not been killed for a good number of years. But it reminded Pyke of his fractious visit to the man's home earlier in the year and the objects that had been stolen from his safe; objects including the Saviour's Cross, which still hadn't been recovered.

Presently they were joined by Guppy's widow Matilda, a frail creature whose otherwise plain face was lifted by dark, liquid eyes. Her nose and cheeks were mottled from her tears, and after she had blown her nose a couple of times and wiped her eyes, she described, in halting tones, how her husband liked to take the air at night, especially after dinner, to think about what he might say in his Sunday sermons. She told them that she had been sewing in the living room when Fricker – the churchwarden – had brought her the awful news. He'd come straight from the churchyard, she explained, where he'd heard the constable's shouts. At this point, she burst into tears, and Fricker reiterated what she'd just told them; that he had heard the policeman's shouts and rushed into the yard, only to find the rector already dead. He concluded with a perfunctory remark, perhaps for the widow's sake, that Guppy was a very generous man.

Nutt, the beadle, nodded vigorously. 'I think it'd be fair to say the rector was universally loved by his parishioners.'

Clearly not by everyone, Pyke thought. He exchanged a quick glance with Whicher and asked who had last seen the rector alive.

'That would be me,' Nutt said. 'I was doing my rounds when I happened to spot the goodly man perambulatin' in the church grounds. We conversed about the chill in the air and I enquired after Mrs Guppy's health. He assured me Mrs Guppy was quite well and we went our separate ways.' Anticipating Pyke's next question, he added, 'This would have been at approximately eight o'clock. I remember the bells chiming shortly afterwards.' He smiled to reveal teeth that were yellow and black at the roots.

Beadles were a throwback to a system when the parish had assumed responsibility for policing; they were untrained, poorly paid and universally derided. Despite the new policing provisions, some parishes had decided to retain their beadles, perhaps out of personal loyalty, but their work was now largely pastoral.

'Did you notice anything unusual? Did he seem anxious, for example?'

'A little anxious, maybe. He did seem keen to go about his

business, now that you mention it. But other than that, he was perfectly normal. He was wearing his surplice; he said he was preparing his sermon and wearing the surplice always helped put him in the right frame of mind.'

'A surplice?' Pyke had already conferred with Fricker inside the church, and no mention had been made of such a garment.

The churchwarden confirmed that Guppy *hadn't* been wearing his surplice when he'd come across the rector's battered corpse and explained that the garment itself was rather unusual in that it had strips of rabbit fur lining the shoulders. Pyke made a mental note to go back to the churchyard, once he had finished at the rectory. The fact that the garment appeared to be missing added a new dimension to the situation. When he asked whether anything else had been taken, Fricker shook his head and added that there were a few coins in Guppy's pocket and his gold wedding ring was still on his finger.

At the mention of Guppy's ring, the wife broke down in tears again. 'Did your husband perhaps mention that he'd arranged to meet someone at the church?' Pyke asked, when her crying had stopped.

She stared at him through weary eyes, seemingly perplexed. 'If my husband had intended to meet someone, why would he have not invited them to the rectory?'

A little later, while tea was being served in the drawing room, Nutt took him aside and ushered him into the hallway. 'I hear Fricker has already told you about this chap, Francis Hiley. The rector called him his odd-job man, and seemed fond of him, although I couldn't see what the fuss was about.'

Pyke stared into the beadle's podgy face. 'You didn't like him, then?'

'It's not that I disliked him.' Nutt lowered his voice to a whisper. 'But he was a strange fellow, if truth be told. He never said very much but he was always around, looking, keeping an eye on things.'

'How did he come to be working here?'

'He was recommended by the Reverend Martin Jakes from one of our sister churches, St Matthew's in Bethnal Green.'

Pyke's thoughts turned immediately to the search earlier that evening, which had been focused on the area around St Matthew's.

He thought, too, about the scavenger he'd arrested and then let go, when it became clear that the man knew nothing about the murder.

The picture that Nutt sought to paint of the rector was one of a generous and selfless man who had given food and shelter to a lowly ex-convict, but he couldn't really say what Guppy had hired Hiley to do, except tend the graves and keep the yard tidy, which, Nutt admitted, was also the duty of the gardener. Nutt told Pyke that he'd heard Hiley had spent time in Coldbath Fields, possibly for killing his wife, but his information was sketchy. Like Wells, he had already made up his mind that Hiley had killed the rector and was trying to push Pyke in this direction. Tapping his nose, Nutt explained that no one had seen Hiley since the murder and that they weren't likely to. Nutt was rather less helpful in providing a motive: he told Pyke he had no idea why Hiley might have wanted to kill Guppy but suggested that some men were just predisposed towards violence.

Back in the drawing room, Pyke asked Whicher what he'd been able to find out. Whicher said that the police constable's description of the man he'd seen in the yard matched Fricker's description of Hiley.

'No chance the two of them could have conferred?' Pyke asked. Whicher shook his head.

It was late, already well past one in the morning, but Pyke had insisted that all of the servants and household be summoned, so that he could question them about their dealings with Guppy.

Pyke conducted the interviews in the drawing room but no one had very much to add. All the servants, gardeners and stable-hands were polite but tight lipped about their employer, and none of them could give any reason why someone might have wanted to kill him. They were a little more forthcoming about Francis Hiley. None of them seemed to have liked him, and to a man – and woman – they backed up the beadle's belief that Hiley was a little odd. A loner, someone said; a thief, another reckoned. When Pyke asked Matilda, the wife, about Hiley, she seized the chance to praise her husband's philanthropy; the fact that he'd been willing to give a felon another chance when the rest of society had turned its back on him. The implication was clear: *look how the scoundrel repaid his generosity*. She clearly felt, as Nutt did, that Hiley had killed her husband.

How long had Hiley been employed by her husband? Pyke asked. She'd thought about it and said since April.

And had there been any indication that Hiley had a temper?

No, she conceded. He had always behaved in a respectful manner.

Later Pyke accompanied Whicher back to the church, where the body was waiting to be taken to the nearest public house for the inquest. To Pyke's relief, Wells had already left.

Pyke had never liked churches, their cold, draughty interiors and the hard, functional pews that people, in some instances, had to pay to occupy. Their size was supposed to convey something of God's majesty, but standing in the aisle, looking towards the altar, all Pyke could think about was how many men had been needed to build it and the pittance they'd doubtless been paid.

Candles had been lit and placed on the table in front of the altar, casting their flickering light upwards and illuminating the plain wooden crucifix that hung above it. It made Pyke think about the Saviour's Cross and the three men who'd been killed in Cullen's shop in the summer; even more so since the archdeacon himself was shortly expected at the rectory.

'So what do you think, Jack?' Pyke circled around the body, trying to keep warm. 'Did Hiley kill him?'

'People here certainly seem to think so. And I have to say, it doesn't look good for him.'

Pyke nodded. It was a fair conclusion, even if the investigation was still at an early stage. Since the summer, he had come to rely on Whicher more and more, and now they both seemed to feel comfortable in each other's presence. Pyke had started to treat him as an equal rather than a subordinate, and the others in the Detective Branch had noticed this. Increasingly, they had formed their own faction, from which Pyke and Whicher had been excluded. Whicher hadn't expressed any real concern at this situation and, in actuality, it suited Pyke very well.

'Doesn't it strike you as odd that a rector should live in such comfort? Five servants, two gardeners.' Then, almost as an afterthought, he added, 'And yet he still needs to employ an odd-job man.'

'Apparently it's a wealthy parish, one of the wealthiest in the city.

That might explain the servants. But you're right about the need for an odd-job man.'

'What about Guppy himself? Aside from Nutt, none of the servants spoke particularly warmly about him.'

Whicher nodded. 'I know; and what kind of man would wear his surplice just to take the night air?' Earlier, they'd looked for, and been unable to find, the surplice anywhere in the church or the yard.

Pyke smiled at Whicher's remark. 'We also shouldn't lose sight of the *way* he was killed.'

'The fact that someone took a hammer and went to work on Guppy's face until there was nothing left.'

'Exactly. Whoever did it didn't just want to kill him. If they did, they could have used a knife or a pistol.'

'To be that close to someone and swing a hammer at their head: you'd really have to hate that person.'

'We also don't know what Guppy was doing in the churchyard,' Pyke said. 'I don't believe for a moment he was simply going for a walk.'

'It's bitterly cold. Why would you venture out unless you had to?'

'Perhaps he'd arranged to meet someone.'

'To do what?'

'I don't know,' Pyke said. 'Why do people meet up in places like churchyards late at night?'

Whicher was smiling. He had come to appreciate Pyke's dark sense of humour. 'Maybe that's why he took off his surplice.'

'Just his surplice?'

'But he was fully clothed when they found him,' Whicher said, still smiling.

Pyke shrugged. 'Maybe Guppy didn't get as far as he'd expected to.'

When Pyke finally arrived home, he found Felix asleep in the armchair beside Godfrey's bed, a Bible resting in his lap. Pyke's gaze drifted between his son and his uncle, and as he stood watching them, he tried not to think about how little time he had spent at Godfrey's side since he had collapsed two weeks earlier.

'You're up early,' Felix said, lifting his head and forcing open one of his eyes. 'Or back late.'

After Pyke's injury in the summer, there had been a rapprochement of sorts between them, but throughout the autumn the distance had gradually started to open up again and Godfrey's sudden collapse had put them at loggerheads once more. The issue, for Felix, was Pyke's apparent lack of concern. For his part, Pyke had done all he could; he had paid for the best doctor and a full-time nurse. Deep down, he was as desperately worried about the old man's health as Felix, but he simply couldn't give up his work, and Felix had started to resent this.

Pyke took the other armchair and pulled it closer to the bed. 'How is he?'

'No better, no worse, according to the doctor.' Felix sat up, stretched his shoulders and yawned.

'What did he say?'

'Just that. No change in his condition. He told us to keep trying to give Uncle Godfrey food and water.'

Pyke stared at the plate of uneaten food and the glass of water on the floor next to the bed. Since the collapse, Godfrey had said very little and had barely eaten a thing, and now the skin was hanging off his face and neck.

'At least it means he's not getting any worse,' Pyke said, mostly for Felix's benefit.

He wasn't sure how much his son knew, how much the doctor had told him, but as far as Pyke was aware, the prognosis was not good. Certainly there seemed little chance that Godfrey would make a full or even a partial recovery. Pyke looked at the bags under his son's eyes and asked how he felt. Felix shrugged and said he was fine, even though it was clear he'd had almost no sleep. Since the collapse, Pyke had allowed Felix to stay at home, to be with Godfrey, but in recent days he'd been forced to question the wisdom of this decision. Was it healthy for a boy of his age to sit indoors all day with nothing to do and no one to talk to? Still, Pyke knew he wouldn't be able to raise this issue without Felix coming back at him. *I have to be here, because you never are.*

'Seriously, you look terrible,' Pyke said. 'Go and lie down. I'll sit with him for a while.'

'You don't look too good yourself. What kept you up all night?'

'Work.'

Felix rolled his eyes and they sat for a while in silence, both staring down at Godfrey's sleeping form.

'I see you've been reading the Bible.' Pyke gestured at the book, which had fallen on to the floor.

'So?'

'I didn't know you'd embraced religion.'

'I haven't *embraced* religion.' Felix sighed. 'I was just reading aloud to Godfrey. Where's the harm in that?'

Pyke considered this for a short while. 'I'm sure Godfrey appreciates what you're doing for him but I know he's never found solace in the Bible.'

Felix reddened slightly. He went to retrieve his copy of the Bible and held it closely to his chest.

'Did they give you that at school?'

It was a trick question and Felix knew it. 'You know they don't teach us the Bible, so why do you even ask?'

'So where did you get it from?'

'Believe it or not, Pyke, the Bible is freely available.' Defiantly, Felix held his gaze. 'I pray for Godfrey to get better. What's so terrible about that?'

'And you think it's in God's power to make Godfrey better?' Pyke paused. 'He's a very old, sick man.'

'I know he's sick. Remember, *I'm* here. *I'm* the one tending to him.' Felix stopped, sensing he'd said too much, and then shook his head. 'I'm sorry, Pyke. I didn't mean ... I know you're as upset as I am.'

Pyke went over and put his arm around his son's shoulders and to his surprise Felix did not push him away.

'I'm scared, Pyke. I'm scared he's going to die.' Suddenly there were tears in his eyes. 'Aren't you scared, too?'

Pyke was mute but just about managed a nod of his head. He had known that this time would eventually come, that Godfrey couldn't live for ever, but now it was here he felt as lost and frightened as a boy.

SEVEN

'I don't like to speak ill of the dead, sir, but Guppy was a rather objectionable creature; the kind who'd refuse to feed a starving man because he hadn't washed his hands.'

Martin Jakes's whole house could easily have fitted into Isaac Guppy's drawing room, and the study, where they were now sitting, their knees almost touching, was not quite as large as the cupboard under Guppy's stairs. The fact that Jakes had found himself at a church like St Matthew's, Bethnal Green, at the age of fifty, rather than serving out his days in the country, struck Pyke as something to be admired. It suggested Jakes hadn't bothered to cosy up to men like the archdeacon. Jakes had an open, honest face and wasn't shy about speaking his mind. Pyke cast his eye up at the books on his shelves and saw Marcus Aurelius and Blake there, as well as Erasmus and St Augustine. Jakes's features were weathered and craggy; he was interesting to look at and this told Pyke that he had lived a life; that he hadn't tried to hide behind the robes of office.

'Please don't misunderstand me,' he said, after he had given Pyke his impression of Guppy. 'I was shocked, horrified even, when I first heard the news and I'm desperately sorry he's dead. His wife, Matilda, is a fine woman. She'll take this very badly.'

'But you didn't like him as a man?'

'It's not that I liked or disliked him.' Jakes loosened his collar. 'It's just ... how can I put it? St Botolph's is one of the wealthiest parish churches in the whole city. I would guess it raises in excess of two thousand a year from the rate alone. Now, I know a healthy proportion of that goes towards maintaining the rectory and its grounds ...'

'But you just get the crumbs from the table?'

Jakes winced slightly. 'I don't know how knowledgeable you are about parish arrangements. St Botolph's is our mother parish; all of the rate goes there. To make ends meet, we have to rely on what we can earn from funerals and marriages.'

'St Botolph's gets the oysters, you get the shells.'

Jakes smiled at Pyke's analogy. 'We try to do as much charitable work with the poor as we can. Offer them food, hot soup in the winter. Coal and firewood if we can afford it.'

'But you could do more if you were given more.'

'*So* much more,' Jakes said, emphasising each syllable.

Pyke glanced around the cramped, dusty room and thought about the accommodation at the rectory attached to St Botolph's. It was easy to see why Jakes might be frustrated with the situation.

'I was told you recommended an odd-job man to Guppy.' Pyke waited, and studied the vicar's reaction. 'A former felon, by the name of Francis Hiley. Is that correct?'

'It is, indeed.' Jakes's expression was earnest. 'Can I enquire why you're asking about Francis? Has something happened to him?'

'Not as such. But it would seem that he packed up and left just before or after Guppy was murdered.'

'Ah, I see.' Jakes's expression darkened. 'And everyone at St Botolph's believes Francis killed the rector.'

'Is that such an unreasonable conclusion to reach? Given Hiley's sudden flight?'

'No, I suppose not,' Jakes said, sighing. 'It's true that Francis is a deeply troubled man. Nonetheless, I don't doubt that some people have been more than forthcoming about his past.'

Pyke couldn't help but smile at Jakes's insightful reading of the situation. 'I was told he served time in Coldbath Fields.'

Jakes nodded. 'I first made his acquaintance when I moved here from St Luke's, Berwick Street. He was a bright lad, and always showed a keen interest in the Bible, but he was let down by his temper. He found out that his wife had been unfaithful to him; they fought and she fell down the stairs. The jury returned a verdict of unlawful manslaughter but when it came to his trial, the magistrate was lenient. Francis hadn't contested the charges and anyone could see how distraught he was. He liked a drink but that doesn't make him a bad man, does it? I enjoy a tipple every now and again myself. So I spoke up for him at the trial and the magistrate gave him two years. After Francis had served his sentence, he came here and offered to help out, in return for his room and board. I had to go to Guppy to gain his consent and initially he was hostile. He warned me about the dangers of consorting with hardened criminals.

'In the end, and after a great deal of posturing, Guppy gave me his consent. I offered Francis a bed in this house but he insisted on sleeping in the church. And he proved to be a useful man to have around. I'm not as young as I used to be, and he would fetch and carry things for me; mend what needed to be mended. And when I did my rounds, I felt safer when Francis was with me. As you might expect, the church is not universally liked in a district like this one. In the past, I've been pushed to the ground and spat on, but with Francis at my side, no one bothered me. You see, he was big, a physical man. Folk around here respect that more than the word of God.'

'So how did Hiley come to work for Guppy?'

Jakes adjusted his position in his armchair. 'About seven or eight months ago, Guppy came to see me here at St Matthew's, which was a rare enough occurrence, as he would usually summon me to St Botolph's. I could tell something had upset him but he refused to take me into his confidence. For him, that would've been an admission of weakness. But he'd heard all about Francis; the fact that people in the parish respected him on account of his size and physical presence. He told me he needed someone to keep an eye on the church and he offered to take Francis off my hands; that was the phrase he used. He even promised to pay him a wage.'

Pyke tried to weigh this up against the sense he'd got from the churchwarden and the rectory servants that Francis Hiley had been an unwanted presence at St Botolph's and that he'd been spoiled or indulged by an overly generous rector. He put this view to Jakes.

'As I said earlier, life at St Botolph's is comfortable, respectable. Francis comes from rough stock. It's no surprise that most people there would have taken against him or been suspicious of him.'

Pyke rubbed his chin and nodded. 'And how did this arrangement work out? Was Hiley happy with it? Was Guppy?'

'Guppy never complained, at least not to me.'

'But Hiley did?'

Jakes sighed. 'Guppy promised to feed him and pay him a wage but more often than not Francis would turn up here hungry and looking for food.'

'You're saying that Guppy didn't honour his commitment?'

'Francis was grateful for the work and even more grateful for the chance to atone for his sins. He never criticised Guppy directly.'

Pyke was about to ask another question when a younger woman put her head around the door. Honey-coloured hair surrounded her pale, pinched face. She wasn't unattractive, he decided, but there was something unsettling about her. Perhaps it was just that she was so thin. She was introduced to Pyke as Kitty, but Jakes made a point of describing her as his ward. It made Pyke wonder whether Jakes was married or not.

'Can I fetch you anything, sir?' She bowed her head, avoiding Pyke's eyes. He put her age at twenty-five or thereabouts.

'Martin, my dear. Please call me Martin.' He offered Pyke an apologetic smile. 'Perhaps you can tell Inspector Pyke here about the goings on at the rectory. He's investigating the murder. You're friendly with some of the girls who work there, aren't you?'

Kitty reddened and she tucked her blonde hair behind her ears.

'Please, my dear.' Jakes hesitated. 'If you know something that could help the inspector, it is your responsibility to tell him.'

'No one liked him at the house,' she said, eventually. 'None of the servants, at least. He was a tyrant, so he was.'

'That may be so, Kitty, but surely you can't be suggesting that someone might've killed him for that reason alone?'

Kitty shrugged. 'I didn't say that, did I? I just don't think anyone there will be weeping into their pillows.'

She excused herself and Pyke turned back to face Jakes. 'Do you know where I might find Hiley?'

'So you can throw him to the wolves?'

'So I can talk to him and determine whether or not he is implicated in what happened.'

Eventually Jakes said, 'Francis's mother and father both died in the cholera outbreak in the early thirties.'

Pyke stood up and pulled on his greatcoat. 'And what if Hiley came here to see you or tried to make contact with you?'

Jakes was frowning, apparently not grasping the nuance of his question, so Pyke added, 'Would you pass this information on to me?'

'Ah,' the vicar said, now understanding why Pyke had asked the question. Later Pyke realised he hadn't actually given an answer.

Pyke found Adolphus Wynter taking tea with Matilda Guppy in the drawing room of the rectory. The December sunshine was streaming through a window at the front of the room and the archdeacon seemed relaxed. When Pyke entered, closely followed by one of the servants, who needlessly introduced him, Wynter was stirring his tea with a silver spoon.

His face immediately tightened. He glanced over at Matilda Guppy and rose to his feet.

'Archdeacon,' Pyke said, nodding once. Wynter simply stood there and didn't offer Pyke his hand.

'Mrs Guppy here was informing me about this felon, Hiley.' Wynter's eyes were as grey as slate. 'I'm told that a man matching his description was seen standing over Reverend Guppy's body.'

Pyke's expression gave nothing away. 'I was hoping you might be able to answer a few questions about the roles Guppy performed as rector here and in the wider church.'

Wynter looked over at Matilda Guppy and said, 'Perhaps you might excuse us, my dear. I shouldn't like to bore you with our conversation.'

Only when she had left the room did Wynter turn his attention back to Pyke. 'So what exactly do you want to know?'

'I'm told St Botolph's is a wealthy parish. By implication, that makes or made Guppy an important man. I'd like to inspect the parish accounts, for a start.' Pyke stopped himself before he drew a comparison between the rectory and Wynter's impressive home on Red Lion Square, which he'd found out, to his great disappointment, had been purchased with his wife's inheritance.

Wynter adjusted his cassock while he considered this request. 'Reverend Guppy is the victim here, Detective Inspector. I think you would do well to remember that fact.'

Pyke had hoped that he wouldn't get riled by the archdeacon's manner but already he could feel his stomach knotting. 'I don't need your permission to consult the parish accounts. Nor to conduct a search of Guppy's study and private papers.'

Wynter wetted his lips. 'Then why are we having this conversation?'

Pyke met his stare and held it. 'I have to say I'm surprised to see you back here so soon after last night.'

'If I didn't know you already, Detective Inspector, I would be deeply offended by your peculiar insinuation. A highly respected and much loved man of God has been murdered in the most ghastly of circumstances. I'm simply trying to do what I can to bring comfort to those he cared for.'

'You're quite right about the circumstances. Someone didn't just kill the rector; they *decimated* him. It's my guess that whoever picked up that hammer believed that Guppy had done him a great wrong.'

'That may turn out to be true, sir, but our city is a dangerous and violent place.'

'So you think this might have been a random attack?' Pyke didn't bother to hide his scepticism.

'What I think, Detective Inspector, is that you should establish some facts before you jump to any conclusions.'

'Perhaps you're correct, Archdeacon, in which case I'll offer you my humble apology. Perhaps an escaped Bedlamite took a hammer to the poor rector for no ostensible reason. But in my experience the way someone commits a murder tells us something about their reasons for doing so. This attack suggests, to me at least, a great deal of anger.'

Wynter eyed him cautiously. 'I am just as keen as you are, sir, to see the monster who perpetrated this act facing justice in a court of law.'

Pyke waited for a moment. He still didn't understand why the archdeacon had returned to the rectory, having been there only the previous night. 'I'm intrigued, Archdeacon. What was the precise nature of your relationship with the rector?'

'What do you mean?'

'Did you know him well?'

'Reasonably well.'

'As I understand it, you occupy the second-most important position in the Church hierarchy after the bishop. The rector of a parish like St Botolph's is an important man in his own right but I would imagine there would be canons, sub-canons and deans to deal with such lesser mortals?'

'The rector of St Botolph's is an important post in our Church family, sir. Perhaps you didn't know that our much-beloved bishop once occupied this very office?' Wynter allowed himself a faint smile. 'I have liaised closely with Guppy on matters relating to the administration of this parish.'

'So you would consider him to be a friend?'

'In my capacity as archdeacon I know him well, in his capacity as rector.'

Pyke nodded. He had to admit it was a good answer; slippery but good. 'But what does a rector actually do?'

'How long do you have, Detective Inspector?' Wynter offered him a patronising smile and Pyke had to suppress an urge to slap his face.

They talked like this for another five minutes but Pyke learned little or nothing that he didn't already know or couldn't have worked out for himself. Then, for the following hour, Pyke conducted a fruitless search of Guppy's study and sought in vain to make head or tail of the parish accounts that Wynter and the churchwarden had set aside for him.

To his surprise, Wynter was still there when Pyke emerged from the study.

'Your dedication to the pastoral needs of your flock knows no bounds,' Pyke said to Wynter, while one of the servants fetched his greatcoat.

The archdeacon smiled, aware that Pyke had been trying to mock him. 'I hope you don't feel that your time here was wasted, Detective Inspector.'

The servant appeared and Pyke took his coat. 'Tell me. Did your crucifix ever turn up?'

Just for a moment the archdeacon seemed thrown by this sudden shift of focus. 'Sadly I think it's lost to the Church for ever.'

Mayne kept Pyke waiting for about a minute or two. There was no chair for him to sit on, so he stood, looking around the room, while the commissioner attended to the papers on his desk.

'I believe you went to the rectory at St Botolph's today and exchanged words with the archdeacon.' Mayne put down his pen and looked up at Pyke.

'The archdeacon was there and yes, we had a conversation. But I went to St Botolph's to conduct a search of the dead man's study.'

Mayne nodded, as though he already knew this to be true. 'Would I be correct in assuming you don't much care for the established Church?'

'Whether I care for the Church or not is beside the point. I'm investigating a murder.'

Mayne glanced down at the pile of papers on his desk and then back up at Pyke. 'I'm just asking you to treat men like the archdeacon with some sensitivity.'

Pyke didn't want to give Mayne any indication of the anger he could feel building inside him. 'Are you telling me, Sir Richard, that the affairs of the deceased are somehow not relevant to this investigation?'

'There are ways and means, Pyke, ways and means,' Mayne said, not bothering to hide his frustration. 'If a high-ranking figure in the Church is displeased, his displeasure will be made clear to figures who, in turn, have dominion over my operations here at Scotland Yard. Do you understand my predicament?'

'Some might understand that as interfering with an official police investigation,' Pyke said, perhaps too quickly.

Mayne's expression remained distant but Pyke could tell from the hardness of his mouth that he was disappointed. 'It isn't often a member of the clergy is murdered, and in such dire circumstances. More particularly, the public's appetite has been whetted by reports of the manhunt conducted yesterday in Whitechapel and Bethnal Green.'

Pyke waited and said nothing. Mayne continued, 'It is imperative we find the brute who perpetrated this act as quickly and, may I say, as *efficiently* as possible. As such, I have decided to make Superintendent Wells and his men available to you for the investigation.'

This was a humiliation that Pyke had hoped to avoid, but ever since Wells's meddling on the night of the murder he'd known it was a distinct possibility. 'Superintendent Wells is to take charge of the investigation?'

Mayne gave him a hard, dispassionate stare. 'I am hoping that the two of you will work together.'

'May I ask why you've taken this decision?' Pyke waited for an answer but Mayne had already turned to the papers in front of him.

'You do know that by constantly drawing upon the assistance of the Executive Branch you run the risk of undermining the autonomy of the Detective Branch?'

This time Mayne looked up at him, his brow furrowed. 'That will be all, Detective Inspector.'

At the door of the Detective Branch's main office, Pyke listened as Lockhart and Gerrett teased Frederick Shaw about a woman he had apparently met at a dinner hosted by one of his father's friends. 'I hope her mind was as ample as her figure, Frederick,' Lockhart was saying. Gerrett just guffawed. Hearing footsteps in the corridor, and not wanting to be exposed as an eavesdropper, Pyke opened the door. The office suddenly fell silent and Pyke was surprised to see not just Shaw, Gerrett and Lockhart but also Whicher and Walter Wells. Wells was grinning, enjoying the good-natured banter in the room. The idea that his detectives were more comfortable talking to one another in front of Wells than him baffled and disappointed Pyke in equal measure. 'Find out anything new at the rectory?' Whicher asked.

'Nothing I didn't already know.' Pyke turned to Wells. 'Superintendent. I believe we'll have the pleasure of your company on this investigation.'

The others nodded in agreement. Billy Gerrett made a point of telling Wells how much he was looking forward to working with him. 'I'm presuming you will be in change of the investigation as superintendent,' he added.

If anything, Gerrett had put on even more weight during the autumn. It was the fat under his neck which most repulsed Pyke; the fact that his chin had all but disappeared into a mound of stubbly flesh.

Wells glanced over at Pyke and smiled. 'I'm merely here to assist Detective Inspector Pyke. That is all.'

It was a gracious concession and it made Pyke wonder whether he'd judged Wells too harshly. But almost immediately, Wells said, 'I'm presuming our first task will be to determine how to conduct the search for Hiley?'

'It's certainly one avenue we need to pursue,' Pyke said, wondering whether Wells had briefed the men in his absence.

'There are others?' Wells asked.

'I talked to the curate of a neighbouring church. He's known Hiley for much of his life and told me he didn't believe the man was capable of such a cold-blooded murder.'

'And yet, according to the superintendent here, all of the evidence would seem to point to the contrary.' There was a note of confrontation in Gerrett's tone and Pyke wondered what had emboldened him.

Wells must have seen Pyke's expression because he smiled apologetically. 'I should have waited, I know, but I talked to the police constable who saw the man in the churchyard. The description he gave exactly matches one provided by those who know Hiley.'

'But did he actually see this man attacking Guppy?'

Wells shook his head. Pyke exhaled loudly. This wasn't new information and yet Wells had presented it to the men as exactly that.

'The question surely is,' Lockhart said, to Wells rather than to Pyke, 'if Hiley *is* innocent of all wrongdoing, then where is he? His flight is surely indicative of his guilt?'

It was a good point and almost impossible to refute. Gerrett and Shaw nodded briskly. Feeling cornered, Pyke said, 'It's true we need to find Francis Hiley as quickly as possible, but we also need to establish or disprove his culpability. In that sense, we need to know as much as possible about him.' He turned to Lockhart. 'I want you to visit Coldbath Fields, see what you can find out about him there; what kind of a prisoner he was, whether he received any visitors.'

Lockhart nodded. Pyke then shifted his attention to Gerrett and Shaw. 'I want you two to consult the court records. Hiley was found guilty of manslaughter but he was only sentenced to two years in prison. Maybe there were others, in addition to Jakes, who spoke up for him.'

Wells nodded approvingly at Pyke's proposed course of action. 'I will lead the operation on the ground. Even as we speak, twenty of my finest men are scouring the streets of the East End for witnesses who might have seen Hiley on the night of the murder.' He paused and added, 'If he's out there, if he's hiding, I predict he'll be in our custody by nightfall.'

Later, after the others had departed, Whicher handed Pyke an envelope that had been left for him earlier that morning. Pyke inspected it. There was no indication of who had sent it.

'I take it you have your doubts that Hiley is the killer?' Whicher said.

Pyke shrugged. 'I just don't like the way everyone is already measuring him up for the noose.'

Almost as an afterthought, he added, 'Do you know if Gerrett and Lockhart are still on friendly terms with Pierce?'

'I don't know.' Whicher took out his handkerchief and wiped his forehead. 'They both seemed to like him when he was head of the Detective Branch.'

Pyke nodded, trying to assess where their loyalties now lay. 'And Shaw?'

'Frederick would never turn against you. He's too beholden to hierarchy and you're his superior.'

'But?'

'It's probably nothing. It's just I've noticed he's spending more time with Gerrett and Lockhart after hours.'

'Is that such a surprise? Given they all billet in the same quarters?'

Whicher shrugged. 'I think maybe you should keep an eye on him. Lockhart, too. That's all.'

Pyke looked down at the envelope in his hand. The words '*Detective Inspector Pyke*' had been written in careful, looping letters. Retrieving a letter opener from his desk, he slit it open and pulled out a piece of writing paper. It looked like a poem; indeed, the words were vaguely familiar. He read and reread the lyrics: *Now the sneaking serpent walks / In mild humility, / And the just man rages in the wilds / Where lions roam.* Still puzzling over the poem, he almost didn't see the address penned at the bottom of the page.

28 Broad Street.

'Broad Street.' Pyke handed Whicher the note and added, 'How good's your knowledge of London?'

Whicher took the note and studied it. 'Better than my knowledge of poetry.'

EIGHT

Broad Street was typical of the district; a ramshackle place with two irregular rows of terraces facing one another. It had once been a respectable, even fashionable, address, but its wealthy residents had long since crossed Regent's Street to Mayfair and the once grand buildings had now been carved up into apartments and rooms that were let, sublet and sublet again until upwards of fifty people might be crammed into the same space. No. 28 stood at the junction with Marshall Street. To get there, Pyke had to walk past a row of shops and businesses: a grocer, apothecary, machinist, tailor, bonnet-maker, beer shop and an ironmonger. The building itself was a stucco-clad terrace house from the time of Queen Anne and, as with the other buildings on the street, there were numerous plates and bells next to the front door. Pyke picked one of the bells at random and pulled it, waiting on the front step while the chimes echoed somewhere in the belly of the building.

A stout, middle-aged woman wearing a cotton dress and a woollen shawl opened the door. Pyke introduced himself as a police detective and explained that an anonymous note had been passed to him bearing a few lines of poetry and that address.

'So?'

'I'm just trying to determine why someone might have sent the note.'

Still blocking his path into the building, the woman looked at him and sighed. 'When you told me you were a policeman, I assumed you were here to rake over what happened in the summer.'

Pyke looked past her into the entrance hall. 'And what exactly did happen in the summer?'

Crestfallen, the women lowered her voice and said, 'A young child died. Poor mite fell to his death. It was said that one of the lodgers who resided on the top floor deliberately dropped him over the banisters. There was a trial and the man was found guilty. I don't know any more about it than that.'

'Who lives up there now?'

'No one, as far as I know.' The woman looked at him and sniffed. 'No one's lived there since it happened.'

Pyke found out which room the woman rented – her name was Mrs Morris – and told her that he'd like to talk to her further, after he'd taken a look upstairs. The air in the hallway smelled of stale food and mildew and paper was peeling and flaking from the soot-blackened walls. He ascended the creaking staircase two steps at a time and paused for a moment on the first-floor landing. The building was absolutely quiet. Perhaps, he surmised, the residents were all working. The stairs leading up to the top floor were a little wider and, as he mounted them, Pyke wondered whether this was where the child had fallen – or been dropped. He did remember reading about the incident and the subsequent trial but that was all. On the landing there were three doors, all closed but none of them locked. Pushing the first one open, he waited on the threshold and called out, 'Hello?' No one answered. Light flooded in through two large windows and there were some pieces of old furniture but otherwise the room was deserted. The other two rooms were also empty. It was just as the woman had said: no one had lived up here for months.

Having got the name and address of the landlord from Mrs Morris, Pyke stood outside on the pavement and looked up at the building. Who had sent him the note and what were the few lines of poetry meant to suggest?

Jabez Sylvester ran his practice from the ground floor of a building in nearby West Street. After a brief conversation with one of the clerks, Pyke was shown into the lawyer's office, where Sylvester was sitting at his desk reading, a selection of leather-bound volumes lining the bookcase behind him. He was sixtyish, and had grown plump on his modest success. He dressed like a gentleman and greeted Pyke with little enthusiasm. With some cajoling Pyke finally managed to elicit the full story of what had happened at No. 28 and later that afternoon he was able to corroborate the lawyer's account with the official record of the trial.

Brendan Malloy, a former Catholic priest from the west of Ireland, had been the main witness for the prosecution, alleging that on the tenth of June a man called Ebenezer Druitt, who also lodged in one of the upstairs rooms at No. 28, had deliberately and with malice aforethought dropped a ten-month-old child down the stairs to his death. During the trial, Malloy had alleged that Druitt had committed this 'vile, wicked act' out of jealousy over his own attachment to the infant's mother, Sarah Scott, also a resident in the building. Druitt had pleaded not guilty to the charges and during cross-examination had sought to paint the former Catholic priest as a Devil worshipper and a man who'd been forced to leave the Church as a result of perverse sexual desires. In the end, the judge, Mr Justice Parks, had ruled that 'intent to kill' had not been proven and the charge was reduced from murder to manslaughter. After an hour of deliberation, the jury had found Druitt guilty of 'fatally mishandling' the infant and the judge had sentenced him to five years' imprisonment in Pentonville. During his summing up, the judge had remarked on Druitt's sneering indifference to the fate of the child and to the suffering of the mother, Sarah Scott, who hadn't been called as a witness.

'Do you think this man, Druitt, intended to kill the infant or not?'

Sylvester rubbed his chin and frowned. 'I have no opinion on the matter. The jury made its decision and I see no reason to question the verdict.'

'Do you know what became of Malloy and Sarah Scott?'

'I don't know about the woman,' Sylvester said, relaxing into his chair. 'Malloy, I'm afraid, fell into the bottom of a whisky glass. You can find him most days in the Black Lion on Berwick Street. Either there or the Crown and Anchor on Broad Street.'

'He moved out of your property shortly after the incident?'

'They all did.'

'Then why haven't you rented out the rooms? Surely as long as the rooms remain empty, you're losing money.'

'I've tried, believe me.' The lawyer gave him a baleful stare. 'But folk around here are superstitious and they have long memories.

No one wants to move into a place where a young child was killed.'

Pyke nodded. 'What kind of tenants were they?'

Sylvester shrugged. 'They paid their rent on time.'

'What did the other tenants think of them?' Pyke asked, sensing some reticence.

Sylvester rubbed his chin again. 'The one who was the priest was quite well liked.'

'But not Druitt?'

'No, I don't think the neighbours much cared for him. I'm told he brought a lot of people into the building. Footsteps on the stairs all hours of the day and night.'

'What did you think of him?'

'He was the first one who came to me, wanting to know whether he could rent any of the rooms. Apparently the poet, William Blake, was born in No. 28, and Druitt admitted to being a great admirer of Blake's work. To be honest, I always found him rather charming.'

Pyke silently admonished himself. He knew Blake's poetry quite well and should have recognised the lines. His realisation didn't explain why someone had sent him the quotation but it gave him somewhere to start.

Later, after Pyke had arrived home and eaten his supper, he went upstairs to check on Felix and his uncle, who was awake and sitting up in his bed. In the past few days he'd seemed a good bit better and had some colour in his cheeks. When Pyke quoted the lines of the Blake poem, Godfrey smiled. 'Blake's *The Marriage of Heaven and Hell*, if I'm not much mistaken.'

'I didn't recognise it. But you knew it straight away.' Pyke handed Godfrey the note he'd been sent. 'I presume it's well known?'

'Are you questioning my literary knowledge, dear boy?'

That made Pyke smile. It lifted him to see his uncle in better spirits.

'It's an illustrated edition: Blake's great paean to Milton.' Then by way of explanation, Godfrey continued, 'Blake wanted to human-ise the Devil, just as Milton had done in *Paradise Lost*. Turn him into a figure of justified rebellion. Blake described Milton as "a true poet of the Devil's party without knowing it".' Godfrey was sitting upright and his white hair had been combed back off his face. He looked better than he had done in a long while, Pyke thought, although he was still desperately thin.

'So what do those lines mean? Why does the sneaking serpent walk in mild humility?'

'The snake's always been understood as Satan in another form.' Godfrey looked down at the piece of paper. His hands were frail and bony and the paper shook as he studied the contents. 'You see here the snake *walks* in mild humility. How many snakes do you know that can walk? But I'd say the emphasis is on the just man who's raging in the wilds.'

'You'll see on the note that Blake's old address, 28 Broad Street, is scribbled under the lines.' Briefly Pyke explained what had happened there in the summer, half aware that, as he was telling the story, something about it was bothering him.

Godfrey digested this information, seemingly glad to be distracted from his condition. 'And this note was addressed to you, in person?'

Pyke nodded. 'Hand delivered. Of course, none of the clerks remember who delivered it.' It made no sense. 'Why would someone want me to visit a couple of empty rooms?'

'I'm afraid I don't know,' Godfrey said, sinking back into his pillows. 'But give me Milton over Blake any day of the week.'

'Well, I'm sorry for lowering the tone,' Pyke said, smiling. 'You seem a little better tonight,' he added, a few moments later.

'Do I? Nice of you to say so. I feel tired and very weak. Everything seems such an effort, even turning over in bed.'

A little later, once Godfrey had drifted back to sleep, Pyke retreated to the landing and knocked on Felix's door. Not waiting for an answer, he went in. Felix, who was lying on the bed, hurriedly stuffed whatever he'd been reading under the blanket.

'Godfrey seems a little better tonight, doesn't he?' Pyke said. Without being invited, he sat down on the end of the bed.

'Perhaps.'

'He told me he ate a little soup and even managed a few sips of wine.'

'The nurse said he should eat.'

Pyke nodded and a short silence passed between them. 'I don't want you to think I'm indifferent to what's happening to him.'

Felix stared at him blankly. 'Then perhaps you should spend some more time with him, while you still can.'

'I know. You're right.' Pyke hesitated, not sure what else to say. He didn't want to make promises he wouldn't be able to keep. 'I'm not sure I'd even be here, if it wasn't for that man next door.'

'What do you mean?' Felix asked, interested now.

A vague memory he'd suppressed for a long time began to form at the edge of his mind. Perhaps it had been there all along. He didn't have much time to mull it over but he felt an urge to tell Felix what was on his mind. Maybe it would help the lad understand the debt he owed Godfrey, explain that he wasn't indifferent to the old man's suffering.

'I don't think I've ever told anyone about this,' he said carefully. 'Not even your mother.'

Felix sat up on the bed. 'Told anyone what?'

Now he'd mentioned it, Pyke didn't want to go ahead with the story; there were too many parts associated with it that he'd rather not think about. But Felix's face told him he had no choice.

'After my own father died, I spent a year in an orphanage. I can still remember the smell of camphor and waxed floors and the taste of the gruel they used to serve at breakfast.' Pyke hesitated. He'd meant the story to focus on Godfrey but other memories were now assailing him.

'Each night, after the candles had been blown out, a man – well, a reverend, because it was a church-run orphanage – would make his rounds. If he stopped at the end of your bed, it was a sign that you were meant to go with him.' Pyke could feel his heart beating faster. 'I'd lie there, under the blanket, with another lad, there'd be two or three of us in each bed, willing him not to stop. And in almost a year, he never did. None of the other boys ever talked about where they went or what they did. But I'd hear them return, later in the night ...' He looked up at Felix and smiled. 'We used to call him the Owl on account of his eyes; they would follow you wherever you went.'

It felt strange to think about these things after so many years. Pyke looked down and saw his hands were trembling. Felix reached out and touched him.

'Godfrey took me out of there. Do you know something? I don't think he really was a blood relation of my father, though our families were connected. He didn't have to do what he did. But he found me and insisted on giving me a home. I can't even imagine how my life would have turned out, if he hadn't rescued me.'

They sat for a while in silence, Felix's hand still pressed against Pyke's. Eventually Felix said, 'What was it like, the orphanage?'

'Cold ... lonely.' Pyke looked at him and shrugged. 'You got used to it after a while, like anything else.'

'Is that why you don't care about God?' Felix asked in a quiet, small voice.

Pyke tried to laugh. 'I haven't thought about the man we called the Owl in many years. But to answer your question, I don't think they treated us well. In fact, I think we were treated very badly.'

Felix bit his lip, evidently thinking about what Pyke had just said. 'Did you recognise Godfrey when you first saw him?'

'I don't know. I can't remember.' Pyke closed his eyes and opened them again. 'I might have. He was a good friend of my father's. He used to come to our room from time to time.'

'You and your father lived in the same room?'

Pyke smiled and squeezed his son's hand. 'Us and another family. But it was a different time.'

'Do you still think about him?'

'Who, my father?'

Felix nodded.

'Not often. When I do, I find it hard to remember the good things. He used to drink a lot.'

'I'm lucky by comparison, aren't I?' Felix's tone was gentle. 'What I've got. What we've got.'

'We're both lucky.' Pyke squeezed his son's hand one more time. 'But when someone you love falls ill, it's not always easy to remember that.'

NINE

Pyke had often wondered exactly how old Frederick Shaw was. At first glance, he didn't look any older than twenty; his face was freckled, his skin free of blemishes and his frame wiry and slight. But Pyke also knew that Shaw had first joined the New Police eight years earlier, which had to put him in his mid to late twenties or even his early thirties. Indeed, when you looked at him closely, the lines around his eyes were just about visible and his skin wasn't quite as flawless as it seemed. Sometimes Pyke wondered whether Shaw used his apparent innocence and naivety as a mask to keep the rest of the world at arm's length, for when he had observed Shaw's work at first hand there were signs of a sharp and even cunning intellect. It was a clever strategy, in a way: people always underestimated someone who smiled at them and doffed his cap.

That morning, Pyke had asked Shaw to accompany him to Soho to find the former Catholic priest. He had suggested that they walk from Whitehall Place.

'It was a good job Eddie did at Coldbath Fields, wasn't it?' Pyke said, as they crossed Trafalgar Square.

Lockhart had informed them at the morning meeting that he'd spoken to the governor of the prison and consulted the records and that Hiley, according to the governor, had been a model prisoner. He had not received visitors and had seemingly made no friends while he was incarcerated.

Shaw seemed momentarily thrown by this compliment.

'He's a good detective,' Pyke added. This much was true; Lockhart was a methodical, competent investigator.

Shaw nodded. 'But sometimes he likes to assume authority over me and Gerrett, even though we're the same rank.'

'He tells you what to do?' Pyke turned this notion over in his mind.

'In the summer, when I found out the name of the other victim, he told me not to say anything until we had proper corroboration.'

'The victim in the Shorts Gardens robbery?'

'A man by the name of Gibb,' Shaw declared.

Pyke wondered whether there was anything in this, but perhaps Lockhart had been acting out of caution, as Pyke had told them to do. They were walking at a brisk pace and when Shaw didn't offer anything else, Pyke said, 'I can't say he has much of a sense of humour ... and I know he was close to my predecessor.'

Shaw shrugged. 'He's a private man. Never talks very much about himself.'

This was not unusual. Pyke knew very little about the personal lives of his men and was happy to keep it that way. 'You and Billy did well yesterday, too,' he said, referring to their trip to the Sessions House at Old Bailey to consult the official account of Hiley's trial.

'I don't like working with him,' Shaw said.

Pyke had always assumed Shaw and Billy Gerrett were friends. He tried to say as much but Shaw interrupted, clearly agitated now the subject had been raised. 'He borrowed money from me to pay a gambling debt. But instead of paying me back, he's gone and run up another debt.'

'How much did you lend him?'

'Twenty pounds.'

Pyke whistled. It was a sizeable sum; it would take a detective sergeant a couple of months to earn that amount of money.

'And now this other person, the one he's run up a new debt with, is ahead of you in the queue to be paid back?'

Shaw nodded grimly. 'The other one who lent Billy money is the landlord of a public house ...'

They were walking up St Martin's Lane and the pavements were full of people. 'Which pub?' Pyke asked, as innocuously as possible.

'The Engineer,' Shaw said. 'Holywell Street in Millbank.'

Pyke nodded, as if he knew the place well. 'It must be difficult, having to do without things yourself when Gerrett is making light of what he owes you.'

Shaw started to walk a little more quickly, as though to try to exorcise the pent-up anger he doubtless felt, but he made no further comment.

Brendan Malloy lived alone in a dingy room above a printer's shop on Silver Street, and by the time they had dragged the former priest out of the Black Lion tavern and fed him sufficient mugs of steaming black coffee to sober him up, it was early afternoon. They had managed to find out that he'd grown up and taken his orders in the west of Ireland. Once ordained, Malloy, by his own account, had volunteered for missionary work in London and had been given letters of introduction to prominent Catholic figures in the south of England who had, in turn, funded, though not generously, a mission he had established in some stables on Cambridge Street. Three times a week, Malloy had led prayers and taught the Irish poor of Soho the catechisms, and on Sundays he had heard people's confessions and taken mass. When Pyke asked why he had left the church, and whether it was of his own accord, Malloy pretended not to have heard the question.

His dishevelled appearance wasn't helped by a slight stoop, nor by the squint that meant you were never quite sure whether he was looking at you or not. His ink-black hair was unkempt and, because of his crooked back, he walked with a faint limp.

'Until recently you rented a room on the top floor of number twenty-eight Broad Street, didn't you?' Pyke said.

Malloy didn't seem particularly taken aback by the question. 'You here to rake over that old ground again?'

'Which old ground?'

'I said all that needed to be said in that there courtroom.'

Pyke looked over at Shaw, who was inspecting the titles of books on Malloy's mantelpiece. 'Were you the child's father?'

A look of irritation flashed across Malloy's face. 'What kind of a question is that?'

'You see, I'm curious,' Pyke said. 'The mother, Sarah Scott, didn't give evidence against Druitt at his trial. Can you tell me why not?'

'I still don't understand why you're here, or what you want from me. I thought the judge had ruled on all this ...'

Pyke noticed that Shaw had picked up one of Malloy's books

and was inspecting the cover. 'When was the last time you visited number twenty-eight Broad Street?'

'I haven't been back to that godforsaken place since the night it happened.' This time Malloy looked directly at Pyke. 'The night the child died.'

Pyke removed the note he'd been sent and handed it to Malloy. 'Do you recognise the handwriting?'

Malloy took the letter and held it up to his eyes. 'No, I'm afraid I don't.'

'Someone sent it to me anonymously. Clearly they wanted me to visit your old address.' He waited and then added, 'Do you know why?'

'I haven't the slightest idea.' The former priest took another look at the letter. 'But I recognise the poem from somewhere ...'

'Blake.'

'Of course.' He looked at Pyke. 'If you don't mind me asking, what did you find there?'

'Nothing. The rooms on the top floor are empty. It seems no one's lived there since the summer.'

Pyke took a moment to assess Malloy's reaction; his blank, glassy stare. Then he noticed that Shaw was troubled by a book he'd taken from the former priest's shelf. 'What is it, Frederick?' Pyke asked.

'*Malleus Maleficarum*,' Shaw said, to Malloy rather than Pyke. He'd been reading from the spine of the book. 'What does it mean?'

'Literally? The hammer of witches.' Malloy must have realised he'd said something of interest because almost at once he added, 'Why are both of you lookin' at one another like that?'

'Like what?'

'Like I'm guilty o' something.'

Shaw turned the pages until he found the engraving he was looking for. He showed it to Pyke: a Dominican monk was standing over the disembowelled body of a young man with a hammer in one hand and an axe in the other. Pyke nodded: they both knew he'd dug up something important. Shaw showed the engraving to Malloy. 'What did he do, to deserve such an end?'

'That there is a Devil worshipper.'

'And the monk is punishing him for his sin?'

'These days we tend not to think of Satan as flesh and blood.'

He tapped his right temple. 'But those monks knew better; they knew Satan was someone you had to fight out there, not just in here.'

Pyke noticed the change in the former priest's demeanour. He was sitting up straighter, and his eyes suddenly seemed clear and lucid.

'You think that's a fair punishment?' Shaw asked.

Pyke was watching Malloy's reaction carefully and he was impressed with the subtlety of Shaw's questioning.

'Those were different times, sir. Different times.' Malloy struggled to find the right words. 'If the Devil doesn't exist, at least as flesh and blood, then how come he's still able to sow his discord?'

Pyke picked up the leather-bound edition and had a look at it himself. The words were Latin but the few engravings were truly horrific. 'I don't understand ...'

Suddenly Malloy sat forward and gripped the arms of his chair. 'How can we believe in Heaven if there's no such place as Hell? How can we believe in God, if the Devil is just a figment of our imagination?'

Pyke and Shaw exchanged a quick glance. It was the first indication that Malloy had a temper, if sufficiently riled. 'So you believe that the Devil is walking among us?'

'I do,' Malloy replied solemnly.

'Have you seen him?'

Malloy looked around the tiny room and bowed his head without answering the question.

'Have you ever come across an Anglican vicar by the name of Isaac Guppy?' Pyke asked, suddenly.

The former priest's face remained entirely blank.

'He was the rector at St Botolph's, Aldgate.'

'So?'

'Guppy was murdered the day before yesterday in the grounds of the church. Someone beat him to death with a hammer.'

'I never heard o' him.' Malloy's gaze drifted over Pyke's shoulder. 'May God bless the poor bugger's soul.'

'Are you quite certain?'

'I don't make a habit of befriendin' Protestant clergy.' He waited and then added, 'You can search this place, too. Regardless of what I might read, I don't own a hammer.'

'And you don't have any idea who might have wanted me to visit number twenty-eight Broad Street?'

Shaking his head, Malloy stood up and went over to his desk. There, he retrieved a clutch of papers and thrust them into Pyke's hand. 'That's my handwriting, sir. Just so you can be sure it wasn't me who sent you the letter.'

Outside, Pyke buttoned up his greatcoat and took shelter from the freezing rain under the awning of a butcher's shop. Gaslit flares illuminated wooden trays of unappetising meat in the window. 'It was good work, finding that book.'

Shaw's freckled face reddened; he wasn't used to being praised. 'He didn't seem to know about the letter, though – or Guppy's murder.'

Pyke nodded ruefully. 'Guppy dies at the hands of someone wielding a hammer. And Malloy owns a book called "The Hammer of Witches".'

Shaw looked at the dark clouds gathered overhead. 'Do you think he had something to do with the rector's death?'

Considering the question for a moment or two, Pyke shook his head. 'Why? Do you?'

Later that afternoon, Pyke found Martin Jakes in front of his church serving meat and vegetable broth to a line of poorly dressed men, women and children; there was no pushing and everyone seemed grateful for the chance to fill their stomachs. As Pyke watched Jakes and his ward, Kitty Jones, fill the bowls with wooden ladles, he tried to imagine the archdeacon performing such a service and wondered whether Wynter ever come into close proximity with the city's working poor.

Jakes must have seen Pyke at the gate but he waited until the crowd had been fed before he came over to join him. 'Welcome to my church, Detective Inspector,' he said, taking Pyke's hand and shaking it firmly. 'Would you care for some broth?'

Pyke thanked him but declined. Those who'd been fed had fanned out across the yard and were chatting in small groups. 'I was wondering if you'd heard from Francis Hiley.'

Jakes nodded his head, as though he'd been expecting Pyke to ask this. 'Unfortunately not. It would seem he's vanished into thin air.'

Pyke wiped his forehead with the sleeve of his coat, wondering how to proceed. 'There's a growing feeling among my colleagues that Hiley killed Guppy. I can see their point of view, but I'm trying to keep an open mind. Do you understand?'

Jakes nodded. 'That only by coming to you first of all will Francis get a fair hearing.'

'And you'll advise him to do this, if he tries to contact you?'

Jakes's genial expression vanished. 'I don't concur with your colleagues' poor opinion of Francis, but I do understand and respect my obligation to the law.'

'There is an eyewitness, a police constable no less, who's willing to swear that he saw a man matching Hiley's description standing over Guppy's body in the churchyard.'

Jakes assimilated this new piece of information with a stony face. 'Maybe Francis came upon the body by chance and fled for fear of being accused of the murder himself?'

Pyke had considered this scenario but decided to keep his views on the matter private. 'When I visited you at the vicarage, you told me that Guppy had come to you to request Hiley's presence at St Botolph's.'

'Yes, that's correct,' Jakes said.

'But he never told you why he wanted to have Hiley around.'

'Not in so many words.' Jakes paused. 'It was clear that someone had upset Guppy. He wasn't his usual belligerent self.'

'When would this have been?' Pyke asked.

'March, April.'

'Could you be more precise?'

'Late March or early April.' Jakes paused and suggested that they take a walk around the yard to keep warm. When they'd taken a few steps, he turned to Pyke and added, 'I hope you don't think I'm speaking too harshly of the man. Guppy had his faults, as we all do, but he was my immediate superior and I respected the work he did as rector.'

'Last time, I think you said there were other vicars under Guppy's wing.'

'That's right,' Jakes replied. 'Seven of us at present, all stipendiary curates. You can see for yourself that St Matthew's was built in the last century, but the others were all appointed in the last year or two to new churches: St John's, St Peter's, St James's the Less, St James's the Great, St Bartholomew's and St Jude's. There are three or four other churches being built.'

'And St Botolph's is the mother parish for all these churches?'

Jakes nodded. 'That's why I said that the rector of St Botolph's is an important figure.'

The idea of traipsing around all these churches and talking to the curates depressed Pyke, but it was clear this needed to be done.

'A parish,' Jakes went on, 'especially one as wealthy at St Botolph's, is like a small kingdom. The rate is collected and the income has to be dispersed. The rector is ultimately responsible for everything that happens.'

Pyke turned to face Jakes. 'Do you know if Guppy had a disagreement with any of the other curates?'

'Not a public one. But I think it's fair to say we all felt like poor relations of the mother parish.'

'And such resentments can fester.'

'Perhaps,' Jakes said, 'but I certainly can't imagine any of the curates going after the rector with a hammer.'

Jakes walked ahead and Pyke increased his stride to catch up. 'Tell me, was Guppy involved in the planning and building of these new churches?'

'I'm not sure. I'm only a perpetual curate, so I'm afraid I know very little about the administration of our church family. But the situation we face here in London is quite anomalous, as the bishop realises. There are thirty clergymen attached to St Paul's, some with incomes in excess of fifteen thousand. But just a mile or two to the east, here in Bethnal Green, there's one clergyman for every ten thousand souls.'

'The bishop is keen on reform, then?'

'He's keen but the Church as a whole is a tradition-bound beast, inured against change.' Jakes hesitated, perhaps wondering whether he had said too much. 'Please don't misunderstand me. I respect the bishop and wholeheartedly agree with the reforms he's attempting to push through.'

'And the archdeacon?'

Jakes chose not to answer Pyke's question but his silence was damning.

'Tell me something. When you were the vicar at St Luke's in Soho, did you ever come across a Catholic priest by the name of Brendan Malloy?'

Jakes's face had scrunched into a frown. 'The name's familiar ...'

'He left the Catholic Church under a cloud a few years ago and fell into the bottom of a gin bottle.'

'Ah, yes, I do believe I remember hearing about such a chap.' Jakes looked searchingly into Pyke's face. 'Why do you ask?'

'No reason. His name was mentioned. I just wondered whether you knew him or not.'

'Not personally, I'm afraid.' Jakes dug his hands into his pockets. 'I have to admit that I miss those days, Detective Inspector. Soho isn't a wealthy district but compared to here, well, there is no comparison. And there was such intellectual vigour. In a tavern, I might find myself in conversation with a philosopher or a poet. Here,' he added, 'the poverty is overwhelming and, rightly or wrongly, the locals resent anyone who claims to speak for the establishment.'

'It wasn't your choice to come here, then? You would have happily stayed in Berwick Street?'

Jakes didn't appear to have heard the question. Instead he waved at his ward, Kitty Jones, who was collecting the discarded soup bowls. 'Do you have children, Detective Inspector?'

'A son. He's fourteen.'

'A grand age,' Jakes said, smiling. 'Kitty was a little older when she first came to me. That would have been almost five years ago now. I've tried to convince her to think about marriage, a life of her own, but she tells me she's wedded to the Church.'

Pyke hadn't intended to say anything else about Felix but this last reference, as casual as it was, changed his mind. 'Recently I'm afraid to say my son's been showing an unhealthy interest in the Bible.'

'And such a thought upsets you?' Jakes asked, amused rather than wounded by Pyke's insinuation.

'I visit a man like the archdeacon and I'm truly horrified.' Pyke looked around him and shrugged. 'Then I come here and I'm not so sure.'

Matilda Guppy didn't seem angry or resentful when Pyke was ushered into the drawing room at the rectory, but there was no warmth in her greeting. She was wrapping wineglasses in sheets of paper and packing them into a wooden crate.

'I suppose the servants could do all of this,' she said, in a dull tone, 'but it helps to keep my mind occupied.'

Pyke looked at the pile of china plates stacked on the sideboard. 'On my last visit, I was led to believe, by others more than by yourself, that your husband had grudgingly agreed to give Francis Hiley food and shelter. Now I'm told it was the other way around; that he actively courted Hiley's presence because he wanted someone to keep an eye on things.'

Guppy's widow looked straight through him. 'I'm afraid my husband didn't consult me about the decisions he made.'

'This would have been in late March or early April. Can you think of something that happened just prior to this, something that might have upset or unsettled him?'

'As I've just explained to you, Detective Inspector, I wasn't privy to my husband's affairs. Now if you'll excuse me, I have a lot of work to do.'

'Perhaps your husband mentioned something. Perhaps he'd been threatened by one of his parishioners, or he had money worries. Perhaps you noticed a change in him. Or someone came here to the rectory ...'

'I won't say it's been a pleasure, Detective Inspector, because that would be lying.' She picked up a china plate from the sideboard.

Pyke stood his ground. 'Please try to think, madam. It could be important.'

Matilda Guppy put down the plate and rested her hands on her hips. 'This would have been in late March?'

Pyke nodded.

She wandered across to the bay window, and when she turned around to face him, it was as if she had finally reconciled herself to answering his question. 'A strange fellow came here to the rectory about that time. After he left, I could tell that my husband was upset. I tried to find out what this man wanted, and what they'd discussed, but my husband wouldn't tell me. He was still upset for at least a couple of days after that.'

'Can you describe this man, the one who visited? I mean, did you actually see him?'

'See him? I was introduced to him, sir. It would have been before he'd spoken to my husband.'

'Do you remember his name?'

'Not his name but I remember he was a funny-looking man. Rather shabby, if truth be told. I do remember his brogue, though. Rather nice, even if it was Irish.'

'If you saw him again, would you recognise him?' Pyke waited. 'Would you be able to pick him out of a group of men?'

Pyke arrested Brendan Malloy on suspicion of murder, transported him back to the station house at Great Scotland Yard and locked him in one of the cells in the basement. Later he would think it a little strange that Malloy had remained in his room; that he hadn't tried to make a run for it as soon as he'd realised Pyke had gone to see him regarding Guppy's murder. In that sense, staying put didn't seem like the action of a guilty man, but then again, when Pyke had found him for the second time, the man had imbibed a bottle of gin and needed to be carried to the carriage.

By late afternoon, when Malloy had sobered up enough to be able to stand, Matilda Guppy had presented herself at the Detective Branch. Malloy was led up the stairs and told to line up in a parade of similarly dishevelled men. Guppy's wife filed up and down all of them, like a sergeant major, and picked out Malloy at the first attempt.

An hour later, after he'd penned a route-paper and sent one of the clerks upstairs with it, Pyke was summoned to Mayne's office. The commissioner had someone else with him, and when Pyke pushed open the door, Mayne and his companion looked up, a little startled.

'Could you give us a moment, Detective Inspector?' Mayne said, glancing at the well-dressed man with him.

'Is that necessary, Sir Richard? I think our business here is complete.' The man was in his fifties; his silver hair was smooth and smelled of lavender oil. He carried himself with the air of someone who had done well for himself.

Mayne grunted and looked over at Pyke. 'Detective Inspector Pyke, this is Sir St John Palmer.' He waited as they acknowledged one another. 'Sir St John has kindly agreed to oversee the renovations of the old station house.'

Pyke had another look at Palmer. He was in good shape for his age; his hair was thick, and his complexion clear. 'I never trust a businessman who's being kind to me.'

Palmer regarded him with interest. 'I couldn't agree with you more, Detective. Sir Richard was just being diplomatic. I plan to take the department for all I can get.' He grinned at his own joke.

Palmer acknowledged Mayne with a nod of the head and then let himself out of the room.

'This is good work, Detective,' Mayne said, when they were alone. He was holding the route-paper Pyke had written. 'Thorough and imaginative.'

'Thank you, sir.'

'This Catholic priest, the one you arrested, lied about not knowing Isaac Guppy?'

'It would seem so; I plan to question him further.'

'So, you have two lines of investigation. This priest constitutes one; Francis Hiley the other.'

'That's correct.'

Mayne looked down at the route-paper in front of him. 'Question the priest but don't forget about Hiley.'

Pyke wondered why everyone seemed to be so keen to implicate the ex-convict.

'That will be all, Detective Inspector. Good afternoon.'

There was a woman waiting for Pyke in his office when he returned from his exchange with Mayne. She was respectably dressed in a dark-coloured blouse, a grey flounced crinoline skirt and a woollen shawl covering her shoulders. It took Pyke a few moments to remember where he'd seen her before.

'Mrs Morris.' He gestured for her to take the chair on the other side of his desk. 'Now what can I do for you?'

'I have a son, he's twelve. Not a bad lad but he never listens to his mother. I found this among his possessions,' she said, rummaging around in the cloth bag she'd brought with her. 'I asked him where he'd got it and he told me he'd found it in one of the upstairs rooms at number twenty-eight.' She removed what looked to be a garment of some kind and shook out the creases. 'Apparently it was just hanging there on an old nail.'

Pyke took it from her and inspected it more closely.

Made from black cloth, it was a surplice with thin strips of rabbit fur attached to both shoulders.

TEN

Brendan Malloy sat on the hard floor of the cell, back against the wall and arms wrapped around his knees, shaking. Neither his ankles nor his wrists had been shackled but he still looked pathetic. The gin fumes from his breath filled the small space and mingled with the scent of his body odour. In the light of a solitary candle it was hard to see his face beneath the dark, tangled morass of whiskers.

'Get me a pint of gin and I'll tell you anything ye want, sir. Just get me some gin. Please.' He held up his hands in supplication.

'If you answer my questions in a manner I consider to be satisfactory, I might give you what you want.'

Pyke took a step into the cell. 'When we last met, I asked you whether you knew or had ever met Reverend Isaac Guppy. You told me you'd never heard of him.'

Malloy's stare fell to his boots; he didn't make any attempt to deny the lie he'd been caught in.

'Why didn't you tell me you'd visited Guppy in March?'

'Is that why I'm here? 'Cos I mighta been to the man's house on one occasion?'

'So you don't deny you went to see him?'

Malloy just shrugged.

'Why did you go to see him? And why did you lie to me about knowing him?'

'I didn't kill him.' He looked up at Pyke, his eyes wide and pleading. 'Isn't that the important question?'

'The hammer of witches. Is that just a coincidence?'

Malloy seemed puzzled.

'Guppy was beaten to death with a hammer.'

The former priest held up his bony, trembling hands. 'Does it look like I could kill a man with these?'

It was true that Pyke couldn't imagine Brendan Malloy wielding a hammer to any great effect. 'Where were you last Tuesday night, between the hours of eight and midnight?'

Malloy's stare drifted back to the floor. 'I couldn't exactly say; these days I can hardly remember what I did yesterday. But I'd say I was where you found me earlier or in the Black Lion. I don't tend to venture much farther 'n that.'

Pyke made a mental note to send Shaw to check with the landlord and drinkers there, to see whether anyone remembered seeing Malloy that night. 'You still haven't answered my question. Why did you go and see Guppy?'

Malloy wiped his hand across his forehead. 'To warn him, that's all.'

'Warn him about what?'

'Before I can tell you, you have to understand something about Ebenezer Druitt.'

Pyke nodded for him to continue.

Malloy's hands were trembling violently now. 'Do you know what a mesmerist is?'

'I think I know what a mesmerist does. Or claims to do.'

'Folk would come and see Druitt at number twenty-eight. Folk with ailments, problems. Druitt would put them to sleep and pretend he was curin' them. They'd pay him good money, too.'

Pyke nodded. He remembered reading about Franz Mesmer, who'd studied medicine in Vienna and had initially believed that cures could be achieved by rubbing diseased bodies with magnets. Eventually Mesmer had come to realise that the power of suggestion was even more potent and he had travelled to Paris to try to convince experts that his findings had medical uses.

'You're suggesting Druitt was a fraud?'

'A fraud?' Malloy laughed bitterly. 'No, I don't think he was a fraud. But he was a dangerous man – still is. He could terrify and charm in equal measure, but he also claimed he had the gift of prophesy, said he was visited by spirits. If you'd seen one of his acts, you mighta believed him too.'

Pyke felt his frustration rise. 'What's any of this got to do with Isaac Guppy?'

'I was just tryin' to explain. Earlier this year, Druitt told me he'd foreseen that an Anglican vicar called Guppy would die. This was when we were still on speakin' terms. I asked him whether he felt he had a duty to warn this Guppy. Druitt just laughed, said that one less vicar in the world would be a good thing. At first I didn't know what to do, but I didn't feel I could sit back and do nothing, so I went looking for him.'

'You just approached him, a total stranger, and told him a man called Druitt had prophesied his death?'

Malloy nodded.

'Did he believe you?'

'Not at first.'

'What changed his mind?'

'I don't know. At the time, I thought I'd convinced him that Ebenezer Druitt wasn't a man to be taken lightly.'

'But afterwards?'

'It was only when I told him my name that his whole attitude changed.'

Pyke contemplated this. 'You think he knew who you were?'

'I'd say so,' Malloy replied, nodding.

'Only you'd never met him before.'

'That's right.'

'Maybe Druitt wanted you to tell Guppy. Did you ever think about that? I mean, why else would he go to the trouble of taking you into his confidence?'

Malloy shrugged. 'That could be true, I suppose. Druitt could've had some business with Guppy I didn't know about. It would have been like him, too. Wantin' to frighten the man and gettin' me to do it for him.'

Pyke studied Malloy's face for signs that he was lying. 'And did you tell Druitt what you'd done?'

That elicited a gallows laugh. ''Course I didn't tell him. Druitt's not just a mean man, sir, not just a man with violence in his blood. If he were just that, I wouldn't have been afraid of him.'

Pyke dug his hands deeper into the fur-lined pockets of his greatcoat. 'Then tell me why you were afraid.'

'Still am, sir. Still am.'

'Even though he's locked away in the Model Prison at Pentonville?'

'Evil recognises no walls, sir, and that's the truth. Look into his eyes and you'll know what I'm talking about. You'll feel the chill in your soul.'

Pyke considered this for a moment. He believed that Malloy was telling the truth but he had no way of knowing how mentally disturbed the former priest actually was.

'I'd like you to tell me about Sarah Scott,' he continued.

'What about her?' Malloy said, curling up into an even tighter ball. His eyes glistened manically in the candlelight.

'Did the two of you live together at number twenty-eight?'

'She lodged there for a while.'

Pyke nodded. 'Were the two of you lovers?'

'That's none of your business, sir,' Malloy muttered, but his indignation seemed unconvincing.

'It's my job to find out who killed Isaac Guppy, and if I decide your affair with this woman, Sarah Scott, is relevant to my enquiries, then I'll make it my business to dig up every sordid detail, whether you like it or not.'

Malloy said nothing but continued to glare at him.

'Is that why you left the Catholic Church?'

'I had my reasons, sir.'

'Do you know where I can find her now? If I felt you were being co-operative with me, I might allow the gaoler to bring you some beer or even some gin.'

That seemed to do it. 'Last I heard she'd gone to live in a vegetarian colony in Suffolk.' Malloy hesitated and then continued. 'A place called Stratford St Mary, near Ipswich.'

'Are the two of you still corresponding?'

'She's there, I'm here,' he said glumly.

Pyke considered the man crouched in front of him for a moment. 'I read the court transcript of Druitt's trial. I was interested to see that Sarah Scott wasn't asked to testify.'

'She'd just lost her child. Is it any wonder she didn't feel up to takin' the stand?'

Pyke looked into Malloy's proud, gin-ravaged face. 'In the end, it came down to your word against Druitt's. The jury believed you and not him.'

'I was there. I *saw* him. That bastard, he knew I was watchin'' him, and you know what he did, just before he let go of the baby? He looked down at me and smiled.'

'What still puzzles me is the lack of motive. Druitt didn't have any reason for wanting that child dead.'

'Haven't you listened to a single word I've told you?' Malloy said, shaking his head.

'Are you saying that Druitt didn't need a reason?' Pyke made it clear that he didn't believe this for a moment. Instead, he said, 'The surplice that Isaac Guppy was wearing on the night he was murdered turned up the other day in one of the upstairs rooms at number twenty-eight.'

'So?'

'So, it stands to reason that Guppy's murderer took the surplice to your old address. And at the moment you're the only person I can think of who lived at number twenty-eight and had met Guppy. Now, do you see the trouble you're in?'

But Malloy seemed far away. 'I always knew he could still get to me ...'

'Druitt? But he's locked away in Pentonville?'

Malloy held his breath, as if weighing up what Pyke had just said. 'You still don't understand, do you? I thought I'd be safe; I'd be out of his reach.' Malloy started to rock back and forth, his arms clamped tightly around his knees.

'Has Druitt been sending you letters from prison?'

Malloy buried his face in his hands and began to sob. It was a while before he was able to speak. 'When you fall from grace, when you cut yourself off from God, there's nowhere left to hide.' Without warning, Malloy sprung forward and grabbed Pyke's coat sleeve. 'Don't you see what I've been trying to tell you? Druitt isn't just a dangerous creature. He's not just a man. He's the Devil. Druitt is Satan himself.'

For a long while afterwards, Pyke would remember the tortured look in the former priest's eyes.

Pyke turned up the collar of his coat and walked into the wind; it was gusting so hard it felt as if he might even be lifted off his feet. On the other side of Scotland Yard, past the fishmongers and the lodging house where the unattached policemen billeted, was the river. At the wharf stairs, he stopped and looked into the dark choppy water. It was the immenseness of it he liked: up close, the river was merely a heave of scum and sludge, but when you looked at the horizon it was a vast, slow-moving mass of water eddying its way through the largest city on earth. He stood there and thought about Brendan Malloy. It seemed unlikely, to say the least, that the former priest could have carried out such a vicious physical attack on Guppy. But at the same time Malloy somehow seemed to be implicated in the events leading up to the murder. What was clear was that someone had wanted Pyke to find the surplice and make a connection between Guppy's murder and the former occupants of those rooms. But why? He stood for a while under the hissing gas-lamp before turning around and heading back towards Scotland Yard.

The temperature dropped below freezing as the wind continued to gust from the north and by the time Pyke arrived home he was shivering.

'He seemed all right earlier, but he fell asleep at about four and I didn't like to wake him, even though his dinner has gone cold,' Felix said, gesturing at the bowl of soup on the bedside table.

Pyke looked at his uncle's pale, cadaverous face and at the hot coals burning in the grate. At least the room was warm, he thought, as the furious wind rattled the windows. 'Has he eaten anything today?'

'He had some bread and cheese for lunch,' Felix replied.

'Well, that's something, isn't it?' Pyke looked at his son's drawn expression. 'Perhaps you should get some rest, let me stay with Godfrey for a while.'

They were sitting on either side of Godfrey's bed. Neither of them spoke for a few moments. 'This is it, isn't it? He's dying,' Felix said in a whisper.

'We don't know that. Godfrey's as strong as an ox, always has been. He's probably just tired.' Pyke tried to keep his tone upbeat. He hadn't told Felix that the doctor had said it was now only a matter of time. When he'd been told this, Pyke hadn't wanted to believe it. His uncle had lived his three score years and ten and was lucky to have done so; and his life had been much fuller than most.

But this didn't help to lessen the sharp, stabbing pain Pyke felt in his stomach whenever he realised that some time soon Godfrey would no longer be there, even though in his job he had to confront death almost daily.

'And when he's no longer able to fight?'

'When the time comes, he'll be ready. We'll all be ready.' Pyke felt guilty about pretending he'd already adjusted to the idea of Godfrey passing.

Just then, Godfrey opened his eyes and yawned. 'Listen to you, a pair of old fishwives. I'm not dead yet.' Felix helped him to sit up. Godfrey looked around the room and smiled. 'Who said I'm not able to fight?' That made Felix blush and giggle and suddenly he seemed younger than his fourteen years.

Pyke went to collect the soup bowl and said he'd go downstairs to warm it through, but on the landing, hearing Felix and Godfrey happily chatting, he took a diversion to Felix's bedroom. The Bible was hidden under a pile of books on the table next to the bed. There was no inscription in it. Carefully he put it back where he'd found it and headed downstairs to the kitchen. When Pyke returned to Godfrey's room five minutes later, he handed his uncle the bowl of soup and a spoon, then said to Felix, 'I visited a church today, St Matthew's in Bethnal Green. I'd like you to meet the vicar there. I think you'd like him.'

'Why?' Felix asked, only half interested.

'He's clearly a man of God but he wears it lightly. And while others do nothing but talk, he actually helps people.'

'Careful, dear boy. You're starting to sound like a convert,' Godfrey said, a dribble of soup running down his chin. 'We already have one God-botherer in the house as it is.'

If Pyke had said this, Felix would have been offended, but since it was Godfrey, Felix hit him playfully on the arm and smiled. Suddenly uncomfortable, Pyke excused himself, saying he should look in on the pigs.

At the bottom of the garden, Pyke found – to his relief – that his three pigs were huddled together in the sty. There was a small, screened area where they could take refuge from the rain and wind but it wasn't really large enough for all three of them. Either he would have to build a larger sty or one of them would have to be sacrificed. But which one? A farmer would make such a decision on a pragmatic basis: which one would yield the most meat? As such, Alice would be first in the queue, but Pyke liked her best: she was the greediest and most stubborn of the three animals. Pyke fetched another sack of corn from the shed and emptied it into the trough, but none of the pigs stirred from their shelter. He looked up at the row of houses and thought about his uncle. When Pyke had been Felix's age, Godfrey had always known what to do; what to stand firm on, what to let go. Pyke had tried to do likewise with Felix but, in recent years, he hadn't got it right. The boy loved Godfrey, it was so clear, but could the same be said of him? Did Felix *love* him in quite the same way? A sharp gust of wind tore a branch off a nearby tree and in the distance Pyke heard Copper bark. He hurried back to the house, hoping to get to the mastiff before it set off the neighbour's dog.

The following morning, Pyke walked into the offices of the Detective Branch to find Billy Gerrett devouring a meat pie for his breakfast. The whole spectacle turned Pyke's stomach, and he was about to leave and shut himself away in his office when Gerrett said, to no one in particular, 'Looks to me like Superintendent Wells has this one wrapped up.' He glanced towards Pyke and forced the final chunk of pastry into his mouth. 'Confirmed, beyond any doubt, that Hiley did it.'

That stopped Pyke in his tracks. 'Is that so?'

Wells feigned modesty, although he was basking in Gerrett's praise. 'I was fortunate, that's all.'

'What exactly have you managed to do, Walter?' Pyke asked, feeling a tightness in his chest. He looked around for Jack Whicher, but remembered at the last moment that he'd been dispatched to look into another matter: a burglary in Belgravia.

'I took a group of men to Whitechapel High Street. We talked to shopkeepers, market vendors, crossing-sweepers, anyone we could find. Eventually we found a man, a costermonger in fact, who knows Hiley. He told me they often frequented the same establishment. Anyway, this fellow is prepared to testify under oath that he saw Hiley running like a madman along Whitechapel High Street at about eight o'clock on the night that Guppy was killed.'

While Pyke digested this new piece of information, Gerrett offered Wells another slap on the back.

'I'd say that just about settles it, wouldn't you?' Wells added, looking at Eddie Lockhart for affirmation.

Lockhart shrugged but said nothing. For some reason, he didn't seem persuaded by this new piece of evidence.

Pyke looked at him, surprised he hadn't fallen in behind Gerrett. 'That was good work, Walter, but when you think about it, it only tells us what we already know: that Hiley was in the vicinity of the church yard at the time of the murder and fled as a result of what he saw. What it doesn't tell us is whether Hiley actually killed Guppy.' As he was talking, Pyke noticed Eddie Lockhart nodding in agreement.

'But why would an innocent man run?' Billy Gerrett said, looking at Lockhart rather than Pyke.

Pyke waited. 'Let's assume for a moment that Hiley heard the attack, heard Guppy's shouts. He would have rushed to find out what had happened. That could have been when the constable saw him and called out. In that moment, Hiley would have made a decision. Run or find the finger of guilt pointed at him. If I were a felon, I know what I would do.'

'If?' Gerrett arched his eyebrows.

Pyke couldn't tell for certain whether Gerrett's remark had been a barbed reference to the time Pyke had spent in prison. If so, it was an unforgivable breach of discipline and, even worse, it indicated that the man was too stupid to fear him.

'You're quite right, of course,' Wells said, choosing to ignore Gerrett's comment. 'Until we find Hiley and force a confession out of him, we can't say for certain that he is the killer.'

Pyke looked first at Lockhart and then at Wells. 'So for the time being, it would seem prudent to explore other avenues of enquiry.'

'Is that why you're holding a papist priest in one of the cells?' Wells asked.

'I know you think we should focus all of our attention on finding Hiley, Walter. But the surplice Guppy wore on the night he was killed was found at number twenty-eight Broad Street in Soho. Malloy, the priest, used to live at this address. And Malloy paid

Guppy a visit in late March, apparently to warn him that a fellow tenant had prophesied his death.'

This last piece of information was new to all of them. 'You've been to see this tenant, I assume – the one who made the threat?' Lockhart said.

'I plan to. His name's Ebenezer Druitt and he's currently serving a five-year sentence for manslaughter in Pentonville.'

'But how can we be sure it's the same surplice?' Wells asked.

It was a good question; all Pyke could do was explain what a distinctive garment it was.

Lockhart looked at him and nodded. 'I'd say we need to take Pyke's finding very seriously indeed.'

Pyke didn't bother to hide his surprise: Eddie Lockhart coming to his defence? If he'd trusted the man, he would have been gratified by the intervention.

'A word, if I may?' Pyke said later, calling Eddie Lockhart into his office and inviting him to sit in the chair opposite him.

Closing the door, Pyke sat down behind his desk and took a moment to contemplate the man's unease. 'I have an important job I'd like you to do for me. There are seven curates attached to the parish of St Botolph's. I've talked to one of them, the Reverend Martin Jakes of St Matthew's, Bethnal Green. I'd like you to go and see the others, to build up a fuller picture of the victim and his dealings with the curates. Maybe some of them saw Guppy in Hiley's company. They might have important details they aren't even aware of.' Pyke lowered his voice. 'You'll have to be sensitive, mind you. Any information will have to be coaxed from these curates.'

Eddie Lockhart regarded him with a cool expression. 'You don't believe Hiley killed the rector, do you?'

'To be honest, I don't.'

'Neither do I.'

Pyke nodded, surprised by the forcefulness of his statement. 'Why don't you believe it was Hiley?'

'Intuition. And the evidence.' Lockhart sighed.

'We need to look more closely into Guppy's affairs. Someone killed him for a reason,' Pyke continued.

Lockhart gave him a sceptical look. 'I've read your report. As far as I can tell, everyone who knew Guppy loathed him.'

'Then this is your chance to talk to the curates and find out what, in particular, they loathed about him.'

Lockhart shrugged. He didn't seem especially keen. 'We need to look at the parish accounts too, you said so yourself. The man lived more like a prince than a priest.'

Pyke nodded. 'You think this might have something to do with money? The misappropriation of parish funds?'

Lockhart sat there awkwardly, not knowing how to respond.

'This task I've given you will be quite an undertaking,' Pyke said, finally. 'Given that all of the churches are in Bethnal Green, I wouldn't expect you to travel to and from your boarding house each day.' He licked his lips. 'I'd envisage the job taking perhaps three days, if you start immediately. As such, I've taken the liberty of booking you into a lodging house in the City. You'll find it comfortable: perhaps a good deal more comfortable than your current accommodation.'

Lockhart acknowledged this with a curt nod.

'You'll do it, then?'

'Do I have a choice?'

Pyke picked up a pen from his desk and fiddled with it. 'Whether you believe it or not, Eddie, and whatever differences of opinion we might've had in the past, I do think you're a good detective.'

Lockhart stood up and waited for Pyke to dismiss him.

'One more thing. I'd prefer it if you kept this assignment to yourself,' Pyke added. 'I wouldn't want the others to think I was treating you any differently to them.'

The Engineer public house was situated a few streets from the river at the end of a mean, yellow terrace, backing on to a burial ground and the prison. It was a grim, industrial district dominated by the brewery, a gin distillery, railway works and an old sawmill. Along the river itself, coal barges were moored at the various wharfs and on the other bank the bone-grinding factories of Lambeth billowed plumes of smoke into already grey skies. The pub attracted drinkers from the factories and the rows of tightly-packed terraces.

Pyke didn't introduce himself to the landlord, Gerald Tompkins, but asked for a private audience. Outside in the yard, the landlord lit his pipe. 'So what can I do for you, sir?' He was a bald, unattractive man with short arms and barely any neck.

'You lent a man called William Gerrett twenty pounds. I'd like to buy that debt from you.' Pyke pulled out a piece of paper. 'I'll give you twenty-five, if you'll sign this and agree never to speak a word of our conversation to Gerrett or anyone else.'

Tompkins removed the pipe from his mouth and blew out a stream of tobacco smoke. 'And why would you want to buy this man's debt?'

'That's none of your business. You'll make five pounds from the transaction. That's all you need to know.'

'And Gerrett?'

'He'll owe me instead of owing you.'

Tompkins looked at Pyke and shrugged. 'As long as I get my money, I don't care who's paying me. Let's go inside.'

In an upstairs room, Pyke watched as the landlord signed the document he'd prepared earlier and counted the twenty-five pounds. As Tompkins put down his pen, Pyke took out his pistol from his holster and pointed the barrel at the landlord's face. 'Just so we're sure. If you tell a living soul about this arrangement, I'll come back here and shoot you through the heart. I need you to know that I'm serious. Nod if you understand.'

The landlord looked at the pistol and nodded.

Pyke found Septimus Clapp where he could be found most after-noons; the taproom of the Cheese tavern on Fleet Street. Clapp occupied a table at the back of the room and no one dared venture anywhere near him. This was partly because he stank – of stale tobacco and sweat – and partly because people were terrified of him. Clapp was one of the most successful and ruthless moneylenders in the city. For each day a payment was late, Clapp instructed his men to snap one of the debtor's fingers. He was also no respecter of age or gender; women and the elderly were just as likely to have their fingers broken as young men.

'I'd like to sell you a debt.' Pyke removed the document Tompkins had signed from his coat pocket and slid it across the table. 'The debt's for twenty pounds. I'm willing to sell it to you for ten.'

'And why would you want to do something like that, Detective Inspector?' Clapp cast his eyes across the piece of paper in front of him.

'You don't need to know. I just want you to treat this debt as you would any other.'

Clapp seemed amused by this proposition. Staring down at the name on the document, he said, 'And where does this Mr William Gerrett reside?'

'You can visit him at his place of work.'

'Which is?'

'Scotland Yard.'

The moneylender clapped his hands together in evident delight. 'So he's a policeman, is he?'

'A detective sergeant.'

Clapp folded up the document and tucked it into his pocket. 'Usually I wouldn't bother with such a trifling sum but the nature of this enterprise appeals to me.'

'Do what you do, Clapp, but keep my name out of it.'

Clapp grinned, revealing bloodied gums and two good teeth. 'You're a worse man than you look, sir. And I mean that as a compliment.'

When Gerrett finally showed up for work the following morning, Pyke could still smell gin on his breath. He said nothing to Pyke about his financial predicament and sat morosely at his desk. Pyke had been out when Clapp and two of his collectors had come to the office the previous day but he'd heard about it later from Shaw. Gerrett had been unable to settle the debt on the spot and had begged Clapp for a week to do so. Clapp had given him until the following evening. Gerrett came to see Pyke and broke down. Pyke told him he would look into the matter and passed it on to Wells, who dealt with all disciplinary issues. At the end of the day, Gerrett was summoned to Wells's office and dismissed, as Pyke knew he would be.

'I didn't have a choice,' Wells said to Pyke afterwards. 'He knew the rules, he'd read the code of behaviour.'

'You did what you had to.'

Wells looked at him astutely. 'Of course, if you'd wanted to protect him, you could have kept the information to yourself.'

Pyke held his stare but said nothing.

'The man in question made what I considered to be an unfortunate remark yesterday. I hope it didn't have any bearing on your decision.'

Pyke was in Wells's office and he went over to the shelves, which were lined with books he didn't believe Wells had ever read. 'It's true I didn't fight for him, as I would have done for Whicher or Shaw.'

'And Gerrett's leaving means that Eddie Lockhart is now isolated in the department,' Wells commented.

Pyke was surprised Wells had been able to work it out. 'Yes, I suppose you could say that.'

'And that's good for you because Lockhart may find it harder to pass information back to Pierce.'

'I don't know for sure that Lockhart is Pierce's spy.'

Wells nodded easily. 'Perhaps it was Gerrett.' This thought made him smile.

'At bottom, he was a poor detective, Walter. That's all we need to be worried about here.'

ELEVEN

The train to Colchester left the Eastern Counties terminus at Shoreditch at 12.30 precisely, the carriages lurching forward, porters and hawkers on the platform trying to keep up with them. Steam from the engine hung in the air like cannon-smoke, then they were moving through the same tenements where they'd chased a man, possibly Francis Hiley, a week earlier. From inside the train, the buildings seemed even smaller and dirtier than they had done previously. Relaxing into his cushioned seat, Pyke let his gaze drift out of the window. Soon they'd passed the worst of the slums and the landscape opened out, brick kilns and allotments replacing row upon row of terraced housing. This was not the first time Pyke had travelled on a train, but he had not used the railways as much as he could have done. Maybe it was because he associated them with his wife's death; in the end, she'd been killed because of her efforts to unionise navvies building the London-to-Birmingham line. Pyke shut his eyes and wondered how his life would have turned out if Emily had lived, how different it would've been.

Soon the city was behind them and they were moving through farmland and green fields. The sky was blue and hard, and the frost on the ground sparkled like tiny diamonds. The view, and the motion of the carriage, soon put Pyke to sleep.

By the time he had caught the stagecoach from Colchester to Ipswich and persuaded a hackney carriage to take him to the colony a few miles outside Stratford St Mary, the light was starting to fade. The land was barren and oppressively flat, mile upon mile of cornfields lying fallow for the winter, broken by the occasional tree or windmill with crows hovering menacingly in the air. It was an empty landscape, sparsely populated, and unwelcoming to the outsider. It put Pyke in mind of marshes and ancient Druids, low clouds rolling in off the North Sea so you could hardly tell the land and the sky apart.

The vegetarian colony was located at the end of a muddy track and it was a more orderly and, indeed, permanent community than he'd been expecting. There were tents erected on the grassland closest to the river but there was also a series of mud-and-stone shacks on the slightly higher ground. From the gate, Pyke counted twenty men and women still hoeing the fields. He stopped a woman and asked her where he could find Sarah Scott. The woman said she didn't think that Sarah had returned from London but directed him to one of the larger mud-and-stone cottages. He peered into the interior and saw someone with their back to him. It took him a few moments to realise the woman was standing at an easel, a paintbrush in her hand. The room was lit by candles and a wood fire smouldered in the brick grate, smoke drifting upwards towards a hole in the roof.

'I'm looking for Sarah Scott,' he said, waiting for her to turn around.

'You've found her.' She took a step towards him, brush still in hand. Her cheeks were smudged with paint. 'And who, may I ask, are you?'

'Pyke.' He waited. 'Detective Inspector Pyke of Scotland Yard.'

She stepped to one side and said, 'You had better come in, then.'

There were two simple wooden chairs arranged around the fire. She invited him to take one of them and waited until he was seated before doing likewise.

She wasn't beautiful by the standards of genteel society; she was too petite for a start, no more than five feet tall. Her skin was smooth but dark, suggesting she spent too much time outdoors, and her hips were straight and almost boyish. It was her hair which marked her as different, though. Rather than scraped back off her face or arranged in loose curls, her ink-black hair cascaded in every direction, a tangled, unruly mess, untamed by a comb or even a bonnet. It put him in mind of Medusa. Clearly she didn't dress her hair for anyone apart from herself. In spite of her height, she didn't seem overawed by Pyke's presence and held his gaze for so long that he had to look away first. When she smiled, laughter lines appeared at the edges of her face, her curious, intelligent eyes taking everything in without giving away what she was thinking.

'Do you mind me asking how you found me here?' she said, tucking a loose strand of hair behind her ear.

'I've been talking to Brendan Malloy.'

That drew a non-committal nod. 'I suspected as much.'

'Why's that?'

'Because he's one of the few people in London who knows where I am.' She waited for a moment. 'Is Brendan in some kind of trouble?'

'How well do you know him?'

'Well enough.' She fiddled with her paintbrush.

'Would it be fair to say that you and Malloy were ... *attached*?'

'Have you come all the way from London just to badger me about my private affairs?' she said, not quite smiling.

'Please answer the question, madam.' Pyke tried to keep his tone civil and disinterested, but he couldn't help noticing the fullness of her lips and the sparkle in her eyes.

'Did he tell you that?'

'Tell me what?'

'That he and I were once attached.'

'No.' Pyke hesitated. 'But I got the feeling that he still cares very much for you.'

That silenced her for a while. Pyke thought he saw her jaw tighten slightly. 'Did he leave the Catholic Church to be with you?'

Her expression remained inscrutable. 'How much did Brendan tell you about his work as a priest?'

'A little. He told me about having to perform mass and hearing confessions in a stable on Cambridge Street.'

Sarah Scott nodded. 'Did he tell you about the exorcisms he used to perform?'

'No.' That took Pyke by surprise.

'That's what first took me there, to see him. I suppose, in our little part of the world, he was famous, or should I say notorious.'

'You mean, you went to him to be exorcised?'

She passed off his question with a shrug. 'Anglican vicars stopped performing exorcisms some time during the last century.'

Pyke tried to reconcile this notion with the sense he'd derived of her so far – a woman who didn't suffer fools. 'And was this exorcism successful?'

Instead of answering the question, she stood up and gestured for him to follow her over to the easel. There was just enough light for him to be able to see the painting.

It almost made Pyke gasp out loud, though later he wasn't sure whether his reaction was one of astonishment or horror. The painting depicted a young woman devouring her infant child, the proportions deliberately askew. The naked woman was clutching her child around its tiny waist, and there was nothing but a bloody stump where the head had once been. But it was the woman's expression which really caught your eye: a maniacal glee mixed with an undertow of sadness or regret, as though she knew what she was doing yet couldn't quite stop herself. The details were exquisitely rendered, as one might find in a painting by Vermeer: the blue-black veins on the woman's forehead, the creases in her flesh, the creamy-white softness of the child's skin and the viscous blood congealed around her mouth. If part of the intention had been to render the scene in as realistic a manner as possible, this was undercut by the lush, sensuous colours of the background, giving the painting an eerie, dreamlike quality. Yet the painting seemed to demand that you understood it literally, that you felt its pain and sorrow as intensely as you might your own. In the end, he had to look away. As he did so, Sarah Scott smiled, as though pleased by his reaction.

'I read somewhere that Goya once painted an image of Satan devouring a child,' Pyke said. 'I haven't seen it, of course ...'

'You know Goya?' She stared at him, hands on hips, seemingly amazed by this notion.

Pyke stared back at her, wondering how *she* knew who Goya was. 'I once saw a book of his engravings in my uncle's shop. The *Caprichos*, I think. I'm told it was extremely rare.'

She gave him a sceptical look but her eyes were still glistening. 'Too rare for a poor country girl like me to know about?'

'I didn't say that.'

'But it's what you meant.'

Pyke tried to gauge whether she felt she'd been insulted. 'I simply pointed out that your work reminded me a little of Goya. That was all.'

This seemed to appease her. She relaxed a little and had another look at the canvas. 'A gallery owner came to see my work a few years ago – actually at Brendan's bidding. He liked what he saw and offered to represent me. I sell the occasional painting. It was he who introduced me to Goya's work. It haunted me for months.'

'I can see the influence,' Pyke said, staring at the violent brushstrokes. The pain and fury seemed to leap off the canvas.

Sarah Scott suddenly seemed distracted. 'For as long as I can remember, I've seen things, grotesque things, things that won't let me sleep at night; at the time I thought Brendan might be able to cure me.'

'It's funny how our worst fears always seem to come true ...'

She gave him a quizzical stare. 'You're referring to what happened in the summer?'

'I'm sorry about your baby. I have a son. He's fourteen. I can't imagine how painful it must be to ...'

She held up her hand, as if to stop him. 'Thank you.' She hesitated and looked up at him, dry eyed. 'Perhaps now you could tell me the reason for your visit?'

Pyke hesitated, trying to decide whether to push for more information about what had happened at No. 28. 'When you lived in London, did you ever come across a man called Isaac Guppy? He was the rector at St Botolph's, Aldgate.'

'No, I don't think so. Why? What's he done?'

'Someone beat him to death with a hammer in the yard outside his church.'

Pyke looked into her dark, liquid eyes and felt something stir deep inside him. He saw her shock, or what he believed to be her shock. But she masked her reaction very quickly.

'Let me guess, Detective Inspector. You're labouring under the mistaken assumption that Brendan had something to do with the murder.'

'Why would it be mistaken?'

'Brendan wouldn't harm a fly. I doubt he's capable of even lifting a hammer, let alone using it in anger.'

'Two days ago I arrested him for the murder of the rector.'

This time the shock on her face lasted. 'But Brendan just wouldn't do something like that.'

'You know him that well?'

Sarah Scott lowered her gaze. 'At one point I did. Or I thought I did. But I don't believe he'd knowingly inflict physical harm on another human being.'

'The dead man's surplice turned up in one of the upstairs rooms at number twenty-eight Broad Street. And Malloy lied to me; he assured me he'd never met the deceased.'

'And he had?'

'He visited this man, Guppy, in late March of this year. Perhaps he might've mentioned it to you?'

'No, I don't think he did.'

'He claims he was warning Guppy that another man, Ebenezer Druitt, had somehow foreseen his death.'

Sarah Scott visibly flinched at the mention of Druitt's name. 'You don't think he's telling the truth?'

Pyke removed the anonymous note, with the Blake verses and the address in Soho, and handed it to her. 'Do you recognise the handwriting?'

She looked at it, squinting, then shook her head. 'You know Blake was born at number twenty-eight; probably in one of those upstairs rooms.'

'Yes.' Pyke hesitated. 'Was that the reason you chose to live there?'

'Me?' She laughed. 'I've no particular interest in William Blake, I'm afraid.'

'Then it was Brendan's decision?'

She shook her head. '*He* was the one who loved Blake. We moved into a room that he rented to us.'

'Druitt?'

Sarah Scott eyed him carefully. 'I'd appreciate it if you didn't say that name again in my presence.'

'I can quite understand your antipathy ...'

'*Antipathy*? Is that what you think this is?' She sounded angry for the first time. 'That bastard murdered my child and the judge sent him to prison for *five* years. Does that sound like justice to you?'

Pyke waited for a moment before replying. 'As I understand it, the weakness of the Crown's case was their inability to prove that he had any reason to do what he was accused of.'

'You think a man like Ebenezer Druitt acts according to the dictates of reason?'

Her face was now glowing with anger.

'I was interested to see that you didn't provide any testimony at the trial.'

'I didn't witness what happened. Brendan did. It was decided that his testimony would be sufficient.'

'Not by you?'

'I would happily have taken the stand and told the court what I thought of him.'

Neither of them spoke for a few moments. Outside, Pyke noticed, it had turned dark. 'Actually,' Sarah Scott said, 'the whole business with the letter and the vicar's surplice ... that sounds just like his sort of thing.'

'Druitt's?'

Her stare was hard. 'He always liked to play games. Let you know how clever he was.'

'But he's in prison. The new prison at Pentonville, I believe.'

'So? You think it's beyond him to arrange this kind of thing? He knows a lot of people and he can be very persuasive.'

Pyke considered what she was implying; either that Druitt might have arranged for the letter to be sent and the surplice to be planted at No. 28, or that he'd somehow planned the murder.

But there was something else he'd noticed, too. *He can be very persuasive.* It was almost as if Sarah Scott had just acknowledged the charm of the man.

'If Malloy's telling the truth, he obviously believed in Druitt's powers sufficiently to want to warn Guppy about this premonition.'

'Like I said, a lot of people believed that Druitt had special powers, not just Brendan.'

'And you?'

She ran her fingers over one of the creases in her dress. 'He liked to see himself as something of an anarchist. I think he's just a man who feeds on other people's suffering, takes delight in turning people against each other.'

Pyke mopped his forehead. It was warm in the room now, with

the fire roaring in the grate. 'Is that what happened to *you*? Did he turn you and Brendan against one another?'

Sarah sat very still on her chair, as though she hadn't heard the question. 'Did you know he'd trained as a mesmerist?'

Pyke nodded.

'For a while, at least, what he did to me made the visions in my head go away,' she said finally.

'And what exactly did he do to you?'

Sarah Scott flinched and her face reddened slightly. 'He put me to sleep, Detective.'

'And this had a beneficial effect? In a way that Malloy's exorcism hadn't?' Pyke found himself looking at her full lips and her fine cheekbones. It had been a while, he realised, since he had been with a woman he liked; a woman he hadn't paid for.

She seemed to sense this interest, the way he was looking at her, and softened. 'You're a perceptive man, Detective Inspector.'

'Then perhaps you'll allow me to make another remark. I was going to say that you don't strike me as a particularly religious person.'

'That depends on what you mean by religious.'

He tried to imagine her with Brendan Malloy; tried to imagine what the exorcism he'd carried out was like.

'You seem composed, quite sane, to be honest.' Pyke managed a smile. 'Malloy, on the other hand, seems a little deranged ...'

'He wasn't always like that,' she said, gently.

'Just before I left him in his cell, he grabbed my wrist and told me that Druitt is the Devil himself.'

'It's been sad, to watch him lose his grip on reality.' Sarah Scott looked away and shook her head.

'And that's why the two of you are no longer together?'

Instead of answering him, she put her hand to her mouth and yawned. 'I'm sorry. I'm tired. I was up at dawn with everyone else.'

'Perhaps you don't want to talk about your relationship with Malloy?'

'Tell me, Detective; who *does* like to talk about their past, especially when there's so much to forget?'

Pyke nodded.

'Do you have much reason to make the journey to London?'

She shook her head. 'I haven't been back to London for a number of months.'

He thought about the woman he'd met by the gate and what she'd told him but decided not to press the issue.

'I'm assuming you're not intending to travel back to London tonight,' she said, bending down to put another log on the fire.

'I thought I might walk back into Ipswich and find a room there.' He had already sent a note to Felix and Mrs Booth saying he wouldn't be back until the following evening.

'The cottage next to me is empty for the next few days. You could always sleep there.'

Pyke assimilated this piece of information. To his surprise, a part of him didn't want to go. He liked the fact that just when he thought he had worked Sarah Scott out, she surprised him.

'In case you're worried about what other people will say, this isn't anything like the society you may be used to. People are honest and open minded, or at least most are, and they don't rush to pass judgement. They accept you for who you are.'

Pyke had a quick look at his watch. 'Well, it *is* late ...'

'That's settled, then.' She was smiling. 'I'll go next door and light the fire.'

While Sarah Scott cooked a dinner of stewed vegetables over the fire, she told him that she'd grown up in the area; that her father had been a farm labourer and her mother had been what was known as a cunning-woman. This, she said, was someone who was believed to have the power to heal the sick, tell fortunes, induce love and ward off evil spirits. She said it in a way that suggested to Pyke she was, at best, ambivalent about such claims. After dinner, though, when she was visited by successive guests, it was clear that they deferred to her in a way that required explanation. She said some people in the colony had known her mother and believed that she had inherited some of her mother's powers. Afterwards Sarah managed to turn the conversation back towards him, and to his surprise Pyke found himself telling her about Felix and about his wife, Emily. She must have sensed his unease because she then asked why he'd decided to become a police detective. Pyke tried to explain the simplicity of his decision: he enjoyed the work, the challenge of it. When she asked him whether he felt that the law was fair, he just laughed. Perhaps it was the cider she'd poured for him, but he felt comfortable in her presence. Once they'd cleared away the bowls, they brought their chairs closer to the fire.

'You don't believe in magic, do you?' she said, sipping the sweet, strong liquid from a clay pot. Her tone was playful rather than accusing. 'Don't worry, I'm not offended.'

Pyke smiled. 'To be fair, there were moments when I could hear the scepticism in your own voice.'

'Really?' Sarah Scott seemed intrigued to hear this. 'Maybe you're right. It's a force of habit. Self-protection. And maybe I didn't want you to think I was some kind of lunatic.'

'I suppose I tend to believe that most things have a rational explanation.'

'You know, most folk around here would rather come to me if something of value has been lost or stolen than go to the local magistrate.'

'And how would you assess your record as a retriever of lost or stolen goods?'

'Honestly?' She giggled. 'I think they would have fared better with the magistrate. I do tell people this.' Her expression became serious. 'I never charge anyone money and I won't deal with anyone I don't personally know.'

'When you see the way the police are used to keep the poor in their place, it's not hard to understand why people might be reticent about coming forward.'

Sarah looked at him and nodded. 'When I was about twelve, a carriage arrived outside our cottage. It had come from the big house, the landowner. His only son was desperately sick and someone in his household had told him about my mother's ... abilities. In the end, and I'm guessing despite her better judgement, she agreed to help. I don't know what she did or didn't do but two days later the son died. That same night, some men on horses came and took my mother; the next day my father found her charred remains about a mile from our village. Later, we found out that she had been burned alive. No one was ever arrested for her murder.'

It was a bleak story, and for a moment or two neither of them spoke, the only noise a log spitting in the grate.

'I'm sorry, Sarah. Really I am.' Pyke wanted to reach out and touch her.

'A wealthy man tells a poor man what to do in order to serve his own interests. That's all the law is.'

Ten years ago Pyke would have agreed with her but his views had mellowed or hardened, depending on the way you viewed it. 'Maybe you're right, but what's the alternative? Without some kind of law, we'd end up devouring each other.'

'A community like this shows that it's possible to live a different life.'

'And in the East End of London?'

She took another sip of the cider. 'You know why I suggested that you stay?' She was staring at him through her long, curly lashes.

Pyke felt his stomach tighten. 'I wouldn't like to put words into your mouth.'

'Nice answer.' She smiled. 'Sometimes it gets lonely out here. The people are good but their experience is limited.'

'So I'm just a bit of company?' Pyke said.

This made her smile and the lines wrinkled at the sides of her eyes. 'Good company. Does that sound better?'

'A little.' Pyke paused, an idea forming in his head. 'If you're starved of good company, why not come back to London?' Realising he'd perhaps given the wrong impression, he added, 'You could help me to unravel this mess with Malloy.'

Her smile vanished and she shook her head. 'I can't. I couldn't . . .'

'But with your experience and the fact you might know some of Druitt's friends, his associates, you could be of real use.'

'To you?' she said, softening a little.

'If this murder is Druitt's work, do you want to see him go unpunished?'

He saw at once he'd hit the target but Sarah Scott hesitated. 'I just can't face going back. Not there. Not yet.' Immediately Pyke felt bad about having pushed the point.

'That's all right,' he said, quickly. 'I understand . . . Believe me, I know how much time it takes to grieve.'

When she looked up at him, the tips of her eyelashes were slightly wet. 'You're talking about your wife?'

Pyke nodded.

'If you don't mind me asking, how did she die?'

'She was shot.'

Sarah's eyes widened. 'By who?'

'A rifleman.'

'Why?'

'Because of her political views.'

She reached forward and touched him on the hand. 'It's not always easy, is it? Being subjected to someone else's personal questions.' Her tone was gentle and disarming.

Pyke stared into the fire, but he was aware of how close her hand was to his and his heart beat a little more quickly.

'The cottage next door should be warm now,' she said, without looking up at him. 'I've left some blankets on the table.'

Pyke was lying in the dark, under the blankets, thinking about how quiet it was, the cider warming his stomach, when he heard the door open and saw a silhouette against the frame. Closing the door behind her, Sarah Scott moved towards him with the smoothness and grace of a cat and, without saying a word, she knelt down next to him, and gently put her finger to his lips. Her eyes had a faraway look that stayed with her even after they kissed. It was a soft, gentle kiss and immediately he wanted more. Her lips, plump and moist, still tasted of cider. He ran his fingers through her coarse black hair and pulled her into an embrace; as he did so, he lifted up the blanket and without further invitation she lay down next to him. She was wearing just a petticoat, and as he ran the tip of his finger across her chest, each rib, he realised, was prominent to his touch. Their mouths came together and Pyke felt a hunger in her that he recognised in himself, and as she fumbled at his undergarments he lifted the silk petticoat up over her head. It was her sadness which touched him most, a private cocoon deep within her, and even as she guided him into her, and they were, for a few moments at least, as close as a man and woman could be, it was as if she wasn't actually present. He could taste her desire, feel her need, but there was another part of her he would never know, never get close to. The thought struck him that it might also feel the same way for her.

Later, once it was over, and they were lying under the blanket staring up at the wooden rafters, he was about to say something when he saw a tear rolling down her cheek. He wanted to wipe it away, to tell her that everything would be all right, but even in his head the words sounded hollow.

'I didn't think you liked me,' Pyke whispered, trying to break the trance she'd seemingly fallen into.

Turning to him, she kissed him on the cheek and whispered, 'You've got rough hands and a weathered face but you speak well. I like that. It tells me you've made something of yourself.'

Pyke thought about the story she had told about her own upbringing and the fact that a gallery in London was now selling the canvases she painted.

When he woke up, it was already light outside and he was alone in the room. Dressing quickly, he laced up his boots and stepped out into the crisp morning air. It had rained during the night but the clouds had moved on and the sky was perfectly clear. The door to Sarah's cottage was unlocked but she was nowhere to be found. Later, after he had rinsed his face in water from the stream, he asked some of the other colonists whether they had seen Sarah and was told that she had left camp at first light and that she wasn't expected back until the afternoon.

At eight, and with nothing in his stomach, Pyke started the long walk back to Ipswich.

TWELVE

In Pyke's absence, the whole of London, it seemed, had been made aware of Francis Hiley's status as the chief suspect in Guppy's murder. But it wasn't simply the newspapers which reported, and indeed exaggerated, Hiley's supposed infamy and apparent predisposition towards violence. The previous day's route-paper, circulated within the police, had also effectively identified Hiley as the only viable suspect. The hunt had been stepped up, with as many as ten constables from the executive department now specifically involved in the search, all under Wells's command. In fact, although Pyke had been away for little more than a day, it felt as if control of the investigation had imperceptibly slipped from his grasp.

Whicher tapped gently on Pyke's half-open door and peered into the office. 'I heard you were back.' He hesitated, shifting his weight awkwardly from one foot to the other. Pyke hadn't seen a lot of him that week, since he'd sent the younger man to investigate the burglary in Belgravia and had also asked him to look into a garrotting incident in Smithfield.

'Jack, come in.' Pyke gestured to the chair on the other side of the desk. 'Please, have a seat. Any developments in the burglary? Or the garrotting?'

Shaking his head, Whicher sat down and gave Pyke a very brief outline of the two investigations. 'But I wanted to talk to you about something else. Well, a couple of things, actually.'

Pyke nodded for him to continue.

'I saw one of the daily route-papers. It said a fence, Alfred Egan, had been arrested on suspicion of receiving stolen goods. I thought I should look into it.'

'Egan? The man who was going to buy the Saviour's Cross?'

'It has to be the same person, doesn't it?'

'We had to let him go the last time ...'

Whicher agreed but he seemed uncomfortable. Pyke knew he still felt responsible for the fact that Egan's accomplice, Sharp, had hanged himself while in their custody.

'Go and talk to the arresting officer, see what he says. What was the other thing?'

'I'm afraid I've got what I suspect will be bad news.' Whicher shifted awkwardly in his chair. 'They let Brendan Malloy go.'

'Who let him go?'

'Wells. But I'm told that he had Mayne's approval.'

'Mayne sanctioned it?'

'This morning.' Whicher pressed his lips together. 'I tried to argue otherwise but I was overruled.'

Pyke stood up and told Whicher to wait for him there in the office. He took the stairs three at a time and pushed his way past the clerks into the commissioners' office. Mayne was sitting at his desk and was clearly annoyed at being interrupted.

'Why did you sanction Brendan Malloy's release without consulting me?'

Mayne peered at him through his spectacles. 'I was told that some business had taken you out of town for a day or two.'

'Malloy is still central to this investigation, sir.'

'I disagree, Detective Inspector. I consulted the available evidence and decided he couldn't possibly be brought before a magistrate.' Mayne removed his spectacles and sighed. 'From now on, the full resources of this institution are to be directed towards the capture and arrest of Francis Hiley. I have consulted widely on this issue. It is a decision that I have approved.'

'Then how do you explain Guppy's surplice? It went missing the night of his murder and turned up at an address in Soho: an address where Brendan Malloy – who'd been to see Guppy in the spring – lived at the time.'

'As one of the commissioners, Detective Inspector, sometimes I have to make decisions, difficult decisions that are, in my opinion, in the best interests of the police.' He looked around, picked up a sheet of paper from his desk and raised his voice. 'We have an eyewitness account, from a police constable no less, that places

Hiley at the scene of the crime; we have another account that confirms his flight from the aforementioned scene of crime.'

'You didn't answer my question.'

'I see your point, Detective Inspector, but do you really believe it was this priest who killed Guppy?'

'Honestly, I don't know. But I do know that if we don't keep this line of investigation open, we might end up looking very stupid, indeed. All of us, Sir Richard.'

'Just find Hiley. Then this other business will fall into place.'

For a moment there was silence. 'Malloy knows something. And now we might never find out what it is.' Pyke wanted to say more but he realised he could not jeopardise his already precarious status further. 'I've made my point. That's all I can do.'

He continued to stand there. The commissioner looked up at him and sighed. 'We'll need to appoint a replacement for William Gerrett. I'll draw up a list of candidates. That will be all, Detective Inspector,' Mayne said, his gaze returning to the document on his desk.

Pyke could taste the bile at the back of his throat.

Whicher was still in his office when Pyke returned to the detective department. He told him about his argument with Mayne. 'Wells is the one who advised him. Maybe he thinks that serving up Hiley's head on a plate will get him the assistant commissioner's position.'

'I don't know about that, but he took Shaw out with him first thing this morning. I think the idea was to look for Hiley in Bethnal Green.'

Pyke looked out of the window and thought about the hidden lines of division within his team. Wells was a more astute political animal than Pyke had given him credit for, and now he was trying to court Frederick Shaw.

'Has Lockhart reported back yet?'

Whicher was puzzled. 'I thought he was just sick?'

Pyke wondered what Lockhart would say when he heard the news about Billy Gerrett. Deciding to ignore Whicher's question, he said, 'Tell me. How did Shaw react to Gerrett's dismissal?'

'I don't know. You'd have to ask him.'

'And you?'

'Gerrett made his bed ...' Whicher paused. 'And you know what I thought about him as a detective.'

Later, Pyke found Frederick Shaw in the main office, picking mud from the soles of his boots. He wouldn't meet Pyke's eyes, at least not until Pyke had summoned him to his office and asked him directly whether anything was the matter.

'No, nothing's wrong,' he said, still not looking directly at Pyke.

'Once I'd found out that a debt collector had visited Billy here, at his place of work, I had no choice but to refer the matter to the acting superintendent.'

In fact, Pyke had been to see Clapp later and had paid off the debt in full. Although he didn't like Gerrett and he didn't want him to be part of the Detective Branch, especially if he was passing information back to Pierce, he knew what it was like to owe money and didn't wish to exacerbate another man's problems for the sake of it.

'But that's just it, isn't it?' Shaw's expression was hot and tight. 'I told you about Billy's gambling in the first place, didn't I?'

'So?'

'So I'm asking: was it just a coincidence that this debt collector came looking for Billy here?'

Pyke held up his hands in a conciliatory gesture. 'Gerrett brought this on himself. No one else is responsible but him.' He put his hand in his pocket, retrieved a ten-pound note and slid it across the desk towards Shaw. 'But I don't want to see one of my men out of pocket. That's for you. It's not everything you lent Gerrett but it should help. If and when Gerrett repays you, you can pay me back. Until then, consider it a loan.'

Shaw looked at the banknote and then at Pyke. 'I just don't like to think I had anything to do with Billy's dismissal.'

'You didn't, Frederick. I promise you.' Pyke tried to smile. 'But it does mean I'll be relying on you and Jack even more than usual.'

Shaw reached out and took the note, as Pyke knew he would. 'Actually, sir, there was something else I wanted to talk to you about ...'

'Call me Pyke, please.'

The young detective sergeant shuffled his chair closer to the desk.

'I was thinking about the letter you received, the lines from the poem about the serpent.'

Pyke looked at him, intrigued.

'The serpent is a symbol of the Devil, right?'

'Some would see the serpent as the Devil himself.' Pyke hesitated. 'Why do you ask?'

'A few years ago, before the Detective Branch was established, I was transferred from D Division to assist on a murder investigation. Perhaps you remember it? A boy from St Giles was beaten to death with what we thought at the time was a cudgel.'

'This would have been about five years ago?'

'I'd say so. I'd have to check the records, though.'

'It sounds familiar, but I don't recall the details.' In fact, Pyke had no recollection of such an incident, but five years earlier he had been imprisoned in Marshalsea for not paying his debts.

'That was the first boy. But a couple of weeks later, another boy was found. This one's hands and feet had been nailed to a door.'

'And that's what made you think of Guppy?'

Shaw shook his head. 'Not exactly, but soon afterwards we made an arrest. A night-soil man called Morris Keate. We searched his tool-chest at his lodging house and found a hammer. It still had traces of dried blood on it.'

Pyke put down his pen. 'And what became of this man, Keate?'

'He was tried, found guilty and hanged.'

'And you think this might have a connection to our current investigation?' Pyke asked, still a little sceptical.

'Not just me. I talked to Eddie about it. He suggested I come and talk to you. Said it might be relevant.'

'All right,' Pyke said, still trying to work out how the various members of his team felt about one another. Certainly there was more to Frederick Shaw than initially caught the eye. 'What can you tell me about this man, Keate?'

'He was a Devil worshipper. That letter someone sent you made me think about the case.' Shaw waited and added, 'Keate used a hammer to kill the first boy, so ...'

'Perhaps you should dig up the old records, see whether there are any files held in the Criminal Returns Office.' Pyke looked at

Shaw and smiled. 'But you were right to bring this to me, Frederick. It's what good detective work is all about.'

'I can't take all the credit, I'm afraid.' Shaw reddened. 'It was Eddie's idea as much as it was mine.'

'And when I next see him, I'll thank him.'

The next morning, Sunday, a frost had turned the denuded tree branches silver. The sky was blue and clear and a weak sun sat just above the rooftops. But it was bitterly cold, and when he looked out of his bedroom window and saw that one of the pigs had escaped from the sty again, Pyke knew that the time had come to take decisive action. The sty and shelter were too small for three fully grown animals and Pyke had also been told that December was the best time to slaughter a pig because they'd fattened up during the autumn. He also wanted Godfrey to have a taste of the meat before he passed away. The idea of a last supper seemed too morbid and an unnecessary temptation of fate, but if he could kill his first pig, then it would be a good excuse for the three of them to sit together around the table.

He changed into an old pair of trousers and a shooting jacket, ate breakfast alone, and let himself out into the garden, Copper hopping along at his side.

Pyke had never slaughtered a pig before but he'd been told how to do it. He fetched a length of rope from the shed and sharpened his hatchet on a grinding wheel, the wan sunlight glinting off the metal blade while he worked.

The three pigs ignored him when he set down the rope and hatchet. Pyke ruled out Alice, his favourite, and the ten-month-old he still hadn't named. That left Mabel, a long-bodied creature with coarse, bristly skin.

Having enticed Mabel out of the sty, Pyke closed the gate, to ensure the other two pigs remained inside, took a length of rope and tied it around her leg. That done, he led Copper back up to the house and, while he was there, had a quick nip of gin from the bottle. The house was quiet. Godfrey was upstairs resting and Felix had already gone out.

Ignoring Copper's howls, Pyke trudged back down through the mud to the sty. He'd hoped the gin might have settled his nerves but his stomach was still tied up in knots. Mabel had wandered across to one of the flower beds, the length of rope dragging behind her. Pyke picked up the hatchet and the other length of rope and went to catch her. Mabel didn't like Pyke manhandling her and started to wriggle and squeal. Perhaps she sensed what was about to take place. Pyke took the hatchet and pulled back on the head to reveal the terrified pig's throat. The squealing was louder, the wriggling more aggressive. That was when he should have drawn the blade of the hatchet across the animal's pinkish throat, but at the last moment he couldn't do it.

A moment later, the pig squirmed free and bolted across the lawn, the rope dragging behind it. Caught off balance, Pyke tumbled to the ground. He sat on his backside staring up at the sky and thinking how close Mabel had come to meeting her end.

Later that afternoon, Pyke went to sit with Godfrey, Copper settling down next to him on the floor.

Godfrey opened his eyes and yawned.

'Earlier this afternoon, I went out into the garden with the intention of slaughtering one of the pigs,' Pyke began.

'So what happened?'

'I couldn't bring myself to do it.'

That seemed to amuse the old man and he started to chuckle. 'I always suspected you were soft at heart.'

Pyke let the thought linger in the air. 'Do you think I'm wrong to worry so much about the interest Felix has taken in God?'

'I can see why you're concerned. I would be, too. But perhaps you should try to see it from the boy's point of view. Or at least ask him. You never know, he might surprise you.'

Pyke reached down and patted Copper on the head. The dog grunted approvingly. 'Does he talk about it with you?'

'Not directly.' Godfrey tried to sit up a little. 'He's at that stage where he wants answers. That's what the Bible, what Christianity, does. It gives answers. Heathens like you and me might not like those answers but they're a help to some.'

Pyke knew he was right but didn't say anything.

'I'll grant you, dear boy, he's been deeply affected. Yesterday, while you were away, he literally pleaded with me to consider a

Christian burial. He said without it, I stand no chance of getting into heaven.'

Pyke didn't know whether to be amused or upset by this revelation. 'And what did you tell him?'

'I told him that when I go, I'm gone for good. I didn't like to be so harsh but I didn't want to lie to the lad, say I'd be looking down on him from some place called heaven.'

'Or that your spirit would inhabit these rooms and keep us company in the dark days to come?'

Godfrey grinned. 'I think you and I are agreed on that particular matter.' The old man adjusted his position. 'I did tell the lad I'd think about it, a Christian burial. I didn't want to disappoint him. But I need you to promise me that you'll put me into the ground at Bunhill.'

'Of course,' Pyke said, taking his uncle's hand. 'But shall I talk to Felix?'

Godfrey shook his head and smiled weakly. 'I think this is one of those situations where the more you do, dear boy, the bigger the hole you'll dig for yourself.'

THIRTEEN

It took Pyke a little more than half an hour to walk from his house to the Model Prison at Pentonville. Once there, he presented himself at the warden's lodge, crossed a neat gravel yard, climbed some steps and entered the governor's waiting room through a freshly painted door. A warder met him and waited while he signed the visitor's book. Then he was escorted through another door into a light, airy corridor, which, in turn, led into one wing of the prison. As someone who'd spent time behind bars, Pyke's abiding impression of the new prison was its stillness and silence. In his experience, prisons were raucous, fetid places where you could get a drink as easily as in a pub, if you had money. But here, even as you approached the cells, there was hardly a sound. It was quite eerie; the warder noticed his reaction and grinned. 'The guv'nor calls it the separate, silence system, says it gives the felons a chance to reflect on the errors of their ways.' In Marshalsea, Pyke had slept in a ward with ten others; here, each man was confined to his own cell and was forbidden to converse with other prisoners. Even during their exercise hour, the warder said, the men had to walk in single file around concentric rings, thereby limiting the opportunities to talk to one another. Pyke asked whether many of them took their own lives. The warder didn't know whether this was a serious question or a criticism and so decided not to reply.

There was room for five hundred prisoners and, if the inmates showed a willingness to embrace the opportunities that were available to them, he claimed, the emphasis was on rehabilitation rather than punishment.

The cells were arranged over two floors; half opened directly on to the ground floor; half on to the iron gallery above. The floors, made of asphalt, were smooth and spotless and the painted brick walls were similarly bare. It was, Pyke thought, like walking into a brand-new factory before production had started, the clean, sterile lines of the building conjuring an image of utter hopelessness. Felons would come here as men and leave as machines.

The cell itself was thirteen feet long, seven feet broad and nine feet high. It had a window cut into the back wall, filled with glass and crossed with iron bars. In the cell there was a stone water-closet pan with a cast-iron top, supplied by a cistern above the cell, and a copper basin. There was also a small table, a stool, a shaded gas burner and a hammock slung across the width of the room. The men usually worked in their hammocks, the warder explained, but slept on mattresses and blankets that, during the day, were folded up and put away.

If Pyke had been expecting a monster, he was disappointed. In his stockings and flannel shirt, and with his cropped hair, Druitt might have looked just like all the other inmates. In fact, close up he was quite a handsome man. His sculpted cheekbones, lantern jaw, pale skin and piercing grey eyes would have set him apart in respectable company. But it was his voice which really caught the attention; words rolled off his tongue as if individually polished and his soft, mellow tone made you want to listen to him.

'I thought the winter would be much colder but warm air seeps in here through these.' He gestured to the perforated iron plates in the floor. 'I'm told the heat is supplied by flues connected to stoves in the basement.' He sounded like a man showing off his new home.

Pyke took another step into the cell.

'So how can I be of assistance?' Druitt smiled.

'I'm Detective Inspector Pyke.'

'Then can I welcome you to my humble abode, sir, and offer you a place to sit.' He gestured at the stool.

'I want to talk to you about your time at number twenty-eight Broad Street.' Pyke elected to stand but almost immediately felt this had ceded a nameless advantage to Druitt, who was languishing in his hammock.

'Oh?' Druitt was apparently intrigued by Pyke's reference to his former address. 'And what exactly do you want to talk about?'

'For a start, I'd like to ask you about your dealings with Brendan Malloy and Sarah Scott.'

Druitt nodded, as though he'd already guessed this was the reason for Pyke's visit. 'So what would you like to know?'

'Let's begin with Malloy. Would you say you and he were friends?'

'At one time, perhaps.'

'What happened?'

'Living in close proximity to others can tell you more about them than you might have wanted to know.'

'And what did you find out about Malloy?'

'Brendan is a deeply disturbed man. I wouldn't care to imagine what passes as thinking inside his head.'

'You would say that, of course. After all, it was his testimony that put you in here. It's revealing that the jury chose to believe him over you.'

'Yes, that was unfortunate,' Druitt said, as though describing a simple mishap.

'What about Sarah Scott?'

'What about her?'

'How would you describe your dealings with her?'

'Before or after her child fell to his death?' Druitt's pink tongue glistened behind a row of white teeth.

'Fell? You mean you didn't drop him?'

'The jury ruled that I did, even if no intent was ever proven.'

'And they were mistaken?' Pyke asked sceptically.

Druitt's stare wandered around the cell. 'I was expecting much worse, to be honest. It's really not too bad. Beef or mutton on alternate days, gruel for dinner, the best bread I've eaten, cocoa sweetened with molasses in the morning. I'm kept occupied by my work.' He gestured to the mat he was weaving. 'I am allowed to exercise twice a day in the yard; I bathe once a week; my clothes are *changed* once a week and the schoolmaster regularly brings me books to supplement the rather dreary offerings provided by the chaplain.' He gestured to the small row of books on his shelf. 'I would hazard a guess that I'm rather more comfortable and well provided for in here than a pauper or a soldier.'

'I asked about your dealings with Sarah.'

Druitt's smile broadened. 'It's Sarah now, is it? Then I presume you've had the pleasure of meeting her. She's rather a comely creature, isn't she?'

'She was less generous in her assessment of you. In the circumstances that's hardly a surprise.'

'No, I suppose not. But it wasn't always so. In fact, I suspect that our ... friendship ... was one of the reasons behind her separation from Malloy.'

Pyke felt his throat tighten and his stomach muscles contract: he hadn't been in the cell for more than a few minutes but already he felt uncomfortable and agitated.

'Would you care to elaborate?'

Druitt had noticed the imperceptible shift in his demeanour. 'Does it upset you, Detective Inspector? The notion that Miss Scott was, at one point, rather taken with me?'

'Were the two of you attached?'

'*Attached*?' Druitt was grinning. 'Now there's a word to stand in for all manner of sins.'

'Did the two of you ever sleep with each other?'

'Better, Detective Inspector. Much better.'

'Well?'

'I rather think the lady should be the one to answer that question.'

'Was the child Malloy's?' Pyke asked, biting back the urge to grab Druitt by the neck and squeeze.

Druitt didn't answer immediately. Instead he rocked himself back and forth for a while in the hammock. 'I couldn't possibly comment on the child's parentage.'

Pyke waited for a moment; he heard footsteps pass by the cell. 'You intimated that the child fell to his death; that it had nothing to do with you.'

'Yes,' Druitt said, matter-of-factly. 'That's exactly what happened.'

'Then why did Malloy take the stand and tell the court that you deliberately dropped the boy?'

'You'd have to ask him. I wouldn't care to speculate on what may or may not go on inside his head.'

'I've read his testimony. He claimed he saw you drop the baby. I asked him about it. He said you were looking at him when it happened. He said he saw you smile.'

Druitt wasn't the least bit concerned by this accusation. 'As I said, Brendan's disturbed. She is, too. Perhaps she told you that she employed my services to soothe her nerves?'

Druitt almost seemed to be enjoying himself. Pyke sat down on the stool and let the silence take root. Lying back in the hammock, Druitt started to hum.

'When you were living at number twenty-eight, did you ever come across a man called Isaac Guppy?'

'Guppy?' Druitt rubbed his chin. 'No, I don't think so. Why?'

'He was the rector at St Botolph's, Aldgate. He's dead now. Murdered.'

Druitt sat up in the hammock. 'I see. And you've been prevailed upon to find the killer?'

'Guppy was wearing a surplice when he was killed. This same garment turned up a few days later in one of the upstairs rooms at number twenty-eight.'

'I find all of this fascinating, of course, Detective Inspector, but I don't quite see what it has to do with me.'

'A note was sent to me, at Scotland Yard, with the Broad Street address scribbled on it, together with a few lines from a poem by William Blake.'

'How delightfully mysterious. Which poem, if I may be so bold? You see, I'm rather an admirer of Blake.'

'*The Marriage of Heaven and Hell.*'

Druitt nodded briskly. 'Ah, Blake's response to Milton's *Paradise Lost*. And the line?'

'"Now the sneaking serpent walks / In mild humility / And the just man rages in the wilds / Where lions roam."' Pyke paused. 'I mentioned the letter to Sarah. She told me it sounded like your handiwork. That you liked to play games with people.'

But Druitt seemed not to have heard what Pyke had just said. 'Minister Beale said that Milton was, and I quote, "too full of the Devil". Likewise, in the poem you just quoted, Blake described Milton as "a true poet of the Devil's party without knowing it". Blake, of course, was paying Milton a compliment.'

'Let me ask you a direct question.' Pyke removed the letter from his coat pocket and handed it to Druitt. 'Did you arrange for someone to deliver this letter to me at Scotland Yard?'

Druitt gave it a cursory glance and let it drop to the floor. 'No, Detective Inspector, I did not.'

'You don't recognise the handwriting?'

'No, sir, but if it would make you sleep easier in your bed, I'll scribble a few lines in my own hand, so you can discount me as the phantom author.'

Pyke went to pick up the letter from the floor. 'Brendan Malloy told me he'd visited the murdered rector, Guppy, in the spring. He said that you'd had a premonition that Guppy was going to die and that he'd gone there to warn Guppy.'

'He told you *that*?' For the first time, there was a hint of what may have been concern on Druitt's face. 'I can assure you he's lying. I possess certain gifts, it's true, but I'm afraid prophesying the future isn't one of them. Would I be here if it were?'

Pyke tried not to show it but he felt there might have been some truth in what Druitt had just said. '*Something* compelled Malloy to go and see Guppy. Part of me thinks you know what it was.'

'Until you came here to see me, I'd never heard of this rector's name.'

'Malloy owns a book, *Malleus Maleficarum*. It literally translates as "The Hammer of Witches".'

Druitt looked at him, seemingly bored now. 'I don't remember such a tome, I'm afraid, Detective Inspector.'

'What if I were to tell you that Guppy was beaten to death with a hammer?'

A flicker of interest passed across Druitt's slate-grey eyes. 'And now you're wondering whether Brendan may have had something to do with it?'

'Perhaps.'

Druitt shrugged. 'To be perfectly honest, I can't imagine Brendan picking up a hammer with genuine malice aforethought. A bottle of gin perhaps.'

Another silence fell between them.

Pyke stood up and stretched his legs. Sitting on the stool for too long had made his leg go dead. 'How would you describe Malloy's sentiments regarding the Devil?' He was thinking about the accusation that the former priest had made in the cell: that Druitt wasn't simply evil but was the Devil incarnate.

Druitt fell back into his hammock and contemplated the question. 'Brendan sees Satan everywhere, in everything and in everyone. A harsh interpretation would be that he had long since surrendered his mental faculties. A kinder one would be that he does so because he wants to; because it suits his view of the world. Heaven and Hell, God and the Devil, good and evil. There are no shades of grey in Brendan's world. In fact, I'd go as far as saying that if Satan was ever proved to be a fiction, there would be no reason for Brendan to exist.'

Pyke found it hard to disagree with Druitt's candid assessment of the former priest.

Druitt climbed out of the hammock and stretched his limbs. 'To say I've enjoyed our conversation would be an understatement. It's been a while since I've talked for this length of time, but I'm afraid it's left me feeling rather worn out. If you don't have any further questions, perhaps you might permit me to get on with my work.' He gestured down at the half-woven mat on the floor.

'I'd like to think I won't bother you again, but somehow I suspect I'll be back.'

'I'll be ready for you, Detective Inspector,' Druitt said.

Pyke banged on the door and the peephole opened almost immediately. 'Are you ready to go?' the warder asked. A few moments later, the door swung open. But Druitt hadn't quite finished with him.

'Tell me one thing, sir. What date *exactly* did this murder take place?'

Without having to consult his notes, Pyke said, 'The third.'

'Of December?'

He nodded. 'Is that significant?'

Druitt yawned, but when he looked up, his eyes were glistening. 'I'd say you were better placed to answer that question than me.'

'Why me?'

'The problem of Milton's poem isn't Satan. It's God,' Druitt said, calmly. 'Because why else would the poem need, or even desire, to justify the ways of God to men?'

By the time Pyke returned to the Detective Branch, it was late, well after ten, and the rooms were occupied by just Whicher and Shaw.

While he removed his greatcoat and hung it on the stand, Whicher explained that he'd been to see the constable who'd arrested Egan, but that there was seemingly no connection between the matter he'd been arrested for, the theft of a few crates of wine, and the Saviour's Cross. Pyke asked him whether he'd managed to question Egan himself, but Whicher shook his head and said it hadn't seemed to be worth his while.

Frederick Shaw was sitting at his desk surrounded by stacks of papers and reports. His sleeves were rolled up and an ink pen was tucked behind his ear.

'Found anything interesting?'

'I've been trying to reacquaint myself with that investigation I was telling you about,' Shaw said, pointing to the reports on his desk.

'And?'

'The first boy, Johnny Gregg, was beaten to death with a hammer, as I said.'

Pyke pulled up a chair and sat down. 'And this other boy was crucified?'

'Stephen Clough. His hands and feet were nailed to a door.'

'Where?'

Shaw took a few moments to find the right file. 'Cambridge Street.'

'Soho?' Pyke felt a jolt of excitement race up his spine.

'That's right.'

'But I thought you said the bodies were found in St Giles.'

'The first one was.'

Pyke could feel the blood pumping in his chest. 'Do you know where on Cambridge Street?'

Shaw had another look at the report. 'An old stables, I think.'

'That's where Brendan Malloy used to perform mass each Sunday.'

Shaw looked up from the report, confused. 'Malloy?'

'The priest. The one we had in our custody until Wells, in his wisdom, persuaded Mayne to release him.'

This was an important piece of information. It suggested that Malloy knew or at least knew of the man hanged for killing Johnny Gregg with a hammer and for crucifying Stephen Clough. If Morris Keate was as plagued by Satanic visions as Shaw seemed to think he was, and in view of the location of the second murder, it was almost inconceivable that he hadn't met Malloy and perhaps even asked for an exorcism.

'When did all this take place, Frederick? I know you've mentioned the date already but remind me again.'

'Eighteen thirty-nine.'

'Which month?'

'December. The first boy, Gregg, was found on the morning of the fourth.'

Pyke felt another rush of excitement. 'So he would have been killed some time on the third?'

'I suppose so.' Shaw looked up and must have seen the heat in Pyke's face. 'Why's that significant?'

'Guppy was killed on the night of the third of December, too. And as far as we know, a hammer was used on both occasions.'

Shaw looked at him, dumbstruck. 'I thought there was a connection. I just didn't think to check the dates ...'

'Frederick, don't feel bad. You've just broken this whole thing wide open. Now, I need you to tell me everything you know about the old investigation.'

Shaw's hands were trembling slightly. 'Do you really think there's a connection?'

'Just take your time,' Pyke said, pulling his chair up to Shaw's desk. 'And start from the beginning.'

The first body was found by a crossing-sweeper early on 4 December at the crossroads of Tower and Little Earl Street in St Giles. The boy was soon identified as Johnny Gregg and was believed to be part of a gang of pickpockets that operated among the theatre crowd in Covent Garden and Drury Lane. From there, it was always easy to slip back into the rookery and relative safety. Gregg had been beaten to death with a hammer or some other blunt object but no family had come forward to claim the body. According to Shaw, no one had been especially concerned to find the boy's murderer, at least not initially, presuming, rightly or wrongly, that, as a petty thief, he had stolen from the wrong person and had got what was coming to him.

But when a second body was found two weeks or so later, this time on the other side of St Martin's Lane in Soho, people sat up and took notice, not least because of the gruesome nature of the death. Stephen Clough had been pinned to the door of a stable on Cambridge Street, six-inch nails driven through his hands and feet. He had also been stabbed in the stomach, and it was this wound, rather than the nails in his hands and feet, which, according to the coroner, had killed him.

Again, few people either in Soho or St Giles volunteered information beyond confirming that Clough, like Gregg, had been part of a gang of pickpockets that worked in the district. Nonetheless, this second murder had sent sections of the city into panic. The fact that children were being murdered, even if the children in question were dirt poor and belonged to the criminal classes, turned the story into a sensation. Rumours began to circulate about witchcraft and an underground coven of Devil worshippers. No one, it was said, was safe. The sales of pistols and knives soared and self-appointed constables joined the official police in patrolling the lanes and back-alleys of St Giles and Soho. In this febrile atmosphere, Shaw told him, the pressure to find the murderer had been intense, so when a man called Keate was brought to their attention, everyone, Shaw included, pounced on him. A night-soil man by trade, Keate lodged in one of the houses on King Street, St Giles, close to where the first body had been found. According to the men he worked with, Keate was a loner who, at nearly forty, was still under his mother's thumb. He was also a deeply religious man, a Roman Catholic, and was troubled by visions of Heaven and, more often, Hell. Other lodgers reported that Keate had not been seen at the house on the night of the murders. His tool-chest was searched and a hammer was found, together with a distinctive hat that was later proved to belong to one of the boys. The hammer had traces of blood on the handle. Keate was arrested and taken to Bow Street police office. At his hearing, it was decided that the evidence against him was sufficient to warrant a trial, and at the trial, in spite of entering a 'not guilty' plea, Keate was found guilty. Two weeks later he was hanged in front of a crowd outside Newgate prison.

After Keate's arrest and execution, no one else had been murdered. And no one, Shaw assured Pyke, had been in any doubt that they had got their man.

*

'So when exactly was the second boy, Stephen Clough, found?' Pyke took a piece of foolscap and picked up his pen.

'The morning of the fourteenth.'

'That means he would have been killed some time on the thirteenth.' Pyke considered what this might mean for their current investigation. The thirteenth was the following day.

'You think whoever killed Guppy will try again?'

Pyke shrugged. 'Tell me a little more about the investigation. For a start, how did you first come to identify Keate as a suspect?'

'One of the lodgers contacted the police, I think.'

'Who led the investigation?'

Shaw looked at him and wetted his lips. 'I know you don't care for the man but I can assure you that the investigation was conducted in an exemplary manner. Everyone said so. It was one of the reasons Mayne was able to make such an effective case for the establishment of the Detective Branch.'

'Pierce?'

Shaw nodded. 'Nothing, and I mean *nothing*, was left to chance. Keate was the murderer and he got what he deserved.'

FOURTEEN

The following morning, at Pyke's request, the top men of the New Police assembled in the commissioners' offices and were ushered into Mayne's chambers. Rowan, the more senior of the two commissioners, was there, as was Wells. Benedict Pierce arrived late and took a chair between Rowan and Wells.

It was a full-scale council of war, and once Mayne had welcomed them, he gestured for Pyke to take the floor. Having done so, Pyke outlined what he'd already found out (omitting all references to Ebenezer Druitt) and what he suspected might happen later that day or night; he spoke fluently and without interruption, and when he was finished, he allowed himself a glance at Pierce. The colour had risen in Pierce's neck and cheeks.

Pyke knew that the assumption he was making – that Guppy's murder was related to events five year earlier and that the pattern of dates might replicate itself in the present – was contentious. Still, his instinct told him that a connection existed. He'd been led in this direction by Druitt's apparently casual remark, and it was highly possible that Druitt was making mischief for its own sake, but could it simply be coincidence that Gregg and Guppy had been killed on exactly the same date and in almost identical a manner?

'But you have no actual proof, no firm evidence, that such an attack will occur today or some time tonight, do you?' It was perfectly clear from Rowan's demeanour that he neither liked Pyke nor trusted his judgement.

'Or any proof that Guppy's murder is linked to the murder of the boys.' This time it was Pierce who'd spoken.

'No proof,' Pyke said, to Rowan rather than Pierce, 'but the circumstantial evidence is strong. After all, Isaac Guppy was murdered in the same way and on the exact same date as the first boy, Johnny Gregg.'

'This is ludicrous.' Pierce looked at Mayne. 'Sir Richard, let common sense prevail. Ignore this man's requests. Let us all go about our duties as normal.'

'I forgot to mention that the second boy, Stephen Clough, was nailed to the door of a stable on Cambridge Street.' Pyke made a point of looking at Mayne. 'The same place that a Catholic priest, Brendan Malloy, used to hold mass every Sunday.' He waited and then said to Pierce, 'There was no mention of this fact in any of the reports at the time.'

Mayne frowned. 'This was the chap you arrested and that Walter here persuaded me to release?'

Pyke couldn't help but smile at the speed with which Mayne had shifted the blame on to Wells. For his part, Wells immediately argued that Hiley was still their man. Pierce muttered that he would have to consult his records.

Mayne looked over at Rowan. 'Well, it wouldn't do any harm to take this threat seriously, would it?'

'What exactly are you suggesting, sir?' Rowan exhaled loudly and folded his arms, glancing contemptuously at Pyke. 'Tell the men to look out for some poor soul being nailed to a door or wall?'

'I think someone is mimicking the events of five years ago in order to draw our attention to failings in that investigation,' Pyke said. Again, this was an assumption not yet borne out by the facts, but it had the desired effect as Pierce jumped to his feet.

'I will not sit here and be publicly slandered by a man whose own reputation is so tarnished.'

'Sit down, Benedict. No one is slandering anyone.' Mayne stared at Pyke. 'We do need to take the detective inspector's concerns seriously. But that doesn't mean we have to panic or announce our suspicions to the public at large. All we can do is make sure there are as many constables patrolling the streets as we can muster.'

'And what exactly do we tell the men, Sir Richard?' Wells said, with an air of contempt. Clearly he didn't concur with this assessment of the situation, either.

'I don't know. That's your job, Walter. Tell them to be on their guard.' Mayne paused. 'We'll use reserves from the Executive Division to bolster our presence in Soho and St Giles.'

'And in the meantime,' Pierce said, looking over at Rowan, 'the real murderer, Francis Hiley, slips through our net.'

Wells gave Pierce, and then Pyke, an uneasy look. 'I agree that Hiley should remain our primary suspect.'

'That remains to be seen,' Pyke said, turning to Pierce for the first time. 'But if, as the head of the former investigation, you have nothing to hide, then what's the harm in having another look at it?'

Pierce didn't rise to Pyke's bait. 'I stand by the decisions that were made during that investigation. We got the right man.'

'Fine. Then you won't mind us using the documents to establish whether or not Guppy's murder is linked to the deaths of the two boys.'

'Consult the documents, if you think it's going to help,' Mayne said, trying to smooth out the disagreement. 'All we're doing is taking the necessary precautions to preserve peace and order, as is our duty as police officers.'

'I fancy Sir Richard's right,' Rowan agreed, unenthusiastically. 'After all, prevention rather than detection has always been the watchword of this organisation.'

Since the two most senior men in the room had spoken, the discussion was effectively over. Rowan made his excuses to leave and was closely followed by Pierce and Wells.

'You *do* realise, Detective Inspector, that I've nailed my colours to your particular mast,' Mayne said to Pyke when they were alone.

'And I'm grateful for your vote of confidence.' Pyke paused. All of a sudden, he didn't feel especially confident. Perhaps it was dawning on him what a risk he was taking.

'Of course, I hope I'm wrong and nothing happens,' Mayne continued.

'Of course.'

'But if it does ... I want you to tread very carefully around this old investigation. At the time there was a lot riding on it.'

'In what sense?'

'The department you now head was established on the back of the hunt for that murderer.'

Pyke nodded; he'd already heard the same thing from Shaw.

'I don't need to tell you, Detective Inspector, that if you're wrong about this, Pierce in particular will be quick to call for your blood.'

Wells was waiting for Pyke in the Detective Branch's office. He told Pyke he'd already authorised an additional seventy-five men from the Executive Division to patrol the streets of St Giles and Soho.

'That was very prompt of you, Walter,' Pyke said, ushering Wells into his private office. 'I'm gratified by your change of heart.'

'I wouldn't call it a change of heart, Pyke. To be perfectly honest, I still think Hiley killed Guppy.'

'Then you're just following orders?'

'Not exactly.' Wells sat down and waited for Pyke to do likewise. 'Right or wrong, I arrived at the conclusion that arresting Francis Hiley would help me steal a march on my friend from Holborn Division. In the meantime, I've shut my eyes to other possibilities, including the admittedly fine detective work that you and your men have been carrying out.' He paused and rubbed his chin. 'The irony is, and I didn't realise this until just now in the meeting, Pierce thinks as I do. Our positions are essentially the same; he also sees the arrest of Hiley as the best route to becoming assistant commissioner. Therefore the political advantage I can glean from this is limited.'

'I did wonder for a moment whether you and Pierce had had some kind of rapprochement,' Pyke said.

'Far from it, Pyke. Far from it.' Wells shook his head. 'In fact, Pierce has been busy pointing out my relative inexperience to Mayne and Rowan and anyone else who'll listen.'

Pyke had fully expected to have a row with Wells. Now he was thrown by Wells's volte-face, even if it was motivated by self-interest.

'When do you expect the post of assistant commissioner to be filled?'

'Within the next few months. I'm told, unofficially of course, that Pierce is ahead of me at the moment.'

'A lot can happen in a couple of months,' Pyke said.

Wells nodded. 'I won't pretend I agree wholeheartedly with your assessment of the situation vis-à-vis Guppy's murder but I do understand that I need to put some clear water between myself and Pierce.'

Pyke eyed him carefully but he was more predisposed to accept Wells's explanation, now he had admitted his self-interest. 'So what do you propose, Walter?'

'I'm offering to support whatever approach you decide to take.' He gave a forced smile. 'I do still have some influence in the building.'

'I don't doubt it and I'm very grateful to you.' They stared at one another across Pyke's desk.

'Good, I'm glad we've got that sorted out.' Wells stood up suddenly. Then, almost as an afterthought, he said, 'Actually there was something else I thought I should mention . . .'

'Yes?'

'It's a little sensitive,' Wells said, his expression serious. 'And it involves our friend from Holborn's plans for you . . .'

Pyke nodded and his entire face darkened, but he tried to make light of the situation. 'Forgive me for not being too concerned. Pierce has been plotting my downfall since we were Bow Street Runners back in the twenties.'

'But this time, I'm told, he seems to think he has the ways and means of fatally wounding you.'

'Who told you this?'

'I'm sorry, I can't say. But I can assure you my informant is reliable.' Wells paused, trying to gather his thoughts. 'If there's anything in your past that Pierce could use, anything he could exploit, my advice would be to bury it.'

'Your informant couldn't be more particular?'

'I'm afraid not. But I'd say you should be extremely careful. Pierce can be a vindictive man and unfortunately he's not stupid.'

After Wells had left, Pyke looked up at the cracked ceiling and the flaking plasterwork and contemplated what he'd just learned. Part of him wanted to catch Pierce in a deserted alleyway and beat him with a cudgel until the man's skull split open, but he knew deep down that winning against a man like Pierce required more than menace or brute force.

*

There was nothing to be done except wait. Instead of patrolling the streets of Soho and St Giles, Pyke spent the rest of the morning and most of the afternoon re-reading the files, reports and route-papers relating to the investigation five years earlier. It didn't take him long to realise that the process hadn't been as thorough as Shaw and Pierce had intimated. Little was known about the victims, the two boys, apart from their age and criminal predilections. Johnny Gregg had been twelve and Stephen Clough eleven. No one, as far as Pyke could tell, had bothered to find out about their families, and it was the same with the alleged perpetrator, Morris Keate. According to the records, Keate had been a night-soil man who worked with three other men, but there was no indication that any of these men had been interviewed. Likewise, there were no further details about Keate's mother and his siblings: two brothers and a sister. As Pyke leafed through the various pieces of paper, he wondered whether anyone had bothered to speak directly to the family. The Crown's case against Keate seemed to rely on the fact that an item of clothing allegedly belonging to Gregg and a hammer with dried blood on it had been found in Keate's tool-chest. The prosecuting lawyer had also tried to portray Keate as a religious madman, a Devil worshipper prone to violent outbursts. As far as Pyke could see, Keate himself had not been well represented and had offered little or no defence.

At three o'clock, Pyke went upstairs to find Wells, but the acting superintendent was 'in the field'. Pyke asked one of the clerks whether there had been any developments and was told that nothing had been reported.

Outside, snow was falling. Pyke took a brief walk down to the river. The pavements and cobblestones had been turned into a carpet of white, dazzling against the dull Portland stone of the buildings, even in the ebbing light. He thought briefly about the scene at home; Felix had always loved playing in the snow; maybe he would be outside in the garden with Copper. For a moment or two, Pyke indulged this particular thought with a twinge of guilt that he wasn't at home to see it for himself, but then it struck him that he'd been thinking about a memory that was eight or nine years old. Was it a coincidence that his happiest memories of time spent with his son were all in the distant past? Pyke suddenly felt very old; his son was now fourteen and wouldn't be at home for much longer. What would become of them then? Would they still see each other?

Pulled back into the present by a barking dog, Pyke's thoughts turned to the matter in hand; Ebenezer Druitt and his casual reference to the date of Guppy's murder. He thought about the anonymous note and how this had brought both Malloy and Druitt to his attention. But who had sent him the letter? Was this person also the murderer and, if so, why had he wanted to bring No. 28 Broad Street into the equation? By the time Pyke got back to the relative warmth of his office, he could barely feel his ears and nose.

Wells visited him at about eight and then again just before eleven. He had nothing to report. It was strange, Pyke thought once he was alone, to be disappointed that no one had died; that no one had been murdered. At midnight, he pulled his coat around him and shut his eyes. He woke at two and then again at four. At half-past six, he got up and went outside to the tap in the yard. He'd intended to wash his face but the water in the pipe had frozen. Everywhere was white, any noise muffled by the covering of snow. At eight, when the first clerks arrived, Pyke's suspicions were confirmed: nothing out of the ordinary had occurred during the night. A flower seller had frozen to death in Covent Garden and a tanner's assistant had been stabbed and wounded in a brawl outside a tavern in Bermondsey. These would have to be looked into by either the Detective Branch or whichever division had jurisdiction for central and south-east London, but Pyke didn't pay the cases any attention that morning. Instead, he paced up and down the corridor, wondering what had happened and how he had managed to get it so wrong.

By Wednesday afternoon, almost two days after the night of the thirteenth of December had passed, there was still no sign of a body. During this time Pyke had tried unsuccessfully to find Malloy and had been told by Mayne to give up on his 'far-flung notion' and concentrate his efforts on finding Hiley. In one ill-tempered meeting, an evidently furious Mayne had held Pyke personally responsible for his 'reckless' prediction that a murder would take place, and had berated himself for lending his support to Pyke in the first place.

'How long would it take for someone to die if they were crucified?' Pyke asked Whicher and Lockhart.

They were sitting in the main office drinking tea that one of the clerks had just brought for them.

'It wouldn't be immediate,' Lockhart said. 'That's the point, isn't it? To draw it out for as long as possible and inflict the most pain.'

Whicher looked at him, frowning. 'Are you saying that our body may still be out there somewhere?'

'Not exactly. Stephen Clough was stabbed, too, remember? That was the wound that killed him, according to the coroner.'

'So?'

'So why go to the effort of crucifying someone, only to stab them in the gut?'

Lockhart considered this. 'Perhaps the crucifixion was some kind of symbolic act.'

'In what sense?' Pyke asked.

'I don't know.' Lockhart brought the cup to his lips and sipped his tea. 'To make it *appear* that the murder was religiously motivated?'

Whicher sat back. 'Clough was nailed to a door in a busy part of the city. Maybe he was stabbed as an afterthought. If the murderer had just left him to die, Clough might have been able to identify him.'

They were both credible explanations.

'What if the second death we've been expecting wasn't reported to the police? Look at these.' Eddie Lockhart showed Pyke the death notices he'd been reading in *The Times*. 'Five of them, all from natural causes.'

'If they all died from natural causes, I don't see how they could be of any interest to us.' Pyke yawned. He'd hardly slept in the past forty-eight hours.

'But that's just it. How do we know for certain that all these people did die of natural causes? Do you see my point?'

'Anyone who dies in suspicious circumstances has to be seen by the coroner. You can't just put someone in the ground.'

Lockhart shrugged. 'It was just an idea.'

But it was the only idea any of them had had and so Pyke sent

Lockhart and Whicher to collect a list from the coroners of everyone who had died in suspicious circumstances since Monday. They came back with three names. A retired bank clerk from Somers Town called Willis, who had stepped out in front of a fast-moving phaeton, a sanitary inspector from Walworth who'd died in his bed, and a bank director and alderman who'd collapsed suddenly and without explanation at his place of work. In addition, four still-unidentified men and women had frozen to death as a result of the cold weather.

Pyke asked whether there was any more information about the alderman. Lockhart shook his head.

'Was the death reported in the newspaper?'

Frowning, Whicher went to retrieve *The Times* from his desk. 'There was something, I believe.' He looked through the copy he'd been reading earlier in the day but couldn't find any mention of it. But when he retrieved the previous day's newspaper from a pile under his desk, he found what he'd been looking for. He handed it to Pyke, open at the relevant page. There were few details about the death itself. Seemingly the man in question, Charles Harcourt Hogarth, had been working alone in his private chambers and had suffered a seizure or stroke. His body had been found the following morning by one of the porters. Pyke read on:

Charles Harcourt Hogarth, 55, was the second son of John Harcourt Hogarth. Educated at Eton college, he entered his father's engineering firm at the age of eighteen. In 1808 he was admitted as a partner in the contracting firm Lovell and Lyne under whose stewardship the London to Sittingbourne and London to Epsom turnpikes were macadamised and part of the Regent's canal was built. In 1820 he joined the board of the Regent-Colonial Bank and, in 1829, he was invited to join the City Corporation as a councilman. In 1835 he was elected for life to a Court of Aldermen which he served until his death and was thought to be a future candidate for the position of Lord Mayor. In his role as court Alderman, he was responsible for improving the state of the City of London's roads and pavements and more recently he had spoken of the need to establish public baths and washhouses in the capital, the first of which is due to be founded in Goulston Square, Whitechapel. Charles Harcourt Hogarth is survived by his wife, Helen, and their children, Mark and George.

Putting down the newspaper, Pyke looked at Lockhart and then Whicher. 'Go back to the coroner, find out exactly what happened and where the body is now.'

They returned about two hours later, and told Pyke that the coroner had confirmed the cause of death as a massive heart seizure and that the body had been taken to the family home in Chelsea in anticipation of the funeral, which was planned for the end of the week.

'He was nervous, though,' Whicher said. 'Especially when he realised it was Hogarth, and not the others, we wanted to talk about.'

'By the end, he was sweating like a pig,' Lockhart added.

'Do you think he was trying to hide something?'

'It was hard to tell.' Lockhart looked over at Whicher. 'You know anything about this man, Hogarth?'

'A man in his fifties, an alderman who's probably eaten and drunk too well, keels over at his desk.' Whicher said. 'It happens all the time.'

'True, but aren't you sufficiently curious to want to pay the family a visit?' Pyke rose from his seat. 'Anyone want to join me?'

Charles Harcourt Hogarth may have inherited his wealth and business from his father but everything about his mansion and indeed his widow suggested new rather than old money. With its pillars, porticos and pediments all designed in the classical style, the property, situated just off the King's Road, screamed 'parvenu' even to someone like Pyke, who wasn't especially knowledgeable about architectural styles. It was as if someone had built the house with the sole intention of impressing others; the white stone walls, the smooth, marble floors, the statues in the entrance hall, all testament to the owner's relentlessly upward mobility. Eventually, when the butler finally granted Pyke and Whicher five minutes with the lady of the house, they saw that Helen Hogarth conformed to the same maxim: she was wearing black, of course, but the style of her dress and the cut of the fabric were remorselessly fashionable. As befitted someone who hadn't been born into wealth, Helen Hogarth treated the two of them with palpable disdain. She shook their hands as though the act itself were a violation of her bodily purity, and as soon as Pyke asked about her late husband, she informed them, with a haughty, almost fey flick of her hand, that she *couldn't possibly* answer any questions about her *darling* Charles, especially since the funeral was still so fresh in her mind.

'Do you mean that the funeral has already taken place?' Pyke looked over at Whicher, unable to contain his surprise.

She looked at him with a puzzled expression. 'That's *exactly* what I mean, sir.'

'But it was my understanding, madam, that your husband only passed away two nights ago.'

'And?'

'It was always my understanding that the arrangements for such affairs always took at least a week.'

They were sitting in the parlour and the butler and another servant were hovering near by.

She smiled blandly. 'I could ask what business is it of yours how I or my family choose to conduct our private affairs.' The rictus smile started to fade. 'But since you've come here as a representative of the law, I'll say only this. Charles had always talked about wanting a small, private family funeral. As such, I saw no reason for dilly-dallying. The parish church was able to accommodate the funeral and dear Charles was laid to rest in the family's mausoleum at the London and Westminster cemetery.'

'But the coroner's inquest often takes a couple of days to arrange ...'

Helen Hogarth nodded, her expression almost pained. 'Yes, I suppose we were fortunate that he was able to expedite things a little.'

Still thrown by her revelation, Pyke said, 'It's Wednesday. Your husband died on Monday and he's already been buried. Do you see why I'm a little puzzled?'

Her face hardened. 'No, not really. I made a decision that I felt was in the best interests of my family and my dear, departed husband. Now you come to my house and imply that I've done something wrong.'

'Not wrong, madam. Just a little unusual. The coroner indicated that your husband died of a cardiac seizure. Is that correct?'

'If that is what the coroner said, sir, why ask me?'

'I'm not disputing the coroner's findings. I'm just wondering how he was able to arrive at this conclusion. Perhaps your husband had a long history of chest pains?'

That drew an exasperated sigh. 'Can you please tell me the purpose of these questions, sir? Are you suggesting that my husband might have done something wrong?'

'Not at all ...'

Helen Hogarth cut him off. 'Because he was a gentle, law-abiding man and I would be greatly concerned if I felt his reputation was being unfairly impugned.'

'I'm not suggesting anything of the sort.' Pyke waited for a moment or two then smiled. 'It's just there are some procedural irregularities that still require an explanation.'

'Such as?'

'For a start, as I understand it, there was no official inquest. In circumstances where the cause of death isn't absolutely self-evident, a jury is required to deliberate on the evidence.'

'Who said the cause of death wasn't self-evident?'

'Your husband collapsed in his office. I'm sorry for being so blunt, but what's to say he wasn't poisoned?'

That drew an irritated frown. 'But why would anyone want to poison my dear Charles? Anyway, I was told the coroner declared it to be a cardiac seizure.'

'Exactly my point, madam. The coroner made this decision, not a doctor.'

Helen Hogarth pulled her shawl around her shoulders and shook her head. 'Really, sir, I'm quite at a loss to understand your interest in my husband's death.'

'I mean no disrespect, madam.' Pyke glanced over at Whicher and got up, as if to leave. 'You've been very helpful. Please excuse our intrusion and accept our sincere condolences.'

That seemed to placate her a little, although, on reflection, Pyke felt that her indignation had been too demonstrable, too forced.

Outside, their driver was waiting for them but another carriage had pulled up and two policemen in uniform stepped out. They introduced themselves as Sergeant Russell and Constable Watkinson from the Kensington Division and asked Pyke and Whicher what had brought them to the Hogarth residence. Pyke showed the men his warrant card.

'One of the servants turned up at the station house,' Russell explained sheepishly. 'He said there were two detectives at the house wantin' to speak to the lady. I think he was afraid you wasn't who you claimed to be.'

'We showed the butler our warrant cards.'

Russell removed his stovepipe hat and cradled it in his hands. 'Well, no harm done, eh, sir? Better to be safe than sorry.'

Pyke looked at the man and frowned. 'Is it usual for you to rush to the aid of one of your rate-payers?'

'We do what we can, sir.'

'But to arrive here as quickly as you did, you would've had to have dropped everything.'

The two policemen looked at one another but said nothing.

'Can I ask you a question, Sergeant Russell? Was there a general command to attend any business at the Hogarth residence as a matter of urgency?'

'I'm not sure what you mean, sir.' Russell banged his hands together to warm them up. He was in his forties, Pyke estimated, with thick black, curly hair, small eyes, a beaked nose and a thin mouth. 'We came as soon as we could because the servant was worried. No harm done, eh?'

As Russell walked away to the waiting carriage, Pyke noticed the man's limp. He didn't pay it much attention at first but as soon as he'd joined Whicher in their carriage, his expression must have given him away.

'You remember the old crossing-sweeper who claimed he saw a uniformed policeman loitering outside the pawnbroker's shop on Shorts Gardens at the time of the robbery? He said the policeman had a limp.'

Whicher regarded him with scepticism. 'You're saying that Russell could have been that man?'

'The description fits.'

'It's hardly conclusive, though. I mean, how many policemen do you reckon walk with a slight limp?'

Pyke shrugged. Whicher was right. It was probably just a coincidence, but in his years as an investigator Pyke had learned not to trust coincidences. Still, rather than pursue it, he asked, 'So what did you make of all that, then?'

'The widow, or the two policemen turning up when they did?'

'Both.'

Whicher shut his eyes briefly. 'I don't know. The widow certainly didn't want to answer any of your questions.'

'An apparently great man dies; a man perhaps even destined to be the Lord Mayor. One might have expected the funeral to be an occasion befitting his office.'

'And in spite of what the coroner told me, it isn't usual for him to rule on the cause of death himself.'

'But is it something we should be concerned about?'

'It's unusual. You were quite right about that. But maybe the old girl was telling the truth. Maybe the family saw no reason to wait.'

They had made a little progress along the King's Road when Pyke made his decision. He didn't tell Whicher about it but slid down the glass, banged on the roof and told the driver to turn around and take them to the London and Westminster cemetery.

Whicher looked at him and shook his head. 'If you're thinking of doing what I suspect you might be ...'

'What? You're telling me you're not the slightest bit intrigued?'

'Go to a magistrate, get an order of court, and I'll be right there behind you.'

'Really? Even in these circumstances, how likely do you think it is that such an order will be granted?'

'What you're proposing is a crime. It's grave-robbing and it carries a sentence of up to fifteen years' imprisonment.'

'I'm going to the cemetery; you can do as your conscience dictates.' Pyke settled into the cushioned seat.

Whicher folded his arms and looked out of the window.

As the wind changed direction, the temperature rose a little and turned the snow into slush. The ground itself was still hard but the air was damp rather than cold and the sleet now fell as rain. In the dark and with no moonlight to guide them, it took almost an hour to find the family's mausoleum. The mist swirled around them, gravestones drifting in and out of sight. Even though Whicher remained silent throughout their search, Pyke could tell he was agitated. Apart from the sound of the wind and the rustling of the branches, the graveyard was silent and Pyke was glad of Whicher's company, even if the man had no desire to be there. It wasn't that Pyke believed in spirits or ghosts, but he knew the tricks that the mind could play in these situations. Unsurprisingly, given the size of the Hogarth residence, the mausoleum was one of the largest and most elaborate in the cemetery, but it was also one of the most fortified. Pyke rattled the steel chain, which was fed through the door handles and secured with a shiny, brass padlock.

Whicher backed away and held up his hands. 'I'm sorry, Pyke, but I can't be party to this. I didn't think I was a superstitious man but I do believe the dead should be left to rest in peace.'

Pyke already had the picklocks in his hand. He noticed his fingers were shaking, more from the cold than because he was frightened.

'I'm not going to stand here while you openly break the law. If you're really going to do it, I'd prefer not to be a witness.'

'Jack, just stay for a while. *Please*. I might need you.'

Whicher dug his hands into his pockets and shook his head. 'I'm sorry, Pyke. I just can't do it.'

'Then go.'

With a mixture of frustration and admiration, Pyke watched Whicher trudge off into the night until he was alone in the cemetery. For a few moments, he stood there and watched the inky darkness, sensing that perhaps Whicher had changed his mind. Something caught his eye and he turned around suddenly. Was there someone out there? In the long grass away to his left Pyke thought he heard something move, a rat or a rabbit perhaps. That seemed to relax him and he told himself again that he wasn't a superstitious man. What was it that Godfrey had said? *When you go, you're gone.* Pyke repeated this to himself a few times.

Holding his hands steady, he set to work on the padlock, his skin exposed to the cold. It took him ten minutes, and by the time the lock sprung open he felt much calmer and was breathing normally. Unravelling the length of chain from around the handles, he opened the oak door and stepped into the cool chamber, which was barely high enough for him to stand up straight. His heart started to beat a little more quickly. As much as it was true that he wasn't superstitious, he didn't relish the prospect of coming face to face with an embalmed corpse. Hesitating, he lit a match and held it up; there were two coffins visible but it was clear which one was newer. The polished walnut glistened in the flare of the match-light. Pyke waited for the light to die out, put down the box and tried to prise the lid from the top of the coffin, only to discover it had been nailed shut. In the end, he had to use a stone to bash it open. The air suddenly smelled of embalming fluid. Now his eyes had adjusted to the near darkness, he could see that the corpse was fully clothed; for some reason he had expected Hogarth to be naked. He took one of the limp arms, undid the cuffs and rolled back the sleeves. With his other hand, he struck a match and waited. Pyke saw it immediately; the blue-black hole in the centre of the dead man's hand. His stomach lurched. Quickly he inspected the other hand and saw the same mark. When Pyke unlaced the dead man's shoes and pulled down his socks, he found similar holes at the top of his feet. But the most visceral proof that Charles Hogarth had been murdered still awaited him. When Pyke tore open the man's pristine white shirt, there was a gaping hole in the middle of the stomach, as though someone had tried to disembowel him.

Heart thumping, Pyke was fitting the lid back on to the coffin when he heard someone or something moving outside. 'Jack? Is that you?'

When no one answered, Pyke remained perfectly still and listened. The only sound was the wind whispering through the trees. He emerged from the mausoleum and looked around him. Something moved in the bushes to his right. Pyke felt his stomach tighten. He moved towards the foliage, wishing he had his pistol or at least a knife. As he neared the spot, he heard another sound, and this time he shouted, his voice echoing around the deserted graveyard. It must have been some kind of animal because there was a rustling of wet leaves and then silence.

Back at the mausoleum, Pyke wrapped the chain around the door handles and snapped the padlock back into place, then retraced his path through the cemetery to the spot where the carriage was waiting. Whicher wasn't there. Pyke told the driver to take him at once to Scotland Yard. He would return to the cemetery in the morning with a warrant signed by a magistrate.

As he relaxed, he thought about what he'd just seen and what it meant. Charles Hogarth had been killed in the same way as Stephen Clough, and yet someone had gone to quite extraordinary lengths to cover it up. Pyke would go to the coroner in the morning and force the truth out of him. The fact that he had lied would be easy enough to prove, once the body was produced; and then there was the porter at Hogarth's place of work who had allegedly found the body. He would also have to be brought in and questioned.

Half an hour later, the carriage dropped Pyke off in Scotland Yard. He noticed that a candle was burning in one of the Detective Branch's rooms. A porter let him into the building and told Pyke that there was a boy waiting for him in his office. He explained that his shift had just started and he didn't know the boy's name. Entering the office, Pyke saw Lockhart before he saw Felix. His son was sitting listlessly in one of the chairs. Lockhart looked up at Pyke, relief on his face. 'Your son was already here when I arrived. I thought I'd better wait with him. We didn't know where you were ...'

'What is it?' Dry mouthed, Pyke looked into his son's face and felt his entire world tilt on its axis.

'I thought you'd want to know,' Felix said, flatly, as though the issue were an academic one. 'Godfrey passed away in his sleep last night.'

Bunhill Fields

DECEMBER 1844–JANUARY 1845

FIFTEEN

Almost a week passed between Godfrey's death and his funeral, and although he had requested a simple, private affair, such was the level of interest that it took Pyke almost that long to send out funeral cards, liaise with the undertakers and make arrangements for the burial. True to his uncle's request, and much to Felix's chagrin, there was to be no religious aspect to the ceremony.

All of the snow that had fallen the previous week had long since melted, and on a dull Monday morning, the hearse, pulled by four horses and accompanied by the undertaker and six pallbearers, left their home in Islington. Pyke and Felix followed in an open-topped phaeton, behind them the assorted vehicles of the other mourners. Pyke wore a plain black cloak over his frock-coat and cravat and an unadorned black hat. Felix was similarly attired in plain black clothes. They sat apart, each lost in his own thoughts, oblivious to the breeze and the drizzle, barely noticing the people on the pavements, their solemn faces and their hats removed as the procession passed by. For days after Godfrey's death, Pyke had wandered around their house, numb, not quite able to comprehend that his uncle had really gone. Then the night before the burial, he'd come across the book Godfrey had written, loosely based on Pyke's exploits as a Bow Street Runner. The *True and Candid Confessions of a Former Bow Street Runner* had upset readers with its frank portrayal of an anonymous man seemingly unconcerned by moral strictures. It wasn't the book which caused Pyke to break down, though – it was Godfrey's simple inscription. *'To my dear boy, who has made my life immeasurably richer.'* Pyke had taken the book with him to bed and had read it over and over, until his tears had run dry.

From the Angel, they proceeded west on City Road, as it curved around what had once been the northern reaches of the metropolis, and was now a ribbon of factories, warehouses and brickyards. They passed the pavements crowded with commuters heading to work in the City, turned on to Bath Street just past the City Basin and followed it across Old Street on to Bunhill Row. Bunhill Fields, adjacent to the narrow street bearing its name, had once been called Bone Hill. Originally a plague pit, it had become a final resting place, just beyond the city walls, for nonconformists, non-believers and religious dissenters.

As the hearse pulled into the burial ground Pyke squeezed Felix's hand and leaned over to kiss him on the head. Godfrey's death had brought the two of them closer, but he worried about the future, how they would get along without the old man's reassuring presence.

Felix seemed bewildered by the scene that greeted them, the sheer volume of people, a seething mass of bodies, all clad in black and wanting to pay their respects. Later, Pyke heard that Harriet Martineau, Francis Carlyle, Charles Dickens and the booksellers John Chapman and John Tallis had attended the burial.

'Godfrey knew a lot of people,' Pyke whispered, by way of explanation. 'He was loved by a lot of people.' Felix smiled and gripped his hand more tightly.

It was a simple affair. At Godfrey's instructions, there were no feathermen, with their trays of black plumes, or mutes carrying wooden staffs dressed with black weepers. The coffin was lifted and carried by the pallbearers, Pyke and Felix following closely behind. They made their way slowly along a path, graves on either side, eventually coming to a halt at a freshly dug plot. The pallbearers laid the coffin down at the side of the grave and the mourners assembled around them. With no vicar to orchestrate proceedings, Edmund Saggers had agreed to assume the role of master of ceremonies, and one by one he invited various speakers to offer their thoughts. John Fisher Murray, a sketch writer, read a piece Godfrey had penned for *Blackwood*'s about the ill-effects of over-indulgence, which, as Pyke had hoped, elicited a few laughs, and Francis Place read a piece Godfrey had written for an unstamped magazine about the terrible suffering of the Spitalfields weavers. This drew a round of applause from the Chartists and trade union leaders who had known Godfrey in his rabble-rousing days. Saggers gave a witty account of one of his prodigious lunches with Godfrey and then invited Pyke to address the mourners.

Pyke cast his gaze around the crowd gathered by the grave, and waited for a few moments. The sky was sealed with thick, grey clouds and the wind whipped at the hats of the mourners, some of the women having to hold on to their scarves and hoods.

He thanked everyone for coming and invited them to join him and Felix afterwards at the Turk's Head Coffee House and Hotel on the Strand.

'I was going to give a long speech about Godfrey Bond's extraordinary life as a writer, journalist, publisher, radical and general thorn in the side of the establishment.' He waited for the murmur of approval to subside. 'I was going to commend his skill as a writer, the fact that you were never bored by anything he'd penned, his eye for a good story, his willingness to take on pieces that no one else would publish, his love of the grotesque and the low, his belief that the published word could excite men's minds and change the way they perceived the world, his refusal to back down from a fight, his willingness to take on the establishment, whatever the cost to him personally.' Pyke felt a tide of sentiment well up inside him and took a deep breath. Godfrey really was dead. That thought struck him with all the force of a sledgehammer.

'I was going to say all these things about the man I called my uncle, the man I loved and respected above all others.' He turned to face the coffin. 'I was going to give a speech about your death being the end of an era, and in many ways it is. You were always a man out of step with our more sober, moralistic times.' He felt his voice begin to crack and looked over at Felix, saw the tears rolling down his cheeks. 'But in the end I just want to say this: you didn't judge me, you didn't desert me, you put a roof over my head and food on my plate; you read to me, you educated me, you nursed me, you made me laugh, you let me do what I wanted to do, you wept with me. You counselled me, you forgave me, you came to my rescue more times than I can remember and you loved me. I owe my life to you and I will never, ever forget you. You were the best of men and my life will be immeasurably poorer now you're gone.'

Pyke didn't remember much as the pallbearers lowered the coffin into the grave, and once they'd done so, no one moved, apparently waiting for him to take the lead. For a moment, he wanted the crowd to swallow him up, wanted to be anywhere else but there at Godfrey's graveside. Then, as if sensing Pyke's paralysis, Felix stepped forward, took a handful of dirt and threw it on top of the coffin. Others followed. Pyke put his arm around Felix and whispered, 'Thank you.'

Afterwards, in the Turk's Head, Pyke greeted the mourners and invited them to partake of the food and drink laid out on the table.

He noticed Jo only once she'd taken off her hood, her flame-red hair visible from the other side of the room. She'd been Felix's nursemaid, governess and friend for the first ten years of his life. She'd also shared Pyke's bed for a much briefer period, an attachment beginning and ending in the same summer about four years earlier. Pyke had often wondered about her, what had become of her, and he was surprised at how pleased he felt to see her. It was just the grief, he told himself, as he strode across the room to greet her; anyway, she had been an important part of their lives for a long time.

'You look well,' he said, shaking her hand. She did, too. Her pale skin was as free of blemishes as he remembered, but now she wore her ginger hair in ringlets, some of which hung down, framing her face.

'I read about Godfrey's death in the newspaper.' She waited and bit her lip. There were tears in her eyes. As Felix's nanny, she had shared Godfrey's apartment for a couple of years, when Pyke served a sentence for the non-payment of debts, and afterwards when he had travelled to Jamaica, and the two of them had become close.

'Thank you for coming.' He looked into her eyes and felt a small tug in his stomach. 'I know Godfrey would have appreciated it.' In fact, Godfrey had always chided him for breaking off their attachment and had often said that he would never find a better or more loving woman.

'What you said at the graveside ... It was very moving.'

They stood there in silence; Pyke thinking about the last time he'd seen her, the tears she had shed. 'Have you seen Felix? He'll want to say hello. You won't believe how much he's grown up.'

'I know. I was talking to him just now.'

'He still misses you.' Pyke stopped himself before he added that he missed her too but he wondered whether it was true. He did miss what they had all once shared, especially after Emily's death. She, Jo, had helped them through a difficult time, and he still owed her a great deal.

Her cheeks coloured slightly. 'How are the two of you getting on?'

'Oh, you know ...' Pyke hesitated. 'Felix has discovered truth and beauty. I, on the other hand, represent all that's ugly and debased.'

That made her smile. 'Don't underestimate how much he loves you, Pyke.' She waited, her eyes not quite meeting his.

Other mourners were waiting to offer him their condolences and Jo moved off without shaking his hand or saying goodbye. About an hour later, he saw her again on the other side of the room, this time chatting to Felix. Pyke had had a few glasses of claret, and gin, and felt a little giddy. A pot-boy wearing a black apron passed carrying a tray of drinks and Pyke took one more and poured it down his throat. It caused him to shudder. For a moment he had to hold on to the back of a chair to steady himself. It was funny that he should be thinking about Jo more than Emily, he decided; that seeing Jo should have unsettled him so much.

Later, he noticed that she was putting on her coat, as if preparing to leave. Outside, it was raining and Jo had pulled a black scarf over her head. Pyke caught up with her in front of the hotel. Startled, she began to say something but Pyke took her wrist and pulled her towards him. Jo tried to wriggle free from his grip and looked up into his face, hot and indignant. He didn't see it or didn't care. He cupped the back of her head and pulled her into a kiss. He half-expected her lips to part but they remained closed. Stamping on his toe, she shoved him in the chest and took a step backwards.

'I'm *married*,' she spat, her eyes burning with anger.

'Married?' He hadn't even bothered to check whether she was wearing a wedding ring.

'An officer in the Fifth Hussars. Peter Hind.' There were tears in her eyes now. 'I had a child of my own last year.'

'I'm sorry. I didn't ...' He couldn't bring himself to finish the sentence.

'You always have to ruin everything, Pyke.' She gathered up her skirt and raced across the street to a waiting hackney carriage.

As he watched her go, Pyke thought about what he'd just done, the awful humiliation he'd visited upon her and himself, and he wondered why, having hurt her once before, he had felt it appropriate to accost her in a public place and reveal himself to her, once again, in all his unthinking ugliness.

SIXTEEN

Two days after the funeral, Pyke returned to work at the Detective Branch. He'd been gone for almost ten days but somehow it felt longer. For him, it was as though the whole world had crumbled. Meanwhile, in terms of the investigation, little or no progress had been made. Hiley was still at large and the coroner's verdict in the matter of Charles Hogarth's death had not yet been overturned, although now it was hard to see how this might happen as Pyke had learned from Whicher that Hogarth's body had been stolen from the family's mausoleum in Kensington, apparently by resurrectionists. He had also found out that the coroner, and the porter who had discovered Hogarth's body in his office on Gracechurch Street, were both missing and had been for several days. Pyke didn't believe for a moment that resurrectionists had broken into the tomb, but without a shred of evidence to the contrary, he had no choice but to hold his tongue. He couldn't even dispute the cause of death, at least not officially, because to do so would be to incriminate himself. Instead, at a meeting with Lockhart, Shaw, Wells and Whicher (who was the only one he had told about the crucifixion marks), Pyke told them they were now to treat Hogarth's death as suspicious.

'It's my working hypothesis that, like Stephen Clough, Charles Harcourt Hogarth was murdered and that to spare the family any shame, and perhaps to obscure the man's involvement in our current investigation, the coroner was persuaded to record the death as he did. I can't prove it yet and I'm perfectly happy to be proved wrong on this matter, but I'd like us to proceed as though Hogarth died in suspicious circumstances.' Pyke looked at Wells and then Lockhart. 'At least until the coroner has been found and can determine otherwise.'

Pyke knew he had to be careful: he couldn't come out and definitively state that Hogarth had been partially disembowelled and crucified. But at the same time, and given that Hogarth's corpse, the coroner and the porter had all suddenly disappeared, there was sufficient evidence to at least raise questions. Charles Hogarth had been killed in one of the most horrific ways imaginable and yet his death certificate suggested he'd died of a heart seizure. How had the true cause of death been kept quiet? More to the point, who was sufficiently motivated and resourceful enough to be able to cover this kind of thing up?

'Hypothetically, I'd also like us to proceed on the basis that the murders of Guppy and Hogarth might be linked. Jack, you've done some preliminary work to try to determine whether the two men knew one another.' Pyke looked hopefully at Whicher.

'It's not out of the question, of course. Guppy was rector at St Botolph's and Hogarth's office was just around the corner on Gracechurch Street. But at present I haven't been able to establish any connection. I asked a few discreet questions and it certainly doesn't seem as if Hogarth had any business with the church or even went to church himself.'

Pyke nodded. 'I'd like you to keep looking into Hogarth's affairs – as discreetly as possible. I don't want his family complaining to Sir Richard, at least not yet.'

Whicher's face was lined with worry. He knew that someone – Lockhart, Shaw or Wells – would relay this hypothesis back to Pierce and maybe Mayne, but there was nothing he could do about it.

'Is it merely a coincidence that Guppy and Hogarth died, or were killed, on exactly the same dates as the two boys, Johnny Clough and Stephen Gregg? *Perhaps.* But let's not forget that Guppy and Clough were both beaten to death with a hammer.' Pyke hesitated, deciding not to say anything about the precise manner of Hogarth's death. 'Frederick here worked on the investigation five years ago and he assures me it was a meticulous and thorough affair. He also assures me that they got their man. Morris Keate was tried and found guilty of killing those boys.' Pausing, Pyke looked up at Shaw and saw him nod in agreement.

'Keate was a Catholic by birth but the prosecution at his trial also intimated that he was a Satanist. The second victim, Stephen Clough, was nailed to the door of a stables used at the time by a Catholic priest called Brendan Malloy as a mission to hold mass and hear confessions. At the time, Malloy was well known for the exorcisms he performed.'

Shaw held up his hand. 'While you were away, we did manage to track down Keate's mother, or we very nearly managed to.'

Pyke looked up at him, interested.

'Eddie and I were able to trace Josephine Keate to an address on Poland Street. We went there and were told by a neighbour that a man and woman had turned up a few nights earlier and moved the old woman out, without leaving a forwarding address. That wasn't the end of it, though. Apparently the next day, three or four ruffians forced their way into the building with knives and pistols looking for the old woman and ended up ransacking her home.'

'When was this?'

This time it was Lockhart who spoke. 'We did the calculations and worked out that the man and woman must have come for Keate's mother on the same night that Charles Hogarth died.'

'You're sure about that?'

'Certain,' Shaw said. 'Of course, we don't know whether the two things are related,' Shaw said. The youngest member of the Branch, Pyke noticed, had become more confident about stating his views in meetings.

Lockhart acknowledged Shaw's concern with a frown. 'Let's just think about it for a moment. What if Guppy's death upset someone – the fact that Guppy was killed on that date in particular and in the same manner as the boy five years earlier? It might have made this person, or persons, uneasy. Then Hogarth dies or, as you say, Pyke, is killed. Let's assume there's a connection between all the deaths. What happens? Immediately some men are dispatched to Keate's mother to see what, if anything, she knows. But someone has already foreseen this and moved the mother to another place.'

Whicher cleared his throat. 'So what you're suggesting, Eddie, is that someone might have suspected the involvement of Keate's family in the reprisals, *if* indeed that's what they are, against Guppy and Hogarth?'

'It's a possibility, isn't it?'

'We need to find out why those men came looking for Keate's mother – and who sent them,' Pyke said, aware of both Whicher's caution and the fact that he was siding with Eddie Lockhart.

'I still don't understand,' Wells said, screwing up his face. 'Why would someone want to rough up an old woman?' It was the first time he'd spoken since the meeting had started.

'Let's assume, and this is still a very big assumption, that Keate didn't do what he was found guilty of five years ago. Someone close to him finds out and sets about trying to right this particular wrong.' Pyke hesitated and looked up at Wells, whose frown had deepened. 'There are too many connections for us to ignore, Walter. If the Keate family are not involved in any of this, why did someone dispatch three or four men with knives and pistols to talk to the mother?'

'So what do you suggest we actually do?' Wells asked.

'Keep looking for Keate's mother, the two brothers and the sister.' Pyke addressed Shaw and Lockhart. 'Did any of the neighbours see the man and woman who came to collect Keate's mother?'

Lockhart shook his head. 'Not a good look anyway. The woman was wearing a headscarf and the man a cloak.'

'And the men who turned up with knives and pistols?'

'As yet, no one's been willing to offer us any descriptions,' Lockhart stated. 'I'd say they were afraid of retaliation.'

'Then bring the neighbours in here and lock them up if needs be. If we can trace those men, perhaps we can find whoever dispatched them.' Pyke looked around at his team. 'Someone is worried enough about what's happening to want to kidnap an old woman and make Hogarth's body, the coroner *and* the porter miraculously disappear.'

The meeting broke up and everyone, except Lockhart, who Pyke had asked to see, drifted out of the room.

'I just wanted to thank you for staying with my son when he came here to find me,' Pyke said once they were alone.

'I just did what anyone would have done in the circumstances. I could see the lad was upset.'

'He spoke highly of you, Detective Sergeant. It made me wonder whether I might've misjudged you.'

Lockhart loosened his collar. 'I ... I have to ...' He took a deep breath and looked around the room. 'I admit I was angry at you for not trying to save Gerrett's position.'

Pyke noticed he hadn't accused him of deliberately trying to engineer it. 'If I'd rated Gerrett's abilities as a detective, I would've fought for him. I still might not have been able to save him, though.'

Lockhart conceded this point with a curt nod. 'I haven't told anyone this. I wanted to talk to you first.' He took out his handkerchief and wiped his forehead. 'I'll be honest with you, Pyke. I do think you could have done more to help Gerrett. But what's done is done. I also think you're a good detective and I think you're right about these murders. While you were away, I went to try and find the coroner. I didn't succeed but I did manage to talk to one of the clerks who worked with him. I could see he knew something so I pushed him around, threatened him a bit. In the end he admitted he'd sneaked a look at Hogarth's body.' His face was now flushed with excitement. 'Do you know what he told me?'

'That Hogarth didn't die of a heart seizure?' Pyke hesitated, wondering how much he should say to Lockhart about what he'd seen in the mausoleum.

Lockhart looked at him and nodded. 'You know what you said, about Hogarth's death and the boy's, Stephen Clough's, being linked?'

Pyke nodded.

'Well, this man told me he saw marks, holes bored into the hands and feet of Hogarth's corpse.' Lockhart wetted his lips. 'He also told me the man's stomach had been cut open.'

Pyke stared at him for a moment, trying to comprehend the gift Lockhart had dropped into his lap. 'You have this man's name?'

'Tom Challis.'

'And he's willing to say this in front of a judge?'

Lockhart looked sheepish. 'He's afraid of what will happen to him if he does. He's afraid of what *I'll* do to him if he doesn't.'

'Bring him in, I'd like to talk to him.' Pyke waited. 'Do it quickly and quietly and don't tell anyone else what he knows. If I'm not here, put him in my office and stay with him.' He smiled. 'I don't need to tell you this is first-rate detective work. More than that, I can now take this to the commissioners.' Pyke waited and added, 'You said just now you hadn't told anyone about this?'

'That's right.'

'No one in the Detective Branch and no one in the police as a whole?'

This time Lockhart's eyes narrowed a little, as he sensed perhaps that his honesty was being questioned. 'That's what I said.'

'You did the right thing.' Pyke reached forward and tapped him awkwardly on the arm. 'And thank you, Eddie.'

Later Wells came to offer Pyke his condolences; he had also sent a wreath to the house, which Pyke had already thanked him for. It felt strange, thinking about the funeral, the fact that Godfrey had died. At times, when he was occupied with other things, Pyke could almost forget about what had happened. It was the same for the first few moments when he woke up in the morning. Then the reality of the situation would sink in and Pyke would feel despair descending on him once more. Could it *really* be true that he'd never again see or have a conversation with his uncle?

'I saw you talking to young Lockhart,' Wells said. 'I trust he wasn't causing you any problems.'

'No, no problems.' Pyke could see that Wells wanted to know what they'd been talking about.

'He seems to have buckled down, got on with things. Perhaps Gerrett's dismissal will be good for him, good for all of us.'

Pyke sat down in his chair and waited for Wells to do the same, but Wells opted to stand. 'You didn't say much in the meeting, Walter. I take it you don't approve of the turn the investigation's taken?'

'I said I'd support whatever course you wished to steer.'

'But you don't think this is the best one?' Pyke raised his eyebrows. 'You still think Francis Hiley killed Guppy?'

Wells's eyes drifted to the small window behind Pyke. 'We'll find him eventually, and then we'll know one way or another.' His expression darkened. 'But I've had to redeploy most of my men to another most disagreeable matter. You won't have heard about it yet, I suppose.'

'Heard about what?'

'A man was shot dead yesterday. The body was found in the river near the Billingsgate stairs.'

Pyke's blood ran cold. 'Who?'

'One of the Rafferty brothers. Sean was his name, I believe.'

The news took a few moments to sink in. 'Do you have any idea who might have done it?'

'Could be one of a hundred thousand, I'd say.' Wells rubbed his hard, waxy skin. 'You know as well as I that the Irish are prone to violence and a wildness of spirit that can be quite lethal, especially if they find themselves under a feebler police than they're used to.'

'And you think that's what's happened here? Sean Rafferty has been shot dead because we, as a police force, have become permissive?'

Wells smiled. 'Indeed, I'd forgotten that your attitudes vis-à-vis our Irish brethren are less hostile than mine. Nevertheless, this murder will have to be investigated with our characteristic thoroughness and the task of doing so has fallen to me. I don't doubt it will be a nasty job; the list of names bearing brutes like the Raffertys a grudge is likely to be a long one and I can hardly expect assistance from the brothers.'

'Except this time the Raffertys are the victims.' Pyke thought back to the summer when Wells had been convinced of the Raffertys' guilt on the pawn shop murder.

Wells's eyes shifted focus. 'I might have leapt to the wrong conclusion about the Raffertys before but you can hardly blame me for doing so: they're notorious for their thieving and general disregard for the law.'

'I'm sure you're right, Walter,' Pyke said, sighing, not wanting to further antagonise the man. 'Actually, now that you've reminded me of the murders in the pawn shop, there was something I wanted to ask you,' Pyke added.

'Oh?'

'You remember I mentioned that a constable in uniform had been seen in the vicinity of the pawnbroker's just before the shooting?'

Wells jaw tightened. 'You said someone saw this man, a beggar or hawker.'

'A crossing-sweeper.'

Wells looked at him carefully. 'What about it?'

'He said the policeman in question had a limp. I met a sergeant matching that description a couple of weeks ago. Man by the name of Russell.'

'Russell?' Wells seemed to give the matter some thought. 'No, I don't think I've come across him.'

'Part of Kensington Division.'

'Still doesn't ring a bell.'

'I didn't expect it would, but it struck me the other day that Pierce was in charge of that division before he moved to Holborn.'

'I'm not sure what you're implying, Pyke?'

Pyke eyed Wells carefully, not sure himself what he was suggesting, whether the matter was worth looking into or not. Perhaps it would turn out to be a dead end. Perhaps it was just the case that Sharp, the tall man they believed had shot the victims in the Shorts Gardens robbery, had acted on his own volition and had taken the secret of the cross's whereabouts to his grave. But that didn't explain how Sharp had come by the cross in the first place, nor why a policeman in uniform had failed to respond to the sound of three loud blasts of a pistol.

'Sergeant Russell?' Pyke waited to see whether the man would recognise him or not. He had presented himself at the desk in the police building on the King's Road and asked whether Russell was available. The man had kept him waiting for a little more than five minutes.

Russell was heavier than Pyke remembered and, without his stovepipe hat, his hair was bushier and more unkempt. He had the same ferret-face, with small, quick eyes, thin lips and a pinched nose. It took the man a few moments to recognise Pyke and when he did, he stiffened slightly.

'Detective Inspector ...' Russell paused and grimaced. 'Trout?'

'Pyke.' He held the man's stare. 'With a "y".'

Russell nodded. 'What brings you to Kensington?'

'I wanted to talk to you about an incident that took place in the summer. I was looking back at our records and I saw that, for some reason, you were the first policeman on the scene after a robbery at a pawnbroker's on Shorts Gardens, just off Drury Lane.'

Russell's expression gave nothing away. 'I'm sorry, Detective Inspector, but you must be mistaken. You say I was first at the scene of a robbery in St Giles? That can't be right. It must have been someone else.'

'Are you quite sure?' Pyke made a point of checking something in his notepad. He reeled off Russell's rank and badge number.

'That's me, but I wasn't in the centre of the city that day and I didn't see or report a robbery.' Russell's manner wasn't aggressive; he just sounded irritated.

Pyke glanced down at his notepad one final time and snapped it shut. 'Then I believe I owe you an apology. Please excuse me. I didn't mean to waste your time.'

'No harm done.'

Russell had said the same thing to him outside Helen Hogarth's mansion on the King's Road.

Pyke held out his hand and waited for Russell to shake it. The sergeant did so, but grudgingly. As he gripped the other man's calloused hand, Pyke stared into his eyes, and looked for any sign that he might have been lying.

Later that afternoon, Pyke went looking for Edmund Saggers in the Green Dragon on Fleet Street and then the Cole Hole, Coach and Horses and Edinburgh Castle, on the Strand. From there, he tried the parlour at Clunn's Hotel in Covent Garden, and eventually found the journalist holding court at the Shakespeare on Wynch Street. In fact, Saggers wasn't talking but eating. As he later told Pyke, he'd wagered a pound with a fellow journalist that he could put away ten steak and kidney puddings in one sitting. By the time Pyke found him, Saggers had managed to consume eight and the strain was beginning to show on his face. A vast man with an even vaster appetite, he was sitting alone at the table, a napkin tucked into his collar. The ninth steak and kidney pudding was pushed towards him and, with a sly glance at the man he'd made the bet with, Saggers took his fork and devoured it in a few mouthfuls. Looking up, he asked for the tenth pudding in a manner that suggested he was still hungry. A sheen of perspiration clung to his rotund cheeks. After a few moments' delay it was brought to him by a harassed pot-boy. Barely allowing it cool, Saggers opened his mouth and shovelled it in, and when he had finished, he washed it down with a glassful of wine.

Once the crowd who'd gathered around Saggers's table to watch him eat had ebbed away and the man he'd made the bet with had paid up, Pyke sat down opposite him. 'Can I buy you lunch?'

'Very droll, I'm sure.' To alleviate his discomfort, the garrulous journalist opened his mouth and let rip with a belch that filled the room.

They hadn't seen one another since Godfrey's funeral, and Saggers asked how Felix and he were faring. Pyke shrugged, not sure what to say. The fact was that he had spent the past week trying not to think about the death and the hole it had left in both his and Felix's life. He was aware that this was not necessarily the best way of dealing with the situation. He was also aware that he and Felix hadn't talked about Godfrey's death for a number of days and the closeness they'd shared around the time of the funeral had already started to fade. Instead of answering Saggers's question directly, Pyke said, 'Actually I wanted to pick your brains about something.'

A few months earlier Saggers had written a piece for the *London Illustrated News* about the detective department in which he'd described the figure of the detective as a secular priest for the modern era. It had been a gauche piece, little more than an advertisement for the department. Pyke had sanctioned it not because he needed the publicity but because Saggers wanted to write the story and he valued his association with the journalist. Then, as now, there was little that happened in the city that escaped Saggers's ears and eyes.

Briefly Pyke told him everything he already knew about Morris Keate and the murders five year earlier. Saggers said he remembered them, though not particularly well.

'So what do you want to know?' he asked, when Pyke had finished.

'Does that sound like a fair summary of what happened?'

Saggers took a swig of wine. 'From what I remember, the two boys did work as part of the same mob.'

'Do you know which one?'

'Not as such, but I can say with some certainty that any dipper who worked the theatre crowds around that time would have handed a part of their take to a mobsman called Horace Flint.'

'Flint?' For some reason the name seemed familiar. 'Didn't someone stick a knife into his belly?'

Saggers nodded briskly. 'That would have been about three or four years ago. I'm assured that anyone who answered to Flint now answers to a fence called Culpepper.'

'Georgie Culpepper?'

'You know him?'

Pyke laughed. 'I used to; if he's the same man I'm thinking of. We grew up on the same street.' This would have been before his father died, before he'd spent a year in the orphanage, before Godfrey had rescued him.

'Well, if he is the same one, I'd tread very carefully. I'm told he's ambitious and he has a nasty bite.'

Even after Pyke had moved away from the rookery, he'd heard stories of Georgie Culpepper's exploits, and he knew the man was active in the city's underworld.

'Do you know where I can find him?'

'You could try the Coach and Horses on Duke Street, or the Rat's Castle. Someone there will know where to find him.'

Standing up, Pyke surveyed the detritus of Saggers's eating marathon and smiled. 'You could try looking into the affairs of a City alderman called Charles Hogarth, if you felt so inclined.'

'And why would I want to do that?'

'He died about ten days ago. The coroner described the cause of death as heart seizure. I think he was murdered. The body was stolen from the family mausoleum and both the porter who found the body and the coroner are now missing, too.'

Saggers's interest was clearly kindled, as Pyke had known it would be.

Pyke found Conor Rafferty in the same place as before, the Blue Dog in St Giles, but this time the back room was closed to the public and Pyke was told to leave his knife and pistol at the counter. A tall, muscular man with a gaol-cropped head took him along a damp, narrow passageway and through two sets of doors that had to be unbolted from the other side. Conor Rafferty was sitting alone at one of the tables, a half-empty bottle of whisky for company. Pyke could see that his eyes were tired and bloodshot, the lids heavy and bloated.

'Come to tell me who killed our brother, Detective Inspector? Or to promise me you'll have the gunman behind bars before the end of the week?'

'I didn't think you had such faith in the police.'

Even though he had agreed to let Wells run the investigation into Sean Rafferty's murder, Pyke wanted to talk to Conor, to reassure himself there was no link to the ongoing search for the Saviour's Cross. He also didn't sufficiently trust Wells to look into the matter with fairness and impartiality.

Rafferty smiled thinly. 'I'm pleased to see that a man of the law can spot irony when he hears it.'

'Can I sit down?'

Rafferty shrugged and pushed the whisky bottle towards him. 'You can have a drink, too.'

'Do you have any idea who might have killed your brother?'

Rafferty's eyes were as cold as ice. 'We can bury our own and we can take care of our own problems too.' The Irishman groped for the whisky and, realising it wasn't in front of him, he laughed and shook his head. 'At home, anyone who blabs to a Peeler ends up at the bottom of a well.'

'And anyone else who crosses you, too.'

'It's a nasty world, Detective Inspector. But I expect you know that already.'

'It's not the world that's nasty. It's the people in it. When I came to see you in the summer, you were enjoying a drink with the rest of the customers in the taproom. Now you're hiding out in one of the back rooms, guarded by a small army of your men. Am I to deduce that someone wants to kill you as well?'

'Tell me, Detective Inspector.' Rafferty gave him a long, cold stare. 'Why did you really come and see me today?'

'I heard what happened to your brother. It reminded me of a conversation we'd had in the summer.'

'I remember now. You reckoned we might have had some hand in that shootin' at the pawnbroker's.'

'Some did; I wasn't one of them.'

'It's certainly true we can't be claimin' too many friends among your colleagues.' Rafferty looked into Pyke's face. 'Every day, it seems, one of our flash houses, our card games, our brothels, our taverns is raided by your lot. Meanwhile, other folk go about their business like their shit smells of roses.'

'If the police are harassing you, it's just because they're doing their job.'

Later Pyke would think about the implications of Rafferty's remarks. Could it be true that someone was specifically targeting them?

'Doin' other folks' jobs for 'em, more like.'

It was the way Rafferty said this which interested Pyke. 'What do you mean?'

But Rafferty waved him off with his hand and said, 'I'll drink a wee drop for the big lad in your name.'

Pyke stood up. 'I'm guessing you'll want to take the law into your own hands and punish your brother's killer.' He paused and added, 'This is just a friendly warning. If the streets start running crimson, I'll come back and drag you off to the cells.'

Rafferty took another swig from the bottle and watched Pyke carefully until he had reached the door.

That night, the rain returned, a faint drizzle turning into a violent downpour, drops of water hammering against the windows and doors. Pyke had tried, and failed, to have a proper talk with Felix and lay in his bed worrying about the way they were drifting apart. Felix had gone back to school, and the return to a normal routine had proved to be comforting. Still, this had perhaps given his son the impression that he had already adjusted to Godfrey's death and moved on, which was far from the case. It also meant that the two of them would be spending less time together. This was one of the reasons Pyke had suggested they both go and see Martin Jakes at his church in Bethnal Green. If nothing else, it would give them something to do.

The following morning, the rain had cleared and the temperature had dropped, a chill wind blowing in from the east. The sky was hard and blue and the pavements and roads were treacherous. Together with Felix, Pyke walked down to the High Street and waited at the stand for a cab to take them to the East End. Inside the carriage, Pyke took off his gloves, unwrapped the muffler from his neck and waited for Felix to do the same. 'It's a cold one, isn't it?'

Felix barely looked at him. Pyke stared out of the smudged glass at a donkey and cart standing in the middle of the pavement.

'I hope you'll like this man I'm taking you to see,' he said, thinking about Jakes. 'I think you will.'

'Because he's a vicar?' Felix commented sceptically. He'd made it very clear the previous night that he was making this journey under duress.

'Because he has a conscience.' Pyke continued to stare out of the glass. 'In a small way he reminds me of Godfrey.'

'What?' Felix's stare intensified. 'Are you looking to replace Godfrey already?'

Before he could stop himself, Pyke reached out and grabbed his son's wrist. 'How dare you doubt my feelings for Godfrey.' The extent of his anger took him by surprise.

When he let go, Felix waited for the shock to wane and inspected the red marks on his wrist. 'I'm sorry. I didn't mean what I said.' His head had fallen and he seemed to be on the verge of tears.

Immediately Pyke felt bad for losing his temper. 'I'm sorry too. I didn't mean to hurt you ... It's a difficult time for both of us.'

'Then why are you carrying on as if nothing's happened?' This time Felix's voice was pleading rather than accusatory.

'Is that what you really think?' Pyke hesitated, wondering whether his son might be right. 'I'm just trying to keep busy, to distract myself, that's all. It's too painful otherwise.'

Felix blew air into his hands and nodded. Pyke tried to ask him how he was coping with Godfrey's death but the lad only shrugged and said he was doing the same thing, trying to distract himself. After that, they settled into an uncomfortable silence for the rest of the journey.

Martin Jakes met them on the pavement at the front of St Matthew's; he was accompanied by his ward, Kitty, and once the introductions had been made, she took Felix by the hand and promised to show him around the inside of the church. Pyke stood with Jakes, watching them disappear into the building. 'We had a bereavement a couple of weeks ago. An uncle. Felix has taken it very hard. He wants to believe that Godfrey has gone to a better place.'

'And what have you told him?'

'Godfrey didn't want a Christian funeral. We buried him in Bunhill Fields.'

'And this upset your son?'

'If the decision had been left to him, I think he would have made different arrangements.'

Jakes was wearing a pair of old trousers and a tatty shooting jacket. He nodded, as if he understood the dilemma. 'It can be hard sometimes, grappling with these big questions.'

'To be perfectly honest, I'm not even sure why I brought him here to see you,' Pyke said eventually.

'I hope you don't expect me to give the lad answers.' Jakes shook his head and laughed. 'What would you say if I told you that sometimes even I'm not sure I believe what I'm supposed to?'

Pyke looked at him, intrigued. 'I'd think you more than sane.'

'It's sometimes hard to maintain one's faith in the face of so much scepticism; hard when men, women and children are dying every day from disease and starvation.'

'But, as a man of the cloth, without faith, what is left?'

Jakes pondered this question for a moment or two. 'I could ask you the same about the law.'

Pyke was impressed by the astuteness of Jakes's comment. 'I have colleagues who believe their role is to keep the poor in their place and make life more comfortable for the well off. I'm sure you could say the same.'

That drew a wry smile but Jakes held his tongue.

'It's also true that greed and cruelty are rewarded whereas compassion earns you nothing.' Pyke hesitated, wondering whether he was talking about himself or men like Georgie Culpepper.

'What you propose is a very bleak way of looking at the world.'

Pyke didn't respond.

'What if I can't accept that you're right, Detective Inspector?'

'My wife was a compassionate person and she was killed for it. I'm afraid I don't subscribe to the view that morality wins in the end.'

The concern was visible in Jakes's eyes. 'But look at you, Detective

Inspector. I don't imagine you're prepared to let murderers line their pockets and succeed with impunity.'

'I don't have any great faith in the law but in the end it's what separates us from the animals.'

'And what about our consciences? Our spirit?'

They stared at one another for a moment. 'You have your beliefs, Reverend, I have mine.'

'Martin, please.' His weathered face softened into a smile. 'And don't think I haven't wanted to take my pistol once in a while and exact a little earthly justice.'

'Now you're sounding like the bandit and I'm the bureaucrat.'

'I'm sorry to hear about your wife,' Jakes said. 'She sounds like a remarkable woman.'

Pyke didn't feel comfortable telling him about Emily but what they had just discussed reminded him of the conversations he'd once enjoyed with her. He decided to change the subject. 'Actually there was something I was hoping to ask you.'

A frown spread across the curate's face. 'If it's about Francis, I'm afraid I haven't seen or heard from him ...'

Pyke held up his hand. 'No, it's not about Hiley – or not directly. I wanted to ask about a murder, two in fact, that happened five years ago in Soho. A young lad, a pickpocket, was found nailed to the door of a stable on Cambridge Street. About ten days before that, another boy was beaten to death with a hammer in St Giles.'

'Yes, of course, I remember it,' Jakes said carefully, choosing his words. 'Given that it happened so close to St Luke's.'

'The stable in question was the same one a Catholic priest called Brendan Malloy used to take mass.'

'Malloy? You asked me about him before, I think.'

'And you told me you'd heard of him but that you didn't actually know him.'

'That's right ...'

'A man called Morris Keate was tried and convicted of killing the two boys. I'd say it's highly likely he knew Malloy and that he'd gone to Malloy to have an exorcism performed on him.'

'Yes, that's why I remember the name, I think. *Malloy*. He was known for carrying out these exorcisms.'

'But you didn't actually know him – or Morris Keate?'

Jakes looked up and waved at Kitty and Felix, who were emerging from the church. 'No, I'm afraid I didn't. Why do you ask?'

Pyke watched Felix and Kitty amble towards them; his son head and shoulders taller than Jakes's ward, even though she was ten years older. 'No reason.' Pyke smiled. 'So you don't mind if I leave Felix with you for the day?'

'Not at all. We'll be serving soup at lunchtime again. If he doesn't mind mucking in, I'd be delighted to have him here.'

Pyke took out his purse and gave Felix enough change for a carriage ride back to Islington. He was going to say something about being good but decided to hold his tongue because he knew it would embarrass his son.

SEVENTEEN

There were many stories about 'Little' Georgie Culpepper that stood out and made you realise you were dealing with a person entirely untouched by traits such as compassion and empathy. The first, which may or may not have been true, was that he had slept for most of his first seven years in a coal cellar with a pack of wild dogs and that he had learned to bark before he'd learned to talk. Perhaps he'd learned some of his viciousness from those dogs, too. Certainly he'd been able to catch rats with his bare hands before he was seven. Not just any rats, either, but the meanest sewer rats, the kind whose bite could take off your hand. Georgie would crawl into cesspits and tunnels and would emerge hours later with a bagful of vermin, some as large as cats, and he would sell them on to landlords for ratting contests. This activity earned him a lot of money and gave him his first point of entry into the underworld. The second story related to a burglary that Georgie had once taken part in. He'd been a runt of a boy, hence the name 'Little Georgie', but he had put his size to good use. Burglars would pay him to crawl through open windows of houses they intended to rob and unlock the front door. On one occasion, he had climbed through a window into the jaws of a guard dog. The animal, a Great Dane, would have been two or three times as large as Georgie but Georgie had taken out his knife and gutted the beast, even cutting off the testicles as a keepsake. The final story related to Georgie as a young adult. By this time, Pyke had lost touch with him, but he had read about his exploits in the newspapers. By all accounts Georgie had got into a fight with another man in a tavern and had cut his opponent's face with a piece of broken glass. But rather than accepting his punishment and keeping quiet, the man had gone to see the magistrate; as a result, Georgie was tried and sent to prison for five years. The day after he was released, the man who'd made the original complaint against Georgie was found in an alleyway near his home. His head had been hacked off with a rusty axe and attached to a pole. Georgie had been questioned by the same magistrate who'd sent him to prison but this time he'd been able to call upon the testimony of twenty men, all of whom had sworn under oath that Georgie could not possibly have committed the murder because he'd been with them, in a pub, on the other side of the Thames.

When Pyke asked for Culpepper in the crowded taproom of the Coach and Horses on Duke Street, the conversation around him fell away. The landlord stepped out from behind the counter and inspected Pyke's expensive coat and leather boots. A coal fire was burning in the grate and the air smelled of soot. 'No one 'ere by that name,' the landlord said, almost without opening his mouth.

'That would be Little Georgie Culpepper,' Pyke added.

The landlord was wearing a green apron smeared with his own fingermarks. He shook his head. 'I think you'd best be on your way, cock.'

'Tell him Pyke's here to see him. Tell him I used to live on Monmouth Street with him, when we were boys.'

The landlord called one of the pot-boys and whispered in his ear. The boy disappeared through a door and returned about a minute later, relaying a message to the landlord.

'It seems he'll see you, after all,' the landlord said, uncrossing his arms. 'But only on the condition that you leave any knives or pistols 'ere at the counter. You'll 'ave to let me search you, too.'

Pyke did as he was told and the landlord ran his hands up and down his greatcoat to check for concealed weapons. Then he stood up, a curious expression on his face.

'Just a word of warning, cock, no one calls him Little Georgie any more. At least not to 'is face. Not if they wants to keep their looks.'

Pyke followed him along a passageway and up a flight of steps to a room at the back of the building where Georgie Culpepper was playing a game of cards with some others. But it wasn't Culpepper who Pyke noticed first. It was a brothel madam he knew: Clare Lewis. Pyke smiled wryly when he saw her: the last time he'd seen her she had been naked. Jo had been Pyke's last serious affair; since then he'd slept with perhaps half a dozen women, some if not most of them prostitutes. Clare had once been a prostitute and years ago Pyke had paid handsomely for her services. But since she'd started to run her own brothel he'd seen her less and less, and on the few occasions he'd visited her no mention was made of money.

Pyke's gaze passed from Clare Lewis to George Culpepper, who was rearranging a pile of coins on the table in front of him. It wasn't the first time Pyke had laid eyes on Culpepper since their boyhood days. From time to time, he had passed the man in the street or spotted him across the floor of a crowded, smoky taproom, but on such occasions neither of them had given any indication that they recognised the other person. In his role as head of the Detective Branch, Pyke had come across Culpepper's name, of course, and had already consulted the information they'd built up on the man in their files. Still, he hadn't been this close to him for more than thirty years, and he struggled to recognise anything of the boy he'd once known. In the end, it was his scrunched, squirrelly features which gave him away: eyes that were too close together and a hooked nose that was too large for his mouth. Maybe it was the same for Culpepper, looking at him, Pyke thought. But the big man seemed bored rather than curious, more concerned with the game and the other players sitting around the table. Pyke moved into the room and Culpepper's expression changed almost imperceptibly, the briefest of smiles passing across his lips.

'Pyke?' He said it as if the name conjured unpleasant memories. 'I do remember you now. If you're the one I'm thinking of, you were a vicious little bastard.'

'Coming from you, Georgie, I'll take that as a compliment.'

Culpepper gestured towards a vacant chair. 'If you've got what it takes, we're playing primero, no limit to what you can wager.'

Pyke remained where he was. 'I'm a poor man on a fixed wage. I'm afraid I wouldn't be able to afford what I'd doubtless end up owing you.'

'So what is it you came here for?'

'Well, I'm now a detective inspector at Scotland Yard. The Detective Branch.'

That changed the atmosphere in the room. Pyke could almost feel the walls closing in on him. In addition to Clare Lewis, Culpepper and the card players, there were five other men. For a moment, all Pyke could hear was the fire spitting in the grate.

Culpepper's eyes were as small and hard as pebbles. 'How in the Lord's name did someone like you turn out to be a Peeler?'

They stared at one another for a moment. 'I want information,' Pyke said, deciding to ignore Culpepper's question.

'About?'

'Two boys who were murdered about five years ago, named Gregg and Clough. Your lads, I'm told. They once belonged to Horace Flint.'

Pyke saw Culpepper flinch slightly. It told him that the mobsman wasn't as good a liar and card player as he thought he was. 'Nothing to do with me,' Culpepper said, scratching his chin.

'Johnny Gregg and Stephen Clough. Both pickpockets. Gregg was beaten to death with a hammer just around the corner from here. Clough was nailed to a stable door in Soho.'

Culpepper ran the tip of his finger across his puckered brow. 'I remember hearin' about those boys at the time. Terrible business. But at least they got the man what did it. A Devil worshipper, I think.'

The fact that Culpepper remembered this as quickly as he did made Pyke suspicious. 'They didn't work for Flint?'

'*Flint?*' Culpepper looked at him, as if the name wasn't familiar.

'Horace Flint. He turned up a few years ago in the gutter not far from here. Someone had stuck a knife into his belly.'

'I remember that one, too, now you comes to mention it. But I don't understand what any of this has to do with me.'

Pyke had hoped that their history together might have inclined Culpepper to give him even a little information, but the man had clearly decided to say nothing. A different approach was needed.

'Well, you never were the most intelligent boy on the street, Georgie.'

Pyke saw Culpepper's forehead tighten. 'I'd be very careful what I say, if I was you.'

Pyke wondered about the men guarding the tavern and the fact he'd seen exactly the same operation in the Blue Dog. 'Don't worry. I haven't come here to reminisce.'

'I'm afraid I don't know anything about the business you mentioned. So you can crawl back under whatever stone you came from.'

Culpepper had effectively dismissed him but Pyke chose to remain where he was.

'It must have been dark in that coal-shed, Little Georgie. But at least you had a pack of wild dogs for company.'

Partly it was frustration on Pyke's part, partly it was sheer recklessness. But he was also curious; he wanted to see what happened when Culpepper cracked.

No one in the room even twitched. Pyke noticed that Clare Lewis was staring down at her shoes. Culpepper regarded him for what seemed like minutes. For his part, Pyke could feel the skin under his collar burning.

'If you wasn't a Peeler, you'd be dead right now. Doesn't matter you knew me a long time ago.'

'I just want to know about Gregg and Clough. Why them? Why did this man, Morris Keate, go after them?'

'I'm gonna count to ten. If you're not gone by the time I gets to ten, I'm gonna kill you with my own bare hands and, so help me God, I'm gonna enjoy doin' it.'

Pyke folded his arms and remained where he was: he could see the beads of sweat popping up across Culpepper's forehead.

'I've just been to the Blue Dog, where I had a more agreeable conversation with Conor Rafferty. He even offered me whisky.'

This time it was impossible for Culpepper to keep the surprise from his face. 'You here to do that Paddy's bidding, then?' he asked.

'No, but he seems to think he's involved in a battle over territory.'

Culpepper watched him carefully but didn't give anything else away. 'I heard about 'is brother. Dangerous city, this one.'

'Is that why you're hiding away? It would take a small army just to fight past the taproom counter.'

'Hidin'? You found me easily enough, didn't you?' Culpepper's smile lacked even the faintest hint of warmth.

'I did, didn't I?' Pyke took a few steps towards where Culpepper was sitting. 'And I'll tell you what I told him. If there are any more bodies, I'll personally see to it that every one of your businesses is closed down and that you and your men spend a few nights in the cells.'

'That so?' Culpepper was grinning. 'In which case, next time you come, I'll be ready and waitin'.'

'I still want to know about the boys,' Pyke said, taking another step towards Culpepper.

'And like I told you, Detective Inspector, I didn't know 'em, didn't know a thing about 'em, except what I read in the papers.'

Afterwards, Pyke wondered whether his next act had been somehow calculated or whether he'd simply wanted to hurt Culpepper. In the end, it didn't matter. It was the suddenness of his movement which took Culpepper by surprise. Before the man could react, Pyke had grabbed a clump of his hair and slammed his face down against the hard surface of the table. He repeated this movement and heard the bridge of Culpepper's nose snap, saw the blood leak on to the table. With air expanding in his chest, Pyke turned suddenly and walked towards the door. If the man standing there had held his ground or if any of them had drawn a pistol or challenged him, he might not have got out of there unscathed. As it was, they were all too stunned to do anything. By the time Pyke stepped on to the street, he could feel the veins corded in his neck.

'Pyke.'

Clare Lewis caught up with him. Her neck was red and mottled, her tone insistent.

'I didn't know you were in bed with a man like Georgie Culpepper, Clare. He's an animal. He once hacked off another man's head with an axe and stuck it on a pole.'

'Exactly,' she said, her whole face flushed with colour. 'Even more reason why what you just did was stupid beyond belief.' She shook her head. 'You think you can just walk all over a man like George Culpepper in front of men who are supposed to fear him and not expect him to retaliate?'

'He knew those boys, didn't he?' When Clare didn't answer, Pyke said, 'He knew them but for some reason he's pretending he didn't.'

She stepped into the space between them and he could smell gin on her breath. It made him want to kiss her. 'And that's why you broke George's nose?'

'They were eleven or twelve years old when they died. Just children.' Pyke waited. 'As far as I know, they both worked for Flint. Even at the time, no one came up with a reasonable explanation as to why two dippers from the same swell mob should've been targeted by a religious lunatic.'

Clare's expression softened a little. 'And you think George knows?'

'He knows something.' Pyke looked around and waited for a beggar to limp past. The air was cool and damp and he felt spots of rain on his skin. 'How well do you know him, Clare?'

'He's a fair partner and he leaves me to run things the way I want to.'

'He has the morals of a goldfish, Clare. He was brought up by a pack of wild dogs.'

'It must be easy to judge everyone else, Pyke, when your own life is so beyond reproach.'

'I'm touched by your sarcasm.' Pyke smiled weakly. 'What I did in there was light the fuse. Georgie knows something about those boys, I'm sure of it. My guess is he'll want to talk to someone. Who knows? With a little prompting, that person might be you.'

'Are you asking me to spy on him?'

'Not in so many words. But if you were to hear something ...' Pyke hesitated. 'Look, I could pay you.'

He knew immediately it was the wrong thing to say. Her back stiffened and there was a wounded look in her eyes. 'For some reason, I never felt you thought of me as a prostitute.'

Pyke watched her trudge back towards the tavern, trying not to think about the hurt he'd just caused.

Walter Wells was waiting for Pyke in the main office of the Detective Branch, ahead of a meeting with Mayne they were both due to attend. He was pacing up and down, oblivious to Shaw and one of the clerks, who were sitting at their desks. As soon as Pyke walked into the room, the acting superintendent took him by the arm and led him into the corridor. 'Just a word of warning, old man. Pierce has heard about your notion that Charles Hogarth was murdered;

he's also been told you're trying to link it back to the investigation of the boys' murder. I'm told he's going to be at the meeting. He's going to come after you with everything he's got.' Wells waited for a clerk to walk past them and added, 'You need to tell me everything you know, if I'm going to be able to help you.'

Pyke wasn't surprised that Pierce was rattled or that he'd invited himself to the meeting. What did concern him was the speed with which Pierce had found out about his plans.

'Someone who was at the meeting in the department yesterday must have gone straight to Pierce.'

'Between the two of us, Mayne's hopping mad. As far as he sees it, you're stirring up trouble with no proof to support your claims.'

They walked to the end of the corridor in silence, and as they started to climb the stairs, Pyke said, 'By the way, you might want to look at a man called George Culpepper or one of his mob as the likely gunman in the murder of Sean Rafferty.'

It had been meant as a casual remark, a bit of help to Wells, but the acting superintendent immediately stopped, turned to Pyke and hissed, 'I, sir, have given you every support, even to the point where it's harming my own standing with the commissioner. The very least I'd like in return is the opportunity to go about *my* job in the manner that *I* see fit.' His face was hot and red, and without another word, he stormed up the stairs, leaving Pyke a few paces behind him.

Pyke managed to catch up with him outside the commissioners' offices. 'I didn't mean anything by it, Walter. It was just a piece of idle gossip. I thought you'd want to hear it, that's all.'

Wells gave him a grudging nod and the two of them entered Mayne's office. Mayne was talking to Benedict Pierce.

Even before Pyke had taken the chair provided for him, Mayne said, 'Is it true, sir, that you have instructed your men to treat the death of Charles Hogarth as *murder*?' The words shot off his tongue like bullets.

'That is correct, Sir Richard.'

Mayne had expected Pyke to deny this accusation and was momentarily flummoxed. 'Even though the coroner has ruled otherwise and the man's funeral has already taken place?'

Pyke glanced over at Pierce, whose face was gleaming with

anticipation. 'Yes, in spite of all this,' he said calmly.

'Then your actions put you at odds with the law of this land and I have no choice but to suspend you from your duties.'

'That would, of course, be your prerogative, Sir Richard, but before you come to a decision, perhaps you should look at this.' Pyke reached into his coat pocket, pulled out a piece of paper, smoothed it out and handed it to Mayne.

'And what in God's name is this?'

'It's an affidavit sworn this very morning before Sir William Wightman, Justice of Her Majesty's Court of Queen's Bench. You'll see that the signatory, Tom Challis, is a clerk at the office of the coroner for the County of Middlesex. He has sworn under oath to seeing, with his own eyes, marks or holes in the hands and feet of the deceased, Charles Hogarth, that could only have been caused by crucifixion.'

Pyke looked at Pierce's face. It told him all he needed to know. Lockhart hadn't said a word to him. For so long now, Pyke had assumed that Lockhart was Pierce's source in the department and now that no longer seemed to be the case. Who else could it be? Not Whicher. That just left Shaw – and Wells.

Mayne stared at the document, seemingly not knowing what to do or say.

'The onus is on the coroner to justify his original finding but sadly he is nowhere to be found. The same is true of the porter who apparently discovered Hogarth's body in the first place. Both men live on their own but neither has been seen at their respective place of residence in over two weeks.'

'What are you saying, Detective Inspector?' Mayne stared down at the document in his hands.

'Let's consider the facts. Johnny Gregg was beaten to death with a hammer on the third night of December 1839. Isaac Guppy was beaten to death with a hammer on the third night of December 1844. Stephen Clough was crucified ten days after Gregg on the thirteenth of December 1839. Charles Hogarth was crucified ten days after Guppy on the thirteenth of December 1844.'

Pierce was on his feet. 'We don't know for certain that Hogarth was crucified and in any case, Detective Inspector Pyke has found no hard evidence linking these murders with the events of five years ago.'

Mayne looked at Pierce. 'Sit down please, Benedict,' he muttered.

'We're not simply dealing with murder here,' Pyke said, raising his voice a little. 'What we have is a wilful attempt to conceal the actual cause of Hogarth's death. The question we should be asking is why? My guess, for what it's worth, is that someone didn't want us to make a connection between Guppy and Hogarth. In other words, if we find how they're linked, we'll find out why they were killed. It also stands to reason that whoever wanted to keep Hogarth's murder a secret has sufficient authority to influence the coroner's decision.' Pyke hesitated and said, 'And perhaps a police investigation.'

That was too much for Pierce. He turned to Mayne and exploded, 'This man is pursuing a personal vendetta against me and the men who carried out that investigation.'

'*I'm* not,' Pyke said, 'but it's clear enough to me that the man who killed Guppy and Hogarth certainly is. What I'm proposing to do is to open up that investigation. To find out once and for all what took place and why someone feels sufficiently motivated to take out their anger on Guppy and Hogarth. Who knows? Perhaps there are others. Perhaps this man hasn't finished.'

Mayne slammed his fist down on his desk. 'Enough.' It was the first time Pyke had ever heard him raise his voice. He held up the document and said to Pierce, 'Can you explain this to me, Superintendent?'

Pierce tried to find something to say but the words wouldn't come. Mayne went on, 'Then it would seem I have no choice but to support Detective Inspector Pyke's preferred plan of action.' He swivelled in his chair and turned to Pyke. 'But woe betide you, Detective Inspector, if you should choose to comment on this matter in public, at least until you've been able to ascertain exactly what happened. Do you understand? You've told your men. That's fine. But you're not to say a word about this to anyone else. And by that, I do mean *anyone*. If word gets out I'll have someone bring me your head on a platter. I don't think I'll have to look hard for volunteers.' With that, Mayne brushed the front of his hair with the palm of his hand and added, 'That will be all for today, gentlemen.'

Pyke caught up with Benedict Pierce at the bottom of the stairs.

'You got the wrong man five years ago and I think you know it. I think you've known it all along.'

Pierce smiled almost imperceptibly. 'Excuse me, Pyke. I have a division to run.'

Thrown by the man's nonchalance, Pyke said, quietly, 'In the past I thought you were just self-interested, the kind of man who'd do anything to ingratiate himself with his superiors. Now I think you're wilfully corrupt.'

As Pyke stood aside, Pierce leaned into him, so close Pyke could smell his breath, and whispered, 'I'm going to break you.'

EIGHTEEN

A cold mist had descended on Islington by the time a hackney coach had left Pyke outside his house, its stagnant breath clinging to the pavements and the bare trees, so that you couldn't see for more than a few yards. Perhaps this was why he didn't notice her, at least until his key was in the front door. She called out his name and as he spun around, she removed the scarf from her head, long curls of black hair falling around her face as she did so.

'How did you . . .?'

Sarah Scott stepped into the light produced by the porch gas-lamp and smiled. 'You're not the only one capable of finding people.' She was wearing a long black velveteen coat over what looked like an old smock.

'Come in, please,' Pyke said, turning back towards the front door, but her gloved hand caught him by the wrist and gently pulled him back.

'Can we just take a walk to the end of the street?'

Pyke looked at her smooth, dark skin, her plump, sensuous lips and her thick eyelashes. Ever since his trip to Suffolk, he'd tried, and failed, to visualise her. Now those memories came flooding back; the feel of her skin, the sharpness of her cheekbone, the brown flecks in her otherwise blue eyes.

'How *did* you find me?' he asked, joining her on the pavement. She was looking up at the house.

'I followed you from Scotland Yard.' She smiled breezily. 'This is rather a grand home for a police officer, isn't it?'

Pyke decided to ignore the question. He started to walk and she fell in at his side. 'What brings you to the metropolis?'

'I was thinking about something you said to me when you visited the colony.'

'Oh?'

For a moment, Sarah stopped and toyed with the silver pendant attached to her necklace. 'You said that if I believed Ebenezer Druitt was in some way responsible for the murder you told me about, the rector, then I should speak up.'

'I also said I didn't want to force you to do anything you weren't ready to do.'

'I know and it was sweet of you.' As she spoke, he could see the air condense in front of her. 'Come on, let's keep walking. Otherwise we'll turn into blocks of ice.'

'After I visited you in Suffolk, I went to talk to Druitt in his cell at the Model Prison,' Pyke continued.

'I hope for your sake you escaped unscathed. That man has a way of infecting one's thoughts.'

Pyke took a deep breath. He didn't want to say what he was about to, but he didn't feel he had a choice. 'Druitt intimated that you and he had been close ...'

He thought he saw her suck in her cheeks.

'Before I knew him, I found him tolerable company. Most people did. As I said, he could be quite charming when he wanted to be.'

'No more than that?'

This time she turned and faced him, the anger in her expression almost palpable.

'He *would* make you think that. It's how he operates. Plants an idea in someone's mind and lets it mushroom. It's one of the reasons I parted with Brendan. Druitt managed to convince Brendan that he and I were lovers. The green-eyed monster did the rest.'

'I take it he was lying?'

Sarah glanced at Pyke, scowling. 'Do you really need me to answer that?'

Pyke walked on for a few yards. The light from the gas-lamp had been swamped by the mist. On one side of the street was a row of terraced houses, but now Pyke couldn't even see their front doors. On the other side was an open field, but it had become a wall of darkness.

'Tell me something,' Pyke said, staring straight ahead. 'When you were living at number twenty-eight Broad Street, did you ever come across a man called Morris Keate?'

'Keate?'

'He was a night-soil man. He was also fascinated by the Devil, I believe. He might have gone to see Brendan Malloy, to be exorcised.'

'No, I don't think I ever met anyone by that name.'

'And you don't remember Malloy mentioning him?'

Sarah shook her head. Briefly Pyke told her about the two boys who'd been killed five years earlier. She told him she remembered the murders and asked why they were of concern to him now.

'Morris Keate was tried and executed for killing those boys.'

'And you don't think he did it?' Sarah asked.

'One of the boys, Stephen Clough, was found nailed to the door of a stable that Malloy used as a venue for mass.' Pyke hesitated and then told her that a City alderman had been crucified a couple of weeks earlier, on exactly the same date that Clough had died, and that Guppy had been murdered in the same manner, and on the same date, as the first boy.

'I still don't understand what any of this has to do with either Brendan or Druitt,' Sarah said, when Pyke had finished.

'Maybe nothing, but Malloy went to see the rector earlier this year, to warn him that Druitt had foreseen his death. And don't forget that the surplice the rector was wearing on the night he was killed turned up at number twenty-eight Broad Street. When I questioned Druitt about all of this, he professed ignorance at first but then, as I was leaving, he told me I should pay attention to the date of the rector's death.'

Sarah paused for a moment. 'So you think Druitt knows who killed the rector?'

'I'd say he wants me to believe there's a connection between Guppy's death and the murder of the boys.'

'But why?'

'I have no idea.' Pyke shook his head. 'Part of me thinks he's just trying to cause mischief.'

'That sounds like him.' Sarah pulled her coat a little tighter around her shoulders. 'And the other part?'

'Like I said, I don't really know what his interest is. But onc thing is certain: if I'm to unravel any of this, I need to find and talk to Brendan Malloy.'

'I thought you said you'd arrested him?'

'They let him go while I was in Suffolk and now I can't find him. He moved out of the room he was renting in Soho.'

A faint smile spread across Sarah's lips. 'So there is something I can do, then.'

'Yes ... I suppose so.'

A loose strand of hair fell down into Sarah's face and she tucked it behind her ear. 'I did live with him for more than a year. I might have a better chance of finding him than you, Detective Inspector.'

'Call me Pyke. Please.'

When Pyke proposed they turn around and head back towards the house, Sarah Scott didn't object. There was a gas-lamp outside Pyke's house and they stopped under it. 'Will you come in, for a hot drink or a bite to eat?' He waited and added, 'If you need a bed for the night, we have a spare room ...'

In the gaslight, her soft skin was the colour of butter. 'That's very kind of you but I have a place to stay.'

'Perhaps you'd like to meet my son,' Pyke said, looking up at Felix's bedroom window. A candle was burning behind the drawn curtains.

'Another time, maybe,' she said apologetically. 'At the moment, I don't think it's such a good idea.'

'How will I know where to contact you?'

Sarah pulled up her scarf and tied it around her head. 'I'll contact you when I've found Brendan.'

Pyke moved quickly to grab her hand and dragged her into an embrace. Her lips were cold and soft but she didn't push him away. In fact they parted just a little and she gave him a short, breathy kiss that was both passionate and withheld, as though she hadn't quite decided what to do. He slid his arm around her back and pulled her in tighter, but just when he felt her begin to yield, she pushed him away, a startled look on her face, her eyes unreadable.

'Not yet,' she mouthed. 'Not like this.' She pulled the scarf back over her head and hurried off down the street.

Felix was in the living room, curled up on the sofa, reading a book. Copper was asleep at his feet. This time, Felix did not attempt to conceal the book when Pyke entered the room. Instead he held it up and said, '*The Confessions of St Augustine*. Martin gave it to me.' It took Pyke a few moments to work out he was referring to Jakes.

'Did you go to St Matthew's after school again today?'

Felix didn't bother looking up. 'Martin said it would be all right. I helped out around the place. He said he was glad to have me.' The way Felix said it made it seem like a barbed remark. 'By the way, the pigs were out again. Mr Leech came here to report it. He was angry. One of them, Alice, I think, had turned his lawn into a quagmire.'

'How could they get out? I've just fixed the sty.'

'You know there's not enough room for them all.'

Sighing, Pyke went over to the window and peered into the darkness. 'I'll go out there and rescue Alice, then ...'

'We already did,' Felix said, gesturing down at Copper.

Pyke sat down at the other end of the sofa and patted Copper on the head. The ageing mastiff looked up and wagged his tail. His formerly black muzzle had turned white. It was a strange life, the one he had made for Felix, Pyke supposed: the fact that it was just the two of them now, that the boy didn't have a mother, someone to nurture him, nor any brothers and sisters. It was one of Pyke's many regrets, both for himself and for Felix, that he hadn't had more children.

'What kind of things does Jakes get you to do?'

'This afternoon, I helped Kitty sweep the floor in the church and then we polished the brass.'

'You seem to be getting on well with her.'

Felix looked up from his book. 'She's nice. Quiet. Doesn't say too much.'

'She's attractive, too.' Pyke noticed his son squirm. 'In a quiet, bookish sort of way.'

'She's ten years old than me, Pyke.'

Pyke had often wondered whether Felix had lost his virginity. At fourteen he was certainly old enough to have lain with a woman, but Pyke suspected that he hadn't. For a start, he hadn't demonstrated much of an interest in the opposite sex. Often Pyke had wondered whether it was one of his responsibilities as a father to educate his son in matters of the heart. Still, no one, least of all Godfrey, had said anything to him. Pyke had just known, and while the first few times had been a disappointment, he had persevered and eventually learned how to enjoy it.

'It's the quiet ones you need to watch out for.'

Felix put down the book and gave him a hard stare. '*Pyke*.' He said it so loudly Copper looked up and barked. In the end they both started to laugh.

'So what about the *Confessions*? Are you enjoying it?'

'Enjoying wouldn't be the right word.' Felix thought about it. 'He's quite candid about his sins.'

'Some wouldn't consider lust to be a sin,' Pyke replied. 'St Augustine certainly seems to have enjoyed himself before his conversion.'

'You've read the book?'

'A while ago,' Pyke said, nodding. 'I have a copy of it in my study.'

'He talks about his inability to remember all the sins he committed as a boy. I sometimes feel like that.' Felix paused, as though he'd already admitted too much.

'Have you ...' Pyke felt the words catch in his throat and swallowed a few times. 'Have you ever ...'

'Have I ever what?'

Pyke inspected his son's face for some sign that he knew what Pyke was talking about. 'Been with a woman?'

Blood rushed to Felix's face, and he looked at Copper, at his book, anywhere but at Pyke.

'I thought I'd better ask. In case there was something you wanted to know.'

'Like what?' There was a haunted look in his son's eyes.

Pyke licked his lips. 'Well ...'

A long silence passed between them. Pyke turned his attention to Copper and stroked the dog's ears.

'But if I did want to know something, you'd tell me, wouldn't you?' Felix's expression was almost accusatory.

'I'd try to.'

'Because I was wondering ...'

When Felix told Pyke what was on his mind, Pyke stared at his son, and not for the first time questioned the wisdom of the sheltered upbringing he'd been given.

That night, Pyke stayed up late reading Mandeville's *Remarks on the Fable of the Bees*, and by the morning he felt neither rested nor ready to confront Ebenezer Druitt. He would have liked to think it was Mandeville's complex treatment of moral sentiment which had kept him awake, but in truth he was thinking about his uncle, trying to remember what he'd said to Pyke the first time he'd brought him back to the apartment in Camden Town.

The following morning, after breakfasting in near-silence with Felix, Pyke walked to the Model Prison at Pentonville, the low winter sun barely rising up above the spires and roofs.

Ebenezer Druitt was just as Pyke remembered him. Lying in his hammock, it was almost as if he had expected Pyke to show up. When Pyke entered his cell, he looked up, opened his eyes and then closed them again.

'I want to know how you knew that the third of December was significant.'

Druitt opened his eyes and yawned. 'Good to see you again, Detective Inspector Pyke. I trust you're well.'

'I told you Isaac Guppy was murdered on the third. You suggested that the date might be significant.'

'Did I? Sometimes I can't remember what I've said. Incarceration does strange things to the mind.'

'Why did you tell me that, Druitt?' Pyke wanted to conceal his frustration but he could see from the smile on Druitt's lips that he hadn't been successful. 'Guppy was murdered on the third. So was a boy called Johnny Gregg. He was killed in an almost identical manner five years ago.'

Druitt's expression remained unchanged. He put his arms above his head and stretched. 'A coincidence, you think?'

'Ten days later, another boy, Stephen Clough, was crucified. Someone nailed him to a stable door in Soho. The same stable used by your former friend, Brendan Malloy.'

Again Druitt received this news with no visible reaction. Pyke wanted to take Druitt into a private room and pummel the truth out of him, but what stopped him was the curious notion that this was exactly what Druitt was willing him to do, goading him so he would lose his temper.

'Clough was killed on the thirteenth of December. So was a City alderman called Charles Harcourt Hogarth. This would have been about three weeks ago.' Pyke noticed a copy of *The Times* on the table next to Druitt's hammock. 'If you'd read his obituary, you would have heard he died from a cardiac seizure.'

Druitt saw that Pyke had noticed the newspaper. 'As a reward for good behaviour, I'm permitted to take *The Times*.' He smiled. 'It's a terrible rag, really, but it's reassuring to know there's a world beyond these four walls.'

'In actuality Hogarth was crucified, just like Clough. But I think you know that. Just like I think you know who killed Hogarth and Guppy – and why.'

'And how would I know that?' Druitt's eyes had lost all of their dullness and now glittered with an intensity Pyke found disturbing.

'You tell me. That's why I'm here. I want to know how Guppy and Hogarth are linked.'

'I'm afraid I can't help you there, Detective Inspector. A shame, because it sounds intriguing.'

'Five years ago, a man called Morris Keate was executed for murdering those two boys. I think Brendan Malloy knew him.'

'Then ask Brendan about it.' Druitt climbed out of his hammock and stretched. He was taller than Pyke remembered from the last visit.

'A poor man is hungry. He poaches some pheasants and is shot by the landowner. His friend sees this and hides one of the stolen birds in the bag of another poor man who is subsequently found out and shot.' Druitt took two paces towards the end of the cell then turned around. 'Should this man be condemned for ensuring his own survival and this other man's death?'

Pyke remained silent, trying to work out why Druitt had told him this story.

'Perhaps the question we should ask is what is the initial crime?' Druitt continued. 'The theft of the bird or the fact they were forced into such an act because they were poor and hungry?'

'I think you should leave the philosophising to those who understand its complexities.'

For the first time, Pyke saw that he'd managed to get to Druitt. Deciding to press home his advantage, he said, 'I had another chat with Sarah Scott. She told me not to believe a word you said.'

That elicited a smirk. 'But you're having trouble with that, aren't you?'

'Trouble?'

'She didn't tell you that the child was mine, then?' Druitt raised his eyebrows and tutted under his breath. 'But why would she? That is, if she was trying to present herself to you as an object worthy of your desire.'

Druitt must have seen Pyke's expression because almost at once he added, 'You'd like to hurt me, wouldn't you, Detective Inspector? I can see it in your eyes.'

Pyke tried to remain calm.

'Admittedly she's a nice bit of quim but if you see her as anything more you'll be disappointed. Brendan was. I was. She'll fuck you and leave you, just as she's done with all the others.'

Pyke tried to put what Druitt had said out of his mind. 'If the child was yours, then why did you kill it?'

'I didn't.' Druitt laughed and shook his head. 'Oh, you are so naive, so easily taken in, Detective Inspector. I didn't kill the child. She did.'

Perhaps it was the casualness of Druitt's lie which pushed Pyke over the edge; perhaps it was the way he ran the tip of his tongue around the perimeter of his lips, as though there was something lewd about the child's death. Or perhaps it was simply that Pyke felt compelled to defend a woman he had grown to like. In any case, he leapt forward, pushed Druitt against the wall and grabbed him by the throat. It felt momentarily good to squeeze it, until he saw the expression in the prisoner's eyes, the fact that he almost seemed to be willing Pyke to hurt him. As soon as Pyke let go, Druitt reached out and pulled a hand-spring.

Moments later, a warder unbolted the door and pulled it open. 'Everything all right in 'ere?'

Pyke looked over at Druitt, who was gingerly touching his throat.

'Everything's fine,' Pyke said.

Druitt looked at the warder but made no comment. He waited until Pyke was almost out of the cell before saying, 'Perhaps Mandeville was right after all; what we claim to value comes not from being good but from greed, cruelty and anger.'

Pyke felt the muscles in his stomach clench. Somehow Druitt knew he was reading that book.

'Wasn't it Francis Carlyle who talked about pig philosophy?' he added a few moments later.

Pyke tried to push past the warder but the man held his ground and Druitt shrank to the back of the cell. Perhaps the warder could see the hotness in Pyke's face.

'I think it would be better if you left, sir, before you did something you might later regret.'

As he went, Druitt said, 'In the end, Pyke, violence demeans its perpetrators much more than its victims.'

The governor was an ugly, diminutive man with almost no neck and arms that seemed to extend sideways out of his shoulders. What he lacked in physical grace, he tried to compensate for in sartorial elegance. His dark blue frock-coat looked as if it had been hand-stitched by the most fashionable Bond Street tailor and contrasted with his pale grey trousers, tucked into polished, knee-length leather boots. He listened carefully while Pyke explained his concern that Ebenezer Druitt might somehow be communicating with a party or parties outside the prison.

'Given our separate and silent system, it would be difficult for the man to communicate with another prisoner, let alone someone outside these walls. I just don't see how it would be possible.'

'Has he received any visits since he came here in June?'

The governor shook his head. 'Prisoners have to serve at least a year of their sentence before they are allowed to receive visitors and, as you can imagine, such visits are heavily supervised.'

It was possible, of course, that Druitt simply knew the man or men who were carrying out the murders and was not in communication with them. But that didn't explain how he knew that Pyke was reading Mandeville's tome or that he kept pigs.

'Druitt receives *The Times* each day. Is that usual for a prisoner?'

The governor sat forward, hands resting on the edge of the desk. 'If we're to convince the felons to alter their behaviour, to see the value of discipline and hard work, then some small inducements are necessary. But if you feel that this prisoner's receiving of the newspaper has in any way contributed to the affairs you speak of,

I won't hesitate to rescind this privilege forthwith.'

'That won't be necessary, for the time being.' Pyke didn't yet know how Druitt was sending and receiving messages, but if he was using *The Times* to do so, it was probably best to keep the lines of communication open.

'I have to say, sir, I'm a little perturbed by your claims regarding this particular felon. Until now, I regarded him as a model for others. A man who works hard, says little, reads the Bible and attends chapel.'

NINETEEN

Scotland Yard had been Pyke's place of work for almost a year but he still didn't feel quite comfortable there. It wasn't necessarily the architecture which he objected to, though in common with all state buildings its intention, he felt, was to overawe and intimidate. Nor did he object to the fact that in a building of such apparent scale and grandeur, the Detective Branch had been housed in such poky conditions. Rather it was the idea that of the hundreds of people who worked there, he could count the people he liked and trusted on the fingers of one hand. More than this, he believed there were at least as many again who were actively trying to damage his reputation. These fears may not have been grounded in hard evidence but the whole place seemed to run on gossip and innuendo, and as he walked by huddles of clerks and policemen they would stop talking, and it was difficult not to feel that he was the subject of their conversations.

Wells had sent word that he wouldn't be able to attend the meeting that Pyke had scheduled for five o'clock that afternoon, so it was just the four of them. Jack Whicher started, telling them he'd still been unable to find anything at all that linked Isaac Guppy and Charles Hogarth; there were no business, social or religious associations. He seemed disheartened. Pyke assured him that he was doing a good job and told him to continue looking into Hogarth's business affairs. Now that Mayne knew the real cause of death, he added, they didn't have to take such care to hide their motives for asking potentially awkward questions. Lockhart and Shaw reported that they had spent the previous two days in St Giles and Soho looking for Keate's mother or his siblings or anyone who might know the family. They, too, had failed to discover anything of interest. Their difficulties had been compounded by the fact that no one from either district had been willing to talk to police detectives.

As the meeting broke up, Pyke asked to speak to each of the detectives separately in his office.

'Ah, Frederick,' Pyke said, as Shaw took the chair opposite him. The youngest detective sergeant had a nervous disposition and Pyke wondered whether this made him more or less susceptible to the kind of pressure Pierce was capable of exerting.

'I wanted to make sure that you didn't have any concerns with the way I'm overseeing the investigation.'

'Me?' Shaw ran his fingers through his brown hair and laughed. 'Why would you think *I* had a concern?'

'You'd come to me, if you did, wouldn't you?'

'Of course I would.'

'Because I remember you saying that the investigation into the murders five years ago had been flawless. I suppose I've been arguing otherwise in public. I think there were avenues that weren't fully explored and I'm not sure how overwhelming the evidence against Morris Keate actually was.'

Shaw nodded vigorously, as though he agreed with Pyke's point. 'I was young at the time and maybe a little naive. It was my first murder investigation. A part of me still wants to think we got everything right.'

'And do you? I mean now, with the benefit of hindsight?'

The younger man shook his head. 'It doesn't seem likely, does it? Not in light of what's happened in the past month or so.'

Pyke looked into Shaw's eyes and tried to imagine him slipping off to see Pierce in his office at Bow Street. Was he capable of such deception?

'Very good,' he said, smiling. 'That's all for now, Frederick. Could you tell Jack to join me for a few minutes?'

As soon as Whicher had settled into the chair Pyke started by telling him about his suspicions regarding Shaw; the fact that he might be the one passing secrets to Pierce.

Whicher held his breath for a moment, as if weighing up the claim in his head. 'Do you know this for certain?'

'He was part of the original investigation. I think he feels a certain loyalty to what was done at the time and hence to Pierce;

and I don't think he quite realises what's at stake here. I'm not just suggesting that the investigation was botched; I'm saying it's possible that Morris Keate was deliberately picked out to take the blame and that Pierce knowingly allowed it to happen.'

Whicher nodded, but said, 'You're sure you're not letting your antipathy for Pierce colour your reading of the situation?'

'All I know is that I need to plug the leak in this vessel as quickly as possible. If Pierce knows what we're doing as a department, he can always remain one step ahead of us, covering his tracks.'

'You're talking as if you've already made up your mind that Pierce is actively seeking to sabotage this investigation.'

Pyke had asked himself the same question: whether his antipathy towards Pierce was causing him to read more into the situation than was appropriate.

'Now you're here, Jack, I did want to talk to you about something else.' He waited for a moment and then gave an account of his visit to the Model Prison and his suspicions regarding Druitt.

'You think Druitt knows who killed Guppy and Hogarth?'

'Either that, or he's pretending he does. But if he is in communication with the murderer, perhaps he might lead us to him.'

Whicher crossed his legs and pondered what Pyke had told him: the idea seemed to sit heavily on his mind.

Pyke rubbed his eyes again and tried to suppress a yawn. He hadn't slept well the night before and had woken up long before dawn. 'I was also thinking about these two boys, Gregg and Clough. They were part of a mob run by Horace Flint. He was murdered a few years ago. Now a man called George Culpepper has taken over.'

'And?'

'If I'm not mistaken, Culpepper is involved in a battle over territory with the Rafferty brothers. The same Raffertys, if you remember, who were initially accused of killing the three men in Cullen's shop.'

'But we came to the conclusion that the Raffertys weren't to blame for that.'

'I know. I was just thinking that no one's ever recovered the Saviour's Cross, have they?' Pyke was still bothered by this idea and the notion that Egan, the fence, might have found a way of locating it without them knowing.

Whicher was still struggling to follow his logic. 'Are you suggesting that this business between the Raffertys and Culpepper is related to the theft of the cross?'

'Not at all.' Pyke leaned back against his chair and sighed. 'I don't know what I'm saying, Jack. I'm just worried that Rafferty and Culpepper are involved in all this and I can't yet see how.'

Afterwards Pyke thought about their conversation and wondered how much he could trust even Whicher. It was surely inconceivable that Whicher was passing information back to Pierce. Pyke liked the man, and in their own way they'd become close since the summer, but he knew very little about the detective sergeant. He was interrupted in his thoughts by a knock on the door as Lockhart peered in.

'Come in, Eddie, please have a seat.' Pyke waited for Lockhart to sit down before adding, 'I just wanted to say how much I appreciated all you did, getting the affidavit from the coroner's assistant.'

Lockhart nodded but said nothing.

'There's something else I'd like you to do for me. It's a little unorthodox.' Pyke saw Lockhart's strained expression and smiled. 'You were once a beat constable in the Kensington Division, weren't you?'

'For a year or so.'

'So you would have come across a sergeant by the name of Russell?'

'I knew him; I couldn't say with any certainty that he'd know me any more.'

Pyke was certain that the man had been told to look out for and protect the interests of the Hogarth family. Why else would he come running as soon as the alarm was raised?

'I want you to go and see Russell. Assure him you've got confidential information about our investigation into Hogarth's death. Tell him you want to trade. He'll ask what you want in return; be vague. Tell him the investigation has uncovered something important that links Hogarth and Guppy, that this information will discredit Hogarth and that his family will want to pay to have it silenced.'

Lockhart looked at him dubiously. 'You're assuming Russell is somehow in the pocket of this family.'

'That's right,' Pyke said. He paused, wondering whether he needed to add that, until recently, Pierce had been in overall charge of the Kensington Division.

'You're assuming that Russell will believe I'm corrupt, too.'

'If he is corrupt, it will be easier for him to believe you are. My guess is he won't question it: he'll be too keen to relay your offer to the family.'

Lockhart thought through the request. 'I take it you're just fishing? You don't really have anything that connects the two murders?'

'Not at the moment. But that's not to suggest a connection doesn't exist. And let's not forget about the issues here. We're up against a man, or a group of men, with the power to conceal a murder and make two other people – the coroner and the porter – disappear into thin air.'

'So what if Russell turns around and accuses me of trying to profit illegally from my work?'

'He won't.'

'But if he does?'

'If he does, just deny it. After all, it'll be your word against his.' Pyke paused and rubbed his chin. 'But I'll bet you a hundred pounds he won't do that.'

'A hundred, eh?' Lockhart looked at Pyke and smiled. 'Maybe I should take you up on that.'

Martin Jakes was waiting for Pyke in the main office of the Detective Branch. At first Pyke thought something might have happened to Felix. Quickly the curate assured Pyke that his son was well and was thriving as a helper. Once they were seated in Pyke's office, Jakes started to explain the real reason for his visit.

'Something's been playing on my conscience since our last conversation. I'm afraid to say I wasn't entirely honest with you.'

Pyke studied Jakes's face and motioned for him to continue.

'You asked me whether I knew Brendan Malloy and Morris Keate …'

'And you told me you didn't. Or that you had heard of them but didn't actually know them.'

Jakes nodded slowly, as though acknowledging the lie. 'Keate was once a member of my congregation at St Luke's.'

Pyke went across to the fireplace and poured more coal on to the fire. When he turned around, he said, 'I'd always assumed he was a Catholic.'

'Most people did; because of his association with Malloy.'

'So Keate did know Malloy, then?'

'When I couldn't help Keate any further, I sent him to Malloy. I didn't know Malloy and to this day I've never met him, but at the time he'd garnered something of a reputation for the exorcisms he performed … For a long time, the Protestant Church has turned its back on the practice of exorcism. It's deemed to be too close to confession; too much power in the hands of the priest. I sent Morris to him because I didn't know what else to do.'

Pyke gazed into the fire and said, 'Tell me about him.'

'Morris Keate was a simple man, in every sense of the word; a little strange, perhaps. Lived with the constant fear that he'd been possessed by the Devil. But in his own way he was kind hearted. Or so I thought.'

'Until he was arrested and accused of killing those boys?'

The memory of this time was clearly painful to the older man. He loosened his collar and wiped his forehead. 'At the time, I was persuaded that Morris had, in fact, done what he'd been accused of.'

'And now?' Pyke tried to read the troubled expression on Jakes's face.

'Now, I don't know. I really don't know. Part of me would like to believe he didn't kill those boys. I don't like to think that any of my congregation would be capable of such a thing. But if he were innocent, that would be even more horrendous: an innocent man killed on the scaffold.' Jakes's eyes remained downcast.

'You didn't campaign on his behalf at the time of the murders?'

'As I said, I was persuaded by the evidence. And Morris failed to provide any kind of defence for himself.'

Pyke went across to the window and opened it. He wanted some cool air on his face. It also gave him a few moments to think about what Jakes had told him.

'What do you know about Keate's family?'

'I think I'm right in saying he was very close to his mother. And he had brothers and sisters. But I didn't know them. None of them ever came to St Luke's.'

'You wouldn't know where I could find them now?'

Jakes shook his head. 'I'm afraid not. It was a long time ago.'

Pyke felt let down by the curate and he wanted Jakes to know it. 'Tell me, Martin. Why did you lie to me, when I asked if you knew Keate?'

Jakes let out a heavy sigh. 'It was a terrible time for me ... for the entire congregation. What Morris did; what they accused him of doing. Somehow the idea of revisiting it seemed too painful for words. I was a coward. I suppose I was hoping the whole thing would just go away.'

'So why put right this wrong now?'

'I don't know.' Jakes stared down at the floor. 'I suppose I didn't want you to catch me out in a lie.'

This made a certain amount of sense. 'If I was to talk to Brendan Malloy, he'd be able to confirm that Keate once attended your church.'

'Yes, he would.' Jakes looked wary, perhaps even sheepish. 'You're a perceptive man, Detective Inspector, but you shouldn't underestimate the damage that a guilty conscience can wreak.'

'And now you've unburdened yourself, do you feel lifted?' Pyke didn't bother to hide his scepticism.

'I should have told you the truth when we last spoke. I was wrong. I apologise.'

It was a grudging apology and Pyke was minded not to acknowledge it. 'I have one more question to ask you and I'd appreciate it if you could answer me honestly. Did you know Guppy at the time?'

'Do you mean when Keate was attending St Luke's?'

'Yes. I want to know whether Guppy knew Morris Keate.'

'That's how I first met Guppy,' the curate said, eventually. 'He came to see me, professing an interest in Keate's circumstances.'

'Was this before or after his arrest?'

'Before, I think.' Jakes's voice was hoarse, his throat dry.

'You're quite sure about that?'

'Quite sure.'

Later, after an apologetic and troubled Jakes had left, Pyke turned over what he'd learned. So Guppy had known about Keate. In itself, this proved nothing, but perhaps it helped explain why the rector had responded so demonstrably when Malloy had visited him the previous spring. According to Malloy, Guppy had only taken his claims seriously when he'd realised who the Catholic priest was. If the two men had never met before, why would Malloy's name give Guppy such a fright? The only answer Pyke could think of was that in Guppy's mind the name was somehow linked to Morris Keate. Still, why would this have unsettled the rector?

Outside the public entrance to the Kensington station house, on the other side of the busy High Street, stood Pyke and Felix. Dressed as costermongers, they were selling fruit from a barrow; Pyke in a full-skirted velveteen coat, a corduroy waistcoat, matching cord trousers pulled tight at the knees, and a pair of heavy ankle boots; Felix in a tatty cloth coat, wool breeches and boots, with a silk handkerchief tied around his neck and a beaver-knapped top hat on his head. Pyke had made sure their hands were muddy and their faces were smudged with soot. Since lunchtime they had sold seven shillings' worth of oranges and apples; the owner of the cart, who'd agreed – under duress – to rent it to them, was watching from the window of a nearby coffee shop.

It had almost been a joke, initially. Pyke had gone home the previous night and without really thinking about it had asked Felix whether he might consider helping him on a job. To his surprise, the lad had leapt at the chance, and ever since then Pyke had been wondering whether he'd made a big mistake. It was true he needed help; you always did whenever you tried to follow someone. But was it wise to use his son on such an assignment? What if something went wrong? He'd never knowingly put Felix in danger, but then again, could he be absolutely certain that Sergeant Russell would fail to spot he was being followed?

Across the road, a man stumbled out of the Farriers tavern. They watched him wait on the pavement, swaying while a wagon with its cargo covered by a canvas tarpaulin rattled past. Their eyes went from him to a man wearing a sandwich board advertising 'SMITH'S JET BLACKING', but before Felix could ask what jet blacking was, an argument flared up between a basket seller and a crossing-sweeper over who should clear up the mess made by the former's donkey. It was bitterly cold and no one paid much attention to their ranting. There was so much to take in, so much to look at, that Felix hardly seemed to know where to direct his attention. Pyke kept his eyes fixed on the entrance to the station house. He had seen Lockhart enter about half an hour earlier and suddenly there he was on the steps, looking one way and then the other, before hailing a cab. Now Russell knew, Pyke presumed, and it was just a question of waiting.

The cold, biting wind made it difficult to stand still, and they moved slowly around the barrow, a few steps at a time. There were men coming and going from the station house all the time; police constables mostly, but also clerks, office boys, messengers and tradesmen. The constant stream of bodies made it hard for Pyke and Felix to stay focused, but the notion that Russell might appear at any second kept them alert. As the light began to fade, Pyke felt the first drops of rain on his face, and by the time the lamp-lighters started their rounds, the rain had become heavier and more persistent.

Fifty minutes after Lockhart had climbed into a hackney carriage, Russell emerged from the station house dressed in his dark blue uniform. He glanced furtively up and down the High Street then turned right out of the building, walking briskly to the first corner and crossing the road. Having pointed out who Russell was, Pyke watched as his son set off after the policeman and waited for a few moments before following. Pyke could just about see Russell's stovepipe hat bobbing up and down among the other pedestrians, their umbrellas raised to shield themselves from the rain. It took twenty minutes to walk from the station house to the Hogarth residence at the top of the King's Road, and once Russell was safely inside, Pyke joined Felix in his hiding place across the road. Despite the rain and cold, Felix's face glistened with excitement. Their wait on the other side of the quiet street was not a long one. About five minutes later, Russell reappeared and, after looking up at the darkening sky, he continued on his way, this time heading back in the direction in which he'd come. Again, Pyke let Felix take the lead and this time allowed a little more distance between himself and Russell because the streets this far away from the High Street were not busy.

About halfway between the King's Road and Kensington High Street, Pyke noticed that Felix was walking more quickly, and moments later he broke into a jog. Pyke was fifty yards farther back, and by the time he reached the place where Russell and Felix had turned on to a quieter street, he had lost them. Pyke raced to the next corner and looked both ways along the residential street, a row of stout terraces facing one another. There was no sign of either Russell or Felix. Suppressing an urge to call out, Pyke turned suddenly, hearing something move behind him. He found himself staring into the ruddy face of a policeman he didn't recognise. Russell stepped out of the shadows, a grin spreading across his face. He had a truncheon in his hand and it was raised. Pyke searched his peripheral vision for any sign of his son; at the same time, Russell whipped his arm through the air and Pyke felt the thick end of the truncheon connect with the side of his head. His legs buckled and a flash of light exploded behind his eyes; after that, he put his hands out to break his fall and slipped into unconsciousness.

TWENTY

Pyke had no idea how long he had been unconscious. It was still dark and the air was damp, although it was no longer raining. His shoes and coat had been taken, as had his purse, knife and pistol. He stood up gingerly, his bare feet sinking into the mud. It took him a moment to remember what had happened and another to remember that Felix had been with him. Panic turned his stomach to ice. He looked around and shouted Felix's name. His voice echoed off the walls of the alley he'd been left in. Pyke's head was throbbing and the pain was acute, but he didn't think the blow had damaged his skull. Limping to the end of the alley, he half-expected to find Felix's body lying in the mud. He shouted his son's name again but there was no response. His feet were entirely numb, and without his frock-coat he was shivering, but the panic meant he hardly noticed the cold. He retraced his steps back to the residential street, and from there it took him another ten minutes to get to the cab-stand on Kensington High Street. There, he was told that it was eight in the evening, which meant he'd been unconscious for two hours. As he waited for a cab, he tried to think what might have happened to Felix and what the best course of action would be. He could go to the station house and confront Russell, if indeed he'd gone back there, but what would the sergeant say? If they were split up, the plan had been for him and Felix to meet up back at the house, so when a cab finally pulled up, Pyke instructed the driver to take him to Islington. It had now been two and a half hours since the assault. If he was safe, Felix would be there at the house to greet him, and for the rest of the journey Pyke clung to this thought.

When the carriage dropped him outside his home, there were no candles burning in any of the windows. Pyke put his key into the lock, turned it and pushed open the door. He shouted his son's name but there was no answer. Only Copper came to greet him. There was a note from Mrs Booth on the kitchen table. She had left supper for them in the pantry. He raced up the stairs to Felix's room but it was empty and the bed was untouched. A fire was still burning in the living room but otherwise the house was cold, dark and unwelcoming. Pyke's panic had returned, together with a feeling of helplessness. What could he do? What should he do? Stay put and hope Felix showed up? Or go back to Kensington and begin his search for the lad there?

Pyke dried his feet and hair with a cloth and put on an old coat and pair of shoes. Then he returned to the street and looked up and down for any sign of a carriage. Apart from a dog barking next door, everything was quiet. Pyke strode to the end of the street and looked up the hill towards Islington High Street. The recriminations could come later but it was hard to hold the guilt he felt in abeyance.

Back at the house, Pyke pushed open the front door and let Copper hobble in ahead of him. In the living room, where at least it was warm, he went across to the window and looked out on to the street. He didn't hear the sound behind him, didn't react until he heard Copper whine. When he turned around, Felix was standing in the doorway. Wordlessly they moved across the room to greet one another, Pyke throwing his arms around Felix and Felix doing likewise. They embraced for what seemed like minutes.

'What happened?' Pyke said finally when they parted.

Felix seemed taken aback by the welcome he'd received. He reached down and patted Copper on the head. 'One moment he was there in front of me, the next he was gone. So I ran ahead to the next corner but I couldn't see him. I doubled back on myself and that's when I saw him with you and some other man at your back. I saw him raise his truncheon and hit you. I wanted to help but I didn't know what I could do. You fell to the ground.'

'And then?'

'I wanted to see if you were all right but I knew you'd be angry with me if I just let him go. I realised if I waited too long, I'd lose him, so I went after him and the other one. He wasn't careful and didn't think to look behind him. I don't think he knew I was with you. They split up and I kept with our man. He hailed a carriage

239

and I did likewise, told the driver I'd pay him double if he kept the vehicle ahead of us in his sight.'

The words were coming out fast and Felix could hardly contain his excitement.

'I didn't know where we were going but when the carriage ahead of us finally stopped outside a big white house. I asked the driver, and he said we were on Kensington High Street. It was dark, of course, but I could see parkland on the other side of the road.'

Pyke listened, not quite able to comprehend that Felix had done all this, and been able to find his way home.

'I paid the driver, and watched as our man presented himself at the gates. There were two or three men guarding the house but they let Russell in. It was a white house, three or four storeys high and twelve windows long. I knew I had to find out who lived there but I didn't want to draw attention to myself. I had to wait a long time for someone to pass by. They didn't know who lived there but a while later someone else came along and told me it belonged to Sir St John Palmer.'

Pyke clasped his arms around Felix's shoulders and lifted him clean off the ground. *Sir St John Palmer.* Pyke had met the man briefly in the office of Sir Richard Mayne.

'Palmer, you say?' Saggers was looking among the glasses in front of him for dregs of wine or porter.

It was a Friday night and the taproom was bursting with journalists and actors, a blur of tweed, wool and kerseymere.

'Sir St John Palmer. He lives on Kensington High Street in a large, neoclassical mansion.'

'*Hmm.*' Saggers scratched his chin. 'I think he's a building contractor. Yes, I'm sure of it now. Quite a significant one, too. Owns his own company, though I can't think what it's called.'

Pyke had gone to Saggers because there was almost no one of repute in the entire city he didn't know or hadn't heard of.

'He's well connected. I believe he's heavily involved in church matters, too.'

Pyke caught Saggers's arm. 'What kind of church matters?'

Saggers pulled his arm free and frowned. 'Dammit, Pyke, will you just let me think for a moment?'

Pyke could feel his heart beating more quickly. This was what he'd been waiting for. He could almost taste it.

'There was a fund set up to help establish a dozen or so new churches in the East End. I think I remember reading he was involved in that.'

'The London Churches Fund?'

'That's the one.' Saggers looked at him, eyes narrowing. 'Are you going to tell me what this is about?'

Pyke tossed a couple of coins on to the table and stood up. 'A while ago, I asked you to look into the affairs of Charles Hogarth. Have you made any progress?'

'I have other things to do, you know.'

'What have you found out?'

'You're very impatient tonight, old man ...'

'*Please*, Edmund. This is important.'

'So I see.' Saggers picked up his handkerchief and wiped the corners of his mouth. 'He was an alderman for the Court of Common Council but I'm sure you already know that. What you might not know is that he was the driving force behind a huge expansion in the number of properties available for rent in the City.'

'Where have all these properties come from?'

'They're domestic residences, mostly. I'd say he's been trying to encourage people who live in the City to sell up and move out. You see, if a public company or even a small business rents the same building, the City Corporation can increase the rate. He was quite successful, I've been told.'

Pyke leaned towards Saggers. 'Keep digging, Edmund; and while you're at it, see if he has an association with Palmer.'

The Bishop of London's official residence was situated in Fulham, but because of its proximity to St Paul's Cathedral he spent most of his time in his chambers at London House, a handsome brick building on Aldersgate Street. Having presented himself at the front door first thing on Saturday morning, Pyke was made to wait for a full hour before the same elderly servant who'd answered the door reappeared and announced that the bishop would see him in the drawing room.

The bishop was a tall, elegant man in his late forties, with grey hair and a gaunt, angular face that seemed to radiate the kind of seriousness his office apparently required. He greeted Pyke with a firm handshake and introduced him to his assistant, a sour-faced man called Taylor.

'Now, Detective Inspector, how can I be of assistance?' He was dressed in a plain black frock-coat along with his episcopal apron and gaiters.

'What can you tell me about the London Churches Fund?'

Bishop Blomfield exchanged a brief glance with his assistant. 'What exactly do you want to know?'

'Just tell me a little about it. What is it? Why was it established?' Pyke tried to keep his tone light and breezy.

'It was created about eight years ago, in order to raise funds for building additional churches in the metropolis.'

'And you felt that it was a project that merited your support?'

'Not just I, Detective Inspector.' He stood up and went to retrieve a document from the bookshelf behind him. 'A report by the Church Commissioners declared that, and I quote, "the most prominent defect that cripples the energy of the Established Church is the want of Churches and Ministers in our cities".' The bishop removed spectacles from his pocket and put them on. 'In the parishes of the East End, there are now in excess of three or four hundred thousand men, women and children but, as of a few years ago, we could provide church-room for barely a thousand souls and just a handful of clergymen. The Commissioners stated that, and I quote again, "the evil that flows from the state of things" would continue unless a remedy was speedily sought.'

'And that's why the London Churches Fund was established?'

'Indeed,' Blomfield said, nodding. 'The plan was to build fifty churches. At present, we have built or are building just ten, all in Bethnal Green. But ten is a decent start, is it not? And we're not resting on our laurels.'

'Quite an undertaking,' Pyke said, pretending to be impressed.

Blomfield beamed appreciatively. 'It is the work of prudence and charity, sir, to impart Christianity to the people of this city.'

'And how is this fund administered? I imagine that with such an undertaking there would be a central committee, and perhaps various subcommittees?'

'Exactly so, Detective Inspector. Many hands make light work. And the Lord guides us always.'

Pyke nodded kindly. He knew he had to tread carefully around Blomfield. As Bishop of London, the man enjoyed serious political connections and he could easily use these to close down the investigation. 'You chair the main committee, I presume?'

'No, that responsibility falls to the archdeacon.'

'Archdeacon Wynter?'

There must have been something in Pyke's tone because Blomfield exchanged another brief glance with Taylor and said, 'Perhaps you might tell me of your interest in our project, Detective Inspector?'

Avoiding the question, Pyke tried to regain a lightness of tone. 'Tell me, Bishop, did the Reverend Guppy serve on one of the committees?'

It took Blomfield a few moments to work out who Pyke had just referred to. He grimaced slightly and removed his spectacles. 'Yes, he did; in a very minor, administrative capacity. In fund-raising, I believe.'

'And Charles Hogarth?'

'No, I don't know that name.' Blomfield looked at his assistant, who also shook his head.

'What about Sir St John Palmer?'

'St John? Of course. He's been one of the leading lights; a very fine man and a personal friend of mine; a man of great vision and humility.'

Pyke could tell the bishop was starting to get agitated. He smiled and said, 'I'm sure he is. But I was wondering if you could tell me how the funds were raised?'

In itself, the fact that Sergeant Russell had gone directly from Hogarth's residence to Palmer's proved very little. But the notion that Palmer was, in the bishop's words, one of the Fund's leading lights had to be significant.

'The Church Building Commissioners provided some of the money; private donations made up the rest. With a board including such luminaries as the Reverend Dr Spry, Mr Joshua

Wilson, Mr William Baines, Sir St John Palmer, the Right Honourable William Gladstone, and not forgetting the prime minister, Sir Robert Peel, we did not experience a problem achieving the necessary subscriptions.'

Pyke had not expected to hear Peel's name on the list but he knew straight away that it would make his task much harder. If there was even the faintest whiff of scandal attached to the Churches Fund, any attempt to expose it would be stamped on from a great height.

'I really must ask you, sir, to explain the purpose of your visit.' This time it was Taylor, the assistant, who'd spoken. 'The bishop has kindly given you of his time and answered your questions with patience and good grace. Now it is your duty to reciprocate.'

'It's nothing for either you or the bishop to worry about.' Pyke tried to smile. 'As you probably know, we're still looking for the man who murdered Isaac Guppy. It was mentioned that Guppy had been heavily involved in the activities of the Churches Fund.'

'Not heavily,' Blomfield said, quickly. 'A very minor capacity, as I said.'

'And I'm grateful to be corrected on that account.' Pyke stood up and nodded to the bishop. 'Thank you for your time, Bishop. I'll show myself to the door. And rest assured, your answers have been most helpful.'

The riverbank at Billingsgate was a rickety forest of piers, steps, wharves and causeways, water sloshing around under the wooden poles, a dirty heave of sludge and scum carried back and forth by the tide. Above, the sky was almost white with seagulls circling for scraps of fish discarded by market traders, the shrill din of their cries making conversation difficult. The air smelled of fresh fish and stagnant water, and out on the river an icy wind whipped against the bowsprits and rigging of moored vessels, the smaller ones, the skiffs and dinghies, clanking against one another.

They paused for a short while and looked out at the vast expanse of river. Sarah Scott had come to him at Scotland Yard and told him there was something he should see. Her grim silence told him all he needed to know. It was cold enough for snow but the skies were clear, apart from the gulls. At the foot of the tide-washed stairs, a plank of wood bobbed up and down in water that looked as black as tar.

Pyke followed Sarah up the narrow, muddy lane leading away from the river, to Lower Thames Street, and into a ramshackle tenement building. Maybe it had once been a warehouse: its size and proximity to the river certainly suggested that. Now it had been carved up into rooms sleeping ten or fifteen, taken over by the district's street sellers and scavengers, toshers and mudlarks, pickpockets and prostitutes. Pyke had no idea who, if anyone, collected the rent, but it was the kind of place you ended up in when there was nowhere left to go. Sarah Scott didn't seem cowed by the lewd remarks directed at her or by the foulness of the air. She paid a shilling for a candle and led him down a flight of crumbling stairs to the basement. At the end of a damp passageway stood a door. She gestured for him to open it. He pushed the door and held up the lantern. He had already guessed that behind it he would find Brendan Malloy and that the former priest would be dead, but nothing could have prepared him for the smell.

Pyke brought the lantern closer and saw that maggots had already started to consume the dead flesh. Still, there were traces of frothing around the mouth, and when Sarah handed him an empty bottle which she said she'd found next to him, Pyke brought it up to his nostrils and sniffed. He knew how Malloy had died. Prussian acid would do that to you, if you imbibed enough of it.

Later, after Pyke had made arrangements for the corpse to be transported to a nearby public house for the coroner's attention, the two of them walked back to the river, now in darkness, and stood in silence at the top of the stairs.

'You still haven't told me how you found him,' Pyke said, staring into the watery blackness.

'We lived together in this city for nearly two years. I know where he liked to go, where he liked to drink. One thing led to another.' She looked at him, her eyes unfathomable. 'You, of all people, should know how that works.'

'Do you still love him?'

She turned to face him. She had an effortless, natural beauty, he decided in that moment, the kind that didn't need to be preened or fussed over. 'Brendan never saw the world as others have conditioned us to. At one point in my life, I was deeply attracted to that view.'

Pyke rested his arm on the metal rail in front of him. 'I just saw him as mentally disturbed.'

'I'm not going to argue there's a certain truth in madness ...'

'But?'

'The Church, whether Catholic *or* Protestant, would have us believe that religious faith is somehow compatible with the advancement of society. Brendan refused to succumb to such a view. He believed that the problem of evil has never been resolved, in spite of what we might tell ourselves.'

Pyke pondered this for a moment or two. 'And you?'

'I'm not an arch-rationalist like you, Pyke. I think there are things we can't see, things we don't know.'

'Don't mistake me, Sarah. I think the rationality we all cling to is paper-thin. Scratch a little and you'll find an ugly world where goodness and morality have no place.'

Sarah seemed to agree with his point. 'That's what I feel when I paint.'

Pyke thought about the image he'd seen in her cottage. 'What I saw in your canvas was either the punishment of a sinful woman by a vengeful God, or a world in which God doesn't exist.'

'That's what I liked about Brendan. Even as a priest, he was able to countenance the notion that perhaps God wasn't, *isn't*, who we're told he is.' She drew closer to Pyke. 'God is never simply vengeful on the one hand, and omnipotent and forgiving on the other.'

Pyke looked into her eyes, wanting to bridge the gap that existed and had always existed between them. He thought briefly about Ebenezer Druitt's claim that she had killed her own child but dismissed it at once. Druitt, he decided, had been trying to play games with him.

'But you do believe in the existence of a spirit world?'

'Just because we can't see something doesn't mean it isn't there.' She paused, seemingly afraid to say more.

Pyke thought fleetingly about what Godfrey had said just before his death: *once you're gone, you're gone.* It was just starting to sink in that the old man wasn't coming back. 'In the end, life is arbitrary.

Things happen for no ostensible reason, good and bad. To acknowledge that, to truly acknowledge it, is terrifying.'

'But patterns do exist, even if we call them coincidences. Or premonitions.' Sarah let her hand settle on top of his. 'I know you don't give any credence to what I might see …'

Pyke wanted to dismiss this idea out of hand but even in the darkness he was aware of the anxiety in her face. 'What is it, Sarah?' he said gently.

'I'm worried about you.' She withdrew her hand and turned away from him. 'The other night I had a dream. I found you in a room. Your nose had been cut off, your teeth pulled out, your fingers had been removed. And your eyeballs were being gouged out by a flock of birds.'

'Some people would call that a nightmare.'

'The last time I had a dream that vivid, my son died the following night.'

They stood for a moment or two in silence. Pyke dismissed her premonition, but there were other less charitable thoughts he couldn't let go of. Since his last exchange with Druitt, he had been racking his brains to think how the felon could have known about his choice of reading. The only answer was that someone had broken into his house and passed the information back to Druitt. And for some reason, he had thought about Sarah. In one sense it was ridiculous, absurd even, to imagine that she would do anything to help Druitt. Druitt had murdered her child; she despised him; the two of them despised each other. But what if they didn't? What if their mutual loathing was just a front? Sarah knew where he lived. She could have slipped in unnoticed, just as she could have sent Pyke the letter directing him to No. 28 Broad Street. Pyke didn't like to believe she might be capable of such deception, but how well did he really know her?

'I'm telling you this because I care for you; not because I'm trying to frighten you.'

'I don't know what I'm supposed to say. If you're right, what can I do? If you're wrong, and I hope you are wrong, well, life continues as before.'

Sarah bit her lip and looked away. Then she threaded her arms around him and pulled him close, her head resting just under his chin. He could feel her shivering. When she next looked at him, her eyes were distraught. She was grieving, Pyke told himself, for her child, and perhaps also for Brendan Malloy. That was it. She needed him and he could help her. That thought reassured him, until he felt the tightness in his stomach, the familiar stirring in his groin.

When they finally embraced, it was a coy, almost chaste kiss, their lips barely touching. Her eyes were closed as she whispered, 'I've taken a room that's not far from here.'

TWENTY-ONE

The following morning was bitterly cold, and despite the fire burning in the grate of the main office of the Detective Branch, they'd all decided against shedding their outdoor clothes. Still, the collective mood was not one that reflected the icy temperature. Shaw and Lockhart had some information they wanted to impart.

'It's about the men who tore up Mrs Keate's room, just after she'd moved out,' Shaw said, beaming.

'We went back to the building and talked to the neighbours,' Lockhart chipped in. 'This time, one of them was willing to talk to us. He said he recognised a couple of the men. Told us they worked for George Culpepper.'

Wells had just walked into the room and Pyke repeated what Lockhart had just said. 'For those of you who don't know him,' Pyke added, 'Culpepper runs what we think is the largest swell mob in St Giles. He's a suspect, perhaps the main suspect, in the matter of Sean Rafferty's murder.'

Given Wells's reaction the last time he'd mentioned this, Pyke half-expected a similar outburst, but the acting superintendent merely nodded.

'The two boys who were murdered, Gregg and Clough, were part of Flint's mob,' Pyke said. 'We think Culpepper killed Flint and took over.'

And now Culpepper's men had gone after Keate's mother. Pyke tried to work out what this meant but for the moment the connection was beyond him.

'What it does mean,' he said, a few moments later, 'is we should make Culpepper's life as uncomfortable as possible.' Looking at Wells, he added, 'Can we rely on reinforcements from the executive department to make that happen?'

249

Wells sucked in some air through gritted teeth. 'I'll do what I can but I'm short on men as it is.'

Briefly Pyke's thoughts turned back to Sarah Scott, the warmth of her body next to his, the softness of her creamy white skin. He had left her unwillingly at dawn and could still taste her parting kiss.

'Culpepper runs gin palaces, brothels, gambling clubs, teams of pickpockets and numerous slop-shops, a whole empire. At the moment, he's secure and in control. We need to change that.'

'Like I said, I'll round up all the men I can spare. But I'll do it in my own way and in my own time.'

Jack Whicher found Pyke in his office; he was carrying a file and placed it carefully on the desk. 'I got that from one of the clerks in the commissioners' office. It's information about Sergeant Mark Russell's career as a metropolitan policeman.' Pyke had asked Whicher to dig up information about the man only the day before, and was surprised at how quickly he'd been able to do so.

Pyke took the file and scrutinised its contents. 'Beat constable for three years, K Division, Stepney, followed by two years in A Division here at the Yard and then a promotion to sergeant and a transfer to Kensington Division.' It didn't tell him much. There was nothing else in the file to indicate that Russell was either good or bad at his job. Given that the man had been promoted, Pyke had to assume the former.

'A Division,' Whicher said, a few moments later. 'You'd think Wells might remember him.'

Pyke had already arrived at the same conclusion. 'Perhaps. But it's the largest division and there must be, what, two or three hundred constables.'

Later, Pyke ran into Wells at the bottom of the staircase. 'Walter, I need your help with something. I'm looking into the way the London Churches Fund has been administered.'

Pyke had thought long and hard about whether to tell him about Sir St John Palmer and his association with the Fund. In the end, he'd decided that Wells would find out soon enough and, anyway, he needed as much support within the New Police as he could get.

Briefly he explained what the Fund was and who sat on its

executive board. Wells's face darkened as he did so. 'Has it occurred to you that they won't allow your investigation to taint the Fund's good name?'

'And by "they" you mean?'

'The prime minister sits on the board. So does the Bishop of London. Doesn't that tell you something?'

'And I'm meant to turn a blind eye to any malpractice that has occurred?'

'I sympathise with your predicament, Pyke, but I've heard of this man, Palmer. He's well connected.'

'His company is overseeing the renovations of the station-house. I met him briefly a few days ago. He was talking to Sir Richard.'

Wells digested this new piece of information. 'That doesn't make your task any easier, does it?'

Pyke waited for someone to pass by and said, 'You remember that sergeant I was asking you about, Russell? He used to be a constable under you in A Division.'

'Russell, you say?' Wells looked thoughtful. 'No, I can't remember the man. Why do you ask?'

'No reason.'

Wells seemed exhausted. 'Look, have you got any evidence to back up these suspicions regarding Palmer and the Churches Fund?'

When Pyke didn't answer, Wells shook his head. 'In that case, they'll flay you alive and throw the morsels to the birds.'

It made Pyke think of Sarah's dream; a flock of birds pecking out his eyes.

The brothel that Clare Lewis ran was situated above a gin and beer shop at the corner of Great White Lion Street and Queen Street, just along from the Seven Dials. There were ten other brothels that Pyke knew of in the vicinity, and probably more that he didn't know of. None of them was especially salubrious, at least in comparison with the gentlemen's clubs of St James's and Haymarket, where you could smoke a cigar and drink a brandy before availing yourself of the services. Still, most of the men who visited these places didn't expect or even demand refinement. They wanted a private room, a solid mattress and a woman who would do as she was told and pretend to enjoy it. Clare's place was as good as any other, was better even, because she treated her women well and paid them a decent wage. But Pyke hadn't known it belonged to George Culpepper. If he had known, perhaps he wouldn't have gone there. It was Clare who kept drawing him back. Her slim, wiry figure, her straw-blonde hair cut unfashionably short in the style of a pageboy and her dirty laugh, which never failed to make him smile. And it was the information she sometimes fed him. As Pyke always told his men, a detective was only as good as his sources.

He found Clare in her room. She had been writing a letter and the quill was still in her hand when he knocked on the door and pushed it open. Clare glanced at his reflection in her looking glass. 'I didn't think I'd seen the last of you,' she said, once he had closed the door behind him.

Pyke took a few steps into the room and stopped. The bed was unmade, and for a brief moment he wondered who else had been there that morning. 'I didn't exactly cover myself in glory the last time we met.'

This time Clare turned around. 'Is that as good an apology as I'm likely to get?'

'I shouldn't have said what I said.' He hesitated. 'I shouldn't have said it in the way I did.'

Clare spun around on her stool, so that she was facing him, and ran her fingers through her short, fluffy hair. 'That'll have to do, I suppose.'

'But I stand by the general sentiment. And I was still hoping you might ask a few well-placed but discreet questions.'

'I've done so already. What master wants, master gets.' She folded her arms and waited.

'Are you going to make me beg?'

'A nice idea but I haven't got anything to tell you.'

Pyke waited for her to continue.

'I mentioned it to someone. They'll remain anonymous. I was told if I valued my life, I wouldn't bring it up again. The last person who did, the mother of one of the boys, ended up dead. Strangled and dumped in the river. I'm told the body was never recovered.' The strain on her face was visible.

'I was under the impression both boys were orphans.'

'They are now.'

'If I didn't know better, I'd think Georgie had done something to those boys himself. Or at least he knows what happened to them.'

Clare fiddled with the brooch attached to her blouse. She may not have remembered but Pyke was the one who'd bought it for her. 'You should have seen him after you left the other day. He beat the lad who was guarding the door, the one you walked past, within an inch of his life. All that was left was a quivering mass. He made us all watch, too.'

'At least now you know who you're dealing with.'

Clare looked at him and shook her head slightly. 'You think I don't know Georgie is an animal?'

'Then why are you still working for him?'

'I don't have a choice. Morals are a luxury of the wealthy. Maybe you've forgotten that.'

'I don't want you to do anything that puts you or anyone you know in danger,' he said.

'Don't worry, I won't.'

'But if you were to hear something about those boys ... or why Georgie is interested in the family of a dead man called Morris Keate ... I'd like to think you'd come and find me.'

'Keate?'

'He was the one who was executed for killing the boys.' Pyke looked searchingly into her face. 'Have you heard the name?'

'No, I don't think so.' Clare turned around and glanced at her reflection in the looking glass.

'But you're not sure?' He had seen the look on her face and heard the hesitation in her voice.

Clare picked up her quill and dipped it in the pot of ink. 'Goodbye, Pyke. I'd like to say it's been a pleasure.'

Pyke had to wait for over half an hour in the marble-floored entrance hall of Sir St John Palmer's enormous neoclassical house before the butler returned and said that Palmer would see him in the drawing room. During this time he'd noted the three men guarding the gates at the front of the property, all armed with pistols, and, after a brief excursion to the back of the house, a similar presence in the rear garden.

As he followed the butler to the drawing room, their footsteps echoed through the building. Palmer was standing in the bay window overlooking the front lawn. Even after he'd been introduced, Palmer's attention remained fixed on something outside, and it was only after the butler had retreated, closing the door behind him, that Palmer finally turned around.

He looked older and frailer than Pyke remembered, his silver hair not quite as neat as it had been, his face thinner and his shoulders slightly hunched. But he moved across the room with a surprising grace and took Pyke's hand, giving it a firm squeeze.

'To what do I owe this pleasure, Detective Inspector?' He smiled easily, as though he and Pyke were old friends.

'I was hoping you could tell me about your relationship with Charles Harcourt Hogarth.' Pyke looked into Palmer's face. 'He died a few weeks ago.'

Palmer's expression didn't change. 'Do you mind telling me why you'd like to know this, Detective Inspector?'

'We're currently investigating a possible link between his death and the murder of Isaac Guppy.'

'And what does this have to do with me?' Palmer asked.

'Well, for a start, I am right in thinking you knew Hogarth, aren't I, sir?'

'Hogarth was an alderman in the City Corporation. Inevitably our paths crossed from time to time.'

Pyke looked around the sparsely furnished, high-ceilinged room. 'Was he involved with the London Churches Fund?'

'No, he wasn't,' Palmer said, without having to think about it. 'Why would you ask that, Detective Inspector?'

'Guppy was, though, wasn't he? I believe he held a relatively minor administrative role,' Pyke said, remembering the words of the bishop.

'I'm afraid I never met this man Guppy. I knew Hogarth slightly, although I still don't understand why you felt it necessary to come to my house to ask me these questions.'

'I'm told that you're one of the leading figures in the London Churches Fund. Is that correct?'

'I've played my own small part in bringing religious education to the darker quarters of the capital.' Palmer gave a bright smile. 'You still haven't answered my question, Detective Inspector. I wouldn't like to think I'm a suspect in some matter or another. For your sake as much as mine.'

Pyke frowned. 'Why for my sake?'

Palmer went back to the window and almost put his face against the glass pane. 'I've made it my business to amass a good number of friends in the New Police – an organisation for which I have a great deal of admiration. If I felt my reputation was being unfairly maligned, I would have to let one of my friends know, and I'm guessing they could make life very difficult for the person involved.'

Pyke looked down at the polished marble floor; he could almost see his reflection in it. Sensing he had to tread more carefully, he adopted an abject tone. 'I didn't mean to imply anything, Sir St John. I'm just making it my business to talk, discreetly and of course confidentially, to anyone who knew both Hogarth and Guppy.'

Palmer nodded firmly. 'Just doing your job, eh? Well, I suppose I can't object to that.'

Pyke took a few steps towards Palmer. Through the window, he could see the men patrolling the back of the house. 'I've never heard of a building contractor having to be guarded by men armed with pistols. Tell me, is that normal in the circles you move in?'

For the first time, Pyke saw the faintest of cracks in Palmer's façade. 'What I do, sir, in the privacy of my own home, is none of your business.'

'Perhaps you're worried that someone might be intending to cause you harm. In which case, maybe we, as the Metropolitan Police, could be of some assistance?' Pyke looked at the contractor and smiled.

Palmer's response was interrupted as the butler opened the door and cleared his throat. 'You wanted something, Sir St John?'

Palmer turned around and looked out on to his perfectly manicured lawn. 'Please show the detective inspector to the front door.'

It was difficult to tell whether anything had been gained from the exchange with Palmer, and as Pyke travelled back into London, he thought about the older man's threat to go over his head and wondered how Sir Richard Mayne would react to such an overture.

Turning his thoughts to Ebenezer Druitt, Pyke pondered something the felon had said during their last encounter, and he realised it needed further clarification. But when, about an hour later, he presented himself at the gates of the Model Prison, instead of leading him directly to the cells, the warder took him to the governor's office and left him there without further explanation.

'Ah, yes, this was highly unusual, highly unusual indeed,' the governor said, once they were alone in his office. 'The prisoner you wish to speak to has been transferred by order of the Home Office.'

'Transferred where?'

'I don't know. The order didn't say. The documentation was in order and I couldn't very well say no. A carriage arrived for him yesterday. The documentation stated it was, and I quote, "in defence of the realm".'

Pyke tried to swallow but his throat was suddenly bone dry. 'You'll have to take it up with the Home Office, Detective Inspector.'

'I will,' Pyke said, already halfway across the room. 'Believe me, sir, I'll do just that.'

'Druitt's been transferred to another location, on the orders of someone in the Home Office.' Pyke had gone directly to Scotland Yard and found Walter Wells sitting alone in his office.

'Really?' Wells looked up at him and put down his pen. 'Why?'

'Someone suspects Druitt knows who our killer is and is using his political connections to try to force this information from him.'

'But that kind of request would have to come from a fairly senior figure.'

'I know.' Pyke thought again about Palmer and his association with Mayne. 'I'd like you to try to find out who gave it – and where Druitt has been taken.'

Wells drummed his fingers on his desk. 'I'll do what I can, old man. But I'm afraid my reach extends only so far.'

'My guess is that someone in the Detective Branch passed this information about Druitt to Pierce, who went directly to the Home Office.'

That seemed to strike a chord. 'I think I might have some

information for you on that front. I was going to sit on it for a day, check it out for myself, but in the circumstances ...'

Pyke felt his stomach tightening. 'Sit on what?'

'I have men loyal to me in Holborn Division; policemen who are close to Pierce. From time to time they hear things and pass them back to me.'

'Go on.'

'I had a visit from one such man earlier this afternoon. He told me the identity of Pierce's source of information in the Branch.'

'And?'

Wells shook his head and offered Pyke an apologetic look. 'I'm sorry, Pyke. I know how much you like the man ...'

Pyke followed Jack Whicher into the privy at the back of the station house and before the younger man had even realised there was someone behind him, Pyke had shoved him into the hut and bolted the door. It was damp and fetid and the stench rising up from the cesspit turned his stomach. As soon as Whicher turned around and saw him, saw the expression on his face, he knew. He didn't even try to hide it. His shoulders slumped forward and his head fell, as though the scaffold that had been holding him up until this point had suddenly disintegrated.

'I knew you'd find out sooner or later. If you can believe it, I *wanted* you to find out. At least now I don't have to lie.'

Pyke swung his fist, felt it connect with the side of Whicher's head. Whicher stumbled but didn't fall.

'Why, Jack?'

'I could make it easy and say I despise you and the way you work.' Whicher must have seen the hurt register in Pyke's eyes because instinctively he flinched.

'I just want to know, Jack. Is that the truth?' Pyke was surprised at how badly he was taking the news, how much he'd come to like and respect Whicher.

'Do you really want the truth?' Whicher exhaled loudly, trying to pull himself together. 'Do you want to know how my son died of cholera? How my wife went insane from the grief? Do you *really* want to know how this grief led her back to the work she'd once done? How she turned her back on me and started to sleep with men for money? How a man, one of her customers, hit her in the face and how she retaliated with a pair of scissors? The madam sent for me, and in my panic, and because I trusted him at the time, I sent for Pierce. And he was brilliant. You should know that, too. Pierce took care of it: he paid off the madam, disposed of the body and had my wife admitted to a sanatorium.'

Pyke stood there, not sure what to say. What Whicher had told him had stripped him of his anger but it didn't diminish the betrayal. 'So you did what you did because you felt you owed him?'

'I did what I did because he said he'd prosecute her and me if I didn't.' Whicher shook his head. 'Pierce's brilliance only lasted until you arrived at the department. Then he wanted his pound of flesh. The quid pro quo for his silence was for me to keep him abreast of all the occurrences in the Branch.'

'But from what you've told me, he's just as implicated as you.'

They stood for a moment or two, each contemplating the other, the damage that had been done. Pyke pursed his lips. He knew what the clever thing to do would be: keep Whicher close at hand and have him pass on false information to Pierce. But he felt so betrayed by the man, he couldn't stand the thought of being in the same room as him. 'I accept your explanation, Detective Sergeant, but I want you out of the Detective Branch immediately. You'll go and see the acting superintendent in the morning and you'll ask for an immediate transfer back to uniform. I'll see that the request is approved. I'll also make sure that nothing of what you told me ever comes to light.'

Whicher cast his head down and nodded. He had already accepted his fate. 'You may not believe it, Pyke, but I've always liked you, as a detective and a man.'

Pyke kicked open the privy door and cleared a path for him. 'Now get out of my sight. I never want to see you again.'

For most people, violence was an abstraction; it was something that happened in other parts of the city; a product of poverty and despair. It was what happened when the poorest of the poor were forced to live cheek by jowl and fight for the crumbs brushed off the rich man's table, crumbs that meant the difference between life and death. The truth was that violence, the kind that came from the blackest place in the heart, couldn't be explained in such simple terms.

Pyke was waiting for Benedict Pierce on the pavement outside the Bow Street station house. He made no effort to conceal his presence and Pierce saw him almost as soon as he'd stepped out of the building. But instead of standing there, Pyke darted into one of the alleyways that ran perpendicular to Bow Street. At first, he didn't think that Pierce was going to follow him. He must have counted to thirty before he saw the superintendent's silhouette in the dark mouth of the alleyway. In the end, hubris had got the better of him, as Pyke had been certain it would. Perhaps he was curious, too. He saw Pyke in the shadows and flashed a crooked smile. He didn't see what was coming; Pyke waited until Pierce was almost next to him before he made his move.

Afterwards, Pyke wasn't sure whether he'd ever intended to try to talk to Pierce. It wasn't until he drove his fist deep into the upper reaches of Pierce's stomach that he realised how deeply Whicher's betrayal, and Pierce's part in it, had wounded him. Pyke saw Pierce's mouth flop open. He swung his fist again and landed a blow on Pierce's chin and felt it shatter, then another to the side of Pierce's head, an arch of blood splattering the sleeve of his coat. Pierce coughed, trying to catch his breath as a spool of saliva dribbled from his mouth. He tried to back away but Pyke caught his head in an armlock and punched him in the nose with his other hand. It was as though a gale were blowing in Pyke's ears and everything he saw had a red hue. Swinging Pierce around, Pyke smashed his skull into the brick wall and then stepped back and lifted him up off his feet with a combination of punches. Too far gone to stop, he allowed Pierce to slither on to the wet ground and kicked him so hard in the stomach that the man vomited blood. Benedict Pierce was no longer moving, a near-silent groan from his face-down body the only indication that he was, in fact, alive. And suddenly Pyke was sickened by what he'd just done.

The first gin barely touched the sides of his throat. He stood at the counter and ordered two more, and then two more again. In the yard he had run cold water over his hands, washing the blood from his knuckles. Later, around midnight, when he could no longer talk without slurring or walk in a straight line, the landlord threw him out and he wandered aimlessly for another hour, the wind and the rain sobering him up a little. He'd taken his first drink in the Green Dragon on the Strand. At two o'clock in the morning, he found himself standing on the street in Soho where Sarah Scott had taken a room, not even sure how he'd managed to find his way there. When he banged on her door, it took her a few minutes to answer it and she did so only after he'd identified himself. She had been sleeping; her hair was unkempt and she could barely open her eyes.

'You'd better come in,' she said, assessing him coolly, perhaps smelling the gin on his breath.

The room was as Pyke remembered it: small, frugal, unfurnished. There were no chairs, just a flock mattress that took up most of the floor space. Sarah had already seen his bruised knuckles. Pyke went to embrace her but she pushed him away. The room started to spin.

'Who did you fight?' Sarah asked, gesturing at his fists.

'A superintendent. I did most of the fighting.'

She gave him a quizzical stare. 'Won't that get you into trouble?'

Pyke hadn't really thought about the consequences of his actions, but he didn't believe that Pierce would come at him through official channels. It struck him then that he should have finished the man off. Now he was injured and humiliated, Pierce was an even more dangerous adversary.

'What did he do to you?'

'It's a long story.' Pyke looked around the small room. 'Have you got any gin?'

'No, I'm afraid not.' Sarah rubbed her eyes and yawned. 'I'm sorry. I can't offer you a thing.'

'How was the inquest?'

'Short and to the point. Brendan died by his own hand – an overdose of Prussian acid. It's the funeral that's proving to be a problem. The Catholic Church doesn't want to have anything to do with him.'

'I tried to see Druitt today. He'd been moved to a secret location by order of the Home Office.'

Pyke wanted to assess her reaction but all the gin he'd drunk had blurred his vision and he couldn't tell whether Sarah was concerned or upset by this news. She just folded her arms and said, 'Is that what you came here at two in the morning to tell me?'

'Someone else thinks Druitt knows who's been killing these men. They're going to try and force the information out of him.'

'And am I supposed to feel sorry for him?'

Pyke's mouth felt as if all of the moisture had been leached from it. 'I shouldn't have mentioned him. I'm sorry.'

Sarah cupped Pyke's face in her hands. 'Don't take this the wrong way but I think you should go ...'

Up close he could smell the perfume on her skin. He wanted to tell her that he needed to be with someone, that he needed to be with her, that he wanted to fall asleep next to her, feeling her warmth on his skin.

She tilted her head upwards and pecked him on the cheek ' ... before one of us says something we might regret in the morning.'

The following day was a Sunday and Pyke staggered from his bed, reached blindly for the commode and emptied the contents of his stomach into the bowl. He splashed his face with cold water and dressed quickly, trying to ignore his shaking fingers and the foul taste in his mouth. Downstairs, Felix had made his own breakfast – Mrs Booth had Sundays off – and was eating it in the living room.

'Have you arrested Palmer yet?' Felix looked up hopefully from the bowl of porridge on his lap.

'I don't even know for sure if he's done anything wrong.'

'Then why did you tell me I'd broken the investigation wide open?'

Pyke put his hand to his temple. 'Not now, please. Let me make myself some coffee.'

'I just thought that since we ...'

'*Not now*, all right,' Pyke snapped.

Felix shovelled a spoonful of porridge into his mouth and looked out of the window. 'I'm going to St Matthew's today. I was there yesterday and the day before. Not that you would know. I heard you come in last night about three. The night before that you didn't come home at all.'

Pyke saw how badly he'd failed the lad and how much he must miss Godfrey's steady hand. He was about to apologise when Felix said, 'Mr Leech knocked on the door earlier. I'm surprised you didn't hear him. It seems one of the pigs has escaped again and is stuck in his garden. I said I'd pass on the message. He wasn't very happy.'

Pyke swore under his breath. The last thing he wanted to do was deal with a stranded pig.

'I should have let you know where I was. I had to work late last night ...'

Felix shook his head. 'I heard you crashing around downstairs when you came in. The whole street probably heard you.'

Pyke couldn't face another argument so he let himself out of the back door, making sure Copper remained in the house.

It was a cool, damp morning and the ground was soft, the sky above sealed with clouds. He found Mabel, the fine-boned short-legged pig, in the middle of his neighbour's lawn. The animal had sunk into the hole it had created and was clearly distressed, its short legs unable to propel it out of the muddy morass. From time to time the pig would wriggle, to no avail, and then squeal as if to underline its predicament. The neighbour, Percy Leech, was out there as soon as he saw Pyke, striding down the garden in his boots, his pet spaniel trotting at his heel.

'I really have to object in the strongest possible terms, sir, about the damage that your vile swine has caused in my garden. I insist that you deal with the matter forthwith and make the appropriate reparations.'

The spaniel was circling around the stricken pig, yapping and taking the occasional nip at its tail. It had an irritating, high-pitched bark that was aggravating Pyke's headache to such an extent that he thought he might have to take a shovel to the dog or at the very least aim a kick at its head.

'It would seem that the pig is stuck,' Pyke replied, having wandered around it a few times.

'I didn't ask for a description of what is obvious to me, sir. I told you to do something about it.' Leech's face was hot with anger.

'What can I do? The pig's stuck. If you'd taken better care of your lawn, this wouldn't have happened.' Pyke looked at the grass;

his pig had clearly gone to work on it and now it looked as if an entire regiment had marched across it.

'You dare to accuse me, sir? Before your swine ran amok in my garden, the lawn was in perfect condition.'

The spaniel was still yapping at his heels and Pyke edged it away from him with a sideways move of his boot. 'Can you be sure it was the pig? Perhaps your little dog was trying to find a bone he'd buried earlier.'

'You think my beloved King Charles would be capable of such an act as *this*?' He pointed at the damaged lawn.

But Pyke wasn't listening. Instead, he was trying to remember what he'd said to Sarah Scott and why she'd asked him to leave. He was also thinking about what he'd done to Pierce, what the ramifications of it might be, and the damage he'd caused, not just to Pierce personally but also to the investigation. In the cold light of day, Pyke could see that his actions had been rash and stupid.

Retracing his steps back to his own garden, and more particularly to the shed where he kept his tools, Pyke collected a shovel and a hatchet then rejoined Leech, who was still trying to pull his spaniel away from the stranded pig. Pyke's thoughts returned to Whicher. It was a hard, unforgiving world and the sooner he remembered that, the better. Standing over the animal and ignoring the sudden protestations of his neighbour, Pyke took the hatchet, lifted up the pig's head and sliced the blade across its throat. Mabel's squeals were quite unlike anything he had heard before. When he looked down at the blade of the hatchet, he saw it was dripping with fresh blood and it made him want to vomit. The pig, which just a few moments ago had been writhing in the mud, had stopped moving. Now a vast pool of blood had extended around its head and was still flowing from the wound. It was really quite obscene. Even in the stiff breeze, you could smell it: at once rich, sweet and rancid.

'There,' Pyke said, wiping the blade of the hatchet on a patch of grass. 'I won't charge you for the meat. Think of it as reparation for the lawn.'

Leech was speechless, and even the dog had stopped barking.

Pyke turned suddenly and saw that Felix had followed him into the garden and had been watching from the other side of the wall. It was hard to make sense of the look on his face but later Pyke kept coming back to the same words. Revulsion. Fascination. Horror.

TWENTY-TWO

Pyke had organised and carried out the searches of many houses, and some time during the previous day it had struck him what a cursory, even half-hearted, job he had made of the search at St Botolph's. He hadn't thought to look up the chimney or search behind the skirting boards or lift up the floorboards or get down on his hands and knees and work his way from one end of the cellar and loft to the other. In light of his suspicions regarding the Churches Fund, or at least the fact that Guppy and Hogarth might have known one another via Palmer, this failure now seemed like a glaring oversight.

On Monday morning, Pyke arrived at the rectory before eight and banged on the door. No one answered, and through one of the windows he noticed that dustsheets were now covering the large items of furniture. He knocked again, then took out his picklocks and had the door open in less than five minutes. The air in the hallway was musty, and the house eerily quiet.

Pyke had decided to start his search in Guppy's study. Pausing at the door, he looked at the desk, now emptied of papers, and the shelves, cleared of books. Perhaps there had been evidence of malpractice hidden there, but it was too late to worry about it. Pyke cleared the room of the remaining items of furniture, took the jemmy he'd brought with him and prised off the skirting boards one by one. He didn't find anything so turned his attention to the chimney. It wasn't a large one and he couldn't fully stand up inside it, so he had to reach in and pat the walls with his hands. Taking up the floorboards was a much larger job, and he moved across the floor looking for any loose ones first. When he didn't find any he returned to the corner nearest to where the desk had stood and started there. Using the jemmy, he had got six rows along when he reached down into the space below and touched what felt like a cloth package. Pulling it up, he put it on the floor and started to unwrap it.

Pyke wanted to believe that his motives were transparent, and that his actions could be explained in terms of the particular task he had to perform. So when he entered St Paul's Cathedral via the west door, and after some minutes found the archdeacon, Adolphus Wynter, dressed in his ceremonial robes, talking to parishioners, he told himself that he was simply going where the investigation took him. But at some deeper level, he knew this claim to neutrality was a lie and that he wanted to cause the archdeacon as much discomfort as possible: to tear off the mask of piety that men like Wynter hid behind.

Sometimes it was best to come at your adversaries from an oblique angle, in a way they least expected. At other times it paid to adopt a more direct approach: to shake the tree and see what fell out. Wynter doubtless believed that he was safe, standing there in his place of worship, wearing his colourful robes, surrounded by people who hung on his every word. Pyke intended to disabuse him of this notion. Wynter saw him as he was walking up the aisle but kept talking to his circle of admirers, as though Pyke wasn't worth bothering about. Pyke pushed his way through and said, his voice slightly raised: 'I want to know exactly what Guppy did for the London Churches Fund and why he was permitted to steal from under your noses.'

For a moment, no one in the circle spoke, all looking towards the archdeacon for reassurance. Wynter seemed unable to comprehend that he had been treated with so little respect not merely in a place of worship – *his* place of worship – but in the most sacred place in the entire city. Pyke couldn't have done a better job if he'd unbuttoned his trousers and relieved himself on the floor.

'Are you insane?' Wynter whispered finally, his small, quick eyes darting around the group.

'Did you know one of your flock was nakedly corrupt? Did you just decide to turn a blind eye, or were you an active participant in his corruption?'

'This, sir, is a place of God,' the archdeacon murmured. 'Take your grubbiness and leave at once.'

Another man, also in robes but older than Wynter, approached Pyke, ashen faced. 'Who are you, sir, and what do you want?'

This interruption gave the archdeacon a chance to recover. His lips puckered with barely repressed anger. 'Your superiors will hear about this.'

Pyke didn't doubt that Mayne would hear about this confrontation, and perhaps also his interrogation of Palmer, but now he had what he'd found under the floorboards in Guppy's study as ammunition, he could throw it back at his accusers. Still, he knew that he was taking a risk, and that his position was now vulnerable. As he pushed his way through the crowd and walked back up the aisle, he could hear the consternation among the parishioners. As he stared up at the cavernous ceiling, his thoughts turned suddenly, and without apparent explanation, to the man he'd known as the Owl.

It took a little over three hours for Sir Richard Mayne to hear about the incident in St Paul's and another hour for him to assemble the necessary people to deal with the situation. When Pyke was finally called up to Mayne's office, he was surprised to see that his friend and the former assistant commissioner, Fitzroy Tilling, was there, together with Rowan and Mayne. There was nothing accidental about the way in which the room had been arranged either. The chair left for Pyke was directly opposite the ones occupied by Tilling and Rowan: they were the jury; Mayne, sitting behind his desk, was the judge. As Pyke entered, they were discussing the injuries that Benedict Pierce had sustained in an assault that had taken place near his place of work.

'Detective Inspector Pyke,' Mayne said, coldly. 'Please take a seat. Of course, you know Commissioner Rowan and Fitzroy Tilling, who is here in his capacity as private secretary to the prime minister.' Mayne paused. 'It would seem that the prime minister was visited a day or two ago by Bishop Blomfield and was forced to reassure the bishop that the Metropolitan Police was *not* investigating the activities of the London Churches Fund which the prime minister represents as a member of the executive board.' The commissioner's face was hot with anger. 'I also received a visit from a good friend of mine, Sir St John Palmer, who told me that you had interrogated him regarding his associations with Hogarth and Guppy.'

Pyke exchanged a brief look with Tilling. He had known Tilling for fifteen years and during this time their mutual suspicion and, at times, antipathy had slowly changed into something approaching friendship. Tilling was a big, clumsy man with olive skin, a receding hairline and dark, bug-like eyes. For most of his working life, he'd faithfully served Sir Robert Peel in one capacity or another, first in Ireland and then in Whitehall. More recently he had served as the assistant commissioner, but after Peel had won the election in '41, Tilling had been called back into the fold.

'Perhaps you would care to tell us what possessed you to walk into a place of worship and accuse one of the most important clerics in the city of corruption?' Mayne asked. His face was tight and hard.

'I didn't accuse the archdeacon of corruption. I asked him why he hadn't acted to curtail the corrupt practices of a person in his charge.'

'But in St Paul's Cathedral, man?' Rowan interrupted. 'And in front of the congregation? Have you no discretion?'

'As the commissioners, Detective Inspector, we've had to field visits from a respected businessman and the archdeacon himself. Both of these men have categorically demanded your head on a pole,' Mayne added.

'Your behaviour, as an ambassador of the Metropolitan Police, has been unacceptable. Totally unacceptable,' Rowan spat. 'I'm proposing that we suspend Detective Inspector Pyke with immediate effect and move to dismiss him, if the accusations made against him are found to be true.'

In spite of the seriousness of these threats Pyke chose to ignore them and direct his remarks to Mayne. 'Perhaps the question you should be asking, Sir Richard, is what drove me to make these accusations in the first place.'

'Defaming a churchman in his place of worship is sufficient to warrant your immediate dismissal,' Rowan said.

'I've just been doing my job, Sir Charles,' Pyke said, turning to look at him. 'But if you'd rather I take what I've found elsewhere, to the newspapers, for instance, that of course is your prerogative.'

Almost at once, Pyke noticed a subtle shift in the mood of his inquisitors. For the first time Tilling spoke. 'I think we should hear what Detective Inspector Pyke has to say and assess his findings on their own merit.'

'Elaborate, Detective Inspector,' Mayne said.

Pyke removed what he had found under the floorboards in Guppy's study and slammed the documents down on Mayne's desk.

'Did you know that Isaac Guppy, the recently deceased rector at St Botolph's in Aldgate, had managed to accrue a little over forty-three thousand pounds in six different bank accounts by the time of his death?'

Tilling shifted uncomfortably in his chair and looked at Mayne, who was inspecting the documents Pyke had presented to him. 'I'd say this changes the situation somewhat.'

'The question is: how did the rector of a moderately wealthy parish manage to squirrel away that amount of money? It would be quite impossible to do so simply out of parish funds. The gross annual income of the parish, I'm told, is no more than four thousand pounds, and out of that salaries are paid and expenses defrayed. It would take many, many years to build up as much as forty thousand from general funds, and Guppy had only been rector for three.'

An uneasy silence descended while all three men digested the information that Pyke had just presented them with.

'But I'm assuming you have nothing to indicate that Guppy took this money from the London Churches Fund,' Tilling said eventually.

Pyke now understood why Tilling had come to the meeting.

'Guppy served in an administrative capacity on the Churches Fund, I believe. It should be investigated.'

'A very minor capacity, as I understand it,' Tilling retorted. 'But I'm told that Bishop Blomfield is happy for the Fund's accounts to be inspected.'

Pyke nodded. He grasped what he was implicitly being told: *you won't find anything amiss.* 'I also want to interview a prisoner who was transferred from the Model Prison at Pentonville to an undisclosed location by order of the Home Office.'

Mayne was about to speak but Tilling cut in and said, 'I think that can be arranged.' It told Pyke all he needed to know; that

Druitt's transfer had been sanctioned at the very highest level.

'You have to learn some tact, Detective Inspector, some basic respect for the offices of church and state,' Rowan stated, glancing over at Mayne. He had clearly wanted to wound Pyke and seemed disappointed.

Mayne nodded vigorously. 'Further outbursts such as the scene today in St Paul's will not be tolerated. Is that understood?' He waited a moment then added, 'And you're to leave Sir St John Palmer alone.'

Pyke composed himself then said, 'Children have been killed. Do you understand? *Children*. And no one cared because they were poor. All you seem to be concerned about is not upsetting men like Palmer and Wynter ...'

Neither Mayne nor Rowan seemed to know how to respond. Perhaps, Pyke speculated afterwards, no one had ever spoken to them in such a manner. He stood and walked over to the door. He'd reached the bottom of the stairs when Tilling called out his name.

'It isn't a good idea to antagonise a man like Sir Richard,' he said, once he'd caught his breath.

'Nice to see you too, Fitzroy.' That elicited a wry smile. Pyke added, 'Even if your role here is to make certain nothing untoward about the Churches Fund ever comes to light.'

A flash of irritation passed across Tilling's face. 'You always did have a flair for making others feel morally soiled. And you never did have much time for the Church.'

'I've never found piety and crookedness to be an attractive combination, if that's what you mean.'

Tilling took out his fob-watch and checked the time. 'You're quite right that Peel won't tolerate the Fund's good name being dragged through the mud.'

'Is Peel telling me how to do my job?'

'No one could possibly do that.' Tilling laughed bitterly. 'Peel knows that, as well as I do.'

Pyke acknowledged the barbed compliment with a nod. 'Tell me, Fitzroy. How did you know about the prisoner being moved from Pentonville?'

'Who said I did?'

'I want to know who put in the request to have him moved.'

Tilling stared at him, as though assessing how much he knew. 'I was concerned to hear about the horrendous assault on Superintendent Pierce.' When Pyke didn't respond, he added, 'You were never on friendly terms with the man, were you?'

Pyke had been wearing gloves to hide the cuts and bruises on his knuckles. Instinctively he put his hands behind his back. Tilling gestured at Pyke's gloves. 'I wonder what I might find if I asked you to take them off.'

'My hands, Fitzroy. You'd find eight good fingers and two thumbs.'

Tilling said as he walked away, 'There's always a line, Pyke. I hope for your sake you haven't already crossed it.'

Two days later, after Pyke's painstaking scrutiny of the Churches Fund's accounts had revealed no evidence of malpractice, he presented himself at Traitor's Gate at the Tower of London. Minutes later, he was escorted over the dry moat and past the Wakefield Tower to the Queen's House, where Druitt was being held. Pyke hadn't realised that the Tower was still being used to house prisoners, and being within its ancient walls made him think about the way in which the authorities had once dealt with threats to their authority: the rack, the press, hanging, drawing, quartering. Such monolithic power had long since dissipated in this enlightened, democratic time, or so they were told, but as Pyke looked up at the Bloody Tower and thought about all of those who had been killed there, he wondered how much had really changed.

After a flight of stone stairs, Pyke was led along a narrow passageway, through a reinforced door guarded by a turnkey, and then to a row of cells, all of which were empty, apart from the final one. The warder produced a key and inserted it into the lock. Then he slid back the iron bolts at the top and bottom of the door and, with both hands, pulled it open.

Ebenezer Druitt was sitting on a pile of straw, head bowed. His ankles and wrists were in chains. When he looked up and saw Pyke, his expression didn't change. He had been badly beaten; his nose was broken, there was bruising around both of his eyes, his cheek was swollen and one of his teeth was missing.

'When I realised they were bringing me here, I expected to be subjected to torture. Unfortunately the methods my interrogators have used have been drearily predictable.' When he smiled, Druitt revealed his bloodied gums.

Pyke stood with his back to the door. 'What have they been asking you?'

'What do you imagine, Detective Inspector?'

'I'm guessing they want to know who killed Guppy and Hogarth. They want the killer's name.'

Druitt moved a little and winced from the pain. 'Unfortunately for them, I was unable to provide this information. I rather fear my relocation has been a waste of time.'

'And do you know who *they* are?' Pyke looked down at him. 'These men who've been interrogating you?'

'Funny you should mention it, Detective Inspector, but to be quite honest, they haven't bothered to introduce themselves.'

'You could always tell me what you're keeping from them.'

Druitt rolled his eyes. 'Very clever, Detective Inspector. Forge a bond with the prisoner by implicitly establishing a common enemy.'

'Who said they're my enemies?'

'Oh, they will be, if you push hard enough.' Druitt tried to smile.

'Push hard enough at what?'

'Do you imagine we're so very different, Detective Inspector? That we want such very different things?'

'I couldn't say. I have no idea what you want.'

'But I can see in your eyes you're less hostile than you were. You've found out some things, haven't you? It's put you in a difficult position vis-à-vis your superiors.'

Pyke tried to conceal what he was thinking. Druitt's grin widened. 'They don't want you to continue with your investigation … they want you to crawl back under your stone and pretend everything in the garden is sweet-smelling.'

'Guppy stole more than forty thousand pounds,' Pyke said, eventually. 'Did it come from the London Churches Fund?'

'The fact that you're good at your job is threatening to many people. I can't emphasise enough how careful you need to be.'

'Perhaps if you were to give me a nudge in the right direction, I could do my job a little better.'

Druitt leaned back against the bare wall and shut his eyes.

'I've seen the Churches Fund's official accounts. Perhaps you know something I don't.' Pyke waited. 'Is there another set of accounts?'

Druitt opened his eyes suddenly. 'Just do your job, Detective, and let me worry about the rest.'

'The rest?' When Druitt refused to answer, Pyke added, 'Is whoever killed Guppy and Hogarth planning to strike again?'

That elicited a subtle shake of the head. 'A predictable question, Detective Inspector. Very predictable.'

'When I visited you in your Pentonville cell, how did you know I was reading *The Fable of the Bees*?'

This time Druitt just stared at the wall in front of him. 'I didn't. But I suspect we're both attracted by Mandeville's bleak vision, his desire to rip off the veil of hypocrisy that surrounds us and see virtue for what it really is.'

The sky was still blue by the time Pyke returned home. Felix hadn't come back from school and Mrs Booth had gone to the shops. With only Copper for company, Pyke let himself out into the garden to check on the two remaining pigs. The ground was still hard from the previous night's frost. As Pyke peered over at the lowest point of the wall into his neighbour's garden, he saw Mabel's carcass still lying where he'd killed her, all the blood having long since drained into the soil.

Back in the house, he had just heated up a pot of coffee when someone knocked on the door. Copper sniffed the air and hobbled on his three legs into the hallway. Shoving the mastiff into the living room, Pyke turned the handle on the front door and pulled it open, expecting to see a delivery boy or a door-to-door hawker.

There were five or six of them; police constables, all wearing their uniforms. Pyke didn't recognise any of them.

Two of them rushed towards him and bundled him on to the floor. The coffee cup fell from his hand and Copper started to bark and scratch at the living-room door. Two of the constables sat on him while the others attached handcuffs and leg-irons. It all happened in the blink of an eye.

'Who authorised this?' Pyke said, thinking it was all a terrible mistake.

One of the men, perhaps a sergeant, ignored him and said to the other men, 'Bring him out into the garden.'

'I'm Detective Inspector Pyke, head of the Detective Branch ...'

The sergeant looked at him, his moustache twitching on his upper lip. 'I know *exactly* who you are.'

Ignoring Copper's increasingly frantic barks, the policemen dragged him through the house and outside into the garden. There, his neighbour Leech was waiting, together with his pet spaniel. Leech followed the dog to a flower bed on the left-hand side of the garden. The policeman in charge joined them, Pyke shuffling along behind, escorted by the four constables. Leech was holding a shovel and, when the sergeant nodded, he started to dig. Pyke didn't have any idea what they were looking for, but he knew they were going to find something.

They all heard the shovel strike a hard object in the ground. It took Leech and two constables another minute to scoop out enough earth from the hole to retrieve whatever was there. Dry mouthed and fearing the worst, Pyke watched as they lifted out a wooden box he had never seen before. It was the size of a small chest. Carefully they placed it on the grass and one of the constables took a hammer and bashed off the padlock. The sergeant stepped in and opened the box; even before he'd done so he smiled, as though he already knew what he was going to find there.

Pyke recognised the object immediately. What he didn't know was how it had come to be buried in his back garden. They had just found the Saviour's Cross.

Bow Street

JANUARY 1845

TWENTY-THREE

Pyke pulled the threadbare blanket over his shoulders and tried to get comfortable on the floor of his cell. The stone was as hard and cold as ice and a bitter draught eddied around the confined space. It was dark but not completely; candlelight from the passageway trickled through the peephole in the cell door, which had been left open so the gaoler could check on him every hour. The handcuffs had been removed but not the leg-irons, and as an extra precaution they had been chained to the wall, which made sleeping difficult. Clearly they, whoever *they* were, were taking no chances. Given that he had been taken to the cells at Bow Street, where Pierce was the commander, it was clear to Pyke that Pierce must have orchestrated the arrest from his hospital bed, and had been planning it for some time. Still, the question of how Pierce had been able to lay his hands on the Saviour's Cross was unclear, as was the question of who had sanctioned his arrest. Pyke assumed it had come from the very highest level and he thought about his last exchange with Mayne.

Since arriving in his cell, Pyke had tried to assess the strength of the case against him; how they would attempt to prove his involvement in the theft. He wasn't naive enough to think his neighbour's testimony alone would be sufficient to get a conviction, which meant there would be other so-called witnesses, and perhaps more fabricated evidence.

Pyke knew this row of cells very well. Little had changed in the fifteen years since he'd left the Bow Street Runners, and while the Runners themselves had long since been disbanded and the building taken over by the Metropolitan Police, the smell of the passage, the sound of clanking keys and the slamming doors reminded him of the time he'd spent there. Then, of course, he'd been the one in charge. It was revealing that none of the constables who'd accompanied him from Islington had wanted to meet his eyes or acknowledge him as one of their own.

It was also true that Pyke had been in this position before. Fifteen years earlier, he had been arrested, tried and convicted of murdering his mistress, Lizzie Morgan, and had evaded the hangman's noose only by escaping from Newgate prison and eventually earning a pardon from Peel himself. As a younger man, he'd had little faith in the legal system and hadn't bothered to defend himself in court, believing that the jury had been instructed to return a guilty verdict irrespective of what he said. Now that he was a serving policeman, however, his view of the law was more balanced. The system was skewed towards vested interests, as all institutions were, but rarely was someone convicted of a crime like theft or murder without overwhelming evidence pointing to their guilt.

That first night, Pyke slept fitfully under the meagre blanket and thought often about Felix and what his son would do when he saw the scribbled note that Pyke had left for him. As watery daylight leaked through the barred window, Pyke listened to the sounds drifting down from the street: the rattle of the drays and carts, horses' hooves, the clanking as street vendors set up their stalls. At seven or thereabouts, a bowl of cold, inedible gruel was shoved through the door, and half an hour later he was unshackled and led to a bare room where Superintendent Walter Wells was waiting for him. He waited for the gaoler to leave them alone.

'I had to fight for this detail, believe me,' he said. 'I'm not sure that Sir Richard trusts me to act impartially, but in light of Pierce's condition, and given that I am the acting superintendent, he couldn't very well deny me the right to question you.'

Pyke thought about his first impressions of Wells, of a barely tethered aggression, but now he saw that the man's heavy features were mitigated by a kindness in his eyes.

'As I've been telling you for months, old man, I knew that our friend from this building had something planned for you but I had no idea what a thorough job he'd make of it.'

'I presume my arrest was sanctioned by Rowan and Mayne,' Pyke said, leaning back against his chair.

'I'm told Sir Richard baulked at the idea initially. In his eyes, he's made a great personal investment in you and knows he'll be implicated in the mess.'

Wells was telling him that the evidence that Pierce had accrued, or that he'd managed to concoct, was strong. Otherwise Pyke's arrest would never have been allowed.

'How about you, Walter? When did you hear I'd been arrested?'

'I only found out after the event. But as I said, I did my utmost to make sure I was the one who would carry out this interview.'

Pyke studied Wells's face. 'Tell me, Walter. How bad does it look?'

'Bad enough.' Wells took out his snuff box, brought a pinch of the powder up to his nostrils and sniffed. 'But before we get to the evidence, I need to ask you a few questions.' Wells gestured to the quire of foolscap in front of him on the desk. 'For the report I'll have to write.'

Pyke folded his arms and nodded.

'Do you have any idea how the Saviour's Cross, a highly valuable religious artefact stolen from the private domicile of the Archdeacon of London on ...' He glanced down at another piece of paper. ' ... on the seventh of March last year, came to be buried in your garden?'

'Someone put it there to incriminate me.'

'So it is your assertion that you were in no way responsible for its theft and the subsequent efforts to find a buyer for it?'

'That's correct.'

Wells took his pen, dipped it in the ink, and scratched a few words on to a piece of foolscap. 'Of course, I know this to be so but I need to make quite sure I have asked all of the questions that Sir Richard will, at some stage, ask me.' He waited for a moment and then continued, 'So by the same logic, the testimony of your neighbour, Percy Leech, who claims he saw you digging in the same spot where the cross was found, is a bare-faced lie.'

'He's been angry at me for a long time because my pigs keep escaping from their sty and ruining his garden.'

'Good, so he can be discredited on the stand.' Wells had moved seamlessly from being Pyke's accuser to his advocate. 'Perhaps we can talk about this fellow Sharp, then. You fought and arrested him earlier this year, apparently on suspicion of him having stolen the cross in the first place.'

Pyke looked across the table at Wells and nodded.

'The Crown is going to try to claim that you and he were partners-in-crime. That the two of you arranged the theft from the archdeacon's home together and planned to split the proceeds.'

Pyke knew Wells was taking a risk by telling him this. 'But if that was true, why would I go to the effort of trying to arrest him? By doing so, I'd be laying myself open to his accusations.'

'The Crown's case is essentially that you decided to claim all of the spoils for yourself while putting the blame on Sharp. They will argue that you intended to kill Sharp before he got anywhere near a prison cell. They'll call on the testimony of witnesses who saw you chase and fight with Sharp in an alleyway behind Field Lane. I've seen some of the statements: you're variously described as an animal and a man hell-bent on murder. You get the idea.'

Pyke turned his mind back to the struggle. 'He punched, kicked and stabbed me; I was fighting for my life.'

Wells smiled. 'I know that. I'm just trying to tell you how the Crown's lawyer is going to come at you.'

'And I appreciate it, Walter. So what else have they got?' He knew this couldn't be the sum of their case against him.

'After you failed to kill Sharp, the Crown is going to claim that you returned to the cells that night and finished him off; that you drugged and strangled him and then made it look like he'd hanged himself.'

Pyke nodded; he could see where this was going, and the potential danger he was in. 'Even though I was two miles away at the time, injured, in St Bartholomew's?'

'They'll claim that since you were well enough to leave your hospital bed the next day, you would have been well enough to have taken a cab from the hospital to Scotland Yard on the night that Sharp died.'

'They have a witness, do they?'

Wells leaned forward over the desk, and whispered, 'The gaoler, for a start. Apparently he'll testify that he saw you go down into the cells on the night in question.'

'So why did he wait this long to come forward; especially as he was dismissed from his position in the aftermath of Sharp's death?'

'I'm told he'll claim he was too afraid of you to want to risk testifying against you.'

'Is that it?' Pyke suddenly felt a lot better about his prospects. The gaoler was a drunk and his testimony would be riddled with inconsistencies, and therefore be demolished in court.

But Wells's expression hadn't brightened. 'I'm reliably told we have a man called Alfred Egan, too.'

An image of the slight, hatchet-faced fence he'd seen that night in the Red Lion flashed through his mind. Pyke knew immediately this was bad news: not only had Egan been in the cells at the time Sharp died; he would also be able to insinuate, from an insider's perspective, that Pyke and Sharp were partners and that Pyke had done what the Crown were accusing him of. In effect, he could make their whole case. But like the gaoler, Egan hadn't come forward with any of this at the time. More to the point, as a receiver of stolen goods with a criminal record, his testimony could not be treated as vouchsafe. A good lawyer would tear him apart on the stand.

'Egan's a fence. A common criminal.'

'But he was there in the cells that night and he's willing to testify that he saw you and that he heard you kill Sharp. He's also going to confirm that you and Sharp were partners from the beginning.'

So there it was. Pyke had to admit that Pierce had done a good job. But the situation wasn't devoid of hope. Admittedly, it did look bad for him, but the evidence against him wasn't as strong as it first appeared. The credibility of the witnesses left a lot to be desired; the length of time since the summer played in his favour; and there was no proof that Sharp had, in fact, been killed. The coroner's inquest had returned a verdict of suicide. The fact that the cross had been found in his garden was a mark against him, of course, but his neighbour's testimony could be discounted because of their long history of animosity.

'So what happens next?'

Wells took another pinch of snuff. 'Well, the Crown's lawyers feel they have sufficient evidence to move directly to trial. Of course, you have the right to a hearing and if you do decide to exercise this right, the various bits of evidence against you will be laid out. You can waive this right on condition that the Crown comes clean and tells you what they've got in their arsenal. In which case, they'll tell you pretty much what I've just told you.'

Pyke tried to make sense of what Wells had just said. 'You're implying I'd be better off going straight to trial?'

'Look, old man, it's my guess that the trial will go ahead anyway. As I've just said, they have enough evidence to convince a magistrate. If you agree to waive your right to a pre-trial hearing, I can arrange for you to stay here. As we speak, I'm having someone prepare the old felons' room, a coal fire, a proper mattress, food, drink – whatever you want, within reason, of course. I can also arrange for you to see visitors here, again within reason. If you have a pre-trial hearing, it's very likely the magistrate will send you to Coldbath Fields and I won't be able to do anything for you there. And the greeting that awaits you, as a policeman, won't be the warmest.'

Pyke could certainly see the logic of what Wells was suggesting; how it would benefit him to remain where he was at Bow Street.

'I'll think about it, Walter,' he said. 'And thanks for everything you've done for me already.'

Wells gathered up the papers on the desk. 'Hang in there, old man. We'll find a way of beating Pierce yet.'

Pyke pondered what he should do next. Egan was the ace in their hand. All Pyke had to do was find a way of getting to him before the trial began.

True to Wells's word, Pyke was transferred to the felons' room later that afternoon and the space had been prepared just as Wells had promised. A coal fire was burning in the grate, a flock mattress, with bedlinen and blankets, had been pushed up against one of the walls, and a tray of food and drink – cold meats, cheese, fresh bread and a tankard of beer – had been left for him. With its barred window and metal-plated door, the felons' room was still as impregnable as any of the cells, but, presumably at Wells's insistence, Pyke's leg-irons were removed, meaning he was free to move around.

Pyke's first visitor was Felix. Pyke offered him the mattress but Felix said he'd prefer to stand. Proudly, he offered Pyke a hip-flask filled with gin which he'd smuggled past the guards.

'Obviously I can't ask him myself but I'd like you to go and stay with the Reverend Jakes, at least until the trial.' Pyke paused. 'Do you know if he has the room?'

'I think so.' Felix bowed his head, perhaps contemplating his future if Pyke didn't earn his freedom.

'Good. I'll write to him and send a note to Mrs Booth. I'll get her to look after Copper.'

'Can't I stay at the house, too?'

'I think you'd be better off at the vicarage with Jakes and Kitty.'

Felix seemed torn and remained silent.

'I also need you to do something *very* important for me,' Pyke said a few moments later. He didn't like the lad to see him in these circumstances, but there were practical things he needed Felix to do. In the past Pyke would have relied on his uncle for assistance but now he'd been forced to turn to his son. The gaping hole that Godfrey had left in his life, in both of their lives, was even more apparent than usual.

Felix nodded. 'Anything. I'll do anything.'

Smiling, Pyke reached out and squeezed his son's hand. 'I need you to find a man called Ned Villums. He has an office on St John's Square in Clerkenwell. I want you to tell him what's happened; that I've been arrested for stealing something called the Saviour's Cross. I want you to tell him the police have Alfred Egan. He'll know what to do, what it all means.'

In fact, Pyke had not seen or heard from Villums since the summer, and he still felt that Villums blamed him for letting Sharp die in police custody, therefore robbing him of the opportunity to avenge Harry Dove's death. Dove had apparently gone to Cullen's pawn shop to inspect the Saviour's Cross. Most likely, Sharp had entered the shop, pistols blazing, and had stolen the cross for himself. So how had it fallen into Pierce's hands, and how had it ended up in *his* garden?

Pyke tried to remember the name of the third victim. Johnny Gibb. Was that the name Shaw had told him?

In a small, quiet voice, Felix looked at the flint walls and said, 'Is it true what they're all saying? That you stole this cross and buried it in our garden?'

'No, it's not true. Someone put it there to make me look guilty. I plan to prove that in court.'

Pyke could see at once that his son wasn't entirely convinced. 'But before ... you *did* steal some gold bars and you buried them at the allotment near our old house.'

Pyke pursed his lips. This much was true: he had acquired the gold during an investigation three or four years earlier and had made the mistake of showing the bars to Felix. Now the lad clearly believed he was in the habit of stealing valuable items.

Clasping his hands around Felix's shoulders, he looked into the lad's eyes. 'I didn't take that cross. I swear it on your mother's grave. I need you to believe me.'

Felix relaxed a little. 'I do believe you, Pyke.' This time it sounded as if he really did.

'I need you to find this man, Ned Villums. If he's not in his office, you'll have to go to his home. He lives on Park Road, overlooking Regent's Park. I don't know which house, so you'll have to ask.'

'Copper must have gone berserk after you were arrested. When I got home, he'd torn up the living room.'

Pyke smiled. 'Come back and see me tomorrow, if you can.'

Felix lingered by the door, biting his lip. 'What if you don't manage to get out of here?'

'I will; one way or another.'

'But if you don't?'

This time Pyke had no answer.

With some decent food and a pint of ale in his stomach, Pyke slept well that night and had already eaten breakfast by the time Fitzroy Tilling was ushered into the felons' room at eight the following morning. Tilling embraced Pyke and regarded him with an expression that combined disappointment and concern. 'God, what a mess you've got yourself into this time, Pyke.'

'I didn't get myself into anything. I was just doing what I'm paid to do. I was fine when my only suspect was a former convict. But as soon as the investigation threatened to implicate men like Sir St John Palmer, the Saviour's Cross suddenly turned up in my garden.'

'So what do you do now?' Tilling asked, looking around the cell.

'The case is going to go directly to trial. Neither the prosecution nor I want a committal hearing. I know the basis of their case against me. It's up to me, and the barrister I instruct, to dismantle it piece by piece.' As Pyke said this, he realised that he'd already made up his mind to accept Wells's offer.

'Is that wise? What if the Crown's lawyer comes up with something you aren't expecting in the trial?'

Pyke considered this for a moment. It wasn't just the question of trusting Wells that he was hesitant about. 'After a committal hearing, the magistrate would be duty bound to send me to somewhere like Coldbath Fields. At least here I can see visitors and prepare my defence with relative ease.'

Tilling glanced around the cell again and said, 'Yes, I suppose you do seem to be rather comfortable.'

'For what it's worth, I didn't steal this crucifix. I'd swear to that, on my son's life.'

'And for what it's worth, I believe you. But I'm afraid there's nothing I can do for you this time. Nothing at all. Peel just wants this to go away. The last thing he needs is a scandal involving a project his name has been attached to.'

'And so I'm the sacrificial lamb?'

Tilling ignored the question. 'Who do you think orchestrated this whole thing?'

'Pierce.'

Tilling made his way over to Pyke and inspected his hands, bruises still visible on his knuckles. 'Because of what you did to him?'

'This has been much longer in the planning. But I should have killed him when I had the chance.'

'I'll pretend I didn't hear that,' Tilling said, impassively. 'So if not Pierce, who is leading this investigation for the police?'

'Walter Wells, the acting superintendent.'

'And is that a good thing? For you, I mean?'

'I think he and I understand one another; I don't think he has any great love for Pierce, either.'

'I don't know him very well, but I've heard on good authority that he's going to be the new assistant commissioner. My old position.'

'Not Pierce?'

'Pierce? I'm not sure he was ever a possibility.' Tilling looked at Pyke and sighed. 'Just don't expect Wells to ride to your rescue. He's going to do as he's told by Mayne and Rowan. The last thing he'll want to do is rock the boat – or let you rock it for him.'

TWENTY-FOUR

Later that night, just before his candle burned out, the gaoler and two assistants came into the felons' room and without explanation put Pyke in handcuffs and leg-irons. An hour or so later, he heard footsteps coming down the stairs. They stopped outside his door. Pyke heard a jangling of keys and waited while the bolt was drawn back. Finally the door swung open. Squinting, Pyke looked up at the cloaked figure silhouetted in the half-light from the passageway. He saw the walking stick before he saw the man's face, which was partly concealed by a top hat. The man limped into the cell and Pyke knew at once who he was. In his other hand, Benedict Pierce was carrying a wooden club. He pushed the door closed.

'I'd like to tell you that I've come here to gloat, Pyke, but that would be a lie.' Pierce looked around the room disapprovingly. 'I can't say I would have permitted such luxury. In the long run, I don't suspect it will matter.'

Each step caused Pierce to wince, and by the time he had made it to where Pyke was sitting, his face was lathered with sweat. Without another word, he raised the club and slammed it against the top of Pyke's arm, the pain arriving a few moments later, a scalding sensation that tore up and down one side of his body. Grunting, Pierce raised the club again and this time drove it into Pyke's midriff, cracking his ribs in the process. Another streak of pain tore across his chest.

Pyke heard the club scything through the air before he saw it, the smooth, round end striking him in the midriff again. Pierce rested for a moment and then brought the head of the club down on Pyke's hand, then his groin. The pain was unlike anything Pyke had ever known, and before he passed into unconsciousness, his agonised shriek bounced off the walls of the cell.

*

When Pyke came around, it was already light and someone had removed the handcuffs and leg-irons, but even the slightest movement caused him to shout out in pain. Keeping as still as possible, he closed his eyes and drifted back to sleep. When he opened them next, he saw that Walter Wells was kneeling down next to him. 'Drink this, old man, it'll help with the pain,' he said, cupping the back of Pyke's head with his hand. Pyke tasted the laudanum on his lips and swallowed. 'I don't know how this could have happened. I left very clear instructions that *he* was not to be admitted to this room. I suppose it is his station house, but I can promise you it won't happen again. Not that I can use this against him. Officially no one saw him. Officially you tripped and fell and did this to yourself.' Pyke sipped some more of the laudanum and waited for it to have an effect. The relief spread from his stomach, a warm, numbing sensation. A few minutes later, his eyelids drooped and his arms became leaden.

When Pyke next woke up, it was almost dark. Someone had lit a candle and a fire was spitting in the grate. Pyke raised his head slightly and grunted from the pain. He felt a hand on his brow, a soft, feminine touch; Sarah Scott was sitting next to him. When she saw that he was awake and had recognised her, she smiled and kissed him softly on the lips. Her skin glowed in the candlelight. She was so lovely to him in that moment that Pyke forgot about the pain. He tried to speak but she put a finger to his lips and whispered, 'Save your strength for now.' She fed him some more laudanum and held his hand, her fingers coiled around his.

He woke later in the night as someone shook him roughly by the collar. Startled, he sat up, the pain from his ribs causing him to wince. He hadn't even heard the door open. Looking up, he saw Sergeant Russell. The man was grinning. There was someone else in the cell, too. Sir St John Palmer stepped out from behind Russell, his expression a mixture of pity and contempt. 'I did try and warn you, Detective Inspector, but you refused to listen.'

'Warn me about what?'

'I have nothing against you personally but I'm afraid there's no way back for you.'

'No way back from what?'

'I've heard about you, Detective Inspector; a curious specimen, by all accounts. I'm told you're not averse to lining your own pockets. It made me wonder whether you were a man I could have done business with. You want to know why you're there and I'm here?'

'Does it look like I'm in need of a sermon?'

'Two men each acquire a hundred pounds. For the sake of argument, let's say that the spirit, if not the letter, of the law has been broken in both instances. The stupid man tries to spend the money and is caught. The clever man takes the hundred pounds and shares it out among his friends. Not as gifts, you understand, but as donations to worthy causes: charities, political campaigns. Very soon most men of a certain rank have received a little of this money. The man keeps some of it for himself, of course, but when questions are asked about the origins of this money, well, the man who's asking the questions is quietly advised to stop. And when he doesn't stop, the consequences are grave. Do you see what I'm trying to tell you?' He was kneeling down in front of Pyke, as though addressing a child.

'And who has benefited from your generosity in this instance? Mayne? Rowan? Pierce? The prime minister?'

'Names are irrelevant. What matters is that the institutions of church and state are protected.' He stood up and stretched his legs. 'After all, no one wants to see socialism or anarchy.'

'But there are plenty who'd pay good money to see you swing from the noose.'

Palmer glanced across at Russell, seemingly bored. 'Now who's giving the sermon?'

'Tell me, then. Just how much did you steal from the Churches Fund?'

But Palmer wasn't listening. Instead he was looking at Russell. 'What do you think? Shall we leave the good detective inspector with a parting gift?'

Russell grinned, leaned over Pyke and drove his fist into Pyke's already cracked ribs.

It was another two days before Pyke could sit up properly and two more before he could think with any degree of clarity about his predicament. The laudanum had kept the pain at bay, but it had slowed him down and made his thinking foggy and vague. During that time, he had received further visits from Felix, who had been unable to find Villums; from Wells, who'd kept him abreast of developments in the case; from Sarah, who sat with him and kept him amused, and from his lawyer, Geoffrey Quince, QC, who Pyke had used before. He went through the Crown's case and tried to work out a plan for their defence.

Since the Crown's case rested on Egan's testimony, they had to destroy Egan's credibility as a witness. Pyke knew that Egan would try to present himself as a businessman who imported silk and wine from the Continent. In part this was true, but it disguised the fact that the man earned most of his money from fencing stolen goods. Egan had been convicted of this crime twenty years earlier, and had served four years in Fleet prison. He had also been arrested within the past month on charges of receiving stolen goods. What had Whicher said? A few crates of wine. Perhaps Egan had offered to lie on the stand in the hope that the charges in this other matter would be dropped. In any case, Quince would tear him apart, if and when he stepped up to give evidence. The key to everything, Pyke decided, was finding Ned Villums, because he would know who had got to Egan. But Ned was nowhere to be found. No one knew where he was, Felix explained, a hint of panic in his voice.

About a week after he had first been arrested, Pyke was visited by Wells and then by Quince. It was a Thursday afternoon. They both told him the same thing: the date of his trial had been set. He was due to go before the magistrate across the road at the Bow Street courthouse at nine o'clock on Monday morning.

That meant he had less than three days to prepare his defence.

'How is everything at St Matthew's? Are they treating you well?' Pyke tried to keep his tone upbeat.

Felix nodded. The trial was just two days away and the boy looked scared.

'As I understand it, you have your own bedroom?'

Martin Jakes had written him a letter, explaining that he was happy to give Felix a roof over his head, but that Pyke would have to find an alternative arrangement if he was found guilty.

'I miss our home. I miss Copper. I lie awake at night and I think about what'll happen if they send you to prison.'

Pyke shook his head, as though this wasn't a possibility. In actuality, it wasn't a possibility. If he was found guilty, it would be the noose.

'And you have enough money for cab fares and to contribute to the expenses at the vicarage?'

Felix chewed his lip and stared down at the stone floor. 'Pyke ... if you're found guilty, they'll hang you, won't they?'

Pyke looked at his son and tried to think of a way of answering that didn't involve telling the truth.

On Saturday afternoon, Pyke was resting on his mattress: he had just finished the last of his laudanum and felt relaxed, even confident that Pierce wouldn't prevail. A thin shaft of light had penetrated the barred window, casting its shadow on to the opposing wall. He heard footsteps and a rattle of keys. Moments later, the door swung open. Jack Whicher had removed his hat to enter the room and stood for a few moments, waiting for Pyke to say something.

'I wasn't sure you'd want to see me ... but then again, in the light of what I've just found out, I couldn't not come.'

In truth, Pyke was glad to see his former confidant, even if the news he'd brought didn't appear to be good.

'You have to understand, Pyke, I had no knowledge that any of this was going to take place.'

'Just tell me what you've heard, Jack.'

'I'm assuming you know that Alfred Egan is going to testify against you? And they've managed to twist the old gaoler's arm, too.'

'Wells told me,' Pyke said.

Whicher nodded; Pyke could see the strain on his face. 'But did he also tell you they've got another testimony?'

Pyke sat up straight and felt his stomach knot. 'Who?'

'Someone called Villums. Ned Villums. I take it you know who I'm talking about.'

Instinctively Pyke dry-retched: he tried to stand up but his legs wouldn't carry him. For a moment, he sat on the mattress, dazed. '*How?*'

'I'm sorry. I don't know any of the details. I have a contact who works as a clerk in the courthouse across the road. He gave me a list of prosecution witnesses.'

Pyke sat there on the mattress, shaking. It was inconceivable, unthinkable, that a man like Ned Villums would testify against him, or anyone else, in a courtroom. But somehow Pierce had got to him; somehow Pierce had broken him; and if Villums stood up and told the court what he knew, Pyke was as good as dead. It wasn't just that Villums could lie about him having stolen the Saviour's Cross; the man had first-hand knowledge of the many crimes Pyke had committed over the years. There were thefts he could talk about. Even murders.

'Wells would have known about this, wouldn't he?'

Whicher pursed his lips and nodded. 'I'd say so.'

And he'd played it quite beautifully, Pyke thought. Convince Pyke to waive his right to a pre-trial hearing and keep him in the dark regarding the true threat to his liberty. Meanwhile, distract him with luxuries and laudanum. It was perfect. But why did Wells want him out of the way? Was it conceivable that he had been acting in consort with Benedict Pierce from the outset?

'Who is he?' Whicher asked, a few moments later.

'You mean Villums? You don't want to know. But he's the one man whose testimony will almost guarantee I'll swing from the noose.'

'That bad, eh?'

'If he stands up and tells the court even a fraction of what I've done, what we've done together, I don't stand a chance.'

Whicher stood still, arms folded. Pyke couldn't tell whether he was appalled by this revelation or not. 'So what are you going to do?' Whicher asked, finally.

Rising unsteadily to his feet, Pyke shuffled across to where he was standing and clasped his shoulders. 'You're a good friend, Jack. I'm sorry about what I said before.'

'I'm sorry too.' Whicher's smile turned into a grimace. 'Pierce isn't interested in me any more, now you're in here.'

'I could always try to delay the trial but I don't think that would help. If Villums testifies, I'm finished.'

Whicher offered an uncomfortable shrug. 'I have no idea where they're keeping him. I don't imagine anyone knows.'

'Don't worry, Jack.' Pyke tried to smile. 'I'm not going to ask you to do anything illegal.'

'Then what *do* you want?'

Pyke returned to his mattress and sat down; he needed time to think. He was in a deep hole and there was no obvious way out.

'I can't ask you to do anything for me, Jack, but I'm hoping you could be persuaded to bring someone to see me.' The first inkling of an idea was forming in Pyke's head.

'Who?'

'You remember Sean Rafferty? He was shot dead some time last month. His brother Conor drinks in the Blue Dog in St Giles.'

'You want me to find him and ask him to come *here*?'

'He'll refuse at first, so you have to try and convince him it'll be in his best interests. He'll want to avenge the death of his brother. Tell him I can help.'

Whicher didn't speak for a moment or two. 'Are you quite sure you want your fate to depend on someone like Rafferty?'

'In a day and a half, I'll stand in front of a judge who'll happily send me to the scaffold, if that's what the jury tells him to do. I don't see I have a choice in the matter.'

The situation was too far gone for Pyke to feel any real anger towards Wells or indeed Pierce. That could come later, if and when he made it out of there. Nor did he have the time to engineer an escape. It was true that he'd been given the freedom of the cell, but he knew there were two men on the door at all times and everyone going in and out of the cell was searched. Still, for a while at least, he imagined what he would do when he next came face to face with Wells. Or Villums. That had been the bitterest of blows. He had known Villums for twenty years and had developed a certain respect for him. The loss of face for Villums was unimaginable, too. Even if he was testifying against a policeman, no one would do business with him again.

Pyke found it hard to settle; he paced around the oblong room until he felt dizzy. And even though the pain from his ribs and broken fingers was almost unbearable, he resisted the temptation to finish the laudanum. That was how Wells wanted him; docile, strolling oblivious into an ambush. No, he had to stay focused and the pain would help him. Turning his thoughts back to Conor Rafferty, he tried to think what he might do if Whicher wasn't able to find him or Rafferty decided not to come. Did he have another idea? It was Sunday tomorrow and the city shut down for the day. He took to counting the hours: thirty-nine until he was due to take his place on the stand.

Later that evening Wells did come to see him. 'You have to believe me,' he said, almost pleading. 'I knew nothing about it. I was just as much in the dark as you. I found out an hour ago and came here as quickly as I could.' He shook his head. 'I assume it's bad news.'

Pyke said nothing for a moment or two. 'Jack Whicher came to see me this afternoon. He broke the news to me.'

Wells nodded. 'It's Pierce. He's played this final card from the bottom of the deck. No one could have seen it coming.'

'But you persuaded me to waive my committal hearing, didn't you, Walter? If I'd taken the hearing, the Crown's lawyers would've been forced to reveal their hand.'

'I know and I feel terrible. Just terrible. Please, old man. If there's anything I can do for you, any way of making amends ...'

'Give me the keys and let me walk out of here.'

Wells simply stared at him. 'Within reason, Pyke.'

'In a day, I go before a magistrate and jury with no chance of refuting the evidence that will be presented to them. What do you expect me to say?'

'Perhaps I could try to find this new witness.' Wells hesitated.

'And do what?'

'Talk to him; persuade him not to testify against you.'

Pyke shook his head. 'It wouldn't do any good; clearly Pierce has something on him. There's no way he would have agreed to testify otherwise.'

'But if I could find him ... and ... What if he had an accident? Something that prevented him from getting to the courtroom?'

Pyke was surprised at this suggestion.

'Things are never as bad as you think they are,' Wells continued. 'When I was a soldier in Afghanistan, our regiment was attacked by the natives. We were ambushed in the mountains and outnumbered. It was hopeless; men were falling like flies. I made a choice. I hid under a pile of corpses pretending to be dead. I stayed there for almost a day. It was baking hot so you can imagine the stench. Eventually reinforcements arrived. I was the only one left alive. Later, I received a medal for my endeavours. It made my reputation as a soldier but not a day goes by when I don't feel ashamed of what I did.'

It was a strange tale. Pyke could see that Wells didn't often tell it and that this confession had taken its toll. But it didn't do anything to change or alleviate the predicament he faced.

Pyke didn't hear anything or receive another visitor until the following afternoon. It took him a few seconds to recognise Conor Rafferty: he was gaunter than Pyke remembered and he'd shaved his head. There was none of his former insouciance, either. His countenance was grim and determined.

'So what is it you think I can do for you, big man?'

Pyke couldn't tell whether he'd used this last term ironically. 'Think of it, in the first instance, in terms of what I can do for you.'

'While you're locked up in here, not a whole lot, I'd wager.' His smile revealed rotten teeth and black gums.

'Perhaps we need each other.'

'How do you work that one out?' He tried to appear indifferent but Pyke could tell he was interested.

'I can give you George Culpepper. In fact, I can serve up George Culpepper's mob on a plate.'

Pyke could see that the name had scored a hit, but Rafferty was still a long way from being convinced.

'Like I said, big man, there's nothing you can do for me while you're rottin' in this place.'

'That's why I need your help.'

Conor Rafferty nodded, as though he'd been expecting this. 'Hell'd freeze over before a Rafferty went out of his way to help the law.'

'How can I be the law if I'm locked up?'

Rafferty scratched his head. 'You have a point there, I'll grant you.'

'Then you'll at least listen to what I've got to say.'

'I'll listen, but at this precise moment, that's all I'm prepared to do.'

'You know I grew up on the same street as Culpepper? We used to call him Little Georgie. For the first seven years of his life, he slept in a coal-shed with a pack of dogs. He learnt to bark before he could talk.'

That, at least, made Rafferty smile.

On Monday morning it was raining. In fact, it had been raining almost continuously since the previous afternoon and the water had gathered in sludge-coloured puddles, carriages and omnibuses spraying brown slush on to the pavements, meaning that pedestrians had to hug the buildings if they didn't want to get wet. The guards had searched Pyke as he'd left the felons' room and the only item they let him take with him was a skin filled with porter, or so he'd told them; they also hadn't noticed a hairpin that he'd smuggled out in his mouth. To get from the station house to the courtroom meant crossing the road but nothing was being left to chance; Pyke was shackled in leg-irons and handcuffs and escorted by half a dozen police constables and an inspector, who carried his pistol at all times. Neither Wells nor Pierce had been back to visit him and he had spent his last night in the cell quietly contemplating all the things that could go wrong. A queue had formed, and it snaked out of the courthouse along Bow Street as far as the Brown Bear. Pyke had already been told by the gaoler to expect quite an audience; after all, as he put it, it wasn't every day folk got to see a copper get his just desserts. Shielded from the onlookers by a phalanx of uniformed constables, they went in to the building using a private entrance and followed a series of narrow passageways that led to the courtroom itself.

Pyke took his place on a small, elevated platform surrounded by a wooden rail on one side of the room, across from the bench. There was a gilt-framed mirror and a large clock on the wall behind him. The spectators had gone quiet when he'd first entered the room, but now there was an excited buzz. Pyke had told Felix not to come, but he knew that his son would probably be there. Perhaps Sarah would come, too, even though she had been given the same instructions. He surveyed the faces gathered in front of him and, to his relief, he didn't see anyone he knew except for Whicher and Eddie Lockhart, who were deep in conversation.

The constables who'd escorted him from the station house congregated on one side of the dock. Pyke hadn't bothered to ask whether he might be unshackled because he knew there was no point. Though no one had said so explicitly, it was clear that the constables, turnkeys and gaolers had been instructed not to let him out of their sight. Pyke studied the faces of the crowd again, this time hoping he might see Conor Rafferty in the room. Instead he saw Sarah Scott and then Felix; they were standing together. Pyke had no idea they had even met, but when he caught Sarah's eye, he smiled and mouthed the words 'thank you'. It was regrettable that they had come but he had known they would. Briefly he wondered how they'd react when the trial got under way. It would be especially hard on the lad, Pyke mused; hard but unavoidable.

'All set, then?' His lawyer, Geoffrey Quince, QC, had aged since Pyke had first met him, but in a distinguished manner. Quince's serene expression indicated he had no idea that another prosecution witness had been added to the list.

'The Attorney-General is conducting the prosecution himself,' Quince was explaining, 'with assistance from Worthington and Chambers.'

As he stood there and numbly listened, Pyke felt for the wineskin he'd concealed under his waistcoat. It would soon be over, one way or the other. He felt closer to the noose than ever.

Soon afterwards the twelve jurors strode into the room and took their allotted seats, just below the bench.

At exactly nine o'clock, the door nearest the public entrance opened and the magistrate, George James Stevenson, JP, entered the room, closely followed by another man wearing robes and a wig, and then a procession of dignities, including Walter Wells and, as it turned out, Benedict Pierce, who hobbled in and was last to take his seat. Wells and Pierce were not sitting next to one another, and while Pierce made a point of not looking over at Pyke, Wells met his eyes almost immediately and gave an encouraging smile. For a moment, Pyke wondered whether this meant he'd been able to get to Villums.

As the chief magistrate banged the gavel to bring the room to order, Pyke looked again for any sign of Rafferty.

'The jury for our Lord the King upon their oath do present that Detective Inspector Pyke, late of Scotland Yard and Islington in the county of Middlesex, on the fourteenth day of July eighteen hundred and forty-four, did with malice aforethought commit the wilful murder of William Sharp and that on the twenty-second day of March eighteen hundred and forty-four did steal the Saviour's Cross and other items from the private residence of the Archdeacon of London. How do you plead?'

All eyes in the room turned to him. Pyke waited for a moment or two then said, 'Not guilty.'

As the magistrate swore in the twelve jurors, Pyke could feel his heart thumping. Briefly he caught a glimpse of Felix, straining on tiptoes to see what was happening, but he still couldn't see Rafferty. He smiled at the lad, trying to exude a confidence he didn't feel.

'I now call on the Attorney-General, Nicolas Tomlinson, QC, to present the case for the prosecution.'

Just as the chief magistrate finished speaking, Pyke noticed a man he didn't recognise, with a cloth hat pulled down over his face, step out of the crowd.

Mr Roland Dunn, a shoemaker from Clerkenwell who had queued through the night to ensure he secured a place for himself at the front of the public viewing area, saw everything and later gave a full statement to the police.

A rough-looking gentleman wearing a hat of some sort and a black, velveteen shooting jacket had pushed his way through the crowd of spectators and, striding forcefully, had ducked under the rail and approached the dock, where the defendant was standing. It had all happened quickly. Too quickly, he stressed, for anyone to have intervened. No one saw the pistol in the man's hand until the last minute; he had concealed it under his jacket. The man screamed the defendant's name, as though angry at him, raised the pistol and fired. The blast, much louder than he'd been expecting, echoed around the room. The defendant, Pyke, collapsed on the stand clutching his stomach. The ball-shot had hit him squarely in the gut and blood was pumping from the wound. The air in the room was thick with people's shouts and screams. The gunman then made for the door behind the dock that the defendant had first appeared from; a police constable moved to block his path but the gunman had raised his pistol, as if to fire, and the policeman had to let him pass. All of this happened, the shoemaker said, in the space of a few seconds. After the gunman had fled the room, pandemonium broke out.

Pyke lay on the floor next to the dock, gasping for air. His hands, his stomach, his clothes were all covered in blood. He could hear the screams around him and his first thought was of Felix, the fact that the boy would have to see him like this. There were faces crowded around him, peering down at him, concerned at the amount of blood he'd lost. He stared at the tallow rings on the ceiling and heard men barking orders at each other. Jack Whicher was one of the first to reach him and he kept the others at bay. Someone shouted for a stretcher and out of nowhere one appeared; a policeman carrying one end of it, a civilian the other end. Whicher and the man in civilian clothes, who'd identified himself as a doctor, lifted Pyke on to it. He clutched his stomach and groaned. The doctor looked around for the constables who'd escorted Pyke from the station house and shouted, 'They'll need to operate; can someone please remove the irons.' It wasn't a question, and one of the constables duly obliged.

Whicher went ahead of them, clearing a path. The doctor was carrying one end of the stretcher, the policeman the other. Pyke heard someone say, 'We need to get him to St Bartholomew's as quickly as possible.' As they carried him through the crowd, he could hear Felix screaming, 'That's my father, let me through.'

Outside, it was still raining but there was a carriage already waiting. Its doors were open and, still on the stretcher, Pyke was pushed inside. He could hear raised voices, a debate about who would accompany him. Eventually the two who had carried the stretcher joined him and the carriage moved off. They all waited until it had turned from Bow Street on to Long Acre, before Pyke looked up at Conor Rafferty, dressed in the policeman's uniform Whicher had procured for him, and at his accomplice, dressed as a doctor, and smiled. Sitting up, he wiped off the pig's blood that he had smuggled into the court in a wineskin, and looked out of the glass at the back of the carriage. There would be others following. Conor Rafferty banged on the roof and the carriage shuddered to a halt. Even before it had stopped, the three of them had leapt through the door, landed on the pavement and darted into one of the side alleyways that criss-crossed Long Acre.

Golden Square

FEBRUARY 1845

TWENTY-FIVE

Up to his knees in excrement, Pyke used the tub to scoop up another load of shit and signalled for Peter, the rope-man, to haul it up out of the cesspit. Somewhere above, the two tub-men, Jimmy and Matthew, were waiting to collect it and empty it into the cart. It would take another fifteen or twenty tubfuls before the cesspit was empty, which, Pyke estimated, meant he would be wading around in faeces for at least another hour. And this was only their second call of the night. By his estimation there were another three pits to clear before they were finished. The tub came scuttling down to him and Pyke filled it again then signalled for Peter to haul it back up. It was monotonous, backbreaking work, but as awful as it was, after two weeks as a hole-man shovelling shit into a bucket, Pyke could honestly say he had stopped noticing how badly it stank. They had been reluctant to employ him at first, even though their hole-man had left to work in a tannery. They didn't know him; no one they knew could speak for him, either. But Pyke had persisted and it had been his efforts to find new business that had finally won around Matthew, one of the tub-men and the leader of the team. In the two weeks since they had taken him on, Pyke had worked hard, spoken little, complained even less, and had proved himself to be a valuable member of the crew. Each night they worked from 11 p.m. until five in the morning; the first part of the night involved emptying the cesspits into a cask attached to the back of their cart; the second part was the transportation of this load to a farm in Hackney, where it would be used as manure. For each cesspit they cleared they were paid five shillings and a bottle of gin, and they might get another shilling or two from the farmer. At the end of the night, after Matthew had taken what was owed to him for providing the cart and horse, they would divide what remained into equal amounts.

That morning they didn't finish until well after five; they had been held up at a house in Shoreditch where it had taken a pickaxe to remove the stone slab covering the cesspit and the entire cellar floor had been thick with the overflowing soil. Matthew kept his horse, Henry, in a stable just north of Golden Square, and if it was especially cold, as it was that morning, they would sit on the straw and pass around the gin they'd been given. Otherwise they would go and sit in Golden Square itself and watch the market traders arrive and set up their stalls. This was the part of the day they liked best; watching other folk start their working day when theirs had just finished. Sitting in a warm pub would have been even better, but no landlord would allow them through the front door on account of the stench from their clothes.

On this occasion, Peter, who was married and whose wife had just given birth for the third time, left after just a few swigs of gin, and Jimmy went shortly after, claiming a headache and fatigue. That left just Pyke and Matthew, and with the gin warming their stomachs, they fell into easy conversation.

'You've settled in well, Johnny.'

That's what Pyke had called himself: Johnny from Northamptonshire. Or the Doc. All he'd told them was he'd once been a doctor until he'd fallen prey to the bottle and had killed a patient in his care. They hadn't asked him further questions. It was what he liked best about them; they accepted him because he worked hard and didn't complain.

Matthew was still handsome in his forties, with short brown hair and boyish dimples when he smiled. All Pyke knew about him was that he lived with a woman called Laura. He untied his boots, slipped them off and rubbed the soles of his feet. Pyke swallowed a mouthful of gin and shuddered.

'You're the best hole-man we've had since Morris.' Instinctively Matthew looked for the others to confirm what he'd said before realising it was just the two of them.

It had been three weeks since Pyke's escape from Bow Street, and this was the moment he'd been waiting for.

Since Matthew was the one who'd mentioned Morris Keate, Pyke now had the opportunity to ask about him. He'd tried to steer the conversation towards the subject of the murders before, but no one had taken the bait.

'Who was Morris?' Pyke asked, casually, scratching the beard he'd grown to conceal his identity.

'Morris Keate, but he's no longer with us.'

'Did the fumes get too much for him?' Pyke smiled, trying to make a joke of it.

'You would've been curing the sick in Northamptonshire at the time it happened, Doc.'

Pyke took another swig of gin and passed the bottle back to Matthew. 'What did he do?'

'Since it's just the two of us I'll tell you. But don't tell the others I've mentioned it. They still don't like to think about what happened.' Matthew drank from the bottle then wiped his mouth. 'They reckon he killed two boys; one not far from here in Soho. Found him guilty, and put him to death on the scaffold.'

'Jesus Christ.'

'I know. Terrible times for all of us. Especially his family.'

'You reckon he was guilty?'

'Guilty? No. No way. Morris was always a little odd. You have to understand, he was a simple man ... gentle, sweet natured, more of a boy than a man, really. But he had these odd beliefs, about God and the Devil. I'd say that's why they picked on him. You see, the second boy was stabbed and nailed to a door. They tried to paint Morris as some kind of religious lunatic – a Devil worshipper.'

'Jesus Christ,' Pyke said, repeating himself. 'Did the Peelers ask you questions?'

'Some, but truth be told, they weren't much interested. Especially when it became clear we weren't going to put Morris into the noose for 'em.'

'But it must have been awful.' Pyke shook his head. 'For you and for his family.'

'At the time they were very close knit, they all doted on Morris. To be honest, I didn't always like the way they treated him, as if he was a lame dog that needed taking care of. But they loved him, would've done anything for him. It hit them terribly hard. Especially the mother. At the time she would've been quite devout. I'd say that's where Morris got some of his beliefs from.'

'I guess it must've shaken them badly. These things always do. You're never quite the same afterwards.'

Matthew took another swig from the gin bottle. 'Morris was the oldest, and the only one fathered by her first husband. That's why he called himself Keate and the rest of them were Gibb.'

Pyke felt a bolt of excitement shoot up his spine. *Gibb.* It had been the name of the third man who'd been killed in the Shorts Garden robbery.

Wanting to prod him gently in the right direction, Pyke said, 'Something like this happens, the whole family can fall apart.'

'Too true in this case, Doc.' Matthew stood up and went to pat his horse. 'Morris had two stepbrothers and a stepsister. One of them, Johnny, was a bad lot, always getting drunk and fighting. I don't know what happened to him. The other, Luke, joined the army. This would have been before Morris was arrested, though. I remember noticing him at Morris's trial, in his uniform.'

'Luke Gibb?' Pyke said, as though he recognised the name.

Matthew came back and sat on the damp straw. 'Dragoons, I think; I remember him telling me he was based somewhere in Cambridgeshire. Morris was always so proud of him.'

'And what became of the others? The mother and the daughter?'

This was a more direct question but Matthew was sufficiently lubricated by the gin, so he didn't seem to mind. 'Last I heard, the mother had gone a little crazy. The sister was an interesting fish. I always thought she was the good-looking one in the family. An artist of some kind. But she was troubled, just like Morris and the mother. She talked about having these strange visions.'

Pyke felt his stomach somersault. *Good looking. Strange visions. An artist.* He had to pretend everything was fine. 'I think I remember reading about it, now you mention it. You know, the murders, the trial. Was the sister involved?'

'Who, Kate?' Matthew screwed up his face. '*Nah*, not her.'

Instinctively Pyke gave a sigh of relief, although he knew the fact that Keate's half-sister was called Kate didn't prove a thing. He took the bottle, had one final drink and handed it back to Matthew. The cheap gin scalded his throat. 'Be hard, I reckon, for them to stay in the area,' he said. 'Everyone pointing their fingers at you.'

'The mother stayed, I know that much. But I haven't seen her for a couple of years.'

'And the beautiful half-sister?' This time Pyke tried to keep his tone light.

Matthew looked at him and grinned. 'Don't go asking me, Doc. My Laura would have my guts on a plate if she heard me talking about another woman.' He stood up and yawned. 'I'm for bed, anyhow. I'll see you tonight at eleven.'

Pyke nodded. He now had all the information he was going to get – at least out of Matthew and the crew. A part of him felt sad that he wouldn't be there in the evening, that they would think badly of him – especially Matthew.

At his lodging house, Pyke took off his clothes in the yard and, in spite of the freezing temperature, scrubbed himself down with soap and cold water. He had done little to his appearance apart from grow a beard and dress in a manner that befitted his status as night-soil man, but, by and large, people had left him alone. In the days just after his escape from Bow Street, when no one seemed to know whether he was dead or alive, he had expected to be recognised at every street corner, but he had forgotten how easy it was to lose oneself in the flotsam and jetsam of everyday life. Still, he didn't take unnecessary risks; he avoided constables walking their beats and he had tried to contact Felix only once since the incident in the courtroom.

Pyke had made a point of seeing Felix as soon as possible, going almost directly from Bow Street to St Matthew's. Still, their reunion had not been a good one. Initially the lad had thrown his arms around Pyke and wept, relieved that he was alive and hadn't, in fact, been shot. But quickly this relief had turned into anger that Pyke hadn't told him of his plan in advance, that he had allowed him to think he was dead. He'd been to every hospital in the city, Felix said, and each one he'd entered, he'd expected to be told that Pyke hadn't made it. Pyke had tried to explain: he told Felix that in time the police would come and question him and if they had an inkling that he knew in advance about the escape bid, he could be arrested. He tried to explain that he'd kept Felix in the dark in order to protect him. At the time, Felix hadn't been ready or willing to accept this and their meeting had ended acrimoniously. Since then Pyke had been back to the church twice, but on each occasion there were too many police constables watching the place, so he couldn't run the risk of trying to speak to his son. He had seen the lad, though, and knew he was safe; and when this whole thing was resolved, *if* it was ever resolved, Pyke knew he would owe an enormous debt of gratitude to Martin Jakes.

He was equally indebted to Jack Whicher, who met him every morning in the middle of Golden Square. Maybe Whicher felt he had to make amends for what he had done, or maybe he simply believed Pyke was innocent and therefore deserving of his help. In any case, Whicher was there on the same bench every morning at eight, and he kept Pyke informed about both the investigation and the status of the manhunt to find him.

The fact that Pyke's escape had taken place under the noses of two of the city's most senior officers was, apparently, the most galling thing, especially for the men involved. They, in turn, had tried to shift the blame: who, they demanded to know, had been the constable who'd carried one end of the stretcher? Who had authorised the removal of the irons? And why hadn't anyone else insisted on accompanying Pyke to the hospital? Whicher, who had been on the scene and, unbeknownst to Wells and Pierce, had known some of Pyke's plan, had attracted a fair amount of ire, but no one had yet accused him of actively conspiring to aid the escape bid. Most embarrassing of all, the authorities had let the gunman – one of Rafferty's men – do what he'd done in front of *everyone* and then allowed him to slip through their fingers. For this, Wells, Pierce and the whole police force had been ridiculed in the newspapers and scandal sheets.

Today Whicher had arrived slightly before him and was drinking a cup of hot chocolate. Pyke sat down next to him and said, 'You remember the third man who was shot in the robbery in the summer?'

'Gibb, wasn't it?'

'Keate's mother and siblings are called Gibb. Keate was the result of an earlier marriage. One of the half-brothers, Johnny, was our victim.'

'So what do you think it means?'

'Well, first of all I think he was there in Cullen's shop to try to sell the Saviour's Cross to this Harry Dove. Cullen was there to broker the deal.'

'So it was Johnny Gibb who stole the cross from the archdeacon's safe?'

'I think so.'

Whicher took a sip of his hot chocolate. 'How does any of this relate to what happened to Keate – and Guppy?'

'I don't know, let's just think about it.' Pyke paused, trying to arrange his thoughts. 'All right. Guppy knew Morris Keate. We know this from Martin Jakes. We know Guppy was sniffing around Keate at the time the two boys were murdered. Let's say the two boys had stumbled on to something they shouldn't have and someone decided to get rid of them. What if Keate was picked to be the scapegoat?'

Whicher nodded but didn't seem convinced.

'Keate is arrested, tried and eventually executed,' Pyke said, confident in what he'd said so far. 'His family and close friends don't believe he did it but the evidence seems to contradict that belief. A few years go by. Then Keate's family, his half-brothers, start to hear rumours. At some point Johnny breaks into the archdeacon's safe; perhaps new information comes to light suggesting their brother's innocence. What would you do? One thing I wouldn't do, in their shoes, is go to the police. Let's just say they opted to take matters into their own hands. Perhaps they learnt that Guppy was involved; Charles Hogarth, too. What we do know is that the deaths were planned to coincide with the dates on which the two boys were murdered. *Why?* It's obvious, isn't it? Whoever killed Guppy and Hogarth wanted to send us a message. They wanted to rub our faces in the truth. Morris Keate didn't kill those two boys. But they also wanted us to look into the original murders again. They wanted us to find out what really happened.'

Whicher nodded. 'I suppose there might be a certain twisted logic to what you've just said.'

'But?'

'It still doesn't explain where the theft of the Saviour's Cross fits in.'

Pyke could see Whicher's point. 'All right. Let's think about what happened to the cross after it left Cullen's shop.'

'Suppose Gibb had the cross with him at the time, and Sharp killed him and the other two for it,' Whicher said.

Nodding, Pyke said, 'We know Sharp tried, almost immediately, to sell the cross on to Alfred Egan. That's when we interrupted them at the Red Lion.'

'Six months later, the cross turns up in your garden,' Whicher said, frowning. 'So how did it get from Sharp to there?'

'I don't know.'

But Pyke had a good idea, even if he couldn't prove it. Instinct told him that he had been set up, either by Wells or Pierce. Therefore, he suggested to Whicher, it followed that one of them had managed to retrieve the Saviour's Cross from Sharp. Perhaps they had been in league with Sharp from the beginning and had taken the precaution of ending Sharp's life before the man had been able to denounce them.

Whicher looked at him, the concern apparent in his eyes. 'You really think one of them is involved?'

Pyke just shrugged.

'Did you bring the daguerreotype we made of Sharp after his death?' he asked, changing the subject.

Whicher dug his hand into his pocket and produced the copperplate. The image looked almost real and Pyke was taken back to the fight he'd had with the man in an alleyway behind Field Lane.

'Any news on Palmer? Or Wynter?'

'By all accounts, Palmer is unwell. He's taken to his bed and hasn't been seen at his place of work for more than two weeks. I'm told his house is better guarded than the Tower.' Whicher sniffed. 'Sergeant Russell's called in sick, too.'

Pyke pondered this for a moment. 'And the archdeacon?'

'He's left the capital on business. No one seems to know where he's gone or when he'll be back.'

It seemed clear that all three men were afraid of appearing in public and had taken the necessary precautions. 'How are things at the Detective Branch, then?'

That drew a wry smile. After Pyke's arrest, Wells had refused to sanction Whicher's return to uniform and he'd been reinstated.

Briefly, Whicher explained that Wells had taken temporary charge of the department. They'd been forbidden to bring up the subject of the Churches Fund; and had been told Charles Hogarth had died of natural causes, that Isaac Guppy had stolen from general parish funds and that this theft was to be treated as an isolated case. 'Wells has gone back to trying to find Francis Hiley. Meanwhile, we're investigating a house burglary in Clapham.'

'What about Lockhart and Shaw?'

'Everyone's trying to keep a low profile. Wells is hardly ever there. It's like a rudderless ship.'

'I'd like you to do something for me, if you have the time. But it's going to entail a trip out of the city.'

'Aside from the burglary, my desk is clear.'

'Keate's stepbrother, Luke Gibb, served in the Dragoons. I don't know, maybe he still does. I was told he was stationed somewhere in Cambridgeshire. I'm afraid that's all I know, but there can't be too many regiments in the county.'

'You'd like me to find out which one he served in and talk to someone who knew him.'

Pyke smiled. 'Exactly.'

Whicher stood up and stamped his boots on the frozen ground to warm his feet. 'Same time tomorrow, then?'

Pyke stood up, too, and looked at the slate-coloured sky. 'I wanted to say how grateful I am, for all you're doing. I'm sorry it had to be under these circumstances.'

'I'm glad to do what I can.'

Pyke thought about their previous encounter in the privy at work, when he'd punched Whicher and told him he never wanted to see him again. It was funny how quickly some things turned around. On that occasion, Whicher had told him awful things about his family circumstances and Pyke had said nothing to him about them since. All of a sudden, he felt ashamed.

'Jack, I don't want you to think I ...' He tried to find the right words. 'What you told me before, about your wife and child ...'

Whicher seemed uncomfortable. 'I know.'

'Do you still go and see her?'

Whicher looked around the square and exhaled loudly. 'Sometimes. Not often, though. She's still in the same ... place.'

'I just wanted to say how sorry I am. I can't imagine how terrible the whole thing must have been.'

Whicher bit his lip. 'Sometimes life has a way of cutting off your arms and legs and then defecating on you from a great height.'

Nodding, Pyke wondered whether he should mention the child, who'd died from cholera, but in the end he resorted to patting Whicher on the shoulder. 'You're a good man, Jack. A good man and a good detective.'

In his dirty workman's clothes, and with a soiled oilskin cap covering his shaved head, it took Clare Lewis a few moments to recognise him. When she did, she smiled and shook her head. 'Somehow I knew you weren't dead.' But she wouldn't turn around to face him and Pyke quickly saw why. The whole left side of her face was swollen and had turned purple and yellow, and her eyes were ringed by smudges of black. She held out her hands, as if to pacify him. 'I know what you're going to say and I'm not interested. Do you understand?'

Pyke gently turned her face towards him. The bruising was worse close up. 'I don't need to ask who did this to you, do I?'

'I'm glad you're alive. I really am. But I want you to leave.'

'And the next time he comes for you, this time with a knife or a cudgel, what will you do then?'

'You don't understand.' She folded her arms and looked up at him for the first time. 'Even your presence here in the building is putting me at further risk.'

'I used the back entrance. Nobody saw me.' As he said this, Pyke wondered how true it was.

This seemed to make her even angrier. She took a few steps away from him and turned towards the window. 'He did this to me because someone told him I was asking questions about those two boys.'

Pyke tried to reconcile his curiosity with the guilt he felt for putting her in danger. 'And what did you find out?'

She shook her head as though she'd expected him to say this but was still disappointed. 'No words of contrition? No "I'm so sorry my demands led to *this*"?' Gingerly she touched the bruised side of her face.

'Would it help if I was sorry? Would it make it more bearable?' When she didn't answer, Pyke said, 'What did you find out?'

'Culpepper is adamant that no one in his mob even whispers those boys' names. The last anyone heard of them, they'd just turned over a house on Cheapside. Number twenty-three. That's all I know; that's all I want to know.'

Pyke decided not to push the issue. Instead he took the copperplate from his pocket and handed it to her.

Reluctantly she took it and glanced down at the image of Sharp's face. Her expression remained inscrutable.

'Do you recognise him?'

Without answering, Clare stared down into the yard. 'I wondered why I hadn't seen him around,' she said, keeping perfectly still.

'So he did work for Culpepper, then?'

This time she turned around and nodded once. 'He wasn't part of the inner circle.'

Pyke didn't smile, but he felt an inner satisfaction spread through him. It was starting to come together, to make some sense. So it was Culpepper who had dispatched Sharp to retrieve the Saviour's Cross, and maybe kill the three men in the shop on Shorts Gardens. But on whose orders?

'I take it you didn't like him.'

'What gave you that idea?' For the first time since he'd arrived, she seemed to relax. 'No, you're right. I always thought he was an animal.'

'And Culpepper isn't?'

'If you've come to judge me, you can go to hell.' Softening a little, she gestured at the marks on her face. 'He did this to me with a leather strap.'

Pyke felt his anger – and guilt – return. He took a step closer to her. 'You have to understand, Clare, I'm not trying to judge you. But ask yourself this: do you still want to be answering to a man like Culpepper in a year or even five years' time?'

That made her laugh. 'And you think I have a choice?'

'We always have choices.'

'In your world, perhaps. But in my world, you do what you're told. And if you step out of line, you're crushed.'

Pyke looked around the nicely decorated room. 'He comes here,

313

doesn't here? Perhaps not to you but he comes here as a client.'

The fact that she didn't answer straight away told him all he needed to know.

'Just go, Pyke. Leave me alone. I've done what I can for you.'

'And the next time he decides you've let him down? Because once this kind of thing starts, Clare, it doesn't stop.' He scribbled his address on a scrap of paper and pressed it into her hand.

'Spare me the cheap sentiments, Pyke. I can make my own decisions.'

It took a few minutes of grubbing around in the scrubland behind the Coach and Horses in St Giles to find what Pyke was looking for: a plank of wood that he could easily hold in his hands. Clutching it, he kicked down the same door he'd used about a month earlier, and swung the piece of wood into the face of the first man who tried to block his path. Another man stepped out of a room leading off the dank corridor and Pyke smashed one end of the plank into his stomach and watched him collapse to the floor. Feeling his fury gather momentum, he kicked open the door at the end with the heel of his boot and looked for any sign of Culpepper: there were two men he didn't recognise from the previous card game but otherwise the room was deserted. From somewhere else in the building, Pyke heard the sound of urgent footsteps. Before the two men could get up, Pyke had taken the plank of wood and swung it against their respective heads. He looked around, the blood pulsing through his veins.

'*Culpepper*. Come on, Little Georgie. Let me beat you like the dog you've always been.'

He felt the jab of something hard and cold against his neck.

When Pyke turned around, one of Culpepper's lieutenants was aiming a pistol directly at his face. Soon there were four others in the room, all armed with pistols, and finally Culpepper appeared, his face relaxed, his gait almost languid.

Pyke took stock of his situation, only now beginning to realise how badly he'd misjudged the situation.

'Drop it,' Culpepper barked. Pyke felt one of the lieutenants jab the end of his pistol into the side of his cheek.

Opening his hand, Pyke let the plank of wood clatter to the

floor. Grinning, Culpepper took a few steps towards him and aimed a sharp kick at his groin. It connected almost perfectly and, for a moment, Pyke felt as if he might pass out.

'Go and fetch the police,' he heard Culpepper grunt to one of his men. 'There's a reward for this one.'

TWENTY-SIX

Pyke stumbled to his feet and looked around him. The route back to the corridor he'd come along was blocked by three men, all armed.

'As much as I'd like to cut you up with an axe, I have to be practical,' Culpepper said, smiling. 'It would be satisfying in the short term, but I'd be pissing good money up the wall.'

One of the men turned and left. Pyke tried to focus. How long would it take him to fetch a police constable? Five minutes perhaps?

'That was quite a performance you put on at the courthouse the other week. I'd say you're about as famous as any man in the country at the moment.' Culpepper paused and touched his chin. 'I'm just trying to imagine the scene when you're led out on to the scaffold.'

'For that, Little Georgie, you need to have an imagination. But they say dogs can't even see in colour.'

Culpepper seemed amused rather than irritated by Pyke's attempt to rile him. 'The other day I was thinking about the street we used to live on. But you know what else I remembered? Your father. He used to coin for a living, didn't he? He was a failure and a drunkard and when he perished in that stampede outside Newgate prison, hardly anyone went to his funeral. I heard folk talking about it afterwards. Said it was an embarrassment. For a moment I even felt sorry for you. I always knew you wouldn't amount to much.'

Pyke felt something as close to pure, undiluted hatred as he had ever experienced. He hadn't thought about his own father in years and wasn't even certain that he could remember what he looked like.

Culpepper continued to grin. 'I know you visit Clare Lewis's place every now and again, just as I knew how you'd react when you saw what I had done to her. I've been *expecting* your visit.'

Pyke looked around him and tried to ignore Culpepper's taunts. They had backed him into a corner of the room: just a window behind him; no door and no way out.

'Who paid you to set Sharp on those men in Cullen's shop? And who paid you to go after Keate's mother?'

'You think you're in a position to ask me questions?'

Fighting off the fear in his stomach, Pyke ran through his options. The window behind him seemed to be the only viable choice but he didn't know what lay beneath it, or whether the storey-high fall might, in the end, do more harm than good.

'Was it Benedict Pierce?'

Culpepper's small, quick eyes gave little away.

Without warning, Pyke suddenly turned and launched himself at the window, his arms wrapped around his head to protect it from the glass. He heard the blast of a pistol as the glass shattered into a thousand pieces. He landed, shoulder first, on a ledge before rolling over and falling ten feet into the yard below. This time he landed partly on his side, the force of the impact momentarily winding him. Up on his feet, Pyke stumbled through an open gate just as a ball-shot tore into the mushy ground where he'd landed. And then he was moving, half-running, half-limping, into the street behind the yard.

But he wasn't free, not by a long way. Behind him, he heard shouting and, somewhere beyond that, the *tat-tat-tat* of a policeman's rattle. At the next junction, he turned into a narrow alleyway and followed it as far as it took him. He turned again and continued deeper into the rookery, the houses becoming more ramshackle. When he reached the end of that lane, Pyke tumbled out on to a much wider, busier street. It took him a moment to work out he'd come as far as High Holborn, and just for a moment the brightness and noise were almost too much for him.

Up ahead, a drover and his two sheepdogs were herding a line of long horned oxen in the direction of the market at Smithfield. Instinctively Pyke moved towards the group. He crossed the road, weaving between slow-moving drays, wagons and carriages, and noticed two constables with their stovepipe hats in the crowd behind him. Pyke kept moving, his head down and hands in pockets. The last thing he wanted was to draw attention to himself.

Out of nowhere he felt a hand clasp his shoulder.

Turning around, he saw the man's dark blue swallow-tailed coat and brass buttons. The young constable had a truncheon in his hand and he swung it through the air. Pyke just managed to duck under it and kick the man's ankles. Another constable saw the tussle and blew his whistle, and soon there were three or four stovepipe hats converging on him from different directions. Without thinking about it, Pyke scrambled into the middle of the herd and started to shout and flap his arms. The first animal reared backwards, its hind legs catching one of the sheepdogs, and another charged forward, ramming the ox in front with its horns. That set off a ripple effect, and soon the beasts were rampaging through High Holborn, panicked pedestrians pushing each other out of the way. It was hard to tell the human shouts from the petrified squeals of the animals as fully grown oxen slipped on the damp cobblestones and careered into traders' barrows. Pyke took advantage of the confusion and slipped into an alleyway running perpendicular to the street. He could hear someone behind him, maybe the same man who'd tried to arrest him, but he didn't stop. Finally, when he couldn't run any more, he came to a halt in a sunless court, wheezing for breath. On the other side of the court was a slaughterhouse, but none of the men standing outside it paid him much attention. He walked past them, avoiding eye contact, and looked over his shoulder. The policeman had just entered the court. He heard the man's whistle, darted into a passageway that ran along one side of the slaughterhouse and found himself in a yard surrounded by ten-foot-high brick walls. It was where the slaughterhouse discarded what they couldn't use or sell – piles of hooves, teeth and cartilage. Flies hovered around the mass, feeding off the putrefying flesh. Pyke heard someone coming towards him down the narrow passage. There was no way out. Covering his mouth and nose, he dived into the mountain of flesh and quickly manoeuvred himself into the centre of the pile. The smell was so bad he retched instantly. He held his breath and counted at first to ten and then to fifty. Eventually he heard the footsteps receding.

*

Every time Pyke walked through the City of London, he was surprised not only at the number of people on the pavements but also the traffic on the roads, omnibuses seemingly disgorging hundreds of bodies every time they stopped. What surprised him just as much were the new buildings; on every street and at every corner, old lath-and-plaster Georgian edifices were being pulled down and in their place would suddenly emerge monstrous granite structures, soaring upwards into the grey skies. There was always a lot of discussion about the new city that was materialising, and when you walked along a particular street and came across one, two, sometimes three gleaming new edifices, it was hard to deny that progress was being made. But at what cost? Certainly fewer and fewer people lived within the square mile. This was now where the new public companies, flush with money following their stock market ventures, wanted to establish offices that were increasingly grand, each a monument to the ambition and vanity of their chairman.

Pyke found No. 23 Cheapside easily enough. It was another newly built structure, this one of modest scale and proportions. A fashionable linen draper occupied the ground floor, offices the upper floors.

The proprietor of the shop greeted Pyke warmly but some of this evaporated when he explained he was a private enquiry agent investigating a robbery that had taken place at the premises about five years earlier. Pyke had changed out of the clothes he'd been wearing and had bathed and scrubbed himself clean, but even so, he could still smell rotten animal flesh on his skin.

'I'm afraid I wasn't here five years ago, sir, and as you can probably see, nor was this building.'

'Do you own it?'

'No, I'm afraid I don't. I rent it from the City Corporation.'

Pyke wondered whether this had anything to do with what Saggers had told him about Hogarth. As alderman for the Court of Common Council, which was an arm of the City Corporation, Hogarth had been instrumental in increasing the number of properties available for non-residential use.

'Perhaps I could ask you just one more question?'

The draper smiled uneasily. 'Of course.'

'Do you remember the name of the contractor who pulled down the old building and put this one up?'

The draper wiped his hands on his apron. 'I should be able to. I liaised with him about the plans.'

'Was it Sir St John Palmer? Was it his company?'

Pyke knew from the draper's reaction that he had scored a hit. The man stared at him, flummoxed. 'Yes, that was it.'

Outside, Pyke wandered along Cheapside and came to a halt outside an older, lath-and-plaster building about six doors down from the draper's shop. At one time it had perhaps been tenanted by one family of means, but now the number of bells and plates on the front door suggested that numerous individuals resided there. Pyke pulled one of the bells at random and, when no one answered, he tried another, then another.

The man who opened the door was elderly, with ash-white hair, stooped shoulders and poor eyesight. He was also hard of hearing.

'What's that, cock?' he said, when Pyke asked him whether he'd known the person or people who'd lived at No. 23 before it was rebuilt.

Pyke repeated the question, this time almost shouting.

'I knew 'im, not well, mind. But I knew 'im. What I call a God-botherer.'

'What happened to him?'

'Eh?'

'What happened to him? Did he move?'

'He died. Sudden, like. Just keeled over one day. 'Is nephew fancied the old boy would leave 'im the property but when the will was read, turns out the old coot 'ad gone and left everything to the Church. More fool 'im, I say, but it must 'ave been a shock to the nephew.' The thought of it made him chortle.

'I just called in there; seems the draper is renting it from the City Corporation now,' Pyke said, trying to rein in his excitement. He knew he was getting close. 'So the Church doesn't own it any more?'

'No, they sold it to the City Corporation, as soon as they got their grubby little hands on it.'

Pyke almost put his mouth up against the old man's ear. 'Did you hear anything about a robbery there? Would have happened about five years ago?'

'A robbery?' He scratched his chin. 'No, can't say I did. But you said it 'appened five years ago, eh? That would've been around the time the old boy passed away.'

The garret room Pyke had rented, on Broad Street, was less than a hundred yards from Sarah Scott's address on Berwick Street, but he had deliberately avoided her ever since his escape because he hadn't wanted to involve her any further. After all, he hadn't known for certain that their relationship, if that was what it was, was entirely secret, and there was always a slim chance that one of Pierce's men, or one of Wells's men, had followed her after her visits to Bow Street. He had left her a note explaining all of this, but now he felt that perhaps he owed her more than that.

He entered the building through the back, and when he knocked gently on her door and there was no answer, he picked the lock and let himself in. It was a small space, barely enough room for a mattress, but Sarah had managed to erect an easel holding a canvas which she had yet to start. A few brushstrokes marked the white background but nothing else. Pyke gave the room a quick search but found nothing apart from some paint and a few brushes. The air, he thought, smelled of her; it made him think of the way the skin at the sides of her eyes creased when she smiled. It was late afternoon and Pyke was more tired than he realised. As soon as he had removed his coat and boots and lain down on the mattress, his eyelids drooped and he quickly fell asleep.

He was woken by a gentle kick, and when he looked up, Sarah Scott was standing over him, wearing a simple white dress and a blue woollen shawl. Her hair was partly held up in a clip.

'So Lazarus rises from the dead.' She said it with a vague sneer, and Pyke knew at once that he hadn't been forgiven. 'It's nice of you to come and see me. Even though I thought I'd locked the door when I left this morning.'

Pyke sat up, yawned and scratched the hair on his chin. 'I left you a note.'

'I got it.'

'When I last saw you, when you visited me, I had no idea I'd have to do something so drastic. I got some news at the last minute which made me realise I'd been set up; that there was no way I'd walk out of that courtroom a free man. I had to make other arrangements; and I didn't want to involve either you or my son because I knew they'd come after you if I did.'

That seemed to soften her a little. 'I met Felix one day outside the station house. One of the clerks told me who he was.'

'Aiding an escape from prison or knowing about it in advance and not contacting the authorities. They can transport you for that.'

Pyke looked at the way her dress clung to her hips. He also thought about how she had come to his aid during his incarceration at Bow Street. But if she was, in fact, Kate Gibb, she had been wilfully deceiving him for the entire time he'd known her.

She saw the way he was looking at her and scowled. 'You didn't explain how you got into my room.'

Pyke made space for her on the mattress next to him and patted it. 'Come on, Sarah. Sit down.'

In the end she did, reluctantly, but kept at least a yard between them. 'I thought you were going to die, Pyke. We all did; everyone in that room.'

'I'm sorry I didn't come to see you sooner. There were things I needed to do.'

'What things?'

'If I said scooping shit out of other people's cesspits, would you believe me?'

Intrigued now, she looked at him and sniffed. 'I thought there was a funny smell when I walked in here.'

'You know I told you about a man called Morris Keate?' Pyke watched her reaction carefully. 'I needed to find out about Keate's family, his half-brothers and half-sister. Becoming a night-soil man was the only way I could do it.'

Sarah regarded him with curiosity. If she was Keate's half-sister, she was hiding it well. 'And did you?'

He shrugged. 'Some details. Enough.'

'Shouldn't you be concentrating on how to get out of the mess you're currently in?'

'The only way I can do that is by proving other people's

culpability. Believe me, there's nothing selfless about what I'm doing here.'

A lopsided smile spread across her face.

In spite of himself, Pyke found her coolness under pressure alluring. Could she really be Kate Gibb? Suddenly he couldn't be sure of anything.

'I missed you,' she said, reaching out and touching him on the shoulder.

It was hard to tell who had pulled who into an embrace. Their mouths met somewhere in between, their kisses hot and urgent. She had already removed her shawl and he helped her with her dress while she tugged at his trousers. He had always liked her confidence, and her experience as a lover, the ease he felt in her company. Did it matter that she might not be who she claimed to be? This thought left his head as soon as he saw her naked body. He pulled her down on to the mattress, and, as he guided himself into her, feeling her breath on his cheek as he did so, he wondered, if only for a moment, whether he might be using her in some nameless, complicated way.

Afterwards, they lay in silence and stared up at the dark stains on the ceiling. He had done what he'd just done because he wanted to, because he couldn't stop himself, because he liked her more than he wanted to admit, but he had done it, too, because he wanted to convince himself that she was who she claimed to be, that physical intimacy was somehow a guarantor of truthfulness. Now, exhausted, he saw this for the lie it was. She had been as ethereal and closed off to him as ever, and he'd used what they'd done as a sly form of interrogation. Where was the truthfulness in that?

'Kate . . .?' He waited for her to turn around and look at him.

Eventually she did, but her expression was quizzical. '*What* did you just call me?'

He felt a slight dampness in his armpits. Perhaps he'd made a mistake.

'Why did you call me Kate?'

Pyke suddenly felt very foolish. He had expected, or perhaps hoped, that having been addressed by her real name, she would turn to him instinctively and answer him. Now all he'd done was given her a reason to be angry at him.

'Did I just call you Kate? I'm sorry.'

She pulled the sheet up over her shoulders and turned away from him. 'Now you've got what you came for, Pyke, I think you should go.'

'I said I was sorry, Sarah.'

She turned around suddenly, her eyes blazing. 'If you call a woman by another name after you've just made love to her, it's never well received. But this was something else. I could hear it in your voice. It wasn't a mistake.' She sat up, folded her arms.

He thought again about Matthew's description of Keate's half-sister and made a split-second decision. It *had* to be her. 'Come on, Kate. You don't need to pretend any more.'

Pyke saw the disappointment register in her eyes and knew at once he had been wrong. She seemed both bewildered and angry.

'I mistook you for someone. I made a mistake. I think I should leave.' Pyke couldn't bring himself to look at her.

Sarah sat there quietly, trying to take it in, then shook her head. 'Do you want to know why I came back here?'

Pyke stood up and found his trousers.

'The main reason was that I didn't want you to find out anything about me that would cast me in a bad light.' She bit her lip.

'And what might I have found out?'

'It all seems so silly now. I should never have been worried about what you thought of me.'

Pyke buttoned up his trousers, thinking about what she had just told him. She had liked him and he had just ruined whatever may have existed between them. He felt sick and empty.

But Sarah's anger hadn't yet abated.

'Jesus Christ. Did you even believe I lost my child? Probably not if you thought I was this Kate person.' She wiped a tear from her cheek. 'What kind of monster do you think I am?'

Pyke could feel the sweat pouring off him. Had he been swayed by Druitt? But there had been inconsistencies in her story; one moment she hadn't wanted Druitt's name mentioned, even in conversation, the next she'd admitted to quite liking him. And she hadn't testified against Druitt at her trial. That had always bothered him.

'If you were certain that Druitt had murdered your child, why didn't you testify against him?' When she didn't answer, he added, 'What is it you didn't want me to find out?'

She was silent for a very long time.

'He … he didn't kill my boy.' Tears were now streaming down her face. 'Brendan did. Brendan did it.'

Pyke was too flabbergasted to speak for a few moments. 'Then why was Druitt tried and convicted? Why did Brendan tell the court that Druitt killed your son?'

Almost whispering, Sarah said, 'Druitt had driven Brendan almost insane with jealousy. I didn't know so at the time, but for months Druitt had been insinuating to Brendan that he and I had been cuckolding him. James, my son, was Brendan's child, or so I always thought. But when James started to grow, it quickly became apparent he looked nothing like Brendan. It was also apparent he was the spit of Druitt. This was impossible, as far as I was concerned. He and I hadn't even kissed, let alone made love. But there it was. The proof was incontrovertible. And one night, after we'd all been drinking, Druitt told Brendan that he was the father – all you had to do was look at the child to know it was true. This was when the two of them were alone; I only found out about it later. Brendan went in to wake up James. I was asleep at the time. He lifted him out of his cot and inspected him. I don't know what happened next. I don't know if Brendan ever understood why he did what he did, whether it was an accident or not. But the result was the same. My dear, sweet, beautiful boy fell to his death. The fall, the thud when he hit the landing floor below, woke me up. I ran down the stairs to him but he was already dead. I do remember looking up at that moment. I could hear Brendan sobbing but Druitt was staring down at me and he was smiling. He was smiling, as if the whole thing was a big joke.

'Afterwards, I remembered this night some time during the previous year. Brendan was away and it was just me and Druitt in the apartment. I felt ill and Druitt was kind to me. He brought me something to drink. I slept well that night but the next morning there was soreness between my legs.' She paused and wiped her eyes. 'I didn't think anything of it at the time, and even after James had been born and looked nothing like Brendan I still didn't make the connection. But that night, before we called the police, I confronted Druitt. He told me as calmly as you like that he'd drugged and raped me and that James had been born nine months later. It was almost as if he was glad to tell someone what he, in his sick mind, regarded as his triumph. That he'd destroyed not just one life but three.'

Pyke wanted to take her in his arms, but it was as if an unbridgeable chasm had opened up between them. 'And you had no idea?'

'That he'd raped me? That James was his child?' Sarah laughed bitterly.

'And was it your idea to implicate Druitt?'

Sarah's face was hard. 'Brendan went along with it because it was what I wanted. But I always knew the guilt would be too much for him.'

'Why didn't Druitt defend himself in court? I read the transcript of the trial. He didn't mention any of this.'

'He isn't like you or me. I don't understand him. I don't think he even cared. It was his lawyer who argued the charge down from murder to manslaughter. All I can think, and I don't like to think about him for reasons I hope you now understand, is that he'd done his work. He'd ruined our lives. That's what he'd wanted to do from the start.' Sarah's face was red and blotchy from her tears. 'I didn't even need to testify in the end.'

'Why didn't we have this conversation at the start?' But he knew why: he was a police officer and she had broken the law.

'You think *that* would've alleviated your suspicions?'

'Someone who knew this woman, Kate Gibb, described her as beautiful, an artist and someone affected by strange visions,' Pyke explained. 'The coincidence seemed too great and I jumped to the wrong conclusion.'

'Then why did you just sleep with me? I don't understand ...'

'I did it because I wanted to. No other reason.'

Sarah was sitting up against the wall. 'Before you go, Pyke, there's something else I should tell you.'

Bending over, Pyke picked up his shirt from the floor and put it on.

'For the past month I've been sleeping very well, nothing bothering me. It's why I haven't been able to paint since, well, since you came to visit me in Suffolk.' Her smile was almost too much for him to bear. 'Well, for the last couple of nights, I've woken up with a terrible sense of dread hanging over me.'

Pyke looked at her but said nothing.

'I know you think this is all poppycock but the dream was very clear.'

Pyke stopped what he was doing and knelt by the mattress. He wanted so badly to help her, to tell her it would all be all right, to make it better, but he knew it was too late. He could tell by the look on her face. 'What is it, Sarah?'

'You should go and see your son ...'

'*Ssshhh.*' Pyke pressed his finger against his son's lips.

'*Pyke.*' Felix sat up in bed, disoriented.

Pyke had slipped past the two constables stationed outside the vicarage easily enough, but it had been harder to creep up the rickety staircase without disturbing Jakes, Kitty or one of the servants. Once upstairs, he had found Felix's room and had watched his son sleep for several minutes.

'I can't stay for long. It's too dangerous. I just wanted to make sure you were all right.' Pyke was crouching beside the bed. He was relieved to see that his son was fine, but he still felt empty from his encounter with Sarah Scott.

'I went back to school. No one's said anything to me but they're all looking at me in a funny way. I don't like it.'

The masters, the parents, they would all have read about him in the newspapers. 'I'm sorry, I really am. If I could've done it differently, I would have.' He was tired of apologising, tired of hurting the people he cared for.

'That's all right.' Felix's demeanour was suddenly belligerent. 'I can look after myself.'

'I know you can.'

Felix went to retrieve something that had fallen down beside the bed. It turned out to be a book. Felix thrust it into Pyke's hand. 'Kitty gave it to me but I want you to have it.'

It was the *Book of Common Prayer*. Pyke's first instinct was to return it, but he saw Felix's expression and relented. 'Are they treating you well?' he asked, stuffing the book into his pocket.

'We say prayers in the morning, prayers before food, prayers last thing at night.'

Pyke did his best to keep a straight face and said, 'That sounds like a lot of praying.'

'We pray for you; for your safe keeping; and for the false charges against you to go away,' Felix added, in a small, quiet voice.

'Martin believes the charges are false?'

Felix nodded.

'I need another week.' Outside, they heard footsteps on the landing and they waited for them to pass by.

'Can I ask you a question?' Felix hesitated. 'I'd like you to answer it as honestly as you can.'

'I'll try.'

'Why do you hate the church so much?'

'If I hated the church, why would I have asked Martin to look after you?'

'I don't *need* looking after.'

'Give you your room and board, then.'

Felix considered this. 'Have you ever wondered why I turned to the Bible when I did?'

'Often,' Pyke replied. He could hear the accusatory tone in his son's voice.

'Or why I got on better with Uncle Godfrey, when he was alive, than I did with you?'

This was something Pyke had expected to hear from his son but he wasn't sure he was ready for it. 'He was gentler with you, more forgiving. I know.'

'That was part of it.'

'And the rest?'

'I was frightened of you.' Felix stared down at his hands. 'Scared of what you're capable of.' He raised his eyes to meet Pyke's. 'A part of me still is.'

'You know I'd never hurt you.'

'That's not what I mean. I lie awake at night and think about the things you've done, things I've seen with my own eyes, and I start to tremble and sometimes I can't stop.'

Pyke fell to his knees. It was like someone had reached inside him and scooped out his insides. 'And that's why you started to read the Bible?'

'It became something I wanted to do for myself.' He paused. 'I hated you for a while. I'd while away the days, imagining what my life would be like if I had a different father. That's why I turned to Uncle Godfrey. It's why I picked up the Bible. I wanted to get as far away from you as possible.'

Pyke couldn't bring himself to look up at his son. He felt the shame wash over him. 'I never knew ...'

'You never asked.'

The next morning was clear, and this time it was Pyke who arrived first at their bench in Golden Square. Jack Whicher was a few minutes late and sat down next to him wordlessly, taking a moment to catch his breath. 'I looked into that thing you asked me to,' he said finally. 'I'm told the Fourteenth Dragoons have their head-quarters near Ely. I plan to go up there later today.'

'Thank you, Jack. I do appreciate everything you're doing for me, and the investigation.' Pyke's mind was still on the conversation he'd had with Felix and how he could have been a different father.

'They found the coroner's body,' Whicher continued. 'Someone had buried it in a shallow pit in Deptford. Wells has taken charge of the investigation.'

'I don't suppose it changes much, does it? I mean, we both knew the man wasn't long for this world.' The porter who had found Hogarth's body would doubtless be buried in another pit.

'I heard yesterday that Ebenezer Druitt has been transferred back to Pentonville.'

Pyke thought about the last time he'd seen Druitt; battered and chained to the wall like an animal. 'You think he told them anything?'

Whicher shrugged.

'I still think he knows the identity of the man we're looking for,' Pyke added.

'Luke Gibb?'

329

'I'd say so.'

'The question is, how might Gibb and Druitt know each other?' Pyke stared up at the dull, grey sky. 'If one or both of the Gibb brothers went to see Malloy at number twenty-eight Broad Street, perhaps they'd heard something about Morris, a rumour purporting to his innocence. Perhaps they felt a need to consult Malloy. After all, he had tried to exorcise spirits from their half-brother. Maybe they trusted him and thought he knew something that might help prove Keate's innocence. They could have met Druitt then. Or Druitt could have heard about Keate's death through Malloy and been intrigued.'

Whicher seemed bemused. 'Whether Gibb knows Druitt or not isn't going to help you, though, is it?'

That made Pyke smile. 'What would help me is if Palmer, Russell and Pierce were rounded up into an iron cage and dropped into the middle of the sea.'

Whicher sat bolt upright, suddenly alert. 'You've just reminded me of something. You know I said that Palmer had become a virtual recluse?'

Pyke looked at him and nodded.

'I heard yesterday about a banquet that is being held in his honour. Wild horses wouldn't keep him away.'

'Whereabouts?'

'The Guildhall.'

'When?'

'Early next week.'

'If Palmer is too well guarded in his house, perhaps whoever we're looking for will try to move against him then.'

'Whether or not you're right the police presence will be enormous. The prime minister is due to attend. The City of London force is asking us for two hundred additional men,' Whicher said, raising his eyebrows.

'And this will be Palmer's first public engagement in a month?'

'More than a month.'

'However many policemen there are, Palmer will be vulnerable in a place as large as the Guildhall. He'll be aware of that, too.'

'But is he really in danger?'

Pyke shrugged. 'He certainly seems to think so, or someone does.

Why else bother to make such elaborate security arrangements?'

They sat for a moment in silence, watching the traders sell their wares. 'I forgot to say, Wynter's back in the city. Wells told us that two constables have been assigned to watch his house.'

'Did he say why? I mean, it's not typical, is it? An archdeacon having to be guarded by two policemen?'

That drew a meagre smile. 'He just said that these are extraordinary times.' Whicher pushed himself up on to his feet. 'If I have to go up to Ely today, I may not be back in time for our meeting tomorrow. Why don't you come to my apartment tomorrow evening, say around six?'

TWENTY-SEVEN

Edmund Saggers was eating a lunch of roast venison in the Cheese on Fleet Street; he saw Pyke out of the corner of his eye and put down his knife and fork, waved him into the alcove where he was sitting. 'It's good to see you, old chap,' he whispered, looking around to make sure no one was watching them. 'That's right. Just keep your hat pulled down over your face and sit with your back facing the room. We'll be safe for a few minutes.' His face was wet with excitement. 'I won't be so vulgar as to ask for your side of the story now but I do want an exclusive at some point. Whether they hang you or not.'

'Nice to see you haven't lost your sense of humour.' Pyke looked down at the remains of the venison haunch. 'Or your appetite.'

'That was quite a trick you pulled at the courthouse. I wish I could have been there to see it for myself.'

'Much as I'd like to chat, there are more pressing matters at hand.'

'Such as?'

'Such as, I was wondering whether you'd got any farther with your investigations into the matter we discussed.'

'Funny you should mention it, old chap. I spent a rather revealing afternoon in the land registry office the other day. In the last five years, Palmer's construction company, Palmer, Jones and Co., has sold quite literally hundreds of properties all over London to the City Corporation.'

'Go on.'

'Well, that's pretty much the sum of it, at the moment.'

'I take it Palmer, Jones and Co. hasn't always been so well endowed with properties to sell.'

'That's just the thing. I didn't have time to conduct a particularly thorough search but in all the sales I looked into, the City Corporation was always the buyer.' He looked up at Pyke, not quite finished. 'And the previous owner was almost always the same too.'

'Let me guess. The Church of England.'

Saggers seemed disappointed that Pyke had already guessed this. 'Well, not exactly. A company wholly owned by the Church of England called City Holdings Consolidated.'

'So this company, City Holdings Consolidated, has sold hundreds of properties to Palmer, Jones and Co. in the last few years and Palmer, Jones and Co., in turn, has sold them on to an arm of the City Corporation.'

'Exactly.'

'But we don't yet know what kind of money changed hands on each occasion, and who turned a profit.'

'That's right,' Saggers said, leaning as far across the table as his girth would permit. 'As far as I can see, there's nothing illegal about any of these transactions. I mean, they're registered with the appropriate bodies.'

'But what we don't know is how this company, City Holdings Consolidated, came to own these properties in the first place.'

'That's true.' Saggers's expression shifted as he looked over at Pyke. 'But you seem to have your suspicions ...'

'About five years ago, a fund-raising campaign was launched to raise enough capital to build as many as fifty new churches in the city. So far, ten have been built or are being built ...'

Saggers finished what was in his wineglass. 'I'm not sure what you're getting at.'

'Just be patient. I'm trying to think ... One aspect of this campaign was to persuade as many people as possible to leave an endowment to the Church in their wills.' Pyke thought about what the old man living on Cheapside had told him. 'Let's assume that the campaign was a success, but that people didn't just leave money to the Church, they also left their properties.'

'That seems plausible enough.'

'But in order to turn these properties into capital, the Churches Fund, or those overseeing it, would've had to put these properties on the open market.'

'There's nothing illegal about that,' Saggers said.

Pyke rubbed his beard, the part under his chin that itched the most. 'But what if City Holdings Consolidated sold these properties to Palmer's company for well under the market value and then Palmer, Jones and Co. sold them on to the City Corporation at the full price?'

That seemed to prick the journalist's curiosity. 'If we're talking about a lot of properties across the entire city, and if the mark-up was great enough, we could be talking about a vast amount of money.'

Pyke was thoughtful. 'Did you know that Isaac Guppy, rector at St Botolph's, died with more than forty thousand pounds to his name, in six different bank accounts? And Guppy served in an administrative capacity on the fund-raising arm of the Churches Fund – the arm that tried to persuade people to leave endowments to the Church in their wills?'

Saggers took out a handkerchief and wiped the sweat from his face. 'None of this has been reported, has it?'

'Not yet.'

'I take it no one has yet proved that the forty thousand was stolen from this fund.'

Pyke shook his head. 'Before all this happened ...' He gestured at the cap and clothes he was wearing. 'I was allowed to inspect the Churches Fund's accounts. Everything seemed to be perfectly in order.'

'Seemed?'

'It struck me just now. What if there was another set of accounts? A set that gave a fairer sense of the large sums that were paid into the Fund and the much smaller sums that were made available for the church building programme.'

'You're saying there might be a discrepancy?'

Another set of accounts.

Pyke had said the words without realising what they meant. Saggers must have seen his expression because he reached across the table and touched his arm. 'What is it?'

Whoever had broken into the archdeacon's safe in March of the previous year hadn't been after the Saviour's Cross – the accounts had been the real prize.

'I know someone who works for Palmer, Jones and Co.,' Saggers said. 'Perhaps I could quietly talk to him. He's involved in the new road they're building through St Giles – the one they had to demolish those slum houses on Buckeridge Street for.'

It was suddenly so obvious that Pyke was astounded he'd missed it for so long. For the second time in as many minutes he sat there, unable to speak.

The last time he had been to the archdeacon's home, on Red Lion Square, it had been summer and the interior had seemed cool and airy. On that occasion, it had been morning, and he had entered via the front door, invited but not entirely welcome. This time, he picked a lock at the back of the house and entered via the kitchen, taking care not to disturb the policemen stationed at the front. Pyke didn't know what he wanted to prove by confronting Wynter with his accusations, and what it would achieve if Wynter acknowledged that a set of accounts had been stolen from his safe along with the Saviour's Cross. Still, as he crept through the lofty, oak-panelled hall and noticed the same Gainsborough and Titian paintings he'd seen hanging there in the summer, he knew he wasn't going to leave until he'd forced the truth out of the man.

It was after midnight and the servants were all asleep. Pyke intended to confront Wynter in his bedroom, if necessary. He'd based this plan on the quite reasonable assumption that Wynter and his wife slept in separate bedrooms; on his previous visit, he'd assessed their marriage as entirely loveless. But as he made his way up the oak staircase, it struck him that he was putting himself in a rather precarious position. All Wynter needed to do was shout and four, five, maybe more servants would all come running; then there were the two policemen outside. What would he do? Fight his way past all of them? At the top of the staircase Pyke paused, noticing light streaming out of a partly open door. He could hear someone moving around there and when that someone, a man, emerged, Pyke withdrew into the nearest room and held his breath. It was dark and the curtains were drawn so it took Pyke a moment to work out that there was someone asleep in the bed. He waited for the footsteps to pass and slipped back on to the landing. Perhaps it had been Wynter he'd seen, but Pyke didn't think so. The man had been taller and younger than the archdeacon. He crept along the landing as far as the open door and peered inside. It was the legs he noticed first. Stepping into the room, he saw the rest of the archdeacon's body. Blood was still leaking from the multiple stab wounds that peppered the corpse, a pool of crimson spreading over the polished floor. It struck him that Wynter had only just been killed, perhaps by the man he'd seen leave the room. Turning quickly, Pyke retraced his steps. At the top of the stairs, he heard a door close at the back of the building. As quietly as possible, he slipped down the stairs and left the house by the route he'd taken earlier. In the alleyway at the back of the house, he looked first left and then right. It was deserted. He turned left, ran to the end of the passageway and found himself on Red Lion Square. He could see the constables at the front of the building, still unaware of what had happened.

Pyke was about to give up the chase when he noticed a lone figure on the other side of the square. The man had stopped and was looking back in the direction of Wynter's house.

Breaking into a run, and not worrying about whether he drew attention to himself, Pyke had crossed half of the square when the figure noticed him and bolted.

The streets were deserted, which meant it was easy, at least at first, to follow the man; and whoever it was made it easier still by staying on the main roads, first Red Lion Street and then High Holborn. It was hard to tell anything about the person he was pursuing – he was too far away and Pyke was running at full tilt – but whoever it was, Pyke decided, was taller and younger than him. And quicker. Just past Gray's Inn Road, the man he was chasing did the sensible thing at last and darted into one of the side streets running north from Holborn. It turned out to be Leather Lane; it was dark and narrow and the cobblestones were slippery from the remains of the daily market. Pyke reached the first junction, looked right and then left, but couldn't see his man. Gasping for breath, he carried on, but at the next junction he still couldn't see him. There was a pub on either side of the street and the man could have gone into either of them. There were another two pubs farther along and at least two more that he knew of on Hatton Garden, any of which the man could have gone into. Not wanting to admit defeat, Pyke stood for a moment or two, trying to catch his breath.

Could it simply be a coincidence, that he had turned up at Wynter's home at the same time as the murderer? Pyke had been told by Whicher, who had found out from Wells, that the archdeacon had returned to London that same day. But how had the murderer known?

'I can't do this any more,' Clare Lewis said, as soon as she'd taken the chair opposite Pyke and removed her headscarf. She had sent a note to his room that morning, asking Pyke to meet her in a tavern just around the corner from her brothel.

'Do what?'

'This. All of this.' She looked angry.

'Tell me what's happened.'

'Nothing's happened. Nothing and everything.' She managed a thin smile. 'I'm not making much sense, am I?'

'Why did you ask to see me, Clare?'

She turned and surveyed the faces in the taproom. 'I don't want to see Culpepper ever again. Is that clear enough for you?' Pyke saw that her hands were trembling.

In the end, it was easier than Pyke could have imagined. A few hours later, Culpepper arrived on Great White Lion Street and left two of his mob guarding the front entrance. He was escorted up the rickety stairs to the prostitute he liked to see, a strong, big-boned woman who called herself Emerald. All Pyke had to do was wait. As he did so, he imagined the scene unfolding in the room: Culpepper removing first his shoes, then his waistcoat, shirt, trousers and socks; Culpepper, naked; Culpepper, waiting for Emerald to do what he paid her to do; Culpepper, oblivious to what was about to happen to him.

As Emerald passed Pyke on the landing, she didn't even acknowledge him. Perhaps, he thought later, she had come to like the man she was paid handsomely to service.

Pyke entered the room quietly and closed the door behind him. Culpepper made an odd, unedifying sight: a sinewy, almost emaciated figure curled up on a bed of crisp, white cotton. Emerald had blindfolded him and tied his wrists and ankles with a silk binding to each of the bed's four posts. To Pyke, he looked older and more wizened than he'd been expecting, and it took some of the sting out of his anger, until he remembered what Culpepper had done.

The first thing he did was check that the binds on Culpepper's wrists and ankles were tight. Culpepper sensed his presence for the first time and, thinking he was Emerald, said, 'Are you going to punish me? I think you should. I deserve to be punished.' Pyke looked at him and noticed his shrivelled penis had begun to stir.

'I have to agree with you there, Georgie. I'm not sure I'll live up to Emerald's standards but I'll do what I can.'

Pyke waited for Culpepper to flinch or struggle but the man remained absolutely still. Perhaps he was trying to place the voice or maybe he thought he could talk his way out of the situation. Pyke didn't allow him the luxury of thought. Swinging the hammer he'd brought with him, he aimed a blow at Culpepper's kneecap and felt the joint dissolve under the force of the impact. Culpepper's cry put Pyke in mind of a cow being crushed under the wheels of a train.

'You should understand, Georgie, that no one is going to come to your rescue. Not the men you left outside on the street nor any of your mob, who, as we speak, are being routed by Conor Rafferty.'

Culpepper's body had gone limp and Pyke noticed that the man had soiled himself.

'You're finished, Georgie. You know it and I know it. But you still have a choice. I can act humanely and slit your throat with a single draw of my razor or I can set to work on you with my hammer the way you did to poor Johnny Gregg.'

'At least take off this blindfold so I can see you,' Culpepper said, his voice barely more than a whisper.

'What's it to be, Georgie? Are you willing to tell me what I want to know?' Pyke reached down and yanked off the blindfold.

Culpepper's eyes were tired and bloodshot. 'I knew I should've killed you when I had the chance.'

'I want to know why you carried out the murders of Johnny Gregg and Stephen Clough five years ago.'

Culpepper lifted his head off the pillow for a moment and tried to assess the damage to his kneecap. 'I didn't think that bitch had the guts to cross me.'

'Well, I suppose this is her way of repaying you for rearranging her face.' Pyke walked around to the other side of the bed, the hammer still in his hand, and gestured at Culpepper's other kneecap. 'I asked you a question, Georgie.'

'There was a house on Cheapside, I think.' Culpepper shut his eyes and winced. 'I sent the boys there to turn it over. They saw this man leave, a gentleman, and thought he was the owner of the house. One of the boys chose to follow him, probably intending to pick his pockets. The other one broke into the house and found a body in the living room – turned out to be the nephew of the former owner, who'd left the place to the Church in his will. The cull was dead but still warm; he'd been strangled. The lad stripped the place of anything he could stuff into his pockets, brought it all back to me. Meanwhile, the other lad had followed this gentleman he saw leaving the place to a church in Aldgate.'

'St Botolph's.'

Culpepper wetted his lips and nodded. 'That's the one.'

'Go on.'

'I waited to read about the murder in the newspapers but there was nothing. Nothing about the robbery either. By then we knew the gentleman one of my boys had followed was a rector by the name of Isaac Guppy. So I paid him a visit, told him what I knew, what one of my lads had seen. The body and him scampering down the front steps. I told him I wanted to be properly recompensed for my silence.'

'You didn't know for certain whether Guppy had strangled this man or not?'

'That didn't matter to me. He'd left the scene of a crime without reporting it. It meant he was involved.'

'Did Guppy tell you what had happened?'

Culpepper shook his head. 'I never talked to him after my first visit. But about two days later I had a visit.'

Pyke nodded, trying to speculate about what may have happened: Guppy and the nephew arguing over the uncle's will. Perhaps the nephew had threatened to go to the police, or the newspapers. Perhaps the argument had turned violent.

'Who from?'

'One of yours.'

Pyke felt his throat tighten – but he already knew what Culpepper was going to say.

'Wells.'

Pyke nodded. 'And he offered you a deal?'

Last summer, Wells had joined the operation in Buckeridge Street to find the men suspected of carrying out the Shorts Gardens murders. But instead of carrying out that detective work, Wells and his men had spent their time clearing the surrounding slums in advance of demolition work to be carried out by the contractor, Palmer, Jones and Co. It all pointed to a long association, and Pyke was sure that if he dug around, he would learn that Wells was the one who'd first put Palmer in touch with Sir Richard Mayne.

'If I made the problem go away, if I was willing to get my own hands dirty, he promised I'd be allowed to run my affairs without interference from your mob. He also said if any freebooter caused me aggravation, he'd personally make sure the cull was stamped on from a great height.'

'What exactly did he order you to do?'

'Later I worked out that he'd already planned for that cully to take the fall ...'

'Keate,' Pyke said, interrupting.

Culpepper nodded. 'At the time, Wells just said he wanted something to scare the rest of the boys, make sure none of them blabbed. Told me he wanted it to look like a religious lunatic had done it.' His eyes were blank, as if he was just describing what he'd eaten for lunch. 'I was going to nail them both to a door but then the older one, Gregg, got a bit uppity so I had to finish him with a cudgel. I reckon the other one, Clough, got wind of what was happening and went on the run. I found him in the end. I had to finish him off with a knife first, of course. Didn't want to cause the lad any unnecessary pain.'

'But they were both your boys.'

'So what?' Culpepper's eyes were hard and small. 'You think I'm attached to any of my boys? That I can afford to be sentimental?'

'Sharp was one of your men, too, wasn't he?'

'He was a good boy but he was always a little too quick to reach for his pistol. I only used him when I had to.'

'You sent him to Cullen's pawn shop, to recover some goods that Walter Wells wanted back? The Saviour's Cross, for a start.'

Culpepper shook his head. 'Wells was never interested in that cross. He just wanted some ledger book. I could see he was desperate. For good measure, he arranged for one of his men to patrol the street outside the shop. A Peeler.'

This had been the man the crossing-sweeper had seen. Sergeant Mark Russell. Part of Kensington Division but formerly of A Division. Wells's division.

'Go on.'

'Sharp had his orders but one of the culls in the pawnbroker's went for his pistol and all hell broke loose. My lad had just got a new Darby, could fire five times without having to reload. Next thing, all of them culls were dead and Sharp scarpered out the back. He didn't get the ledger; but he took the cross and a few things from the safe which was already open.'

This fitted with what Pyke had already worked out. Luke and Johnny Gibb must have suspected, or known, from the beginning that their half-brother, Morris, was innocent of the crimes he'd been accused of committing. Maybe they also suspected that someone had deliberately picked him out to shoulder the blame. Perhaps, over the subsequent years, they had followed a trail of evidence that led back to Guppy and Wynter, although at the time Wells's identity must have remained obscure; maybe it was simply the case that someone had tipped them off about the Churches Fund. In any case, it now seemed likely that, having been alerted to the Church's collusion in the matter of their brother's execution, Johnny and Luke Gibb had broken into Wynter's safe and taken the cross along with the genuine copy of the Churches Fund's accounts ledger. The accounts, Pyke guessed, would have told them all they needed to know about the embezzling of funds and who'd been involved; the cross had just been an added bonus and Johnny had gone to see Cullen to arrange a quick sale. Cullen, in turn, had contacted Harry Dove as a potential buyer and all three men had met that morning in Cullen's pawn shop on Shorts Gardens. Somehow Wells must have found out about the rendezvous. Doubtless he had been frantically scouring the city in the aftermath of the robbery, desperate to recover a set of accounts that set out, clearly and unequivocally, not only his own guilt but also that of Palmer, Guppy, Hogarth and maybe others. Pyke didn't yet know whether Sharp or Sergeant Russell had been able to recover the accounts ledger, but Sharp had certainly made it his business to retrieve the Saviour's Cross before he shot and killed Johnny Gibb, Harry Dove and Samuel Cullen.

'And when Wells wanted someone to find and perhaps frighten Keate's elderly mother and his family, he came to you again.'

'Look, I didn't ask questions or demand reasons. I just did what I was told. In return, Wells was supposed to step on the Raffertys for me. I suppose he did a good enough job on one of the brothers.'

'That was Wells?' Pyke didn't bother to hide his surprise.

Culpepper laughed, in spite of his predicament. 'You have no idea how deep this thing goes, do you? How many of your mob are involved.'

Pyke went over to the window and peered outside into the late afternoon gloom.

'Untie me, Pyke. I'll walk away and I promise you'll never see me again. I'll pay you five thousand.'

Pyke turned around and surveyed Culpepper's naked form sprawled on the bed. It was a grotesque spectacle.

'I asked folk about you. I was told you're not opposed to wetting your own beak from time to time.' Culpepper stared at him and licked his lips. 'Ten thousand.'

Pyke walked slowly towards the door but he stopped just before it, his fingers resting on the handle. 'You know I said I'd put you out of your misery quickly, if you talked to me. Well, I'm afraid I lied.' He turned the handle and opened the door. 'There's a man waiting outside who wants to make your acquaintance. His name is Conor Rafferty.'

'Untie me, you fucking coward!' Culpepper suddenly bellowed, yanking on his bindings. 'Do you know who I am?'

Outside on the landing Conor Rafferty was waiting. Pyke looked him in the eye. 'So we're clear now, you and I.'

Rafferty nodded, walked into the room and closed the door behind him.

When Pyke returned to the building where Sarah Scott lodged, he found that her room, such as it was, had been cleared out. The landlord told him that she had departed the previous afternoon and hadn't left a forwarding address.

From there, Pyke took a hackney carriage to Whicher's address in Camberwell. Whicher lived in a stout, red-brick terraced house belonging to a retired navy captain and his wife. They had been told to expect Pyke and escorted him up the stairs to the top floor, all of which, they explained, belonged to the detective sergeant. Having offered him tea, which Pyke politely declined, the couple left him in what passed as a living room and told him that Whicher was expected by seven at the latest.

In fact, it was after eight when Pyke finally heard a carriage stop on the street outside and the front door open. By that time, Pyke had given all of the rooms on the top floor a quick inspection; there were few books, no papers, no personal touches, nothing to suggest that the occupant spent any time there at all. The bedroom contained a bed and a wardrobe, the living room a sofa and a chair. As he contemplated these living arrangements, Pyke thought about the death of Whicher's child and his wife's illness and wondered whether the emptiness of the rooms spoke of the man's inner life; and whether this, in turn, mirrored his own situation.

Whicher mounted the stairs three at a time and Pyke could see straight away that he had made a discovery.

'Luke Gibb left the regiment three years ago.' Whicher's eyes were gleaming with energy. 'Guess what. He joined the Metropolitan Police.'

'Gibb is a policeman?'

Nodding, Whicher said, 'First thing on Monday morning, I'll go to Accounts. They have records of everyone who's ever joined the force.'

'We're talking about a lot of men,' Pyke said, aware that his heart was beating faster.

'The man I spoke to in the Fourteenth remembered Gibb. He said he was a quiet, competent, articulate soldier. He also gave me the approximate date of Gibb's inauguration as a policeman. March 1842.'

'That should make it easier.'

'I know, but I'll still have to go through the names of fifteen divisions, with a couple of hundred men in each.' Whicher removed his greatcoat and put it on the back of the chair. 'Have you been here long?'

'Not long.'

'I'm sorry; the train leaving Cambridge was delayed.' Whicher looked around the room. 'There's not a lot to entertain you, I'm afraid.'

Pyke shrugged. 'Late last night I went to see Wynter. Someone, maybe Luke Gibb, had just beaten me to it. I found the archdeacon lying on the floor of his room: he'd been stabbed a dozen times in the chest and stomach. I gave chase to a man I saw leaving the place but I lost him in the lanes just to the north of Holborn.'

'So you think it was Gibb who killed the archdeacon?'

'Seems likely, doesn't it?' Pyke nodded.

Gibb had both the motive and opportunity. And it was certainly true that if he had the accounts in his possession, he would know who had been culpable of embezzling the church funds: the men who had, implicitly or otherwise, sanctioned Keate's arrest and execution.

'One thing's for certain,' Whicher said. 'With Wynter dead, Guppy's murder can't now be treated as an isolated incident.'

'What Wynter's murder also means is that anyone else involved will be scuttling for their holes. Palmer among them.'

Whicher considered this for a while. 'Usually I'd say you were right.'

'But?'

'I'm told he still plans to attend this event on Monday evening at the Guildhall. They're giving him the freedom of the city. It's the highest honour a man of his rank can expect.'

All of a sudden, Pyke felt exhausted. 'Palmer's barely ventured out of his house in the past month. This is too good a chance for someone to pass up.'

'Someone like Gibb?'

'In his uniform, it'll be easy for him to slip through the police lines without being noticed.' Pyke waited a moment, debating whether to tell Whicher what he'd just found out. 'Wells is implicated, too.'

Whicher listened while Pyke outlined what he'd discovered about Wells's likely involvement with Guppy, Hogarth, Palmer and the rest of them. When he'd finished, Whicher sat down in the chair and stared wordlessly at the fire.

Pyke could understand Whicher's reaction; he had been taken in by Wells, too. He had written him off as a man used to following orders, not giving them. In fact, Wells had played a careful double game, quietly conspiring with Pierce to engineer Pyke's downfall and allowing Pyke to think he was sympathetic and that Pierce had orchestrated the arrest from the beginning. Whether Pierce was wholly innocent of everything Pyke had believed him guilty of remained to be seen.

'So all along he's been trying to divert attention away from the activities of the Churches Fund?' Whicher said eventually.

'If Guppy died with forty thousand in his account, I don't doubt Wells has accrued as much if not more. In the end, this has been about money and greed, simple as that.'

'So what do we do now?'

'You mean about Wells? If it was just him, it might be simpler.'

'There are others?'

Pyke thought about the slum clearance that Wells had overseen. Maybe some of these officers had been used on other details; maybe some had even killed on Wells's command.

'It looks that way.'

'Jesus Christ.' Whicher's face had turned a pale grey. 'I assume you haven't got any proof of this.'

'Not at the moment.' But Pyke suspected that Luke Gibb still had the Churches Fund's secret accounts or knew where to lay his hands on the ledger.

'Which means you can't go to Mayne.'

Pyke nodded. 'Assuming Mayne's not involved, too.'

'No, that's impossible, Pyke, and you know it. One thing I'd swear to. Mayne's as straight as they come.'

'So is Peel but he's on the Fund's executive board. I was told by his private secretary – who also happens to be a friend of mine – that the prime minister won't allow the Fund to be mired in suspicion.'

Whicher stood and paced to the other side of the room. 'Wells will be there on Monday night, as well as Palmer.'

'And don't forget the prime minister,' Pyke added. 'It could make for an interesting night.'

'Wells has no idea Gibb is a policeman?'

'I don't know. We found out, so it's possible he has, too.'

'Wells has personally liaised with a superintendent in the City of London police to oversee the security arrangements.'

'I want to be there too,' Pyke said, firmly.

'There's no way you'll get past the ring of officers posted around the Guildhall.'

'Not if I dress like this. But I had a quick look in your wardrobe earlier. I hope you don't mind. I found your old uniform and tried it on. The trousers are a little short but otherwise the fit is quite good. I'll take off the buttons giving your old division and number. No one will ever trace it back to you.'

Whicher folded his arms and scrutinised Pyke's face. 'What do you hope to achieve by going to the Guildhall? I mean ... you must have some sympathy for Gibb, for his position.' Whicher hesitated. 'I know I do.'

'I'm a policeman, Jack. I've sworn an oath to uphold the law.'

'And when you come face to face with Wells?'

'I don't know.' Pyke hesitated. 'For a while now, I've been trying to work out why someone wrote me that note directing me to the address on Broad Street.'

'And?'

'I think whoever it was was hoping I'd talk to Druitt and dig a little, find out what really happened to the boys. That man clearly knows something.'

Whicher looked at Pyke waiting for him to elaborate but Pyke had nothing left to say.

TWENTY-EIGHT

The following morning, Pyke woke early but lay on his mattress in the tiny room he'd rented, savouring the quiet. It was a Sunday and the street beneath was almost deserted, just the occasional carriage or cart disturbing the silence. Because he had nothing to read, Pyke reached for the tatty prayer book Felix had given him and started to thumb through it, the words utterly alien to him. Flicking to the first page of the book, he noticed an inscription – Kitty's name in her own handwriting: Kitty Jones. He froze. Big, looped letters. He recognised the handwriting. It was the same hand that had penned the note sent to him in December, with an epitaph from Blake. Kitty Jones. Kitty? Another name for Kate? The words of the tub-man echoed in his head: *Good looking. Strange visions.*

Pyke dressed in a matter of seconds. Five minutes later, having run the entire way, he arrived at the cab-stand on Charing Cross Road to find there were no people waiting and no carriages. He tore across Trafalgar Square to the Strand, where eventually he managed to flag down a carriage. Just as long as Felix was safe, he kept repeating to himself. The streets outside passed in a blur as the traffic was light, and the journey from the Strand to Bethnal Green took less than half an hour.

Pyke went first to the vicarage, and when he was convinced that no one was watching the house, he slipped around the back and banged on the door. It was answered by one of the servants, who told him that Jakes was at church and that Kitty and the boy had gone out earlier, perhaps to attend the morning service as well. Pyke was not sure whether or not he was relieved.

St Matthew's was much fuller than Pyke had been expecting; every pew was packed with bodies, and there was standing room only left at the back of the church. If the building had seemed gloomy when it had been empty, it was now utterly transformed. Almost immediately Pyke could feel the sense of outrage that Martin Jakes, who was standing up in the pulpit wearing neither gown nor robe, was doing his best to stir up.

'If you were to listen to our Church fathers,' he was saying, his arms raised before him, 'you would come away thinking that the single most pressing issue of our times is whether to side with Newman's Tractarians and pay a higher regard for the sacrament, whether to light a candle on the altar and put a cross and flowers alongside it. Meanwhile, I say to you, and I say it because you know it to be true, thousands of men, women and children are perishing in our city every day either from starvation or disease or a general hopelessness borne of poverty and inequality.' There was a loud murmur of approval. 'Our Church fathers are wrangling among themselves about issues that are, at best, trifling, while honest folk can't afford to put bread on their own tables. Of course, these same men have worked to ensure that churches like this one have been built and for this we must be grateful. But if they also want me to stand up here and tell you not to be concerned about this life, to trust and love God and wait for your reward in the next life, I will *not* do it. If all we do is endure our suffering, if we are passive in the face of the ills of the world, then nothing will ever change. For if we accept and endure, then those who exploit us for profit, those who feed off our misery like leeches, grow fat off our travails. Should I tell you to endure? Will God listen to your prayers and put food on your table? This I cannot say. But if Jesus did exist as flesh and blood, and if the gospels are even partly true, we can say that he did not passively accept his lot. He railed against the established Church and he threw the moneychangers out of the temple. He made it clear that the hypocrisy and sometimes even corruption of our supposed betters cannot and *should* not be tolerated.'

Almost in unison the congregation broke into an avalanche of applause. Pyke surveyed the faces in the crowd for any sign of Kitty or his son, and as Jakes brought his sermon to a climax, he thought about what the man had achieved: yoking the righteous fury of the poor to a message about the relevance of the Christian faith. It was an almost impossible task, and yet somehow Jakes had made it work.

At the end of the service, Pyke pushed his way through the congregation, eager to say a few words to Jakes and shake his hand. It took the curate a few minutes to field the handshakes and slaps on his back, and by the time he finally joined Pyke, the church was almost empty.

'Where is my son?' Pyke asked.

'He's out with Kitty.' Jakes seemed puzzled by his concern. 'I assure you he's quite well, Detective Inspector.'

Pyke showed Jakes the name scribbled in the front of the prayer book Felix had given him. 'That's the same hand that penned a note sent to me in December. Why didn't you tell me that Kitty's real name is Kate Gibb and that she's Morris Keate's half-sister?'

'She isn't.' Jakes smiled kindly. 'Morris's half-sister, Kate, died from the pox two years ago.'

Thrown by this revelation, Pyke took a moment to recover his stride. 'Then whose writing is this?'

Jakes looked searchingly at him. 'Mine.'

Helpers were clearing things away from the pews. Jakes led Pyke to an alcove, where their privacy was assured.

'I suspect that you and I are quite alike in one respect, Detective Inspector,' he said, sitting down. 'We both find it hard to countenance the hypocrisy of those we purport to answer to.'

Pyke rubbed his forehead while he considered what Jakes had just said. 'When did you find out that money had been embezzled from the Churches Fund?'

'In the summer, just before Johnny was killed in the pawnbroker's shop.'

'You knew the Gibb brothers?'

Jakes nodded briskly. 'They came to see me some time last year; told me they knew for a fact that Morris hadn't murdered those boys.'

'How did they know?'

'Because they'd found a woman who'd spent the whole night with Morris on the date he was supposed to have killed the second boy. She said he hadn't left her side for a moment. She also said she'd given this information to a policeman and that he hadn't wanted to know – that he threatened to lock her up if she persisted with such claims.'

'Did she have a name?'

Jakes shook his head. 'I suppose I'd never really believed that Morris could have done what he'd been accused of. After the Gibb boys left, I felt a deep sense of shame. I promised myself I'd do all I could to see that those responsible for inflicting such misery on Morris, and those two boys, would suffer. I won't pretend my thoughts were especially holy.'

'You told me before that you knew the Gibb family, and Keate, from your time as the vicar at St Luke's.'

Jakes nodded. 'And I saw what it did to the family, thinking that Morris had done the things he was accused of. I saw how it tore them apart. And I did nothing. In effect, I colluded with the wrong that had been done to them. I hid behind my robes. In my naivety, I assumed that the police could, and would, never make a mistake on what was a life-and-death issue.'

For the first time, Pyke could hear the sting of anger behind his words. 'You told me before about Guppy's interest in Morris Keate.'

Jakes gave him a wary nod. 'But it was the archdeacon who came to talk to me about Morris. I assumed at the time his interest was purely a doctrinal one; whether it was appropriate that a man christened into the Anglican Church should've undergone an exorcism performed by a Catholic priest.' He gestured to one of the helpers, who was waiting to be dismissed. Turning back to Pyke, he said, 'Shortly after Keate was executed, I received word from the archdeacon that I was to be moved from St Luke's to become perpetual curate of St Matthew's. I didn't want to move, but then again, I could hardly refuse to go. Later, of course, I realised I'd been moved here so that Guppy could keep an eye on me.'

'You didn't suspect an ulterior motive?'

Jakes shook his head. 'At the time, I assumed I'd fallen out of favour with the Church authorities. Believe it or not, I've never been their favourite son. Not that my sermons were always as unconventional as the one you heard today. I won't deny that the last year or so has radicalised me in ways I can barely explain to myself.'

It was hard not to see the truth in what Jakes had just said. 'And what did you think when you heard that Guppy had been murdered?'

'I learnt about what had happened from Francis Hiley. He turned up on my doorstep that same night. He'd seen a man attack Guppy with a hammer and he'd been too afraid to do anything about it. But then, when he'd gone to see whether Guppy was alive or dead, a policeman had spotted him and shouted at him to stay where he was. He told me he'd run because he knew they'd try to blame him.'

Pyke regarded him sceptically. 'You didn't know at the time that Luke Gibb had been the one who'd carried out the attack?'

'Not immediately, but when Hiley described the man he'd seen, I did wonder.'

'But that didn't stop you from giving Francis Hiley shelter and then lying to me about not knowing his whereabouts.'

'I sent him away to a friend in the West Country.' Jakes looked at Pyke and shrugged. 'I knew he was innocent and, after our little conversation, I also knew that some of your colleagues would try to hold him responsible. I couldn't let that happen again.'

Pyke felt he would have done the same thing in Jakes's position. 'So what did you do then?'

'I went to find Luke.'

'And were you successful?'

'Eventually. I put some things to him and he didn't refute them.'

'You accused him of Guppy's murder?'

Jakes loosened his collar and wiped his forehead. 'He didn't deny it but by way of explanation he showed me the accounts for the London Churches Fund. He explained that he and Johnny had stolen the ledger from the archdeacon's safe earlier that year.

'He said it had taken them two or three years of digging to get anywhere close to Wynter and that, in the end, someone from the archdeacon's office had tipped them off. Anonymously, of course. Even to a layman, it was abundantly clear that enormous sums of money had been misappropriated from the Fund.'

'What kind of sums?'

'Hundreds of thousands, Detective Inspector.'

'You're saying the Fund was *that* rich?'

'I'm saying, Detective Inspector, that the fund-raising campaign had been extraordinarily successful.'

Pyke thought about what he had been told by the elderly man on Cheapside. 'I suppose I'd already worked that out.'

Jakes looked at him, his brow furrowed. 'So you know what they did?'

'I think so. The money went directly into the Fund's coffers but the properties were annexed by a subsidiary company: City Holdings Consolidated. They were then sold to Palmer, Jones & Co., at significantly less than their market value, and were in turn sold on to the City Corporation for their full market value. The difference was pocketed by the directors of City Holdings Consolidated, who, I'm told, included Palmer, Hogarth and Guppy.' He decided not to mention Wells's name, at least not yet.

Jakes seemed impressed by this assessment. 'Luke also told me that Morris had been sacrificed in order to draw attention away from a potential scandal involving Guppy that had threatened to expose the whole operation.'

Pyke stared up at the ceiling and then at the cross hanging above the table at the end of the nave. 'So why didn't you just come to us then and tell us what you'd found out?'

'Us, meaning the police?'

Pyke nodded.

Jakes looked around them, to check they were alone, and whispered, 'Because Luke had already told me that he suspected police involvement; that the fraud, and cover-up, had been perpetrated with the assistance of individuals within the Metropolitan Police.'

'I assume you know that Gibb is a policeman himself.'

'But in a rather lowly position, I understand. I think he was struggling to make any headway on the matter.' Jakes dug his hands into his pockets and sighed. 'That's why your name came into our conversation, Detective Inspector.'

'*My* name?'

'He said you'd taken over as head of the Detective Branch and that, as someone who'd crossed swords with the authorities on numerous occasions, you might be sympathetic to the cause. Luke had reached a dead end and he still didn't know who exactly was involved. I think he toyed with the idea of simply giving you the accounts he'd stolen from the archdeacon but he was afraid that, if word got out, they would come after you; and if that happened, he'd never find out which members of the police force were involved.'

'And so you agreed to write this anonymous note, sending me to number twenty-eight Broad Street?'

Jakes lowered his head, as if a little ashamed.

'You planted Guppy's surplice there, knowing I'd find it.'

'Luke did. I just wrote the note.'

'Why?' Pyke could feel his anger gathering strength. 'Did you actually want me to arrest Brendan Malloy for Guppy's murder? To see another innocent man go to the scaffold?'

'No ... We wanted to lead you to Druitt, not Malloy. We hoped you would see Malloy for who he was – a broken man, incapable of inflicting harm on anyone but himself.'

'But why to Druitt?' Pyke asked, beginning to see the logic behind their machinations.

'Because Druitt would help you make the connection to the old murders and the injustice done to Morris Keate.'

In fact it was Frederick Shaw who had first brought the murder of the two boys to his attention – Druitt had merely toyed with him by suggesting the date.

'You – a man of God – would employ someone like Ebenezer Druitt to do your bidding?'

'It was Luke's idea. He had met Druitt and realised they shared a dislike of the established Church.'

'But did you ever meet the man?'

'Once, last winter.' Jakes hesitated. 'I didn't like him. I never felt comfortable in his presence. But Luke assured me he would be useful.'

'So Luke had told Druitt about his plans?'

'As much as he felt Druitt needed to know. But Druitt's propensity for mischief nearly jeopardised the whole operation.'

'How?'

'For a start, he managed to convince Malloy that he'd foreseen Guppy's death and then Malloy, who knew nothing about Luke's plans, tried to warn Guppy. That alerted Guppy to the possibility that someone might be trying to right the wrong that had been done to Keate.'

Pyke considered what Druitt had known about his private life: the book he was reading and the fact he kept pigs. Had Luke Gibb passed him this information too, and if so did this mean Gibb had broken into his home?

'Did Luke Gibb actually visit Druitt at Pentonville or did he just find a way of passing messages to him?'

'I'm afraid I don't know.'

Pyke stared into the curate's weathered face and tried not to think about the sense of betrayal he felt. 'Doesn't it concern you that, in effect, you've given your blessing to three murders?'

'I did that one thing, Detective Inspector. I sent you that note. All I ever wanted was for you to find out the truth.'

Pyke folded his arms. 'And now I know the truth, what do you want me to do with it?'

'I won't insult you by assuming your faith in the institution you serve.'

'You're not answering my question.'

Jakes's smile vanished. 'I want you to do as you see fit, Detective Inspector. That's all I've ever wanted.'

'To get my hands dirty so you don't have to?'

Jakes sighed. 'I'm not naive enough to believe that God will forgive me for the sins I've committed.'

'I'm not interested in God. I just want to find Luke Gibb and put a stop to this madness.'

'And let those who have murdered to line their own pockets live out their days in peace?'

'What's Gibbs's rank and division?'

'I don't know.'

'Really? Or is that just another lie?' Pyke saw the pained expression on Martin Jakes's face but he didn't care.

TWENTY-NINE

A bitter wind, coming in off the river, rushed across the wide open space around Great Scotland Yard. A brittle silver frost still lingered and Pyke had to keep moving in order to stay warm as he positioned himself on the far side of the yard, across from the public entrance to the police building so that none of his fellow officers would see him and raise the alarm. There was a large clock on the wall overlooking the yard, and it gave the time as midday. Whicher had been inside the building for nearly two hours. In another corner of the yard, a constable in uniform emerged from the boarding house and hurried across the open space to the police headquarters. To kill some time, Pyke walked down to the river at a brisk pace and stood for a while at the top of the tide-washed stairs. Retracing his path back to Scotland Yard, he passed a constable coming the other way and kept his head bowed, the brim of his crushed billycock hat veiling his eyes.

Whicher was waiting for him in the corner of the yard farthest from the police building. He glanced behind him, to make sure no one had followed him, and started to move off in the direction of Whitehall before Pyke caught up with him. 'Well?'

'Luke Gibb joined on the twenty-third of March three years ago. He was dismissed for drunken conduct on the fourth of June last year.'

Stopping, Pyke turned to face Whicher. 'That doesn't sound like our man.'

'It's all they had. But I've got an address for him in Bermondsey, near the leather market.' He held up a piece of paper.

'What Gibb has done requires discipline, intelligence and planning . . . I can't imagine him risking it all by getting drunk on the job.'

'We need to go to Bermondsey to find out.'

'Why don't I go to Bermondsey? You could go to the Model Prison. I think Gibb might have visited Druitt. If so, there could be a record of it.'

'It couldn't do any harm, I suppose. Dividing up and going our separate ways,' Whicher said, although he didn't sound convinced.

'Each time I visited the prison, I had to show my warrant badge and sign the visitors' log. But I didn't have to specify the prisoner I was there to see. You'll just have to go through the log for the last few months. See if there are any names that stand out.'

'Do you think Gibb might have solicited help from one of his former colleagues?'

'It's possible. I'm not sure what finding a name in the visitors' book will tell us, but if I can't find Gibb in Bermondsey, or anyone who knows him, it might give us something.'

Whicher glanced up at the clock on the wall of the police building. 'I'll meet you back at my apartment at four.'

There was no answer at the address Whicher had given him, and when Pyke forced the door it was apparent that no one had lived there for several months. When he asked the residents whether they knew a man called Luke Gibb and explained he'd once been a policeman, one or two remembered someone fitting that description and suggested that Pyke look for him in the taverns and ginneries of Bermondsey Street.

The air was rotten and the stench produced by drying cow skins and the astringents used to clean them made his eyes water. Pyke made his way to the top of Bermondsey Street and entered the first place he came to, but neither the landlord nor any of the servers knew of a man called Gibb. Next door, the taproom was equally packed, and yet again no one admitted to knowing a Luke Gibb. On the street, refuse from nearby scum-boilers, tripe-scrapers and bladder-blowers collected in the gutters. A wagon with a cargo covered with a wet tarpaulin rattled past, followed by a wolfish dog trotting behind a man with a limp. Pyke walked past an eating house where a big-armed woman was stirring a large pot of tripe stew. Next door, he stepped into the Duke of Argyle and asked the landlord whether he knew Luke Gibb. The man shook his head, but when Pyke explained that Gibb had once been a policeman and that he'd been dismissed for drunkenness, the landlord seemed to perk up. 'You could ask for him at the King's Arms; the one with a blue door about three or four houses along.'

At the zinc counter, Pyke asked one of the aproned pot-boys to fetch the landlord, and cast his gaze around the room. Unlike the other places he'd visited, this one was nearly empty, a few early afternoon drinkers huddled around the old wooden tables.

'I'm looking for an ex-Peeler, name of Gibb, likes to wet his throat,' he said to the landlord when the man appeared behind the counter.

The landlord gestured to a man sitting on his own, a forlorn pot of ale in front of him. He was younger than Pyke but his skin was rough and his face overgrown with whiskers. Up close, Pyke could smell the beer on his clothes and his breath.

'Is your name Gibb?'

'I ain't been called that since the summer.' The man grinned, revealing a gap in his front teeth large enough to put your thumb through. 'I'd say you must be a Peeler, cock. That right? One of 'em Jacks, don't 'ave to wear a uniform?'

'Why would you assume that?'

'Gibb was my name when I was a Peeler.'

Puzzled, Pyke asked, 'Luke Gibb?'

'Aye, that was it.' The man stretched his arms above his head. 'I never liked the name Luke, mind.'

'And what name are you calling yourself nowadays?'

'You ain't lookin' for me. You're looking for the other cully.'

'And which other cully would that be?'

'The one I swapped my name with. Met on the day we signed up and he paid me well for it, too. What did I care what folk called me? I was new in the city and I didn't know a soul.'

Pyke tried to appear uninterested. 'You don't want to tell me what your real name is?'

'I could do but you're gonna 'ave to let me wet my beak first.'

Pyke dug into his pocket, retrieved a five-shilling coin and put it on the table. 'Your name?'

The former constable took one look at the coin and grinned. 'May as well give me a kick in the teeth while you're about it.'

Pyke had checked his pocket watch before he'd entered the taproom and it was already three. He didn't have time for this, so he produced a sovereign. He let the man see its colour, see the gold, but kept it in his hand. 'That's the carrot. I want the name. But if you try to draw this out, I won't think twice about showing you the stick.'

'Tough sort, eh? Let's say you make it a couple of 'em megs, we might just 'ave a deal, cock.'

Pyke flicked the sovereign into his lap. 'I'll give you the other one when you've told me the name.'

The man picked up the sovereign, bit it with his teeth and finally started to smile.

Whicher was in his apartment, pacing up and down the living room as he waited for Pyke.

'I checked the visitors' book.'

'And?'

'The name said Gibb but the division and number didn't match the one I saw in his file this morning.'

'What was it?'

'A25,' Whicher said.

'Do you recognise it?'

Whicher looked nervous. 'Do you?'

Pyke nodded. He told Whicher what he'd found out from the man in Bermondsey, whose real name was Eddie Lockhart. 'I didn't suspect him for a minute.'

'Neither did I.'

'But then I remembered Shaw telling me that Lockhart had tried to bury the identity of Johnny Gibb during the Shorts Gardens investigation. And there was the time he came to my rescue, over the confusion surrounding Hogarth's death. It's obvious now: he needed me; needed me to keep digging. And he would occasionally do something to push me, us, in the right direction. Shaw came to me with the suggestion I look into the murder of the two boys but he gave Lockhart some of the credit.'

Whicher still seemed in shock.

Pyke gave what he'd just said a little more thought. Lockhart could have tried to bring Guppy and Hogarth before the law but had instead chosen to exercise an older form of justice. He'd tried to steer their investigation in a particular direction, not to expose the various perpetrators to the strictures of the law, but rather to try to smoke out the parties he couldn't identify. Men like Wells and Russell. In doing so he'd risked his own freedom.

'He was always very private, never said a word about his family, where he came from, what he did before,' Whicher said.

Lockhart must have been the one who gave Druitt the information about him keeping pigs, and he could easily have gained entry to Pyke's home. But why? All he could think of was that Druitt had somehow put him to it; that Druitt had been able to convince Lockhart that provoking and unsettling Pyke would produce results.

'So what do we do about Gibb? Or should I say Lockhart?'

Pyke said, 'We go to the Guildhall and we try to find him.'

'And then?'

Pyke looked down at Whicher's old police uniform, already laid out on the table for him. 'Did you manage to lay your hands on a pistol?'

Wordlessly Whicher went across to a cupboard and pulled out a wooden case. Placing it on the table next to the uniform, he unsnapped the fasteners and opened the lid. Inside was a flintlock pistol with a smooth walnut butt.

'Do you really think you'll just be allowed to walk in there with this gun, no questions asked?'

'Inspectors are permitted to carry pistols. I'm an inspector, or I was until about a month ago.' Pyke picked up the weapon. 'No one will be looking out for a policeman in uniform. I'll be as good as invisible.'

A moment passed between them. 'Pyke?'

'What is it, Jack?'

'I know my betrayal hurt you and I've done my best to make amends ...'

'But?'

'But I want no part of whatever you're planning to do tonight.'

'And what do you think I'm planning to do?' Pyke stood there, wondering how honest he could be with Whicher. 'It's tempting to let Gibb finish what he started, I suppose, but that would be to abdicate our responsibilities as police officers. Do you want him to kill again?'

Whicher didn't answer the question. 'And when you come face to face with Palmer? And Wells?'

Pyke said nothing.

'These were the men who set you up. For all I know you could still be facing the noose. You're just going to shake their hands and let bygones be bygones?'

'What do you think I should do?'

'I can't answer that. I'll just say this. I sincerely hope to see you back in the department before too long, sir.'

The Guildhall was an imposing stone structure in the middle of the City that looked like a cross between a church and a castle, its Gothic entrance, pre-dating Wren, juxtaposed with a frontage built at the end of the previous century. Coming at the building from King Street, Pyke passed through the first ring of police constables unchallenged, and walked briskly past a second line at the point where the cobblestone street gave way to an open yard in which carriages and liveried broughams were depositing soberly attired men and women dressed in flounced, brocaded silk.

At the entrance, major-domos were collecting invitations. There was a policeman in uniform standing there, seemingly in a supervisory role. Certainly the way he was barking orders at other officers attested to his seniority. As Pyke tried to slip past, the man put out his arm and read the division and number on Pyke's collar: E17.

This was the division and letter he'd chosen because E was Holborn, Pierce's division, and Pyke had met an inspector who worked there a few months ago. 'Inspector Connell, Holborn Division,' he said, 'I'm to report to the Court of Aldermen.'

The man may have seen his pistol but he didn't comment on it. Raising his hand, he muttered, 'Up the main stairs, you'll see it on the left-hand side.'

Pyke had never worn a uniform before, at least not during his time as commander of the Detective Branch, and he was surprised at how uncomfortable it was, the woollen material coarse and scratchy against the skin. It was also hard getting used to the stovepipe hat, the way it didn't quite sit comfortably on top of his head. Still, the anonymity it afforded him was priceless. No one batted an eyelid at him and he was allowed to pass freely through into the main banquet hall.

Pyke had been there once before, about four years earlier, and on that occasion he had dragged a murder suspect into the kitchens and thrust his arm into a boiling vat of soup. The hall hadn't changed much in the intervening years. As austere as it was grand, it was filled with long tables that ran in three lines the full length of the room, and which were now decorated with the finest linen, glass and china. There were monuments to great men who had plundered and murdered their way into the history books, and at each end of the hall were two vast stained-glass windows. Pyke had walked past the City Arms on his way into the hall and had noticed the motto: *Domine, dirige nos.* Lord direct us. Direct us to do what? he wondered. To embezzle? To murder? The contented hum of a thousand polite conversations rippled around the room. These were the great and the good, come to slap one of their own on the back, a man of sixty years who had lied, cheated, even killed.

Pyke approached someone who appeared to be the major-domo in charge and muttered, 'Palmer around? I've got an urgent message for him.'

The man glanced down at his fob-watch. 'There's a private ceremony for him about to start in the Common Council room.'

At the top of the stairs an orderly line of guests was waiting to be admitted into the room. He saw Hogarth's widow and quickly turned his back to her. There were no other policemen in the vicinity and, worried that he was too visible, Pyke hurried past the queue and turned a corner at the end of the corridor. He made sure that no one was following him then tried the first door he came upon. It opened and he let himself into the room. It was an antechamber off the main council room but was connected to it via a narrow door cut into the stone wall. On the other side, he could hear the excited buzz of conversation.

Emboldened, Pyke opened the narrow door and entered the chamber as the first guests began to stream through the main door. He made his way to the front, where a man he presumed to be the Lord Mayor was whispering in the ear of a guest. Pyke cleared his throat. 'Urgent message for Sir St John Palmer, sir.'

'M'lud.' He peered at Pyke through his monocle and frowned. 'You should refer to me as m'lud.'

'I need to pass a message to Sir St John Palmer as a matter of urgency,' Pyke replied, through gritted teeth.

'I believe he was called down to the library a few minutes ago by another of you chaps.' It was the other man who addressed him.

When Pyke turned and began to hurry towards the door, the man called out, 'You tell him we'd like to make a start here in the next five minutes.'

Back in the vast atrium at the top of the main staircase, the queue had dwindled to almost nothing. Pyke had already started to descend the stairs when he saw Fitzroy Tilling and Sir Robert Peel coming up in the opposite direction. They were deep in conversation, and Pyke thought he might be able to slip past them unnoticed. But as they drew level Tilling turned to him, as if startled from a reverie, and their eyes met. Pyke nodded once and kept on walking. Only when he had reached the bottom of the stairs did he glance behind him. Tilling was still talking to Peel but Pyke knew he wouldn't let this go, which meant he had even less time than he'd imagined. The library was somewhere on the east side of the building, so he now broke into a run, no longer worried about drawing attention to himself. Passing a servant, Pyke paused momentarily and asked where the library was, then started running again, almost even before the man had pointed it out.

It was quiet at this end of the building, away from the guests and the servants scurrying in and out of the kitchens, and he stopped at the entrance to the library, vast oak bookcases towering from floor to ceiling ahead of him. He couldn't hear any voices; there weren't even any librarians or porters around. The library was lit by gas-lamps affixed at regular intervals along the panelled walls, and the jets of light produced a slight hissing sound. He saw a shadow pass across one of the bookcases and moved forward very slowly, his pistol drawn. Making as little noise as possible, he came to the end of one of the cases and peered around the corner. That was when he saw them; Palmer and Wells both dressed in their formal attire. They weren't talking, they weren't even moving, and it wasn't until he moved out a little farther that Pyke saw why.

Luke Gibb, the man Pyke had known as Eddie Lockhart, had a shiny, twin-barrelled pistol aimed in their direction. As far as Pyke could tell, no one had noticed him. He slid silently along to the far end of the bookcase, so that he would be nearer Gibb when he made his move.

Unless he acted quickly, Gibb would squeeze the trigger and it would all be over. Gripping his pistol in his right hand, Pyke raised the barrel and stepped out into the light.

Wells saw him first and instinctively turned his head. Perhaps he assumed Pyke was a policeman and was there to save them.

Pyke had his pistol aimed directly at Luke Gibb.

'Put it down, Luke. Just put down the pistol and we can talk.' Pyke took another step towards him.

'Listen to him, Gibb,' Pyke heard Wells say. 'We can arrive at an arrangement suitable to all parties. Isn't that right, Detective Inspector?'

So Wells had recognised him. It changed nothing. Pyke took another step towards Gibb, the pistol still aimed at the man's head. He was now equidistant between Gibb, Wells and Palmer.

Gibb's pistol was now trained on Palmer. 'This is your chance, too, Pyke. These are the men who would've seen you step out on to the scaffold.'

In the distance, Pyke could hear raised voices and footsteps. Tilling, and perhaps others, would be looking for him.

'Let me do what I came to do, and you'll never see me again,' Gibbs continued. 'I'll send you the accounts. You can do what you want with them.'

Wells said to Pyke, 'Like it or not, Detective, you're one of us now.'

'If we let them walk away, it means my brother, both of my brothers, died for nothing.'

This was the man, Pyke thought, who had taken a sledgehammer to Isaac Guppy, who had nailed Charles Hogarth to a wall and who had stabbed Adolphus Wynter.

Without warning, Pyke squeezed his trigger, the blast shattering the eerie stillness of the room. The shot struck Gibb on the side of his face and tore off part of his cheek, mouth and nose. He slumped to the floor, crashing against the bookcase behind him.

Palmer and Wells remained rooted to the spot, too stunned to move. Calmly Pyke bent over and retrieved the pistol from Gibb's warm grasp.

Now the shouts were close by and Pyke could hear an avalanche of footsteps closing in. Wells started to say, 'I knew you'd come around in ...' Raising the barrel of Gibb's pistol, Pyke shot him squarely in the face, the rest of the sentence lost in a bloody gurgle. Without hesitation, he turned towards Palmer, who had started to run, and fired the other barrel; the shot hit him on the back of his head and he stumbled forward. The air was thick with the smell of powder, and it was hard to see more than a few paces in front of him. But while no one knew or could see what had really happened, Pyke knew the smoke would clear quickly and the others would soon be upon him. Bending down, he put the pistol back into Gibb's hand and, retrieving his own weapon, he held it up in the air and shouted, 'Three men down. Gibb shot Wells and Palmer, I got here too late. He tried to run; I didn't have a choice.'

Domine, dirige nos.

Lord direct us.

Pyke let his pistol slip through his fingers and it clattered on to the hard, polished floor. Then there were four, five, six men around him, policemen in uniform shouting at him to yield, the ripe, acrid smell of blood.

THIRTY

The immediate aftermath of the shootings was swift and moment-
ous; with Palmer, Wells and a policeman dead, rumours swirled
uncontrollably among the guests that a murderer with a lust for
blood was still rampaging through the building, and five hundred
guests fought with one another and the army of policemen to
escape from the building. Wealthy men wearing satin cravats, silk
neckties and velvet waistcoats trampled over panicking women who
could barely move in their elaborate crinoline skirts, frantic to reach
their carriages and broughams, backed up all the way along King
Street and Aldermanbury. It would have been amusing to watch
except for the fact that the guests included some of the most
powerful figures in the country, not least the prime minister, the
home secretary and, as it turned out, both Metropolitan Police
commissioners. This meant someone had to shoulder the blame,
and quickly, and without it being agreed in any formal sense,
Pyke was selected for this role. It helped that he was still wanted
on another charge. Very soon the whole debacle, the crushing
humiliation it heaped upon the New Police, was dumped at Pyke's
feet.

Escorted by a phalanx of policemen overseen by Rowan himself,
Pyke was pushed into a fortified police carriage and transported to
Great Scotland Yard, where he was locked in a cell while Rowan
and Mayne decided on the best way to proceed. For the next three
days, Pyke was questioned over and over about his role in the
proceedings and asked to explain why a man they all knew as
Detective Sergeant Edward Lockhart had killed not just Walter
Wells and Sir St John Palmer but also Isaac Guppy and Charles
Hogarth. Unsurprisingly, Mayne and Rowan were not happy with
Pyke's answers, and at first didn't believe him. They wanted

proof, hard evidence, which Pyke was unable to provide. But after recounting the events for the fourth or fifth time, even Pyke's severest critics had to concede that there was some truth in his version. And bit by bit, elements of his story were confirmed: that Lockhart was in fact Luke Gibb; that Luke Gibb had been the half-brother of Morris Keate; that Gibb's brother John had been one of the victims in the Shorts Gardens robbery. This left Pyke's inquisitors in a difficult position. With a welter of circumstantial evidence indicating that Gibb had good reasons for wanting Palmer and Wells to suffer, they couldn't very well charge Pyke with the murders, even though some in the executive department believed that Pyke had in fact pulled the trigger himself. Nor could they pat him on the back and congratulate him on a job well done, or dismiss him from his position with immediate effect – he knew too much and he could go to the newspapers with what he knew, causing lasting damage to both the Church and the police. No one wanted this, least of all the prime minister, who had taken a personal interest in the situation.

Palmer had been a friend of the police department. But now his role in the fraud was becoming clear, his supporters were running for cover. Later, Pyke was told that Wells had introduced Palmer to Mayne and had arranged for Palmer's company to secure the contract to refurbish the station house at Scotland Yard. He was also told that Sergeant Mark Russell had been found in his bed, shot in the face.

Pyke's circumstances improved further when it became apparent that the charges against him regarding the theft of the Saviour's Cross and the apparent murder of Billy Sharp were not going to stand up. With Wells dead, the case against him quickly fell apart. First, Ned Villums withdrew his evidence, then Alfred Egan followed. The gaoler admitted that Wells had offered him money to testify against Pyke and finally Pyke's neighbour Leech admitted that he had not witnessed Pyke bury the Saviour's Cross. At the same time Leech put his house up for sale and Pyke never saw him or his dog again. In the end, Mayne and Rowan had no choice but to let Pyke go free and, with the charges against him shown to be not only false but concocted by a fellow policeman, they couldn't very well do what they may have wanted to and dismiss Pyke from his position. Instead they suspended him temporarily, pending a hearing, which was set for a week's time.

Throughout his extensive questioning Pyke had never made it clear to his inquisitors what he wanted, though he did occasionally hint that the price he was likely to demand would be more than they were prepared to pay. He knew, however, that his success or failure in this respect depended on him finding the true Churches Fund accounts.

That week was cold and bright and, having collected Felix from Martin Jakes's care and returned to their Islington home to be reunited with Copper – who was both excited to see them and disgruntled by their absence – Pyke kept Felix out of school and they spent a couple of afternoons together in the garden erecting a new shelter and sty for the two remaining pigs. They didn't talk about the conversation they'd had in Jakes's vicarage but Pyke tried to show the lad a gentler side of his character.

Pyke made only two trips. The first, to the New Prison in nearby Pentonville, was short and unsuccessful. He went there to persuade Druitt to give up the location of the true Churches Fund accounts, if indeed he knew where they were, but all Druitt seemed to want to do was discuss *Paradise Lost*.

'Why, according to Milton, did Satan rebel against his maker?' Druitt swung lazily on his hammock. 'It was, we are told, because he saw no reason for the extreme inequality of rank and power which God had assumed.'

'I know Gibb visited you here on a number of occasions. I need you to tell me where the accounts ledger is. The one that was stolen from the archdeacon's safe.' Knowing what he had done to Sarah Scott, Pyke could barely look at the man.

Druitt didn't appear to have heard him. 'Of course, Satan, who presents a case against tyranny, also became a tyrant himself. Perhaps this was inevitable. Still, I don't know about you, Detective Inspector, but I would take the earthy rambunctiousness of Pandemonium over the austere dictatorship of Heaven every time.'

Pyke no longer had the patience for these games and he turned to leave.

'You've disappointed me, Detective Inspector. I had higher hopes for you, to be quite frank.'

Pyke stopped and stood facing him, his back to the door.

'I thought you'd want to rock the boat, at the very least; I've heard stories about you. I didn't think that you'd lie down and roll over; whimper in the face of authority. I have to admit, I'm very disappointed.'

'Without evidence, what *can* I do?'

Druitt shook his head. 'And what would you do, if you had this evidence? Do you see what I'm suggesting? Feather your own nest, no doubt. Meanwhile, the tyranny of the Church and state goes unpunished.'

Pyke felt his skin prickle. 'You drugged and raped a woman I admire and then exploited Malloy's jealousy to destroy them both. That's all I see when I look at you. A pathetic, inadequate man unable to sow his seed ...'

Druitt smiled. 'What? In the way God intended?'

That was the last time they spoke. As Pyke walked through the prison and tried to put the image of Druitt out of his mind, he wondered what pleasure, if any, Druitt had gained from what he'd done. Malloy had died believing him to be the Devil in human form. In reality, he was just a bitter, broken-down man.

Pyke's second visit was to Stratford St Mary in Suffolk, but he quickly discovered that whatever had existed between him and Sarah Scott had been lost. She greeted him warmly and they talked at length about what had happened, Sarah listening carefully while he tried to explain why he'd suspected her and how terribly mistaken he'd been. But a gap remained, a gap that couldn't be bridged, and when Pyke asked her whether she might consider returning to London, she chuckled as though the idea was unthinkable.

'I liked you, Pyke. But, in all honesty, given what you did and given the lack of faith you had in me, how could I ever trust you again?' When he didn't say anything, she added, 'Perhaps we're just too different.'

Pyke didn't bother to disagree with her. On the train from Colchester back to London, he thought about the canvas she'd been working on: a naked woman being eaten alive by a pack of wild dogs. One of the animals, its snout wet with blood, was tugging her entrails out of a gash in her stomach.

Early the following morning Pyke found Ned Villums in his Clerkenwell office and for a while, as Villums poured them both a whisky and they sat in silence contemplating each other, it was as though nothing had happened. But eventually Villums began to explain how Wells had been able to turn him.

'He had enough on me to make it a straight choice between you or the scaffold . . . Maybe with hindsight I made the wrong decision.'

Pyke stared at his old friend, sad at what they had become. 'It would be better if I never saw or heard from you again. At present, only a few people know you were, in effect, a police informer. For old time's sake, I'm prepared to allow that to remain a secret. But you need to retire, disappear, for good.'

Villums nodded and even managed a smile. He didn't need to say it – Pyke could tell he knew it was too good an offer to turn down.

At the end of the week, a ceremony for Luke Gibb was held at an unconsecrated burial field in Limehouse. Martin Jakes said a few words, mostly for the sake of the mother, a frail, broken woman who had now lost all of her four children. Pyke attended it, as did Jack Whicher and Frederick Shaw, out of respect for the man they had worked with for almost two years. Afterwards, as Whicher and Shaw helped the elderly mother back to a waiting carriage, Pyke and Jakes stood and watched the masts and rigging of ships as they glided past on the Thames. Earlier that morning Pyke had risen from Clare Lewis's bed; she now owned the brothel that she had run for the past ten years. Conor Rafferty had taken over the rest of Culpepper's concerns.

'I'm told a new archdeacon is about to be appointed. The bishop's choice; a reformer,' Jakes said, eventually.

'You think it will make a difference?'

'He's promised to recover every penny that was taken from the Fund and put it back into the church building project.'

It was as Pyke had expected. The Church was going to try to clean up its own mess. 'To do that, he will need the real accounts.

He'll need to know exactly what was stolen and by whom.'

Jakes stared out at the expanse of water in front of them. 'I was hoping you would be able to help there.'

'I'm afraid not.' Pyke turned to him and added, 'I have no idea where the accounts are. I think the only person who knows is Druitt.'

'And what's his price?'

'Druitt wants to rip down the Church brick by brick. And I don't know what he wants to put up in its place.'

'At one time I might have wanted to do that, too.' Jakes tried to smile. 'Anger can do terrible things to you.'

'Not any more?'

'Collectively, we can do terrible damage, but if we give up, if we turn our backs on everything that's made this world what it is, what's left? It's the dilemma we will always face.'

Pyke pondered this while he looked at the ships sailing past in front of them. 'I've tried to do what I can, not always what's best, but what suits the circumstances best. Yet somewhere along the way I've lost my son. Do you think that's the price I have to pay?'

'I always tell my congregation that no one's lost to Him for ever.'

'I'm not talking about God ...'

'I know. But in your case, it's not too late. That's all I meant.'

The ceremony for Luke Gibb had taken place on Friday afternoon. On Sunday morning, when he woke up, Pyke found that a package had been left on his front doorstep. It was wrapped in brown paper. Taking it into the kitchen, where he'd left a mug of coffee, Pyke put it down on the table and tore off the paper. When he had had the time to inspect them carefully, the missing accounts revealed that more than a quarter of a million pounds had been embezzled from the Churches Fund coffers. Pyke had no idea who had delivered the ledger to his doorstep but perhaps that wasn't important.

Pyke's hearing had been scheduled for Monday morning at nine; he'd already been told that his fate would be decided by the two commissioners alone. No one else would be present. In the entrance hall of the police building, Pyke ran into Benedict Pierce. Pierce, Pyke noticed, still walked with a limp, and you could still see the discoloration around his face where the bruises had been. Later, Pyke realised that Pierce knew about the hearing and had been waiting for him.

'I'm prepared to acknowledge that you were misled by the acting superintendent about my intentions towards you, as I was misled by him about your intentions towards me. As such, I bear no ill will towards you regarding our altercation. I would hope you might do me the same courtesy regarding my actions towards you while you were incarcerated.'

Pyke had the accounts ledger for the Churches Fund under one arm. He transferred it to the other. 'It's not what you and I have done to each other that concerns me, Pierce. One of my officers went to you in good faith, in the aftermath of a tragedy, and you knowingly exploited this knowledge and in the process almost ruined a good man. That tells me more about your character than I ever wanted to know.'

'I did what I did to protect myself. I was led to believe that you were conspiring against me. I needed someone in the department to confirm or disprove this suspicion.'

Pierce had always been able to get under his skin and this time was no exception. Even when he was wrong, when he *knew* he was wrong, Pierce would never admit it.

'Five years ago, you led the investigation into the murders of those two boys. If you'd done your job properly, Keate would still be alive and none of this would've happened. You'll have to live with that for the rest of your life.'

Pierce started to say something but Pyke walked off. Pierce caught up with him on the stairs. 'I want you to know I put in a good word for you with Mayne and Rowan.' His cheeks were red and blotchy and he seemed to want something from Pyke; either gratitude or approval. Later, Pyke realised what had brought about this change of heart. With Wells gone, Pierce would now become the new assistant commissioner.

'And you *do* know that Palmer contributed ten thousand to Peel's election campaign; that he belongs to the same lodge as Mayne and that Rowan is a non-executive director of City Holdings Consolidated?'

He left Pyke with that thought.

As he walked up the rest of the stairs, Pyke wondered whether Rowan – one of the men about to decide on his future – was really implicated in the Churches Fund fraud. He considered what Culpepper and others had said to him and realised he had no idea how far or how deep the corruption in the New Police went.

With these thoughts in his mind, it struck him, not for the first time, that he still didn't know what he planned to say. Did he want his old position back? Whicher and Shaw had made it clear they wanted him to return, but was it what *he* wanted? Wells was gone but some of the men he'd commanded, and who had perhaps killed on his orders, remained in their jobs. Still, he was reminded of Martin Jakes and what he'd been able to achieve, despite the lack of support from his seniors. The clerks in the commissioners' office looked at Pyke but wouldn't meet his eyes. Gathering himself, Pyke clutched the leather-bound ledger under his arm and made his way towards Mayne's office.

At the door, he paused and took a breath, then he knocked hard and waited for an answer.